MOONSHINE CREEK

DUSTIN STEVENS

Moonshine Creek
Copyright © 2022, Dustin Stevens

Cover Art and Design: Christian Bentulan
Formatting: Jamie Davis

You set alight,
in my heart and mind,
the most beautiful chaos.
—Atticus

Because brothers don't let each other
wander in the dark alone.
—Jolene Perry

PROLOGUE

"Cort...you don't..."

Remington knows exactly the words he wants to say, though there is a disconnect that keeps them from coming out. A blockage existing somewhere between his mind and his mouth that has nothing to do with Tyrell and Val and Brady all standing nearby, their assault rifles still raised before them.

An audience that Remington is only vaguely aware of, much the same as the mansion littered with bodies behind them, or even the man with gunshot wounds to either knee laying nearby, audibly groaning in pain. Background noise that has been filtered out, his entire focus on his twin brother a few feet away.

A man who has not been baptized into this life the way Remington has. A divergent path that he would have never treaded anywhere near if not for the events of the last week.

Pausing his slow and stilted walk forward, his features twisted into a pained grimace, Cortland turns and looks at him. The over-sized M17 handgun hangs by his side, an anchor tugging his arm straight down from the shoulder.

"It's my turn," he mutters. "I got this one."

1

CHAPTER ONE

"Oh, my *gawd*," the woman exclaims, raising her voice loud enough to carry out into the central Texas evening. A declaration of amazement, altered by alcohol and delivered at a volume much louder than necessary. Sounds that roll well beyond the veranda extended from the back of the mansion, crossing over the stucco barrier and down to the compound below.

A space of more than twenty acres, all of it enclosed by a wall standing ten feet tall.

The bare minimum required for housing the very specific pets Leo Garcia keeps inside.

A landscaping feature that Garcia is certain the woman has not even bothered to notice since the small party moved outside just moments before. A planned march from the open dining room on the second floor, past the crackling fire pit and out to where they now stand.

A relocation prompted under the ruse of stepping outside to enjoy the sunset. The last few gasps of daylight still resting above the horizon, sending rays of neon orange outward like spokes on a wheel.

Stripes of light broken up by pockets of gases and wisps of clouds, turning the evening sky into a kaleidoscope of color. Vibrant pinks and purples, interspersed with shades of tangerine. A painting that people in other parts of the country will pay thousands of dollars to hang on their walls, playing out before them in real time.

A stunning visual firmly entrancing the woman by Garcia's side. Same for her husband on her opposite shoulder.

Maribelle and Johnson Kleese, otherwise known as Garcia's newest business associates. Owners of The Char Pit restaurant chain, with a pair of locations in the nearby Austin area and the promise of many more on the way. Expansion made possible by their acceptance of his offer for investment, the potential of cash infusions making them blind to what else might be attached.

Not that there is any reason for them to fear the worst. Nothing on Garcia's resume hints at the real source of his prodigious wealth. There is not a single hint of anything nefarious to be seen inside his home.

Never has one of his other various associates throughout the area been foolish enough to whisper a word about what partnering with him truly entails. Complete compliance ensured through displays much like the one that is now just minutes away.

A visual, bringing a stark end to the pleasantries of the evening. An abrupt halt to any pretense of this being an equal working relationship.

He now owns them, in every way. A fact that is the reason for their relocation to the veranda overlooking the grounds below. A display that will make the full extent of their hasty agreement quite apparent.

And will ensure their compliance with whatever Garcia dictates from this moment forward.

"Would you look at that view?" Maribelle gasps. A simple question eliciting a nod from her husband. Eagerness to please, mixed with stunned disbelief.

"Yes," Garcia replies. Turning at the waist, he raises a hand, pointing to the third floor of the mansion above. From it extends a pair of window panes, folded out to allow an unobstructed view of the grounds below. "When we built this place, we made sure the back of the home was facing the west so *mi madre* could watch the show every night from her room."

"Aw," Maribelle says, again raising her voice louder than necessary, drawing the word out to several syllables. More Texas excess, matching the overblown plume of blonde hair encircling her head, and the smear of bright pink lipstick on her face, and the absurd cowboy boots that have been clomping throughout Garcia's home all evening.

A walking caricature, matched by her diminutive husband beside her, desperately trying to overcompensate with a massive belt buckle and oversized hat atop his head. Lifts in his boots giving him an extra three inches.

Little Man Syndrome taken to the most extreme degree.

Baseline attempts at physical expansion made even more pronounced in Garcia's presence. An effect he has seen on multiple occasions, his own physical mass the sole thing his father ever gave him worth remembering.

"It is quite a spectacular sunset," Johnson adds.

"It is," Garcia says, "though that's not the show I am referring to."

Rotating back to face forward, Garcia waits as the sun continues to slip lower along the horizon, leaving just the top quarter of it visible. A steady descent pulling the residual light with it, casting long shadows across the compound below.

Darkened pockets form along the base of the outer walls. Long stripes extend from the clumps of post oak and pecan trees dotting the grounds. Old growth interspersed with low-growing shrubs and tumbleweeds.

The sole part of Garcia's estate not meticulously maintained, left wild for this exact purpose. Habitat playing as vital a role in his enterprise as the security staff roaming the property or the storehouses kept in secret throughout the area.

"Tell me," Garcia asks. "Have you heard about my nickname around town?"

The lead-in question for each of these displays, it is received much the same as usual. One of two evoked responses, the pair before him opting for one of each.

Pure confusion on the part of Johnson, offset by more faux mirth from his wife. Levity that again evokes her damnable cackle, extending a hand and placing it upon the sleeve of Garcia's tailored suit coat. Fingers that just moments before were eating dinner and holding a wine glass, not so much as washed before daring to touch the cream-colored linen.

"Oh, of course," Maribelle says. "Laughing Leo!"

"Yes," Garcia replies, flashing his gaze from her face down to her hand resting on his arm. An obvious hint that she completely misses, too entrenched in her wine and her ongoing display to notice. "That is correct. Though I must ask you, have you seen me laugh once this evening? Or in any of our previous meetings?"

For a moment, there is no response. The perplexed look on Johnson's face grows more pronounced. Maribelle pulls her hand back, her own smile fading.

The start of realization that Garcia relishes. People about to be impaled on the full weight of their new reality, made to watch it happen.

"The answer is, you have not," Garcia says. "Just as the sunset is not the reason I brought you out here this evening, at this exact moment."

Taking a step forward, Garcia brings himself up to within inches of the textured stucco railing lining the veranda. An optimal viewpoint allowing him to peer down into the compound below as a lone figure appears. Dressed in khaki slacks and a white undershirt, he is plainly visible in the semi-darkness of dusk.

Staggering along the dirt path carved through the center of the landmass, twice he falls to the ground, losing his balance as he turns to stare back in the direction he just came from.

A mistake they always make, as if looking toward the people who just released them for aid will somehow work out in their favor.

"I am a man with a great many business interests," Garcia says. "And for the most part, we get along very well. Just as if you do what I say, when I say, and how I say, you and I will get along just fine."

Extending a hand before him, he points to the figure fighting to regain his balance more than seventy yards away. A frantic flurry of hands and feet against loose soil, puffs of dust rising around him.

A vain try to rise and flee, as if there is a single thing he can do to save himself at this point, the time for such a thing long past.

"If you do not," Garcia continues, "if you try to renege on our arrangement, if you ever whisper a word of what really goes on here to anybody, you will find yourself in the same position as my former partner here."

Beside him, Garcia can hear Maribelle gasp. The first sounds of horror, bullying past the alcohol in her system and the shock of what they are seeing.

A few feet beyond, Johnson begins to huff, not yet aware of the pair of men moving in from either direction. Trained security who are Garcia's personal detail, a tiny subset of his larger staff.

Men who have watched the entire interaction this evening from afar, ready to insert themselves if need be.

A show of force that is unnecessary – the man of absolutely zero threat to someone as skilled as Garcia – but is a means to an end. Another layer to the spectacle put forth for the Kleese's benefit.

One final time, Garcia pauses. A planned break that lasts nearly a full minute before the sound he has been craving all evening pierces the air. A siren call that reverberates out into the night, passing through the compound and up onto the veranda.

A shrill whine that never fails to bring palpitations the length of Garcia's core as the narcotic release of adrenaline and anticipation surges into his bloodstream.

"You see," Garcia narrates, "the nickname is actually a misnomer. *I* am not the one who laughs. It is my friends down there."

On cue, a quartet of dark shadows move into view. Animals sitting low to the ground and moving fast in formation, following the exact same path as the man in white just minutes before.

"The spotted hyena. Average weight of one hundred and ten pounds, possessing a top speed of forty miles per hour and a bite force of up to eleven hundred PSI."

Letting that resonate for a moment, he adds, "Clan animals who prefer to hunt at dusk, and emit that sound you are hearing whenever they are agitated or smell prey."

It takes only an instant for the pack to disappear from sight. Speed and precision that Garcia admires for a moment before looking away, turning to stand perpendicular to the rail.

A change in vantage allowing him to watch the terror-stricken faces of the Kleeses beside him.

Maribelle leaning forward, bracing herself against the edge of the railing as she tries to pull in ragged breaths.

Her husband rooted in place, his jaw sagging, all color drained from his features.

A pose all three maintain until the first pained wail of the man below can be heard rising in the distance.

CHAPTER TWO

The worst part of the assignment isn't the long hours Enzo is forced to sit outside the small law office on the north side of Austin. A repurposed brick building that has probably seen many iterations throughout its life, the squat structure and corner lot making it conducive to everything from a bank branch to a diner.

Construction making it very similar to most of the others on this end of town, providing ample parking and plenty of clear sight lines for him to hide in plain sight.

It isn't the two solid weeks Enzo has been forced to tail the woman with a curtain of glossy dark hair and Asian features. An endless parade of tasks related directly to her job or her home, those two places monopolizing nearly every waking moment.

A monotonous cycle of trips to the courthouse or the grocery store or to the dry cleaners to pick up the stacks of business suits that she rotates through each week. Wardrobe choices matching the gleaming Tesla she drives around town, making it plainly obvious that she is a woman working beneath her station.

A recent career shift from the gleaming edifices of Big Law in the city center to this outpost in the suburbs. A conscious trade from the long hours and big money of firm life to something more controlled, driven by health or fatigue or even moral reasons.

Motivating factors that probably seemed like good ideas at the time.

Enzo's presence now proving how faulty such an assumption really was.

The part of the assignment Enzo despises the most isn't even the dozens of fast-food meals he's been forced to endure behind the wheel. The number of snap-button shirts he's sweat through while resting against his leather seat. Even the number of plastic bottles he's been forced to relieve himself into.

Far and away, the worst part is the time of day the woman chooses to call it quits. The exact stroke of six, never failing to step outside as the hands on the manual clock imbedded in Enzo's dash draw themselves into a vertical line.

Timing that means by the time she stops for an obligatory errand or two and sits through a bit of evening traffic before breaking free into the countryside for the latter half of her journey, they find themselves driving west toward her home as the sun rests right on the horizon.

A blinding spotlight that no sunglasses can keep at bay and no amount of adjusting the visor can fully block out. Mother nature's addition to the plan Enzo has spent days concocting, honing it to perfection in his mind before running it by his boss for approval.

A schematic satisfying their only two goals as far as the woman is concerned: to silence her permanently, and to do so without drawing too much attention. Nothing more than a cursory glance, ensuring that the safeguards they have in place can aptly deflect.

One less problem for them to worry about. Another cautionary tale for them to eventually leak once any interest has died down, preventing any other enterprising individuals from going down a similar path.

Eyes pinched tight against the searing glare of the evening sun, Enzo grips the steering wheel of the oversized Ram pickup in both hands. A rig chosen for this specific purpose, taken from the stock amassed in the warehouse at his employer's estate. One of many purchased for various business uses, this tonight the final task it will ever be assigned. A job it is perfectly designed for, towering over the Tesla growing steadily closer before it.

A difference in size and shape that becomes more apparent as the gap between them closes and the world around them grows ever tighter. A transition from city streets with multiple lanes and wide sidewalks to two-lanes beyond the edge of town. A route pieced together by the woman connecting her new office and her home well past the outer belt.

A daily drive through the countryside that she probably extolls to her friends as being peaceful, passing through farmland and open pastures. Picturesque settings resplendent with the full of autumn glory.

Sights that Enzo counts on the woman being lost in, too busy fighting against the intrusion of light before her and the panoramic beauty to either side to bother glancing to her rearview mirror. An insistence on always looking forward that keeps her from seeing him continue to lean on the gas, cutting the distance between them from fifty yards down to forty.

From forty on down to thirty.

What transgression the woman has performed to have earned so much attention from him, Enzo only vaguely knows about. Tertiary considerations that he doesn't need the full details of, knowing only that she is a threat. A direct menace to the operation he serves and the people he considers family.

A target as imposing as an intruder with a gun, there to do them harm.

And bound to receive the same untimely ending.

More than fifty times, Enzo has driven the path. Circuits following the woman to work each morning and home again every night. Dozens more in between, when he knows she is sleeping or sitting in a court hearing or visiting with the ongoing parade of clients there to see her. Sad saps arriving with hats in hand and forlorn expressions, their entire existence worth less than the vehicle he is now staring at.

Repeated trips that have ingrained every dip in the pavement in Enzo's mind. Every gentle jog to either side, and even the small gravel bars acting as turnouts for slow moving farm equipment in the area.

A route he knows as well as his own way home, meaning he is able to anticipate when she inevitably notices him in her rearview mirror. The hulking black machine taking up her entire backward view, causing her to tap on the brakes.

A futile first attempt that he cuts off, staying with her further as she attempts to drift to the side of the road.

Again, a moment later as she leans on the gas in a straightaway, attempting to outrun him.

The start of a chase that isn't really one at all, leading her exactly where he wants her to be.

CHAPTER THREE

"Moving to the next item on the agenda," Ed Pritchard announces, putting an end to the interminable discussion that has been playing out for the last twenty minutes. A final knell to the conversation that most around the elongated conference table seem intent on continuing, many still with mouths open or fingers raised before them, ready to make one last point. Summations that will somehow override the deep-seated convictions of the other board members gathered around the table, bringing a quick and peaceful détente to the ongoing battle.

A fight that Cortland Alder had found quite amusing for the first few minutes, before boredom and eventually frustration set in.

There being only so damn much a disinterested third party such as himself can listen to a debate about staying with the existing landscaping crew or bringing in a new team.

To the point that more than once he even considered inserting himself into the talk, if for no other reason than to point out whoever they hired would be culling from a matching pool of Mexicans to come in and provide essentially the exact same service.

"We will now be receiving an update from Mr. Cortland Alder,"

Pritchard continues, raising his voice to be heard over the continued prattling.

Flicking a glance to the side, he raises a palm toward the ceiling, motioning to Cortland seated along the edge of the room. One of a trio of outside consultants invited to speak at the monthly gathering, made to wait in the wings before being granted their turn at the adult table.

A trial by fire that has already rendered the two ladies beside him on the verge of catatonia, nothing he is about to share likely to improve their condition.

"Mr. Alder is a CPA with Cooley and Piper, who as many of you may remember, we hired to do an analysis of our proposed acquisition of the property in Tarrytown."

Many of the people still entrenched from the previous exchange, it takes a moment for recognition to set in. A slow transition from battle-ready positions to registering what was just alluded to.

A shift Cortland gives an extra thirty seconds, knowing better than to jump right in with a crowd that is still seated in the previous topic. A matter so far removed from what he is about to share, the likelihood of most people being able to process – let alone absorb – the new information is extremely low.

Like a sudden cloudburst on a desert floor sunbaked to concrete, it will merely run off before ever having a chance of being soaked up.

A retention rate Cortland couldn't care less about, his pause more rooted in self-interest. The desire not to have to go through it repeatedly, forced to make his presentation in duplicate to a host of befuddled people still trying in vain to get their last word in about who cuts the grass.

Making a point of avoiding eye contact for the moment, Cortland glances down to the trio of pages before him. Notes and facts and figures he knows verbatim, this matter having taken up the bulk of his work hours the last couple of weeks. A chore steeped in tedium, almost making him long for the monotony of tax season just a few months in the future.

His gaze sweeping across the papers, he makes it almost halfway through the second sheet, checking to ensure the graph in the center still says what it did earlier this afternoon, before his focus is drawn to his cellphone resting beside it. A sudden burst of light as the darkened screen comes alive, a single name splayed across the center.

MAYLINN.

"Mr. Alder, whenever you are ready," Pritchard prompts, drawing Cortland's attention up to the host of faces aimed his way.

The last thing Cortland told his wife before they went their separate ways this morning was that he had to attend the board meeting this evening. A throwaway line that she probably forgot after arriving home to find his side of the garage empty, her own thoughts still on whatever case she was working just minutes before. A load that has increased exponentially in the time since she opened her new practice, seeming to grow more with each passing day.

"Thank you," Cortland says, extending a hand to deny the incoming call. A single tap on the red button at the bottom of the screen before folding his hands in front of him. "And thank you all for having me here this evening. As Mr. Pritchard just alluded to, I am from Cooley and Piper, and have been doing a cost analysis of the proposed acquisition on Garnet Avenue."

Extending a hand before him, he continues, "If you will all kindly look to the packets that were disseminated prior to the start of the meeting, you will see my preliminary analysis, which is essentially broken into two pieces: the purchase itself, and the needed expansions and upgrades to bring the existing structures up to code."

The words still hang in the air - barely even heard, let alone grasped - when a hand shoots up from the far corner of the table. Belonging to a woman in a pink blazer with thick-framed glasses, her packet still rests facedown before her.

"I'm sorry," she declares without waiting for acknowledgement. An unusual choice of opening, her tone alone making it clear she is not about to apologize for anything. "But can we please take just two more minutes on the landscaping discussion. I'd like to..."

How the sentence ends, Cortland can't be certain. Knowing full well the direction the conversation is about to go, he allows his focus to drift downward, focusing on the screen of his cellphone lit up for a second time in as many minutes.

An announcement this time not to let him know of a missed call, but of an unheard voicemail. A message left by his wife just moments before, lasting more than a minute in length.

Lifting his attention for a moment, Cortland hears Pritchard beside him say, "Ms. Tiernan, as we just got done outlining, the existing contract is no longer advantageous for what we ask of the crew, and they have been unwilling to either reconsider parameters or renegotiate the pay structure."

A verbatim repeat of an answer given twice already. A stock response that is received the same as in previous attempts, setting off a round of verbal responses.

The start of another shouting match Cortland has no interest in hearing, instead sliding his phone up from the table. Tapping on the voicemail icon, he holds the phone to his ear, using his heel to push himself back a few inches from the table.

The start of a hasty retreat coming just seconds later as he turns and sprints from the room, leaving his presentation materials and a host of confused board members in his wake.

CHAPTER FOUR

Cortland Alder's left hand is curled over the top of the steering wheel, clutching it so tight that all blood has long since left the digits. White knuckles stand out plainly beneath pale skin, flashing along the bottom edge of his vision as they whip back and forth, pushing him through evening traffic.

The closest he has ever come to a Formula One driver, he slides through every small gap in the steady flow of vehicles, accelerating at each available chance. A slalom run that has almost assuredly infuriated more than a few drivers in his wake, inspiring horns and obscenities and middle fingers on both sides of his SUV.

Minor distractions that have barely registered, his focus alternating between the road in front of him and the cellphone gripped in his right hand. Now pressed to his cheek for the fifth time since sprinting out of the boardroom ten minutes earlier, one ringtone after another sounds out. Shrill beats that pass directly into his ear canal, each successive one feeling like a jackhammer to his brain.

Harbingers for what his wife's continuing refusal to answer might mean.

Unanswered calls causing new images to sprout up. Harrowing

visuals making his pulse race and his foot nudge further toward the floorboard, spurring him onward.

"*Shit!*" Cortland spits, hearing the same automaton tell him that the party he is calling cannot be reached. A message he doesn't bother listening to in its entirety, not needing to hear the same canned response or to leave another frantic plea for Maylinn to call him back.

"Come on, hon," he mutters, twisting his arm up and swiping the sleeve of his dress shirt across his face. An impromptu sweat rag, stripping away the perspiration dotting his brow and stinging his eyes. Heavy droplets that easily pass through the pale blue fabric, leaving a damp streak the length of his forearm. "Pick up your phone."

Glancing to the road in front of him, Cortland rotates the screen back toward the ceiling. Swinging out into the far lane, he punches the gas, causing the vehicle to lurch slightly before evening out just shy of triple digits.

A rate of speed sure to draw the attention of whatever police might be in the area, though right now he can't bring himself to care.

Already, he has listened to the message twice. That first time while sitting at the conference table, listening to some busybody go back to the conversation about who should be handling the flowerbeds and thin strips of grass outside. An inane topic that he can't imagine any of them actually caring about, most people barely looking up on their short walk to or from the car each day. Maybe an extra couple of minutes while sitting at their desk and daydreaming in the afternoon.

A completely superfluous matter they have somehow attached personal vestment to, their childish vehemence benefitting Cortland only in allowing him to check the message and make a hasty exit before another precious moment passed.

The second time he heard the strained sound of his wife's voice on the recording was shortly after getting into his car. Peeling out of the parking lot and whipping his way through the thinning crowd still dotting the city streets, he played it once more, forcing himself to ensure that what he thought he heard was actually what was shared. Words that might have easily been contorted through his initial shock, his mind making connections and drawing conclusions that weren't there.

Hopes that were proven faulty, the same thing waiting for him a second time, spiking that initial burst of emotion. Fear and dread and urgency that started deep in his core, clutching at his stomach before rising upward.

A bile climbing along the back of his throat, forcing its way up until he can now taste it as he considers listening a third time before deciding against it.

Doing so will only make him even more frantic. Another burst of chemicals that may become too much, inhibiting him from getting to her side.

The only possible way any of this can possibly be worse than it already is.

The V8 engine of his SUV bucks hard as he punches the gas once more, the red needle on his tachometer swinging to the right before dropping off as he jerks his vehicle to the side. A quick lane change followed by another, and then a third in order.

A swing from one side of the freeway to the opposite as his exit comes into view, reducing the world to stripes of horizontal lights in his side and rearview mirrors. Vehicles and roadside signage rendered as blurs as he hurtles across the pavement, hitting the offramp at just north of sixty.

Flicking his gaze to either side, he checks to ensure there are no vehicles sitting at the waiting intersection before barely tapping on the brakes. A small drop in speed intended not to obey the red octagons ordering him to stop, but to allow him to jerk a wide left turn. A change in direction while operating the steering wheel hand over hand, feeling his side of the vehicle rise on its shocks. A weightless feeling that carries him through the intersection before settling out, allowing him to mash on the accelerator again.

A surge in speed that flings him back in his seat, taking him away from the freeway and all of the assorted sights and sounds associated. Neon signage from passing businesses and the bright glow of overhead lamps and the harsh red flecks of brake lights flaring up around him. Peripheral distractions that fade to the background, replaced by the growing tranquility of the countryside north of the city.

Farmhouses and open meadows that Cortland hurtles past, leaning forward behind the wheel, willing the vehicle to go faster. Bit by bit, his right foot descends toward the floorboard, again bringing his speed up past eighty miles an hour.

An SUV feeding directly off his own adrenaline, using it as a nitrous oxide boost to go faster. A journey on the verge of recklessness, careening toward an endpoint Cortland isn't even sure of until seeing the faint flicker of red and blue lights arising over the treetops in the distance.

CHAPTER FIVE

The young deputy planted in the center of the road looks to be no older than twenty or twenty-one. Straddling the double yellow line in the center of the asphalt, his legs are flexed. Both arms extend straight out from the shoulder, palms upturned toward Cortland.

Two hundred and twenty pounds of muscle and baby fat that barely two years before was probably playing high school football, now attempting to act as a corporeal barricade to keep Cortland at bay.

A self-appointed task he doesn't have a chance in hell at completing, regardless of the uniform he wears.

"Sir! I have to ask—"

Cortland doesn't hear another word the kid says. Nor does he bother slowing his pace as he tears forward, the textured bottoms of his dress shoes gripping the pavement beneath him.

Arms both hooked into ninety-degree angles, he pounds straight ahead. A sprint that started the instant he spilled out of his SUV, forced to stop fifty yards back by the pair of patrol cars blocking the road. Leaving the door open and the lights on behind him, he'd made it through the gap separating the two vehicles before either of the deputies standing alongside them could so much as yell for him to stop.

Fates the young man before him would be wise to share, stepping aside before Cortland either runs around or through him.

"Sir!" the deputy calls again. A single word pushed out from a face shining crimson beneath a head of blonde hair shorn tight.

Twenty minutes solid now, Cortland has been pushing to this moment. A frantic dash spurred by wanton fear and thousands of mental images.

Horrific visuals, most of them containing at least some elements of what waits before him. Patrol cars and ambulances parked at haphazard angles, the rotating lamps atop them painting the darkening scene in hues of red and blue. The smells of charred rubber and wood chips in the air. People in uniforms of various kinds all moving about.

None with the sort of urgency he would expect.

Signs of resignation that causes a pained cry to rise from his throat as he pounds out two more strides, barely looking at the young deputy as he drives straight ahead. A determined path that the young man tries to circumvent, sliding just a few inches to the side before their right shoulders slam into one another.

Even avoiding a direct collision, the contact is hard enough to send the force of impact down Cortland's arm. His entire body twists to the side, momentum carrying him forward as hands reach for him from behind. Errant grasps at the tail of his shirt, jerking it free from his waistband.

Additional impediments he spins away from, his body listing to the side as he continues to push forward, the sounds growing louder from within him. Carnal cries driving him ahead, every bit of him needing to get to the cluster of vehicles just ahead. The epicenter of the nightmare scene, his every thought on what he might find there.

"Stop, dammit!" the young man yells from behind him, the voice backdropped by the sound of additional footsteps. His two cohorts having caught up to Cortland, aided by the deputy sacrificing his body in the name of slowing him down.

A pursuing mob Cortland continues fleeing, driving his knees forward, fighting to get to the twisted assemblage before him. Ambulances and cruisers becoming increasingly fuzzy by the moisture blurring his vision. Emotion growing too strong to be held back, manifesting in every way possible.

Sweat and snot and tears and even the noises emitted from deep within, his only thought of getting to his wife's side.

A goal thwarted by the trio of men at his back finally catching up to him, the collective weight of the first two hitting him at once. Hard sprints that overcome his uneven balance as he fights to keep himself upright, toppling him to the pavement in the center of the road. Several hundred pounds wrapped in shades of brown uniforms, added to a moment later by the third in their group piling on for effect.

A sum total coming it at over six hundred pounds, pinning him to the asphalt.

"Dammit, we told you to stay back!" the young deputy continues to bellow. "This is—"

"This is my wife, you assholes!" Cortland screams up from the bottom. Words that take every bit of remaining air he has, the force of their bodies leaving him unable to expand his lungs.

"Sir-" the young man begins again, still trying to gain the upper hand. One last stab at establishing dominance, assuaging his bruised ego for getting blasted just minutes before.

An attempt that, just like the previous, is cut short, this time by the sharp bite of a third voice added to the mix.

"Jesus Christ, what the hell is going on here?" a graveled voice spits, pulling Cortland's attention up to see a pair of faded Tony Llama boots extended from the frayed cuffs of Levi's jeans.

"This guy-" the deputy begins. One more shot to try and assert himself, getting control of the situation by being the first to share his story. A hardworking public servant wrestling with some miscreant who refuses to heed orders.

Words Cortland has not the slightest interest – or ability – to hear, cutting him off by yelling, "I'm trying to get to my wife!"

The boots come two steps closer before stopping, their owner squatting to peer straight at Cortland, his visage matching the voice heard just a moment before. Wearing just a plain white t-shirt, the tan of his arms and face is made especially pronounced. Silver hair is buzzed into a flattop.

Central casting for a Texas lawman, right down to the square jaw and the glares he gives to the men piled atop Cortland.

"Jesus H. Christ," he says a second time, adding a middle initial for effect. "Get your asses off him!"

Saying nothing more, he remains squatted down, continuing to scowl as the weight on Cortland decreases. Drops in mass as each one climbs free, allowing him to press his palms into the rough asphalt and drive himself upward.

A resumption of what he was just doing, about to go tearing forward again. A return to his rabid sprint, stopped only by the man stepping forward. Much like the young man earlier, he approaches with palms raised, placing them lightly against Alder's chest.

"Sir, before I can let you go over there, can you tell me your name?"

His every thought on pushing the hands away, running straight into the tangle of vehicles ahead, Cortland pulls in loud breaths. His weight shifts from one foot to another, his body refusing to keep still.

"Alder. Cortland. We live not far from here."

Once more, the man's gaze flicks to the officers standing behind Cortland. A scathing glare that he sweeps between the three of them, holding the stare, before saying, "Mr. Alder, I'm Sheriff Jeff Daubenmire. I apologize for the actions of my men."

Taking a step to the side, he pulls his right hand away from Cortland's chest. His left he slides up over Cortland's shoulder, using it to guide him forward. A tandem march, working their way past an SUV with a star painted on the side of it and an ambulance with lights flashing above.

Vehicular obstacles providing perches for men and women of various races and ages to sit and stare, their lack of movement causing the tightening feeling in Cortland's chest to grow. A clench that grasps even his lungs, making it difficult to draw in air.

More heat rises to his features as bits of moisture leak down his cheeks.

"My wife..." he mumbles. "Is she...?"

Daubenmire's only response is to tighten the hand resting on his shoulder. A silent reply that he uses to steer Cortland around the front grille of another emergency squad parked at an angle, blocking much of the road.

The final blockade, behind which the full breadth of the scene becomes visible.

The towering post oak with the front end of Maylinn's Tesla crumpled against it. The trio of EMT's in matching uniforms grouped around a gurney in the center of the street.

The single mass resting upon it, nested inside a black plastic bag.

A sight that causes Cortland to wrench himself free of the sheriff's grasp, charging toward it even as the full weight of his world crashing around him begins to register.

CHAPTER SIX

The cool kiss of night air blows in through the roll top doors standing open along the front of the building. Floor-to-ceiling openings intended to allow vehicles to pull inside for service that tonight serve the dual purpose of acting as windows to the outside world. A source of blessed relief, the sweltering heat of an Indian summer having finally subsided to the more temperate touch of autumn.

Days that are warm enough to draw a sweat, followed by evenings such as this one that pull it away.

The top half of his coveralls stripped off, Remington Alder lets the sleeves hang alongside his legs on either side. In their place is only his ribbed undershirt, the previously damp material dried by the steady pass of air into the garage.

A persistent rush that slides across the ink lining his exposed left arm, strong enough to even occasionally pull a covering of goose pimples to the surface.

Dragon's skin, as his old commanding officer used to call it. The body's reflexive action, bracing it against intrusions of all sorts, whether they be heat or cold or adrenaline.

The base of his left palm braced against the frame of the engine well to a 1969 Cadillac Eldorado, he extends the head of a half-inch wrench down into the tangle of engine machinery. A probe of sorts, allowing him to assess the mess currently staring back at him.

An assemblage that was nothing short of pristine when it first rolled off the line, untouched in the fifty-plus years since. Time and neglect at their worst having reduced the inner workings to a mono-chromatic palate of grease and dust.

"I'm not sure which is worse," Remington mutters. "That they let things get this bad in here, or suddenly decided they wanted us to fix it."

Three feet away, Remington's friend and business partner Tyrell Walters smirks. Bent forward so his bare forearms rest on the side of the car, he leans in under the upraised hood.

Above a gold cross hanging down from his neck, his wide eyes sweep to either side, taking things in.

"I mean, on the upside, this thing alone ought to pay the bills around here for at least the next month or two."

"At least," Remington agrees. Rolling his gaze to the side, he adds, "Assuming this isn't like the last Eldorado we had roll in and the guy is actually good for it."

A wide grin creases Tyrell's features. Teeth exposed to a monthly whitening regime, made more pronounced by his dark skin and close-cropped hair. "You weren't around when this one came in. If you saw the truck he pulled it here with, you'd know he's good for it."

"Ford or Chevy?"

The smile becomes wider. "Mercedes."

"Damn," Remington mutters, his expression trending not to mirth, but confusion. "And he brought it here?"

Raising his palms in a sign of surrender, Tyrell rises to a standing position. The smile lingers, a follow-up about to be lobbed, cut short by his attention being pulled to the side.

"I know, I know," Tyrell calls instead. "It's time to head home. We're just taking a look so we know how bad tomorrow's going to be."

Still bent over the engine of the Cadillac, Remington swings his attention the opposite direction to see the third member of their team extended from the door to the office tucked along the side of the garage. One hand clasping the frame of it, Valentina – Val - Sanchez leans out at an angle, bare arms extending from her grease-stained lavender tank top to match the headband holding back her dark hair. A half empty bottle of beer in hand, she uses the top of it as a pointer, aiming it at Remington.

"It's way past quitting time," she calls, "but I know better than telling you two that. Rem, your phone's blowing up in here."

"Who the hell is calling him?" Tyrell fires back. "He's only got two friends, and we're both here."

"True," Val agrees, "but he also has a brother, and he's called twice now."

Pushing himself back away from the open hood of the Cadillac, Remington starts with Tyrell, asking, "When the hell did we become friends?"

Not bothering to wait for a reply, he turns back in the opposite direction. Raising his voice, he says, "Answer and tell him I'll call him back, will you?"

Tipping the top of her bottle his way, Val swings back through the doorway, disappearing from sight.

"You sure you want to do that?" Tyrell asks. "Putting off the owner like that could be bad for business."

"Worse than taking on something like this?" Remington asks, dipping his chin toward the wreckage before them. "Besides, it's not like that, Cort's the only one here who seems to understand what the term *silent* partner really means."

"Ooh!" Tyrell says, his glowing teeth again flashing in a wide grin. Leaning back at the waist, he says, "Man might not have friends, but he's got jokes!"

Feigning confusion, Remington scrunches his features. Tilting his chin to the side, he asks, "Was it a joke, though?"

Tossing his head back, Tyrell lets out a loud crack of laughter. A sound that easily carries through the doors and out into the night, bringing a grin to Remington's face as well.

The latest round in an ongoing battle of words that has lasted since their first days together in basic training, this one of the few recent bouts to be decided in his favor.

A victory that is short lived, cut off by Val again appearing in their periphery. Leaning out to assume the same position as a moment before she says, "He says to tell you, MCB?"

"MCB?" Tyrell repeats, as if trying the phrase out. A search that renders nothing, prompting him to ask, "What the hell is MCB?"

"MCB," Remington replies, "means I have to take this."

Adding no more, he circles around the Cadillac, the sleeves of his jumpsuit slapping against his legs as he goes. Each successive step becomes quicker, propelling him across the floor of the shop and toward the phone clutched in Val's hand.

Accepting it from her outstretched arm as he passes, he walks on through the open doorway, out into the cool night air.

"Cort? What's wrong?"

"How fast can you get here?" his brother replies. A question that alone is enough to spike the feelings Remington was already starting to have, taken further by the tone of his voice.

A breathy, aching voice that he hasn't heard from his twin brother in years.

"Fly or drive?" Remington replies.

"Borrow Tyrell's truck. Pay cash."

Remington's hand tightens on the phone. His eyes narrow as he stares out at the street running past the front of the shop. A collection of small businesses all standing dark for the night.

"I'll see you in the morning."

———

"Thank God, it's the Moonshine Creek Boys!"

Pausing his walk halfway down the center aisle of The Smoke-

house, Bill Ketchum threw his hands in the air, the effort lifting the tail of his tank top to reveal several inches of stomach hanging over the elastic waistband of his shorts. His preferred attire whenever running the smoker out back, regardless of time of year. Clothes that had been through more than a few trips around the calendar, soiled with smoke and sweat and barbecue sauce.

Stains splashed in amoebic shapes across the fabric, making it difficult to determine what color either originally was. A look much in line with the interior of the place, the walls and furniture all made from wood that had been plastered over by an assortment of graffiti. Signatures scribbled in marker and dollar bills embellished with rave reviews and ancient posters of local sports teams.

Not that it much matters, people driving for miles around not for the presentation, but the final product.

"I was starting to get worried you boys weren't going to make it."

Placing the wooden crate he was carrying down onto the nearest table, Cortland Alder extended a hand before him. "Come on now, Bill, have we ever let you down before?"

Dressed in his own variation of the same outfit, a blue tank top with lighter horizontal pinstripes hung from square shoulders. Cargo shorts stopped just shy of bony knees, his total mass coming in at less than half of Ketchum's, despite being a full eight inches taller.

Just days past his eighteenth birthday, thick dark hair was bunched in tight around his forehead. Locks with the slightest hint of a curl, caused by the Texas humidity and his own sweat.

"That's true," Ketchum replied, thrusting a meaty paw into Cortland's, the skin moist with grease and perspiration, "but I've never called in an order like this before. Your grandpappy must have been running nonstop for the last week now to get me filled."

"Week?" Remington Alder snorted, stepping up beside Cortland and dropping a matching crate down onto the table. A basic box constructed of thin wooden slats, capable of holding five rows of quart-sized Mason jars.

Five gallons per box of clear liquid representing the most potent alcohol available in Texas.

"Most of the damn month," Remington said. Grinning widely, he thrust his hand out as well, grasping Ketchum's in his own. "You know how folks get around Memorial Day."

Cortland's younger brother by all of seven seconds, his face and general shape matched that of his older sibling, though the two were easily differentiated by Remington's hair buzzed tight to his scalp and an extra thirty pounds draped across his frame.

A build that had made him a star tight end at the local high school and had even brought around a few salivating college coaches, all of which were summarily dismissed by Remington informing them that he would never set foot in a classroom again.

"Can you blame them? This is the kickoff to summer!" Ketchum shot back, practically yelling at the two of them. His general proclivity for theatrics, taken to a higher level by the smoked brisket and beer already working through his digestive tract and the promise of a good party just hours away.

The man's entire reason for being, distilled down to three simple pleasures.

"Speaking of which, I expect you two will be back for it later?"

"It depends," Cortland replied, casting a sideways glance to his brother. "Like Rem said, we've got a lot of deliveries still to get to this evening."

From somewhere in the back, a woman called out for Ketchum. A meat emergency that caused him to turn and start drifting that direction, his upper half still twisted to face them. Raising a stubby finger, he said "Don't give me that. I'll drive out there and get you myself if I have to! Your grandpa, too!"

CHAPTER SEVEN

Leo Garcia's worldview has narrowed to the lane directly in front of him. His periphery blocked on either side by the padded headgear he wears, he can see straight ahead and nothing more. A window allowing him to focus on the younger man directly across from him, all else obscured for the time being.

The way he prefers each day to start. Not with business meetings or phone calls from a thousand miles to the south or any of a hundred other fires that seem to perpetually demand his attention.

This, right here.

Physical combat. A means of measuring himself. A test of virility.

A daily rite of proving that while he might be getting older, now more than two years past his fortieth birthday, he isn't getting slower or weaker. The competition is not gaining on him.

A personal credo that the young man on the far side of the ring is fast becoming acquainted with, as evidenced by the tendril of blood snaking down from his left nostril. The result of a hard right cross Garcia delivered just moments before, snapping his opponent's head back and sending up a chorus of calls from the gathered men surrounding the ring. Bodyguards and landscaping crew and warehouse employees, all here to begin their day as well.

A spectacle open to whoever wants to come watch. Team camaraderie, built through the oldest means possible.

Gloved fists raised before him, Garcia bounces from one foot to the other. A rhythmic dance as he circles to his left, forcing his weaker hand to take the lead.

Stripped bare to the waist, sweat slides easily over his chest and down his torso. A midsection built for movement, bypassing the aesthetics of carved abs for the power of mass. Thickness that starts at his shoulders and tapers just slightly to a waist that is still the same size it was two decades before.

A slab of beef weighing two hundred and thirty pounds, kept upright by a pair of legs built through compound movements twice a week. Power lifts, designed for maximizing strength. Size.

Intimidation.

Factors that his opponent tried to ignore at the start of their foray just a few minutes earlier. The usual amount of bravado displayed by new hires, mixing youthful hubris with delusions of grandeur. Misplaced beliefs that whatever bit of strife they may have endured matches in some way to what Garcia has.

A life that started not at zero, but far below it. A mountain to be climbed before ever breaking even, making what he has amassed now that much sweeter.

A daily fight that he will never tire of, knowing all too well what the alternative is.

Already starting to feel the effects of Garcia's jabs, the bounce the young man exhibited before is beginning to wane. His legs are in the concrete stage, meaning that with just a few more blows they will start to turn to jelly. Wobbly supports that will precede his eyes rolling back, the last thing seen before his ass hits the canvas.

A new employee initiation of sorts, damned near every man congregated around the outside of the ring having gone through it at some point. Eagerness or curiosity or whatever else that always eventually pulls them inside, if only once.

The left side of his body twisted forward, Garcia snaps out a straight left. A piston shot extending the limb out from the shoulder, holding it parallel to the floor before drawing it back. Contact marked by the sound of glove and headgear coming together, the respective pads releasing loud puffs of air.

A shot Garcia follows with another, moving into his patented closing sequence. The simplest of combinations, saved for once his opponents have started to feel the effects of his onslaught. A very basic sequence, letting them think they have figured things out.

The boxing equivalent of how he conducts much of his business, fooling them into leaving themselves exposed for the kill shot.

A third time, Garcia pushes out a straight left. The opening of a standard one-two combination, following it with a right cross. Two quick shots that each draw contact, most of the impact absorbed by the padding encasing the young man's head.

Punches that aren't meant to incapacitate, serving only to get him into position for the closing. A precursor for the finishing sequence of an uppercut to lift his opponent into the air, leaving him defenseless, before slashing in with a right hook for the knockout blow.

A crescendo that is just moments away. A delicious ending to the morning's festivities, preparing him for all that awaits.

A decisive victory snatched away by the sound of the bell sounding out behind him. Betrayal from the clock in his own mind, the impending finish making him believe he had the few extra seconds needed.

Gratification that will have to be prolonged a bit longer, a thin smile painting Garcia's features as he lowers his hands just a few inches. Space enough for the young man to come in with a right hook, swiping his glove across Garcia's face. A blow not hard enough to cause any actual damage, but sufficient to snap his head to the side, a single line of spittle striping the canvas beneath him.

A strike that pairs with the audible gasp of the room, every man present inhaling in unison. A collective response that seems to pull away all air, everything inside the gym grinding to an immediate halt. An absence of sound and movement as Garcia stands in the center of the ring, his chin twisted to the side.

"Sir, I'm so sorry," the young man sputters. "I didn't-"

Having no interest in whatever else might come from the kid's lips, Garcia holds up a hand to silence him.

"We're done here," he says, choosing not to so much as even look over, his gaze instead rolling upward to see Enzo standing in the center of the open doorway before him. A darkened silhouette against the green grass and tan sand outside, lit up by the bright morning sun.

Sunglasses in hand, his brows are raised, his jaw sagging at what just took place.

"Get out of my ring. Now."

Behind him, Garcia can hear the shuffle of scurrying feet. A hasty retreat from the ring, paired with every spectator present making for the exits. Well-served desires to get out of his immediate vicinity before the angst he feels boils over, directed at one of them.

Animosity that Garcia makes no effort to hide, or even tamp down, letting it come to rest on his features. Stepping forward, he rests both forearms on the top rope encircling the ring.

"What the hell was that?" Enzo asks, the shade of indoors climbing up the boots and jeans he is wearing. A variation of the same uniform he always dons, today's offering featuring faded blue denim, topped by a dusty rose shirt with snap buttons.

Turning his head to the side, Garcia spits out his mouthguard. A hunk of clear plastic, streaked with saliva and blood.

"That sucker punching bastard was Miguel, the newest member of the landscaping crew."

Tucking his chin to his shoulder slick with sweat, Garcia peers back behind him to the last few men retreating as fast as possible. A swarm of insects bottlenecked around the doors, trying their best to get far away.

Fast.

"I take it you're being back means it is done?" Garcia asks, turning to face forward, his breathing starting to recede to normal.

"It is," Enzo replies. "Last night."

"Any problems?"

Flicking his gaze toward the door, Enzo shakes his head to the side. "None. Any here?"

"No," Garcia replies, "though I need you and your guys to take care of some cleanup in the compound this morning. We had our newest partners over for a little demonstration last night."

Outside of his own mother, Enzo is the person Garcia has known longer than any other. A fellow traveler on the long trek north over the border years before. A co-combatant then and countless times since.

The closest thing Garcia has ever had to a brother. A member in their corporate enterprise long before it could even be considered as much.

A man who needs no explanation of what happened in the compound, or what cleaning up thereafter consists of.

"And what about Miguel?" Enzo asks, raising his chin toward the departed crowd.

"Nothing yet," Garcia replies. "Let him sweat for a while first."

CHAPTER EIGHT

"Remind me why we have these things instead of – you know – *guns?*" Ramon asks from the passenger seat. A question posed to Enzo behind the wheel of the extended UTV, though his focus never leaves the shock stick in his hands. Gripping it at the base, he rotates the tip of it upward and peers directly down the length of it.

A pose that spawns the urge for Enzo to reach out and snap the stun baton upward, answering the man's question with a demonstration. Fifteen million volts passed directly through the soft tissue lining the underside of his chin, sending him toppling backwards.

A total confusion of the anatomical circuitry, rendering him unconscious on contact.

With the added benefit of a nice little scar to remind Ramon of his stupidity each time he looks in the mirror. A burn that will forever be noticeable, no matter how thick he tries to grow the thatch of course black hair encasing his head and chin.

"Because, you stupid *pendejo*," Hector answers from the back before Enzo has a chance. Bisecting the space between them, he stands with his feet planted behind either of their seats. His hands rest on the roll bar across the top of the vehicle.

Dressed in jeans and a canvas work shirt, the wind tugs at the open collar, revealing chest plates stained from years of working in the sun. An ascension pattern that started on the grounds crew, before moving up to security, and now special assignments with Enzo and Ramon.

Reward for time spent, as evidenced by the scars peeking out from beneath the rolled cuffs of his sleeves and the streaks of gray threaded through the ponytail trailing out behind him.

"Those hyenas are worth more to Mr. Garcia than all of us combined," Hector adds. Tilting his chin to the side, he says, "With the obvious exception of Enzo, he'd shoot anybody here before he'd put a bullet in his pets."

Far from the first time Enzo has heard the exchange, he can't help but let his features crack into a grin. A smile with one side of his mouth, meant to avoid tugging on the scar streaking vertically down his left cheek.

A defining feature on an otherwise smooth visage. A war wound received as a young man, coming to the aid of Garcia long before he owned everything around them.

The exact reason why Enzo is now in the position he is in, even if he doubts that – despite what Hector just intimated – it would be enough to save him from a bullet, if things ever came to that.

"Okay, but doesn't that-"

"*Stahp*, you stupid *pendejo*," Enzo says, parroting the same word as Hector just a moment before. "How many times have we had to do this before? Ten? Twenty?"

"At least," Hector chimes in, answering the question even though it wasn't directed his way.

An answer good enough to allow Enzo to continue with, "And have you ever actually *seen* a hyena out here during the day?"

Pushing the UTV along at barely ten miles an hour, he works them over the trail formed into a loop around the periphery of the compound. Twin ruts beaten into the hardpack, with only a thin layer of dust atop the soil baked to a concrete bedrock underneath.

On either side, dried weeds and grass rise like golden bristles, scraping against the sides and undercarriage of the vehicle.

Habitat meant to resemble the African savannah, made much easier during years such as this, when the heat and drought of summer extend deep into fall.

"Well, no, but that's because they're inside, in their pens," Ramon fires back.

An answer that draws another expletive from Hector above, the man muttering something about Ramon's lack of intelligence before slapping at the roll bar. Hitting it twice with the side of his fist, he extends it to the side, pointing into the thickest part of the tree cover.

A favored spot of the hyenas to drag their prey, allowing them to really go to work, stripping the carcass clean, without being seen from above.

"Two o'clock, boss."

Grunting in reply, Enzo lifts his foot from the gas, allowing the UTV to roll to a stop. Placement making their job more difficult, chosen out of respect for the grounds around them and the important function it serves.

"They're only pulled inside right before a hunt," Enzo says, pushing open the small door on his side of the vehicle and stepping out. "The rest of the time, they roam free. The reason you never see them during the day-"

"Is because nobody does," Hector says, hopping down to the ground beside Enzo, his boots scraping against dirt as he lands. Reaching into the bed of the extended UTV, he takes up a square-head shovel and says, "They're nocturnal, you idiot."

"Exactly," Enzo agrees. Climbing out of the UTV, he doesn't bother grabbing up a shovel of his own just yet. Circling around the back, he heads off at an angle, following the thin footpath beaten into the scant vegetation. A winding route carved across the dusty floor of the compound, pockmarked with evidence of recent use.

Paw prints framed with claw marks. Stripes of blood dried black and hardened under the early sun.

Indicators of what they are about to find and the means of disposal that it will likely entail.

"What's the opposite of nocturnal?" Ramon asks, falling in beside Hector to bring up the rear. Walking trailers, complete with the sound of scraping heels and the blade of Hector's shovel planted into the ground with each alternating step.

"Means they're out during the day, dipshit," Hector snaps.

"I know that, *dipshit*," Ramon fires back. "I mean, what's the word for it?"

Letting the two continue their ongoing debate, Enzo follows the path etched into the ground. Looping out to his left, he passes between two small clumps of scrub brush, the smell of blood and death growing heavier with each step. Same for the low buzz of flies, the insects having already found the body and started their assault.

A nuisance that most years has begun to wane by now, enduring this year with the lingering heat.

"The word?" Hector replies. "You want-"

"Diurnal!" Enzo snaps, bringing an abrupt halt to the conversation as the sight of what they're here to fetch comes into a view. The remains of what he guesses was at one point a man, now reduced to little more than a few hunks of gnawed meat and bone, held together by sinew and tendon. A mass of blood and dust with just a few ragged wisps of clothing remaining.

Turning over a shoulder, he adds, "Go ahead and get the bags. There's not enough left of this one to bother with."

CHAPTER NINE

Remington Alder knew better than to ask any direct questions of his brother the night before. Not because there weren't plenty that immediately sprang to mind, information demanding to be known, but because he knew that there was no chance in Hell he'd be able to sit still if he knew the full breadth of things.

Hours spent tucked up behind the steering wheel of Tyrell's truck, staring out at the conical view of the headlights on the pavement in front of him. A trip already lengthy enough, made that much worse by the desire to get there faster.

One of the few times in his life when, if granted any superpower for just a couple of minutes, he would wish it to be teleportation rather than the ability to regrow the missing lower part of his left leg. A trade he would gladly make for the chance to jump right to his brother's side and find out what happened.

How he could begin to help that instant.

The last time Cortland asked for assistance from his brother was more than twelve and a half years earlier. Aid in the form of physicality, needing Remington's help to get out of a volatile situation.

An extension of the two roles they both played in the last days of the original Alder family enterprise, long predating the auto garage. Cortland, the numbers whiz with unending charm who served as the face of things. Remington, with the thick arms and fiery demeanor, there to do the heavy lifting and to make sure any conflicts never escalated too far.

Positions both were well suited to, serving as precursors to their respective careers later in life.

A separation of duties Remington can't imagine being why his brother has reached out now, though without having much information to go on, can't come up with anything more plausible either. Mental gymnastics that have helped while away the time between the pair of stops made for gas and provisions. Sustenance and hydration to keep him going through the night and ensure he is ready for whatever waits once he arrives.

Exercises to keep his mind busy, trying to stem a bit of the anticipation hurtling through him. Tamp down the desire to push the accelerator to the floor, sending the truck hurtling through the night at over a hundred miles an hour.

A journey he wishes no less than a thousand times was already over, the number growing sharply with each progressive sign along the road announcing the remaining mileage into Austin. A silent countdown appearing in haphazard intervals, guiding Remington over the familiar route. A path he has driven enough times to know by heart, not needing to consult the map or GPS on his phone a single time.

By the time the rustic clash of Cape Cod and farmhouse appears just beyond the scope of his headlights, the first faint hints of dawn have started to show outside the driver's side window. A lightening along the horizon signaling that sunrise is still a half hour or more away, just north of nine hours having passed since Val muttered those three letters to Remington, sending him running for the phone.

Time enough for him to have asked Tyrell to borrow his truck, swung by his own place nearby for a few necessary provisions and to swap clothes, and the pair of required stops along the way. A total allotment still shorter than what any GPS program would say it should take, the overnight hours and Remington's excessive speeds cutting the drive considerably.

Feeling his adrenaline rise as he draws near, Remington swings around the towering willow tree just off the side of the road and down the driveway. Following the gentle bend of it, his headlights sweep across the two-story home, illuminating the features he knows so well from his own time residing here a few years before. Architectural choices, such as the porch extended the length of the front and wrapping around the side, underlining the trio of dormers extended from the bedrooms above. The doublewide windows placed to the right of the front door, offset by the picture window on the left acting as the center point of the front living room.

Design aspects picked by his sister-in-law when she and Cortland first moved in, now highlighted by some recent additions. Fall décor underscoring the windows and lining the porch and steps, ranging from sprays of foliage to uncarved pumpkins. In the yard rests a trio of hay bales, piled into a pyramid and lined with mums, a folksy scarecrow peaking up over the top.

Details Remington sees and dismisses in order, checking each one over for signs of damage or hints of struggle. Anything out of place to hint at what might have happened.

Clues that remain painfully out of reach as he jams the truck to a stop at an angle in the drive, barely killing the engine and the headlights before jumping out and heading right for the door. Jogging as fast as his stiff muscles and his walking prosthetic will allow, he crosses in front of the house, peeking through the darkened windows for signs of life.

Actions that earn him the sharp call of a dog barking from within. One shrill bray after another, reverberating through the silent home.

Announcement of his arrival that Remington hopes will spark some sort of movement, though still he sees nothing as he climbs the pair of front steps and goes right for the door. Bypassing the key hidden in the flowerbed nearby, he tries the handle first, the barking growing louder.

A soundtrack to the knob turning easily in his hand, the door swinging inward to reveal a Collie with splashes of mottled gray and black fur, offset by blazes of white across her face and chest. Missing her left front leg, she balances on the remaining three, hopping to maintain balance as her tail swings to either side behind her.

"Hey, Shine," Remington says, lowering himself to a knee. Letting her run her damp nose across his chest and up to his cheek, he slides both hands over her ears and down the length of her neck, his palms gliding easily atop the soft fur. "How's my girl? Huh? How's my girl?"

Tracing his hands down her spine, he pulls her against him, wrapping her in an impromptu hug. A misshapen embrace that draws a series of grunts from her before he releases her and asks, "Where's your dad, huh? Is he here?"

Giving her one more pat, Remington pushes himself to full height. Swinging the door shut behind him, he steps forward into the living room, checking over the wraparound sofa and the adjacent armchair. Dark shapes just barely visible in the faint light of morning that show no signs of use.

"Come on," Remington whispers, Shine falling in beside him as they exit the living room and descend a short hallway into the kitchen. As they go, the urge to call out rises. Simply raise his voice and holler for his brother, letting him know that he is here. Yell and ask what happened to warrant his driving straight through the night.

Desires he holds off on, still not knowing exactly what has happened. If his brother is ill or if Maylinn is injured or any of an untold number of other things he has considered. Possible options that have his nerves pulled taut as he exits the hallway and makes it almost to the island in the middle of the kitchen before pulling up.

Progress stopped by an unexpected sight.

Rooted in place, Remington watches as Shine makes her way

across the room, resuming what was probably her post before his arrival minutes before.

A spot beside Cortland seated on the floor, his back braced against the wall, the crown of his head tilted back to rest against it. Knees raised before him, his hands are clasped around them, blood stains running all the way to the rolled cuffs of his dress shirt.

His right hand is hooked around his left wrist, his thumb tracing the inside of it repeatedly.

"Cort," Remington whispers, coming no closer. "What the hell happened?"

A question his brother replies to by simply whispering, "She's gone."

CHAPTER TEN

More than once, Cortland offered to make coffee. Liquid caffeine it is obvious they both need, neither having been to bed since the previous morning. Long nights that saw them both dealing with enormous levels of stress, the differences in form having no bearing on the physical toll extracted.

Exhaustion that has them staring across the island in the middle of the kitchen at each other through puffy eyes, the whites lined with tendrils of red.

Remington can smell the combination of oil and grease from the garage still on his skin and the nervous sweat that has oozed out in the long hours since. He can visibly see the stains in the underarms of his brother's dress shirt.

The smears of his wife's blood still marring the backs of his hands and lining his fingernails.

Despite the plain need they both have for coffee – to say nothing of sleep and showers – Remington begged off. A bypass not of the jolt it will provide, but of the thought of dropping the acidic drink into his system right now.

An additive that will fry their already frazzled nerves.

Probably roil their stomachs constricted tight as well.

Concentrated emotion that Shine picks up on, posted at the end of the island and steadily pacing from one side to the other. Coming close enough to brush against Remington's leg, she sweeps by, disappearing to the other side to repeat the process before returning again.

Silent assurances that she is near, even if she has no idea what is playing out.

Where her adopted mother might be.

"Let me hear it first," Remington says. An instruction his brother does not object to, merely nodding once before reaching out to the cellphone balanced on the thick slab of wood between them.

Tapping a single button, he pulls his hand back, matching Remington's pose, both braced against opposite edges of the island. Heads lowered, they let their weight balance across their palms, making a point to stare straight down, avoiding both each other and the device as it begins to play.

"Cort," Maylinn gasps over the line. An opening much softer than anticipated, jerking Remington's attention to the phone. His eyes narrow as he focuses on the sound of his sister-in-law's voice, hearing the pain threaded through it.

Agony not of an emotional sort, manifesting in tears or ragged breaths.

Actual, physical, injury. The kind of thing Remington has heard countless times before, in various countries around the world.

A sound he himself made before the shock of losing his foot became too much and he succumbed to unconsciousness.

"Honey, I called 911 first and they're on the way, but I had to hang up on them and call you. I don't have long, and there's some things I need to say."

Pausing there, she draws in a breath. A sound that is audibly wet, pulling in saliva and hinting at blood in her lungs. Indication of an end fast approaching.

"I love you so, so much," she continues, her voice beginning to break. "My life changed the day you walked into the wrong classroom at Tech, all knees and elbows and that terrible haircut, and every day since has been better because of you."

A single sound slides out from Cortland across the island. A noise that is somewhere between a sob and a sniffle that Remington gives him without looking up, affording his brother at least that much privacy.

"I only wish we could have experienced the next ten thousand of them together, just like we always planned. I am so proud of you, so proud to have been your wife, proud to be an Alder."

As she groans softly, Remington can hear as the pain becomes too much. He keeps his head cocked a bit to the side, listening hard, even as a veneer of moisture covers his eyes. Tears that blur his vision, running the length of his nose before dripping to the countertop below.

Sadness at the sheer agony of what he is listening to, paired with the feeling of intruding on a moment that isn't meant for him. A moment of farewell between his brother and his sister-in-law that he is somehow imposing upon.

"I don't have long now," Maylinn adds, her voice fading to just barely audible. "But I wanted to say goodbye, and tell you this was no accident. It was a big black truck that ran me off the road...on purpose..."

Not expecting that last line, Remington snaps his head upward to see Cortland already looking back at him. His eyes puffy, his cheeks damp, he meets Remington's gaze, his chin bobbing just a few millimeters.

"If police don't...promise me...call Rem...find truck..."

Remington's lips part as a puff of air passes through them. Realization of what he is hearing. The scene that was playing out in that moment and the message being conveyed.

The dying missive now including them both.

"Love you guys."

With that, the call ends. An audible beep can be heard, followed by instructions of a mechanized automaton. Options for how to proceed that Cortland cuts short, ending the call right there.

How many times Cortland has heard this message, Remington has no way of knowing. Enough that he doesn't seem to be shocked by what was shared. The initial bit of emotion that threatened to overtake him was contained to the first part, passing as she got on toward the end.

The bombshell Remington was not expecting, his mind spinning as he uses the island to keep himself upright. Bent forward at the waist, he fights to pull in air, balancing the still new blow of Maylinn's loss with what was just shared.

Competing forces of vastly different kinds, tugging him in opposite directions.

"That's why you called," Remington whispers. A bit of dawning, followed by him adding, "I think you better go ahead and make that coffee."

CHAPTER ELEVEN

Feeding off the amount of concentrated emotion inside the house – of every form, ranging from anguish to anticipation – there was no way Shine was going to be left behind. Posting up on the rug Maylinn placed by the door so the dog wouldn't have to sit on the bare hardwood when waiting to go out, she had waited patiently as Cortland and Remington both showered up. Changed their clothes. Finished their first round of coffees and made a second for the road.

The better part of an hour spent in patient vigil, waiting to make sure she was not left behind once they were finally ready to hit the door.

A declaration of intent that Cortland was in no condition to argue with, knowing there was no chance at getting past Shine without an argument. An audible back-and-forth that would have ended with her in the same spot beside the door, throwing her head back and emitting a doleful moan loud enough for every house within three miles to make out.

A sound they didn't need to hear, having been subjected to enough out of her already for the day. A release that was nowhere near a complete break, but rather more like pressure relief.

A continuation of what happened along the road while gripping Maylinn's hand last night. Death by a thousand cuts, each one pouring forth tears rather than blood.

Her weight lowered to her rear haunches and balanced atop her remaining front paw, Shine now sits in the backseat of the SUV. Leaning forward, her muzzle rests just inches above the middle console. Optimal placement to allow Remington to curl his left hand up and around her neck, his right gripping a travel thermos of coffee.

Seated in the passenger seat, gone are the grayscale camouflage shorts and ribbed tank top he wore on the drive down. In their place are a pair of jeans and a polo borrowed from Cortland's closet. Sunglasses rest on the bridge of his nose, the lenses reflecting the world as seen through the front windshield.

A copy of the idyllic fall scene outside, masking the tempest hidden just beneath.

A storm bound to grow more intense as the day wears on, the schedule stretched before them far from enviable.

"I get why you called me," Remington says. Having had more than an hour since they stood in the kitchen and listened to Maylinn's final words, he has managed to clear any breaks from his voice. A return to status quo, having tamped down whatever emotion was present earlier.

An ability to compartmentalize that far surpassed Cortland's, even before he went into the military and was trained to take it to another level. Mental partitioning, putting everything in its individual space so it can be assessed and attacked in order.

"And believe me, I'd be here with or without what she said," he continues. "But I am curious if you took her advice about telling the police?"

As if sensing the pattern of the conversation, Shine turns her head to the side. A spectator sitting center court, waiting to see how Cortland will return the volley.

A stare that he lets linger, feeling the weight of it on his skin, before sighing loudly. "Yes. And I kind of already have."

Beside him, Remington shifts his focus as well. A turn that isn't complete like Shine's, but is an adjustment far enough to bring Cortland into his periphery.

"Meaning?"

"The last thing I did before I left the scene last night was ask the sheriff how this happened. If there was any indication of foul play. A dent in the bumper. Skid marks on the roads. Tracks in the grass to either side. Even a witness who might have seen an animal jump out or something."

Pausing, Cortland pushes out another sigh. A long exhalation not to buy himself an additional moment, but to shove away the bit of animosity flaring within him.

"He shot it down pretty quick. Said he was sorry, but it looked like she was traveling at an excessive rate of speed and lost control.

"No foul play, nobody else had been near the vehicle except for himself and the EMTs."

Remington's head moves another few degrees toward Cortland. A repositioning from eleven to ten o'clock, bringing him into greater focus.

"Was it raining?"

"Not in weeks."

"Dark?"

"Sunset, so not yet."

"Same road she always takes?"

Dipping his chin, Cortland says, "Since changing jobs a while back."

Stopping his barrage there, Remington snaps his focus back to face forward. He pulls his hand away from Shine's neck, sliding it around the opposite side of the thermos. The second half of a clench grip Cortland has seen his brother use thousands of times before. His standard pose whenever pissed or pondering, this one of the rare occasions that checks both boxes.

Fixed in that position, he stares straight out as Cortland maneuvers them toward the northwest corner of the greater Austin area. A route that he has driven only a couple of times before, an equal mix of rural and suburban. Large lawns and open meadows sprinkled between pockets of urban life. Gas stations and chain restaurants and schools of varying grade levels that present a traffic pattern markedly different than what he is used to facing each morning.

A route he won't be traveling for the foreseeable future, having sent his boss an email this morning citing a family emergency. An excuse that will surely spawn a reply of some sort that Cortland can deal with later, having neither the desire nor the capability to share what has happened.

An event so unfathomable, he still hasn't begun to accept it, let alone state it in writing.

"You think it might be a dirty cop? Inside job?" Remington asks.

Exhaling slowly, Cortland considers the notion, letting it roll around. An idea he puts up against the events of the previous night, from getting tackled by the deputies to the sheriff showing up in jeans and a t-shirt.

A veritable shitshow that was much too messy to be completely staged.

Unless that was exactly what they were intending.

"I don't think so," Cortland replies. "I want to say they were just jumping at the most obvious conclusion, but hell, what do I know? I was a mess."

CHAPTER TWELVE

Under Remington's massive right hand, Cortland can't help but notice how small his wife's shoulders are. A physical characteristic he's never put much thought into, especially given that they were so often hidden beneath blazers and suit coats. Padded garments giving her slight frame a little extra size and shape.

Now stripped away to bare skin, her torso covered only to her armpits, the narrow set of her frame is visibly noticeable. Everything from her collarbone to her biceps is hidden from view, swallowed by the paw resting atop her.

A stark contrast not just in size, but also in hue.

Skin stained after a summer and fall spent outdoors or in a garage, juxtaposed by an already pale Asian complexion made lighter by a lack of blood flow and a cooled environment.

A pasty color bringing to mind an old joke Maylinn liked to share after long winter months, saying she looked like someone had bleached a ghost.

"You know you out kicked your coverage with this one, don't you?" Remington asks. Nobody else is inside the small morgue deep within a branch of the Williamson County Coroner's Office, though still he whispers.

A conversation that is meant just for the three of them, nobody else allowed to hear what is shared.

"I do," Cortland manages to mutter in reply. The very first words to pass through his lips since the coroner pulled back the sheet on his wife and excused herself from the room.

Sliding his hand forward an inch, Remington wraps his fingers over the top of Maylinn's shoulder, squeezing softly.

"I remember the first time you sent me a picture of you guys together," Remington adds. "You'd been out in Lubbock for about two years. My ass was somewhere in the Middle East at the time."

As he speaks, Remington keeps his gaze aimed downward. Complete focus on Maylinn, as if etching the bruises and wounds mottling her features into place in his mind. A remembered scorecard to be taken out and used in the near future.

"I never showed another soul that picture the whole time I was out there. Not even Tyrell. Not until we finished up and rolled back stateside."

Exhaling slowly, he continues, "Somehow, I just knew. Even that long ago – we were barely twenty at the time - I knew. I'd never seen you talk about a girl that way. Never seen you grin like that with any of them.

"Sure as hell hadn't seen one look back at you that way."

As he speaks, Remington's hand remains in place. A connection between the two of them, as if imparting the words he is sharing directly into her.

"I knew you two were meant for each other, and I didn't want anybody else looking at her while we were out there. Having thoughts or defiling her image in any way. She was going to be your family, which made her mine too."

The moments are very rare that Cortland can ever remember his brother speaking openly. A collection of instances that can easily be counted on one hand, the most recent being Cortland and Maylinn's wedding reception. A best man's toast that left every eye in the place damp, ending with the three of them hugging in front of a room full of people.

A cherished memory that Cortland never thought they'd be reenacting a version of here, in this place, so soon thereafter.

"She really did love you, Rem."

"I love her too," Remington replies. "Both of you. The way you guys took me in after what happened. Let me stay as long as you did, even with all the shit I was going through..."

His voice trails away as his fingers tighten slightly. Digits curling into talons, gripping Maylinn tight. More unspoken messages pass between them as he tilts his head forward, his breathing becoming more pronounced.

Palpable sadness that Cortland watches for as long as he can before he too is forced to lower his head. Grief slides down the length of his nose on either side. Hot tears that cleave trails across his skin before dropping to the floor between his feet.

"I'm so sorry I wasn't here," Remington whispers. Words that seem out of place, Cortland's gaze rising to see his brother bent forward at the waist, his lips just inches from Maylinn's ears. "You deserve better than this."

Leaning closer, he kisses the top of her head, taking care to avoid the bruises marring her cheek and brow.

A tender embrace between the two most important people in Cortland's world, the moisture covering his eyes growing thicker. His breath seizes, causing his entire body to wrack as he fights to remain upright.

"This is not goodbye," Remington adds. "Not yet. This is me saying I heard what you asked, and I promise – *promise* – that we will see it through."

Remaining fixed in position, he stays there for several moments, the pose again highlighting the differences between them. The sleeve of tattoos covering Remington's arm. The close crop of his hair. The assorted nicks and scars from a lifetime of hard living.

All of it a harsh juxtaposition to the porcelain doll resting silently beside him.

"That goes to both of you," Remington says, lifting himself to full height. Giving Maylinn one last gentle squeeze, he turns on his heel and heads for the exit, pausing halfway there to put the same hand on Cortland's shoulder. "We will see it through."

Releasing his grip, he continues on his way, adding, "I'll be outside with Shine. Take all the time you need."

CHAPTER THIRTEEN

Remington was back in the passenger seat of his brother's SUV when Maylinn's parents arrived. Two people he hadn't seen in years, though he recognized instantly. Would have even if he'd never met them before, the palpable sorrow they both emoted surpassed only by that of Cortland and, arguably, Shine.

Another pair having just received the news that the most precious thing in their life had been ripped away. Their baseline of good and decency was now gone, replaced by grief and misunderstanding at how such a thing could take place. How someone as wonderful as Maylinn could be gone at such a young age, and in such a random fashion.

Questions that would only become more difficult if they were to ever hear the voicemail left on Cortland's phone the night before.

Intent to make good on his promise to let his brother take as long as necessary, Remington had sat in the front seat as Maylinn's parents disappeared inside. He'd even remained there for more than a half hour afterward, replaying his visit with his deceased sister-in-law and compiling questions in his mind, ignoring the building heat within the vehicle. Warmth brought on by the Texas sun climbing higher into the sky overhead, the November date doing little to mitigate.

A post he was content to remain in for as long as necessary, abandoning it only out of concern for Shine in the back. Opening the rear door, he'd followed her across the parking lot and into the patch of thick grass framing the building on three sides. A lawn meticulously watered and maintained, providing plenty of places for Shine to explore and relieve herself, taking care to spread her mark far and wide.

A process she is still in the midst of, Remington trailing behind, as Maylinn's father emerges from the building. Stepping out across the concrete landing extended from the main entrance, he pauses at the top of the steps leading down to the parking lot, swinging his gaze about. A slow sweep that ends with his focus landing on Remington and Shine before stopping, the man staring their way for several seconds, seeming to debate something in silence, before descending and heading their direction.

A slow amble that ends with him stepping up onto the curb framing the parking lot before deciding to come no further.

"You're Cortland's brother, right? I believe we met at the wedding."

"That's right," Remington replies. "Remington."

Taking a few steps closer, he extends his right hand, clasping the much smaller man's grip in his own. "I'm very sorry, Mr. Chen. Maylinn was...well, I don't know that there is a strong enough word for everything she was."

One corner of the man's mouth creases back. The beginnings of a wan smile that rises no further, unable to penetrate the thick sadness blanketing his features. Grief that is only just beginning, and already the wrinkles around his mouth and eyes seem to sag a bit lower. His thinning hair is matted flat to his scalp. The front of the slacks and button down he wears are rumpled beyond recognition.

A look that – minus the bloodstains – is a parallel to how Remington found his brother this morning.

"Thank you," Chen replies. "She really was. And I'm sorry for you and your brother as well."

Releasing Remington's grip, he turns and glances over his shoulder toward the front door of the building, his gaze lingering a moment before he turns back.

"I, uh, had to get out of there for a minute." Once, twice, his lips open as he tries to find the right words. A search Remington can't begin to imagine, himself having difficulty even as a brother-in-law, there no possible way to quantify what Cortland or her parents must be going through. "Too much agony in a space so small."

Moving his focus toward the front door, Remington begins to confess that the same thing happened to him. Emotion that was not exclusively agony, but was too much for him to handle for an extended period of time. An elixir of different evoked responses, filling him with urges better left unrealized. Means of release that would not have been well served by the time or the setting.

Temporary ways of making himself feel better that all would have ended badly.

And most importantly, would have thwarted what Maylinn herself asked of them barely fourteen hours earlier. A direct request that – more than any guilt or anger or sorrow he might feel – has to be his primary goal from this point forward.

A beacon to focus on, helping him to see past what is bound to be a tempest of other things in the days ahead.

Still attempting to find the right words to convey as much, Remington is cut short by the front door swinging open and his brother emerging. Exiting without Mrs. Chen, he steps out and lifts his face toward the sun, going no further for several moments. His shoulders rise and fall a couple times in order. Deep, cleansing breaths in the wake of what must have just been a difficult situation.

A repeat of what he and Remington went through, taken to a much higher degree.

"Looks like you weren't the only one," Remington says.

Repeating the same rotation, Chen turns to glance at Cortland still rooted on the top of the landing. A sight he focuses on for only a moment before turning back. His eyes glassy, he runs his gaze the length of Remington, stopping on the bottom half of his left leg.

The prosthetic now hidden under a pair of jeans, completely undetectable except by those who know to look for it.

A lingering gaze that normally Remington would abhor, but today can't bring himself to mention.

Not to this man, in this moment.

"You know there was not a thing in the world Maylinn wouldn't do for you, right?" Chen asks, tracing his stare up to meet Remington's.

"I do," Remington says, picking up on the obvious insinuation, no matter that it went unstated.

"Both of you?"

Flicking his gaze back toward the front door, Remington nods. "Believe me, he knows too."

———

Barely was the key in the ignition and the engine turned over when Remington looked into the rearview mirror and saw the pair ambling his way. Positioning that was impossible not to recognize, each of the men assuming a post directly behind the passenger and driver's side tires. An effective blockade keeping them from reversing, leaving them with no choice but to climb out or attempt to drive directly through the side of The Smokehouse.

An option that Remington might consider for most anybody but the two men striding their way.

And for the fact that he wouldn't want to risk their vehicle, or the load still stowed in the backseat.

"Aw, hell," he muttered, dropping the gear shift back into park and twisting off the key.

A sequence that caused Cortland to jerk his attention toward the side mirror, spotting the approaching men just a moment later. A quick glance that evoked a smile as he pushed open the passenger door, the metal hinges moaning slightly in protest.

"Sheriff," he said, stepping out onto the soft dirt of the parking lot. Ground that was never paved, instead left to nature for a covering. Pine needles and matted leaves and all the rest, beaten into a thick pad that was almost buoyant.

A springiness that seemed lost on the man approaching, Sheriff Hal Myles shuffling along without ever fully lifting his feet from the ground. Dragging his heels, he pulled up tufts with each step, carving a path tracing clear back to his cruiser parked out by the road.

Already feeling the effects of the early summer heat, his uniform was barely hanging on. The tail of his shirt was out and the front unbuttoned, his hat cast aside revealing a bright red forehead and graying hair matted flat with sweat.

Sliding his gaze over to the other man in the duo, Cortland took in the long and lean figure dressed in starched jeans and a long-sleeve pullover, his hair and beard both recently barbered.

"Judge."

"Cortland," Judge Henry Mason replied, tilting the top of his head forward before moving his attention to the side and repeating the gesture. "Remington."

"You guys leaving already?" Myles asked. Leaning out to the side, he peered at the front door to The Smokehouse standing open. A clear line of sight revealing the place to be completely subdued. A rare bit of quiet before the shenanigans soon to erupt. "Doesn't look like things have even gotten started yet."

"We'll be back," Cortland replied. "Just had to stop by and drop a few things off first."

Knowing better than to say overtly what those things were, he wasn't the least bit surprised by the knowing glance exchanged between the two men. Sideways stares with the corners of their mouths turned up.

"And how is our old friend Garrison?" Mason asked, referencing their grandfather. The man responsible for the jars filling the backend of the Charger they were standing beside before passing them off to Cortland and Remington for delivery.

A three-man operation, affectionally known around town as the Moonshine Creek Boys.

"Keeping busy? Staying out of trouble?"

"One of the two, anyway," Remington replied.

"One of the two," Myles echoed, his fleshy features breaking into a wide grin. "Yeah, that sounds like old G alright."

Nodding his head in agreement, Mason asked, "Any chance we'll see him out tonight? You boys will finally let him off his leash?"

Evoking a round of laughter, Remington said, "Hey, it ain't us. Seems like the whole county is thirsty this weekend."

Hooking a thumb out to the side, Cortland motioned to the car behind them and asked, "Speaking of which, we always make sure to carry a few extra whenever Remington's at the wheel, just in case."

Much like his original comment, he stopped short of stating the punchline. Inuendo that did its job, both men peering past him to consider the offer before snapping back upright.

Waving their hands before them, Mason said, "Oh no, not for me. Not after what happened to Jim Montgomery last year."

Again, a chorus of laughter sounds out from the group. Shared humor at the recollection of the man who was running against Sheriff Myles attending last year's Memorial Day event and getting a little too deep in the moonshine.

A poor choice for the start of campaign season that ended with him walking naked through the streets of town, carrying a yard sign for his opponent.

The start of an election that saw the sheriff win by the largest margin in county history.

"Me neither, for obvious reasons," Myles added, "but if anybody else does, I'm all for it!"

CHAPTER FOURTEEN

Of the various local officials Enzo has been forced to interact with in recent years, Sheriff Jeff Daubenmire isn't his favorite – that honor goes to County Commissioner Rita Piedmont, who kicks ass and looks good doing it – but he makes the top three. A no-nonsense elected public servant who makes no bones about what he does for Leo Garcia or what he intends to do with the resulting monies.

A man who enjoys hunting and fishing, work is something that either sustains or gets in the way of his hobbies, depending on the task and time of year.

A problem to be remedied by accepting the occasional cash payment from Garcia, bringing his official retirement that much closer. An end goal that drives every decision the man makes, the initial pitch from Garcia one of the easiest Enzo ever witnessed. A simple conversation during which one side presented the financial incentives and the promise of a host of endorsements from associated businesses during election season, and the other promised to look at – or away from – anything that was requested.

A negotiation that took less than ten minutes in total, the ensuing display with the hyenas something that Daubenmire took as a fascinating case study in pack hunting rather than as a cautionary tale to be heeded.

Already seated on a picnic table beneath a grove of pecan trees along the side of the parking lot as Enzo pulls up, Daubenmire waits until Enzo steps out before lifting his Mason jar of sweet tea in greeting. Fingers stained with barbecue sauce from the plate of beef ribs and fried okra in front of him, streaks of residue line the glass.

"Enzo," Daubenmire says.

"Sheriff," Enzo replies. Lifting a single leg over the bench seat on his side of the picnic table, Enzo lowers himself into position straddling the plank. Resting his inside elbow on the table, he peers over at the makeshift structure pumping out woodsmoke and the scent of charred meat into the air.

At one point a food truck, it looks to have been a decade or more since the rig actually moved. Resting on concrete blocks in the center is the original hull of the vehicle, a couple of additions having been made in recent years. All the makings of a brick-and-mortar restaurant, built with the side panel of the truck acting as the centerpiece. A serving window from which all else expands, including a concrete block addendum for restrooms and a washing station to one side, offset by a holding pen made of wooden fencing for the smoker on the other.

An open-air structure allowing plumes of light gray smoke to roll upward, perfuming the air and drawing in motorists passing by.

Behind the rig, a structure extends backward, made of the same concrete block with a pitched roof overhead. Space enough for a proper prep area, replete with kitchen and refrigeration, all hidden beneath red shingles and a coat of red paint over everything.

A setup Enzo himself has seen in person, the place being considered by Leo Garcia a while back before being dismissed as too narrow in scope. A single site with no plans – or even possibility – of future expansion.

A mom-and-pop content to be as much, the gathered crowd out front more than enough to keep them busy and their bills paid. A throng of people wearing everything from bib shorts to business suits, all shouting their orders to the aging woman behind the glass.

"You want anything?" Daubenmire asks. Lifting a bone from his plate, he adds, "Wednesday is rib day."

Flicking his gaze down to the plate for only a moment, Enzo looks at the smattering of bones already picked clean and piled high, balanced next to the remainder of the rack still bearing pink meat and covered in barbecue sauce. A collective heap that looks a little too close to what he and Ramon and Hector spent the morning cleaning up for him to even consider.

"No, thanks," Enzo says, waving away the offer. "Does smell good, though."

"Always does," Daubenmire replies. "Can't tell you how many times I've been driving by and pulled in based on that damn scent alone."

Chuckling softly, he pushes his plate away an inch and leans back on the bench seat. Taking up a paper towel, he begins to methodically work through each of his fingers, wiping them clean.

"You didn't come here to talk about lunch, though, so let's get to it."

"No, I did not," Enzo agrees. Turning away from studying the thickening crowd in front of the window – numbers enough to make him think Garcia might want to give the place a second look – he says, "Anything come up after I left last night?"

"Well, things got a little tight there for a minute," Daubenmire replies. "Apparently, she didn't die on impact, which gave her enough time to get a call off to 911. I was just barely there before the whole damn calvary showed up."

Given the rate of speed they were traveling, Enzo thought for certain that the woman would have passed instantly. Either the violence of her head hitting the dashboard screen or the weight of the front end coming right in on her.

A collision not unlike many he's helped orchestrate before, his mind replaying it twice through before the difference between those and this one becomes obvious. A detail he should have picked up on before snapping into place, causing his jaw to flex as he mashes his molars down. Turning his head to the side, he mumbles out a couple of expletives.

"Damn Tesla doesn't have an engine. Any other car would have cut her in half."

Offering nothing more than a raise of his eyebrows, Daubenmire bends at the waist. Grabbing up a small canvas duffel from the ground beside him, he places it down on the table beside his plate, oblivious to the traces of sauce now smeared into the straps of the handle.

"Nothing to worry about. The frame still got her, and I was able to get the phone and laptop out, as requested."

Still stewing over his error and the potential repercussions it could have – both personally and to the organization – Enzo leaves the bag where it rests. Staring at it, he considers what he knows to be stored inside and how perilously close they were to not retrieving it.

Items that will soon be destroyed and discarded, their destructive value much too high to leave intact.

"Anything else?"

"Nobody saw a thing, if that's what you mean," Daubenmire answers.

Having traveled that road dozens of times, Enzo didn't expect there would be. The curve he chose wasn't picked solely because of the location of the post oak, but also because it was well over a mile from any of the closest homes. Places that saw little to no activity during the day, the occupants either at work in the city or one of the nearby fields.

"The husband showed up," Daubenmire adds, "but it was what you'd expect. Lot of yelling and blubbering and whatnot."

Flicking his gaze upward, Enzo asks, "Did she call him too?"

"I don't think so. Nothing in the call log, and he was still dressed from the office. Looked to be on his way home as well."

Handfuls more questions rising to the surface, Enzo opts to let them go. Raising his fist, he taps his knuckles twice on the table before reaching out and snatching up the bag between them.

"Thanks, sheriff. Payment was deposited this morning."

"Sure thing," Daubenmire replies. Reaching out for the plate before him, he pulls it over, intent to begin anew, before asking, "Just so I know, there wasn't also another animal attack in the area last night I should be aware of, was there?"

CHAPTER FIFTEEN

"Excuse me, miss?" Leo Garcia says, flagging down the waitress as she bustles by. An empty tray tucked under one arm, she walks with purpose, headed toward the back. A woman on a mission, looking to either drop another order on the kitchen staff or to collect a load of their offerings and hustle them out to the corresponding table.

A moment Garcia has been waiting on, wanting to measure the young woman's mettle.

Anyone can be nice to a customer they are serving. Several times in short order, they are forced to interact face-to-face. Potential social awkwardness if they are rude, heightened by the direct financial incentive of their impending tip.

This young woman – the name tag affixed to her shirt identifying her as Pamela – has neither obligating her. Assigned to the tables in the adjoining room, Garcia has seen her hurry by a couple of times, but has not spoken to her.

A test, both of her and of his newest investment.

Forward momentum carries the woman an extra step before she is able to bring herself to a halt. Her left leg swings out, already beginning her next stride, as she rotates on the ball of her foot to face him square.

"Yes, sir?"

"Can you tell me, are the owners here today?" Garcia asks.

Another quiz, this time to see how such matters are handled. If staff are trained in how to interact with similar requests. How accessible the management and owners are.

People with far better things to be occupying their time than fielding every individual comment or inquiry.

"Is there a problem?" Pamela asks, her brows coming together, forming a divot between them. Glancing from Garcia to his pair of cohorts for the day, men from his security staff instructed to dress in a more casual nature, she adds, "Should I go grab your server?"

Noting the way she didn't directly answer his question, granting him a pipeline to the highest ranking people in the place, but rather asked if there was an issue and offered to fetch the lowest individual in the dining hierarchy, Garcia replies, "No, definitely no problem. The Kleese's and I are business associates and I simply wanted to say hello before settling up and heading out."

"Oh," Pamela answers. "In that case, I can go check the back and see if they are available. I know they're here today, but they handle most of the incoming deliveries and what not."

"What is your name, sir?"

"Tell them Laughing Leo is here," Garcia replies. Seeing the bit of confusion that hits her face, he leans in, adding a smile. "It's an inside joke. They'll understand."

"Uh, oh-kay," Pamela says, turning and heading off in the same direction she was going just moments before. An instant return to her original pace, practically sprinting across the floor.

Speed and purpose matched – or even surpassed – a moment later by the appearance of Maribelle and Johnson Kleese. Two people looking decidedly different than the night before, any pretense stripped away. Out of their fancy evening attire, both are dressed in jeans and canvas button downs, the name and logo for The Char Pit embroidered over their hearts.

Maribelle's enormous puff of blonde hair is pulled back in a ponytail, making her head actually look proportional to her body.

Johnson is wearing black running shoes, lowering his height to barely five and a half feet tall.

Both still exhibiting the same sickened looks as the last time Garcia saw them, they inch closer. Expressions they try to put at bay by forcing smiles onto their faces, their eyes darting to either side, monitoring the crowd around them.

Palpable fear that is the real reason Garcia came by today. One last check to ensure their compliance moving forward.

Obedience that is far more delicious than anything he just consumed.

"Mr. Garcia, good to see you," Maribelle opens. "You should have told us you were coming by, we could have set you up in our private room in the back."

"Oh no, not at all," Garcia replies. "This was just wonderful."

Extending his hand before him, he waits, making her accept his shake. A reluctant grasp with a limp hand, allowing him to wrap both hands around hers.

"And please, what's with this *Mr. Garcia* stuff? We're working together, you've been to my home. It's just Leo."

To either side, Garcia can see people turning their way. Curious patrons and rubbernecking servers, all looking to extract some bit of information from the exchange.

People all who will – if ever questioned in the future – recall the kind guest with the quick smile and booming laugh.

Camouflage for how he really feels, about the Kleeses and all of them.

Hell, even The Char Pit and the city it sits in for that matter, every last bit of it a means to an end. The foundation to his empire.

Nothing more.

"How was everything?" Johnson asks. A weak attempt to insert himself and protect his wife, without actually venturing any closer. A performative effort that confirms every supposition Garcia has had about him. Little Man Syndrome taken to the most extreme degree, surpassed only by his own self- preservation.

The kind of thing that brings a sour taste to Garcia's mouth, the person before him unworthy of being called a man.

A trait shared by so many Garcia has encountered since his arrival. An entire society that has feasted on the largesse of a system they had no hand in creating. People who have known no real strife and have grown soft as a result.

"It was wonderful," Garcia answers. "I was actually hoping I might be able to get some to take home to *mi madre* for dinner. She did so enjoy seeing you both last night and was sad she couldn't make it today."

In unison, whatever bit of feigned bravado the couple might have been able to conjure melts away. A visible wilting at the mention of the night before, causing each to take a step back from the table.

Exchanging a glance, Maribelle is the first to speak.

"We could have it delivered right to the house," she offers. "That way it's fresh for dinner tonight."

"Yeah," her husband adds. "On us, as a way to repay your hospitality."

No matter that a similar situation has played out no less than a dozen times before, Garcia cannot help but smile. Joy steeped in knowing that his work is complete. The demonstration the night before and the display this afternoon have done as intended.

The people before him are nothing short of terrified. Already they have offered delivery and a free meal, willing to do most anything to rid them of his presence.

Palpable fear that he will refresh by stopping in from time to time. A corporeal reminder of what they have agreed to and the constant presence he will be if he must to ensure it.

"Thank you," Garcia replies. "We have a few additional stops to make this afternoon, so I think I'll take you up on that delivery."

Fitting his gaze on Johnson, he adds, "But just like everybody else, I must insist on paying whatever is owed. Nobody eats free around here anymore, remember?"

CHAPTER SIXTEEN

The seating arrangement is an exact inversion of barely an hour earlier. His eyes rendered virtually worthless from seeing his wife stretched out on the stainless-steel table, Cortland had tossed the keys to his brother and climbed into the passenger seat. Sliding a hand up and around Shine's neck, he'd pulled her close, pressing his cheek into the thick fur lining her jowls.

Fingers clenching and relaxing in even intervals, he stares out through the front windshield. Looking without seeing, he barely registers the blurs of shapes and colors that pass by, his complete focus on the room he just left. A scene he will never be able to strike from his memory, everything from the antiseptic scent in the air to the echo of Maylinn's mother's sorrowful howls as she saw her daughter for the first time.

The feel of her fingers clutching him as they stood and held each other, Cortland's defenses no match for the scenario, completely crumbling for the third time in just the last twelve hours. Agony there is no point in trying to keep penned in, the sheer amount of it far too great to be held back.

"You sure you're ready for this?" Remington asks.

Letting the question hang for a moment, Cortland allows the scene in his mind to play to completion. A full pass through the events, feeling the swell of emotion within him crest before slowing starting to ebb.

Blinking twice, he clears his vision, drawing in a deep breath. Twisting his chin to the side, he presses his lips to the side of Shine's muzzle before replying, "Never let them see you cry, right?"

"I don't think that applies here," Remington says, following the silent instructions of the phone resting on the dashboard mount. Making one final turn, he pulls off the main road and onto a lane that is equal parts dirt and gravel. Lined by chain link fencing covered in brown tarpaulins, the bulky shapes of vehicles can be seen on the other side.

Automobiles towed at some point in the past and left behind by owners unwilling or unable to come get them. Cars seized for any number of existing infractions.

Vehicles smashed beyond recognition and rendered inoperable, such as the one they are now here to view.

A sight Cortland has no false belief he is prepared for, made to do so only by his wife's dying wish.

The first stop he and Remington had come up with after listening to Maylinn's message a second time earlier. The start of an investigation, ready to begin once they cleared the unenviable task of meeting with her parents.

A rendezvous that, admittedly, took more from him than anticipated, but is still not enough to keep him from moving forward, discovering who put his wife on that table and why.

Pulling to a stop just shy of the drop arm acting as a barrier to entry and the metal trailer standing beside it serving as an office, Remington leaves the car in gear, his foot resting on the brake. "We don't have to do this right now. Or even today."

Cortland's grip on Shine grows tighter. Pulling her against him, he turns and presses his lips to the side of her face, her tongue darting out in response. A quick flick that just barely catches his cheek as he releases and pulls back to take in the scene before him.

A real assessment of things, looking at what is actually present instead of merely seeing it. Mental processing he offsets with the scene they just left. The sights and sounds of the morgue and the brief conversation they had with Maylinn's father out front.

"The longer we wait, the harder it gets."

Up ahead, the front door to the trailer swings open and a man wearing canvas work pants and shirt steps out. Matching dark blue Dickies, the only identifying marks being an insignia sown onto the chest pocket and a circle name patch attached just below it. Identifiers still too far away to make out, leaving only the man's physical characteristics.

Standing well short of six feet tall, he is carrying an extra twenty or thirty pounds, most of it concentrated in his chest and midsection. Weight that tugs at his shirt in odd intervals, while at the same time causing his pants to slide down his non-existent backside.

Atop his head, most of his dark loopy curls have thinned considerably, his scalp visible beneath the midday sun.

A clipboard tucked under his arm, he makes his way down the rickety set of metal stairs and over to the SUV, soft clouds of dust arising around his ankles with each step. Approaching on the passenger side, he motions with his free hand in a circle, signaling for Cortland to roll down the window.

A silent instruction that is followed a moment later with him sidling up alongside the vehicle and saying, "Good morning."

"Morning," Cortland replies, hearing his brother intone the same beside him. "I'm the owner of a vehicle that was brought in last night and would like to take a look at it."

"Impound?" the man asks, pulling his clipboard over in front of him and flipping back the top sheet on it.

"Accident," Cortland replies. "2020 Silver Tesla."

Stopping his scan of the paperwork where he's at, the man slowly raises his gaze. Looking past the SUV, he peers off into the distance, information visibly lining up in his head.

"Name?" he asks, though his tone and the faint wince lines that form around his eyes make it clear he already knows who they are.

"Alder."

The folds of skin around the man's eyes grow more pronounced as he turns back. Tucking the clipboard back under his arm, he glances across the front seat and asks, "Are you the husband of...the...um...?"

The man's voice trails off. A loss of words coupled with some modicum of social grace or awkwardness and the desire to avoid stating the obvious.

"I am," Cortland replies, saving the man from going any further and himself from having to hear it.

Words that, no matter how well intended, he doesn't have it in him to hear right now.

"And you are?" the man asks, looking past Cortland to the driver's seat.

"His mechanic," Remington replies, his voice letting it be known that he has had enough with this conversation. No matter how well intentioned the gatekeeper might be, he is now just prolonging things. Wasted time neither of them has the patience for. "Here to do a quick damage assessment."

Twice, the man flicks his gaze across the front scat. Back and forth between the twin brothers, visibly debating the veracity of Remington's story. A silent internal debate that eventually ends with him saying, "In that case, Mr. Alder, you might want to stay back. It's not exactly something you probably want to see right now."

CHAPTER SEVENTEEN

Any annoyance Remington might have developed for the guy manning the front entrance to the impound lot melts away the instant he pulls open the front door of his sister-in-law's Tesla and peers inside. A reversal of feelings based on the final warning the man issued, telling Cortland that he might want to hang back and let his mechanic take the lead.

A word of caution that was well put, underselling just how bad things are on the inside. A dramatic escalation from just the initial walk around the outside, with only a smear of paint on the back bumper, but the front end crumpled inward like an accordion. A mash of aluminum and plastic reducing the entire nose to barely a couple of feet in length, threatening to squeeze through the trunk and into the interior.

A scene his brother is not ready for after what happened at the morgue just minutes before.

Or ever, Remington himself forced to look away for a moment, steeling himself to what he sees. An instant of detachment, forcing from mind the thought of Maylinn's battered and twisted form curled up on the driver's seat.

Eyes closed, he keeps his head turned to the side, forcing himself to focus only on what is most important. A process his commanding officers used to call *inventory and dismiss*, the phrase one he must have heard a thousand times. A three-word catchphrase hammered home enough that once he finally found himself in the shit, it was already second nature.

A means of clearing away the extraneous, putting his full attention only on what matters.

A process he can't pretend doesn't feel wrong in this instant, but is the only way he will possibly be able to do what he must. A charge issued to them both with Maylinn's dying breath.

The only reason they are anywhere near this place right now, instead of both sitting at the house or still waiting at the morgue with Maylinn's parents. Inertia caused by devastation that will come with time, but by her own request will have to wait for now.

Black specks of dried blood spatter dapple the front dash and inside of the windshield. Even heavier, it rests across the screen mounted in the center of the dash, emanating outward from a starburst fracture along the left side.

A point of impact explaining the injuries to her face. A concussive blow bad enough to injure, but not enough to be fatal.

That honor is held by the pair of metal spikes protruding up between the gas and brake pedals. Chunks of the frame sheared off and hurled into the main of the vehicle, extending several inches beyond the bottom of the steering wheel.

Spears cut short, their tops still bright and shiny from where first responders had to sheer them away to get Maylinn out. Poles that forced their way into the interior of the vehicle, impaling the poor woman where she sat, as evidenced by the thick crust coating the entire driver's seat. Dried blood that has already hardened and begun to mildew, flies and insects sure to arrive at any moment.

Another mental image that Remington will never be able to rid himself of. A second visual added to the one in the morgue this morning, serving as fuel for the coming days.

A source of rage whenever the sorrow becomes too much, helping to keep him on task. A focusing tool far greater than any caffeine or medication could ever hope to be.

And a font of wrath that will be unending once he finally uncovers the driver who did this to her.

Seeing the sight before him, Remington understands fully the sounds heard on the voicemail. The wet inhalations and the pained gasps and all the rest, the sheer amount of will it must have taken for her to even make the call something to be admired.

One last task she was just able to see through before the combined injuries were too much, there being no way in hell Cortland could have gotten to her side in time, no matter how fast he drove.

Resting with his left haunch on the edge of the passenger seat, Remington sweeps his gaze across everything, taking it all in one last time. A final commitment to memory, making sure he has every detail imbedded, before forcing himself to look away.

Averting his gaze, he clenches his jaw, making himself focus on the reason he is here, before leaning out from the car and looking to his brother still standing by the SUV. Arms crossed, he shifts his weight from one foot to the other, visibly debating whether to come closer or remain where he is.

"Did anybody happen to recover her phone last night?"

"Her phone?" Cortland replies, his chin rising slightly in reply.

"Yeah," Remington answers. "These Teslas start based on an app saved to the driver's phone."

"Oh, right," Cortland answers. Taking a step forward, he reaches for his back pocket. "Not that I know of, but I have a keycard in my wallet."

Wanting his brother to come no closer, Remington pulls himself up from the front seat. Increasing his usual pace, he meets his brother well back from the rear of the Tesla, accepting the small card. A glossy piece of black plastic with a textured letter T in gray in the center.

"Just put this on the middle console," Cortland says. Leaning a few inches to the side, he asks, "You really think it will start?"

The vivid images of the sheared spikes rising through the floorboards comes to Remington's mind. Damage severe enough to have punctured the interior of the car, no doubt even worse on the undercarriage. A mass of metal and electronics destroying the needed functions to make the automobile ever operable again.

"Not a chance in hell," Remington replies. "I just want to take a look at the screen, see if it'll tell us anything."

"Ahh," Cortland mutters, his gaze again drifting to the vehicle. "Should I...?"

"No," Remington replies, rotating on the ball of his foot and heading back the opposite direction. A retrace of his previous route that returns him to the passenger seat just a moment later.

Placing the card down in the middle as instructed, he waits with his breath clenched, watching as the screen before him begins to flicker. Like an aging computer monitor turned on for the first time in years, it comes in fits and stops, starting with nothing more than a faint glow before bits of color start to appear. Fractals of disparate shapes and hues, outlining the shatter pattern from Maylinn's impact.

Flickering more than a dozen times in order, it takes the better part of a full minute before eventually what Remington was hoping for comes to fruition. A frozen image of what was up onscreen at the time of impact, forever imbedded in the busted circuitry.

A screenshot that isn't complete, but gives Remington everything he needs. Not just confirmation of what Maylinn told them on the voicemail, but a schematic to use going forward.

In the upper left corner of the screen is a digital speedometer displaying the number seventy-seven.

Beneath it is an overhead computer rendering of her vehicle in relation to its surroundings, showing the car sandwiched between the approaching tree and her pursuer right behind her, both close enough to have set off the alarm sensors on either end.

A sight Remington stares at, searing it into his mind, until he can take it no longer. Another image for the growing collection, to be unleashed on the perpetrator in the very near future.

Grabbing up the keycard beside him, he waits for the screen to go dark before stepping back out. Walking fast, he passes his brother still rooted in place, headed for the driver's seat of the SUV, his mind already moving to the next stop on their list.

CHAPTER EIGHTEEN

Enzo is waiting in the parking lot when Leo Garcia's white Escalade rolls into view. Coming from downtown, it heads due west through the center turn lane, a thin smattering of afternoon traffic filing by on either side. A great white whale parting the sea down the middle, easily identifiable from a distance.

A distinctive ride most people in Garcia's position might avoid, though Enzo knows the exact opposite to be true in this instance. A deliberate choice made while conducting business, letting associates know he is coming and enemies know to stay the hell out of his way.

A matter of great pride, letting friends and foes alike know he is not afraid.

The same confidence Enzo first saw in that dirt patch twenty-five years ago that made him jump in to help the young boy and his mother. The start of a relationship both personal and business that continues to this day.

It is there every time he looks in the mirror.

And it is the reason he is sitting here now.

Clocking the progress of the Escalade in his rearview mirror, Enzo waits as it pauses before turning, remaining seated until it hooks a left across oncoming traffic and slides into the neighboring stall before stepping out. Circling around the backend of his truck, he is waiting as both passenger doors swing open.

From the rear emerges a member of Garcia's security detail. One half of the pair that travels with him wherever he goes, even if Enzo is present. Added muscle that usually are dressed in matching suits, today dressed down for their earlier engagement at The Char Pit.

The final step in ensuring complete compliance. A detailed sequence that works without fail, eliminating any false assumptions before replacing them with wanton fear.

The greatest known motivator on the planet.

Following just a moment later is Garcia himself from the front seat. Donning a tan suit with a sky-blue shirt open at the collar, a cigar protrudes from the perfect circle of dark hair on his face. A plume of smoke trails out behind him.

"Any trouble?" Garcia asks in greeting.

Not sure which of his morning errands Garcia is referring to, Enzo starts at the beginning. Falling in beside him, they head for the door, the security team bringing up the rear. A perfect two-by-two square marching across the parking lot, easily identifiable on the camera feeds attached to the corners of the buildings.

Security monitors that are usually meant to watch for trespassers – whether they be civilian or law enforcement – that today serve the purpose of announcing their arrival. Letting everyone inside know that the boss is near, the time to look sharp upon them.

"The hyenas did a number on that guy last night," Enzo begins, recalling both the carcass stripped almost clean and the stack of rib bones piled high atop the sheriff's plate. Skeletal remains that have defined his morning, same as more than a few in the past. "Wasn't enough left to play it off as a simple attack, so we had to bury the remains."

"Same place as usual?" Garcia asks.

"Yeah," Enzo answers. "His ass won't be found anytime soon."

Grunting softly, Garcia takes one last hit on his cigar. Turning his head to the side, he shoves out a zeppelin of white smoke, letting the breeze carry it off, before tossing away the remaining stub of his smoke. Flinging it across the parking lot, he gives it no more than a passing glance before stepping up onto the raised walk lining the front of the place.

The start of the window dressing that adorns the building, advertising it as a silkscreen and embroidery shop, replete with signage displaying a phone number and website that is kept current and active. Lists of possible offerings are delineated on some of the windows, outlining everything from hats and sweatshirts to banners and car decals.

The sole remnants of what was previously housed inside. One of the initial companies Garcia invested in, the partnership working out reasonably well for a couple of years until sales started to dry up. A shift in the market that the owner was completely forthright about, enabling him to avoid the same fate as the man the night before.

Instead, he was allowed to transition with the facility, still overseeing a very different staff producing a drastically different product.

"What about the other?" Garcia asks.

"The sheriff says everything from last night is taken care of," Enzo replies. "No calls or witnesses, outside of a 911 call from the woman herself, which has already been scrubbed clean.

"The usual amount of drama and questioning from the husband, but nothing out of the ordinary. Sheriff seems certain he won't be an issue."

Pausing just short of the door, Garcia turns to look at Enzo. His brows come together as he asks, "Remind me, he's the..."

"Accountant."

"Oh, right. The numbers nerd," Garcia says. Jerking open the front door, he waves a hand for Enzo to enter, adding, "Yeah, sheriff's right. You've been gone too much lately to waste any more time on this one."

"Yes, sir," Enzo says, passing through the front door into a shop existing only to keep up the façade splayed across the front windows.

The last remnants of the building's previous incarnation, with wire baskets stacked along the walls and metal racks filling up the center. Display space for t-shirts and sweatshirts of various sizes and colors, their fronts emblazoned with everything from the Longhorns to the more prominent area high schools.

Inventory that gets rotated out seasonally, in the off chance somebody who isn't already on the payroll should happen to stop by.

"Mr. Garcia, Enzo, so good to see you!"

Appearing through the door behind the glass counter on the far end of the room, Milo Beauchamps practically beams, his fleshy face glowing red beneath a broad grin. Reminding Enzo of the main character from *The Sopranos*, he is dressed in pleated slacks and a bowling shirt. Dark hair is combed straight back.

His midsection bulges, made even more pronounced by him standing with his arms extended to either side, as if he might reach across the counter and try to hug them.

"Milo," Garcia says, settling instead for a handshake. "Good to see you as well."

Pumping Garcia's hand twice, Milo moves on to Enzo, thrusting his thick palm into Enzo's.

"Enzo, welcome back."

"Hey, Milo," Enzo replies.

Releasing his grip, Milo raises his hand, waving to each of the security men, before turning and motioning for everyone to follow. "Come on back."

As fast as he arrived, Milo wheels and heads through the door. A gate that looks to be a regular wooden affair from the outside, though as they pass through, Enzo can't help but notice the metal plating several inches thick in the center. Stainless-steel rods are imbedded every foot or so, spring released and controlled by a numeric pad on the wall.

The first layer of security that continues as they pass into the main of the facility with a pair of guards standing along the walls, automatic weapons held at the ready before them.

Oversight for the retrofitted shirt shop, now used to sort and count cash flowing in from various Garcia enterprises.

Businesses that currently look to be doing quite well, as indicated by the trio of machines riffling through stacks of bills and the bales already wrapped in cellophane, ready to be shipped out later in the day.

Waiting for all four men to pass through, Milo closes the door in their wake. Reentering the numeric code, he makes sure they are hidden away from any prying eyes that might appear on the opposite side before circling around, his hands clasped before him.

"So, Mr. Garcia," he says, "to what do we owe the pleasant surprise this afternoon?"

Making a show of scanning everything before him, from the guards in tactical attire to the handful of counters casting furtive glances, Garcia says, "I just wanted to stop by and let you know that The Char Pit is now in play."

"Really?" Milo asks, his eyebrows rising. "They're ready for this?"

Smirking softly, Garcia replies, "They better be."

CHAPTER NINETEEN

Under the full light of day, the crash site looks markedly different than what Cortland remembers. A solar spotlight brings out a multitude of details that were obscured just eighteen hours earlier, hidden by the wigwag lights of the first responders and Cortland's own mental state.

Tunnel vision, focusing on a single item at a time. One thing fixated on and then dismissed in order, running from the first sight of the cruisers blocking the road to the young deputy standing in his path to the sight of the gurney with a black plastic bag on it resting next to the crumpled Tesla.

Mental recollections that come back one after another. Quick pulses separated by milliseconds, as if viewed beneath a strobe light.

Vivid images making him tighten his grip on Shine's neck, a single whine passing from deep in her throat as she presses back into him.

Things that he is in no way ready to revisit, doing so now only to honor his wife's wishes. A directive to focus on, helping to keep him upright.

A way to spend his time right now that is infinitely preferable to the alternative. An endless loop of what happened in the morgue, getting pounded by one crushing wave after another of sorrow.

"I stopped just up there," Cortland says. Extending a hand, he gestures to a small bend in the road, easily identifiable by the grasses matted down on either side. Broad blades bent at an angle, making it clear where some vehicles were parked and others merely turned around. "They already had a roadblock set up when I got here, maybe ten or fifteen yards on further up."

Saying nothing more, Cortland lets his hand drop to the dashboard in front of him. His fingertips come to rest atop it as his gaze drifts forward, landing on the massive post oak tree less than a hundred yards away. The towering hardwood that his wife's car was impaled against on his last visit, the only sign now that anything even took place being a few deep gouges carved into the trunk of it. Blonde wood peeking out, visible even from a distance.

Applying gentle pressure to the brakes, Remington eases the SUV to the side of the road. Pushing the passenger side tires into the grass, he leaves just enough space to make sure anybody who drives past can easily slide by before coming to a stop and jamming the gear shift into park.

"I don't think I've ever been on this road before," Remington comments.

"Probably not," Cortland says. "She started going this way after she changed jobs. It's a back route, shaves a few minutes off the commute and keeps her from having to get on the freeway."

Grunting softly, Remington asks, "You said she took it every day?"

Seeing where he is going with it, the question different than the similar one he asked earlier, Cortland nods. "Without fail."

"At least a hundred times, then," Remington says.

"At least," Cortland agrees.

The remainder of the question goes unstated, there no need to point it out. While the route was one Maylinn knew well – too well to have simply missed a curve and gone into the tree on her own – it was also one that anybody paying attention would have known also. The same path she used every day, providing an easy place to stage something, far from the usual traffic patterns snarled around the greater Austin area.

An ideal way for them to make a hit without it being obvious, leaving barely a smear of paint on her back bumper in the way of evidence. A scheme that practically covers for itself, prodding the arriving sheriff to immediately follow the assumption pattern that has been laid out.

Cracking open the driver's door, Remington pushes it no further. His hand remains on the handle as he pauses and asks, "You want to stay here?"

Wanting has nothing to do with it. As glad as Cortland was to see his brother, not one thing in the last couple of days has gone the way he wants. Starting with that damned board meeting, everything has been radically altered in a way that can never be recovered.

Never again will he be able to stand in his kitchen, or speak to his in-laws, or even look at a damn Tesla, without seeing his wife. Forever, he will immediately conjure what happened, his mind making automatic associations with the horrific images he's been forced to stare at.

None of this is what he wants, but that doesn't mean he can side-step it.

Not and fulfill the last thing his wife ever asked of him.

"I'll go as far as I can," Cortland replies. Popping open his own door, he steps into the grass lining the side of the road. Thick blades growing wild, brush hogged down by the county a couple of times a year, the resulting dead stuff left where it falls and baked yellow by the sun.

Bits of detritus that stick to his shoes and the hem of his jeans. Get caught in Shine's paws as she follows him down, bouncing a few times from the momentum of jumping out onto the uneven ground.

"You can see this is where the cruisers were parked," Cortland says, pointing out the pair of divots in the grass before him. Twin depressions extended perpendicular from the blacktop, separated by five feet or so. "One here, and another over there. Parked nose to nose, they left a gap of maybe a couple of feet."

Dragging his shoes through the thick grass, Cortland comes out on the asphalt a few steps ahead of his brother, Shine bringing up the rear. Spacing he is only vaguely aware of, his mind firmly entrenched in the night before. A horrific dream that still doesn't seem real.

Even less now, seeing it under the afternoon sun, nothing appearing as it did then.

"Just enough room for me to get through before the two deputies who drove them even noticed I was here," he continues.

Raising the same finger before him, he says, "Up there was where the third deputy was. Some young kid, acting like he was a goalie or an offensive lineman or something."

Not wanting to go through the full particulars of the interaction – the initial spin to try and avoid the kid, the shot he took from the arriving deputies, even the bruises now blossomed across both his knees – he instead moves on, gesturing up ahead.

"Right there was an ambulance. The second one on the scene, it was parked at an angle, blocking everything from view."

Allowing it to unspool in his mind, Cortland's hand falls to his side. His vision begins to blur. The warmth of the afternoon sun mixes with the heat rises to his cheeks, beads of sweat starting to form on his features.

"And right about here is where it all came into view," he mutters. "The other ambulance...her car...the..."

Dragging his heels across the asphalt, Cortland comes to a complete stop. His focus fixed on the tree before him, he watches as the surface of it seems to come alive, the trunk shimmering through the sheen of moisture covering his eyes. Each breath is audible as he tries to fill his lungs, willing the surge to pass.

A battle that he is still embroiled in as he feels the weight of his brother's hand rest upon his shoulder.

"You two head on back," Remington whispers. "I'll just be a minute."

CHAPTER TWENTY

The small country road plainly depicts most of what happened the night before. A scene it isn't difficult to put together, once Remington is able to look past the matted grass and tufts of soil left behind by the first responders. Layers added after the fact, obscuring things on a surface level, but unable to truly hide what took place.

Especially after seeing the frozen image on the screen in Maylinn's car. A schematic Remington hasn't been able to banish since, using it as an outline for all that he now sees.

Whether or not the decision to begin using the small country road is what eventually led to his sister-in-law's demise is a matter of some debate. On a most basic level, it does provide a fairly remote locale that certainly made things easier for her attacker.

The last house they saw was over a mile back. A simple farm spread sitting more than fifty yards off the road, any inhabitants unlikely to have even been looking out at the road in the brief instant the Tesla and whoever was chasing it drove past, let alone to have seen anything of note.

Odds are, when they load up and drive on back to Cortland's house, the same will be true in the opposite direction. An occasional home or farm outbuilding, interspersed with enormous swaths of crops or pastures. Spots filled with rows of corn, dried and brittle from months of standing in the fields, most stalks already broken off at half-mast, just waiting to be taken in.

Places such as the one where they now find themselves, with gentle hills stretched to either side. Acreage covered with grasses of varying height, left to be cut and baled a couple times a year or as sustenance for rotating herds of cattle.

No witnesses to be concerned with. No chance of traffic or ATM cameras to see a single thing.

An optimal location that anyone who knew Maylinn's schedule probably salivated over, tailing her until out of sight from the rest of the world and then running her off the side.

At the same time, without knowing who the attacker was or what their motivation might be, it is hard to know how much worse an alternative might be. If they had been willing to make a spectacle on a busy freeway, or even if they would have followed Maylinn all the way to her house.

An option leading to all sorts of possible outcomes, ranging from Cortland intervening and diffusing to becoming collateral damage himself.

Quite certainly the only thing that could have happened that would make things even worse. An eventuality Remington allows to linger for but a moment, his molars clenching together in anger, before twisting his head to either side. An angry shake meant to dispel the thought, and all others like it.

Another moment like that in the front seat of the Tesla earlier, when he must consciously center himself. Cast aside all bits of wonder or conjecture, focusing only on the most immediate. The task given to him and the details that serve it directly.

Everything else is distraction.

Starting at the point where Cortland said he was wrestled to the ground by the trio of deputies, Remington lifts his gaze, studying only the narrow expanse of the road and the bits of grass lining it. Everything else stretched wide in both directions is pushed away, extraneous information that serves no purpose.

Eyes narrowed, Remington traces the asphalt path before him. A stretch of road split by a dotted yellow line, though it isn't truly wide enough for it. Bright paint that was put down long enough ago to have now faded under the sun, made less obvious by the pair of fresh skid marks knifing across it. A pair of clearly delineated lines that start not far from where Remington is standing. Beginning as faint streaks, they grow more pronounced, culminating in solid black stripes leading to the base of the enormous oak tree that crumpled the front end of the Tesla.

The place where Maylinn made that phone call to Cortland, and ultimately took her last breaths.

Using that as a baseline, Remington puts together a mental depiction. A vivid replay of just what he has seen thus far, inserting the silver sedan into the scene before him. Matching the chassis of the vehicle with the tattoo of scorched rubber on the asphalt, he imagines the approach and the impact.

A starting point, from which he adds the details provided by the screen on Maylinn's dash. The speed she was traveling and the unknown vehicle giving chase.

Additions to his internal reel that he lets play clear through before taking his first step forward. And then another. A slow march not toward the tree and the deep slashes carved into it or the bits of metal and glass and plastic sprayed across the grass at the foot of it, but in the opposite direction.

An angled approach aimed at the far side of the road with his gaze lowered, scanning the far edge of the pavement. A search not for more matted grass or muddy ruts from first responders, but for clues from the chase itself. Hints to help with identification, or to fully flesh out exactly how things went.

Keeping his pace even, Remington passes by the tree. Marking it in his periphery, he pushes onward, feeling the faintest bit of a breeze touch the sweat lining his scalp. In the distance, the last cicada of the Indian summer offers its song.

Small blips registered by his auxiliary senses as he puts his full focus onto studying the ground before him.

A search that makes it nearly twenty yards past the site of impact before revealing a crescent streak cut through the dirt and gravel separating the road from the thick band of grass framing it. A deep trench carved by radial tires after whoever chased Maylinn off the right side of the road was forced to course correct, jerking their rig in the opposite direction.

The last bit of information Remington needed, now armed with a full picture of exactly what took place.

"We're done for today," he mutters, turning and beginning the long walk back to his brother and Shine waiting in the SUV.

———

With each foot the Charger rolled forward down the narrow lane, the woods on either side encroached a little further. Heavy shrubbery and bushes pushing in beyond the rusted remnants of the wire fence lining the two-track. Thick limbs already rife with foliage hung across the top, blotting most of the daylight from view.

A tunnel effect that rather than lowering the temperature actually heightened it, trapping in any bits of residual moisture. A veritable sauna that had both Remington and Cortland sweating as they rolled along, unable to get up the speed to push enough air through to cool them.

"Gawd, I hate this place," Remington muttered. His left wrist draped over the wheel, he leaned forward, peering past the shadows crawling slowly up and over the windshield.

"Yep," Cortland agreed. "And is it just me, or does this damn road seem to get longer every time we come here?"

"You're not wrong," Remington agreed, nudging the gas just slightly. An increase to almost twenty miles per hour that he main-

tained, pushing them through potholes and a thin trickle of water laying across the lane. "Almost expect to start hearing banjo music any second now."

Snorting loudly in reply, Cortland said nothing, his gaze watching the woods slide past just outside his window. A slow march deeper into the forest stretched out for more than a mile before mercifully ending in a clearing a couple hundred yards across.

Arranged in a wide circle, the only structure of any kind was a massive barn with a pitched center roof and lean-tos extended from either side. A building that, once upon a time, was probably meant to store farm equipment or hang and dry tobacco. In the decades since, it was left to a state of disrepair, most of the original red paint long since faded. Same for the underlying boards, many having lost nails, falling to the ground or hanging lopsided.

Positioned as the endpoint for the lane, the door covering the end had been removed, allowing for a clear view into the interior. Ample space for agricultural purposes, since reconstituted into a makeshift arena. Wooden stairs and folding chairs surrounding a ring held together with little more than duct tape and fishing line.

The third iteration of an underground fighting venue that simply refused to die.

A client Cortland and Remington would both just as soon do without.

Nudging the car around the outside, Remington circled wide before pulling back down the center. Middle positioning with the front grille aimed back up the lane they just traversed, making for an easier exit the minute they were done.

Foresight Cortland couldn't help but appreciate as he grabbed up the small leather ledger that accompanied them on all trips. Lined pages all filled with his and his grandfather's handwriting, outlining every transaction for the last couple of months.

The latest in a line of matching books going back years, everything done by hand on the road before being entered in an Excel spreadsheet on the aging computer at home.

Cortland's addition to the enterprise, implemented after much urging and even more grumbling from their grandfather the year before.

"How many?" Remington asked, drawing the Charger to a stop and twisting off the ignition.

"Twelve," Cortland replied, folding the ledger shut. "You want me to take it up?"

"Definitely not," Remington answered. "You go on in and talk to the old man, I'll be right behind you. Let's get this done as fast as we can."

CHAPTER TWENTY-ONE

The delivery driver from The Char Pit was waiting in front of Leo Garcia's mansion when they pulled in. A young woman wearing the same outfit and dark ponytail as Pamela earlier, she was standing beside her sedan with an insulated bag resting on the hood by the time they climbed out. A smile affixed to her features, she extracted a sack with three Styrofoam containers from within and handed the food over, stating very clearly the amount that was owed.

A sign of sure progress, Johnson Kleese having learned from their earlier encounter.

Nobody eats for free. Not even the man whose money was paying for their impending expansion.

Leaving his security team to deal with the girl, Garcia had gone on inside. Heading directly to his office, he'd shed his coat and poured himself a double shot of Patron, relishing the bite of it as it passed down his throat before returning to the kitchen to find the food already re-plated onto fine China and arranged atop a serving tray.

Flanking it on either side was a cloth napkin and a set of silver utensils. Completing the arrangement was a flute of sparkling water, a matching one in the opposite corner sprouting a pair of fresh daisies.

The exact same spread that awaits him at five-thirty every evening, the only variation being the food atop the plate. Rotating selections that tonight consists of barbecued pork chops, collard greens, and cornbread.

One of his mother's favorite meals. A rare outlier from her usual preferences of Mexican fare, predilections brought north over the border when they first immigrated decades before.

"*Gracias,*" Garcia says to the pair of women busy preparing dinner for the rest of the compound. House staff and security members and assorted other employees who will all receive their meals at six, after his mother has been served first.

Only then, once everybody has had their fill, will Garcia take his own dinner.

"*De nada,*" the women both answer in unison, adding a slight bow as they turn from the stoves to address him.

A ritual that is another carbon copy repeated daily, Garcia leaving them both to their work as he circles out of the kitchen and climbs up to the main level of the mansion. Passing over the polished Spanish tile, he nods to the guard at the base of the stairwell before ascending on to the third floor.

Following the path he has used no less than a thousand times before, he makes his way to the far end of the building and steps through the door cracked open at precisely half past the hour.

"Good evening, *mi madre,*" he announces, turning along a short hallway extended from the door before entering into the master suite for the home. A room much larger than even Garcia's own on the opposite corner, measuring more than fifty feet in either direction. An open space with a square ceiling, exposed beams crossing it every five feet, each one providing a base for light fixtures or ceiling fans.

Additions that are all in use at the moment, casting down a bright glow or spinning lazily, keeping a bit of air moving throughout. An effort that is made much easier by the floor-to-ceiling windows Garcia pointed out to the Kleeses the night before standing open, inviting in a light breeze. Wind enough to push at the thin gossamer curtains hanging over them, bringing with it the scents of lavender and sage from the gardens below.

Herbs planted specifically for this purpose, perfuming the mansion more than ten months of the year.

"Bout damn time," Sofia Garcia replies. Already seated beside the round table in the corner where she takes all her meals, she stares out through the window beside her, watching whatever she is fixated on to completion before turning to address her son. "Thought for a minute there I was going to have to go down and get it myself."

A lifetime smoker of unfiltered cigarettes, what remains of her lungs has been reduced to tissue paper. Weak internal organs decidedly at odds with the woman who otherwise would be a picture of virility, even now well into her early sixties. A setback requiring that she always wear the clear plastic tubing pumping oxygen through her nostrils, forever tethered to the green canister resting on the cart by her side.

An endless source of embarrassment, causing her to banish herself to the suite on all but the rarest of occasions.

Going back to Garcia's earliest memories, he can never remember his mother being what one would call kind. Or doting. Or empathetic. None of the usual adjectives given to parents, any such thing beat out of her long ago by a life marked by strife. Hardship that began when her own mother passed suddenly when Sofia was but seven and grew exponentially when she was forced to run away from her father just two years later.

A brief window of time marked by abuse and alcoholism that Garcia has no doubt marked her forever moving forward, the fact that he was ever conceived – much less born – about the closest thing to a miracle to be found in family lore.

Knowing better than to engage his mother's comment directly, Garcia remains silent as he places down the tray on the edge of the table. Stepping back, he waits as she peers down the length of her nose at it, visibly considering the newest offering, before asking, "Is this from the people last night? The new ones?"

"It is," Garcia replies.

"With the big hair?"

"Yes."

"And boots?"

"Yes."

"And that annoying-ass laugh?"

For decades, Garcia himself was the subject of his mother's rapid-fire barbs. Unending quips and observations that he occasionally shared with Enzo, but for the most part shouldered alone.

A load he is now glad to foist onto others, especially those as easily targeted as the Kleeses.

"Definitely, yes," Garcia says, pulling out the closest chair and lowering himself into it. "They own a small chain of places called The Char Pit. Two locations now, more than three times that by this time next year."

Sniffing loudly in reply, his mother reaches out and slides the tray closer. Resting the sleeves of her blouse against the edge of the table, she inspects the food a second time before taking up her knife and fork. Sawing off a small corner of one of the chops, she takes it down and chews slowly, a food critic considering their latest review.

"Not bad," she comments. "Not great, but good enough."

"I'm glad you like it, *madre*," Garcia replies.

Jabbing her fork out at him, Sofia snaps, "I said it's not bad, I didn't say I like it." Slowly lowering the utensil before her, she starts in again, going for a second bite. "And I sure as hell didn't say I like them."

The start of a discourse Garcia has heard too many times to count, he rotates his gaze out toward the window. Peering through the break in the swaying curtains, he focuses on the compound down below, the sun still a bit too high for the shadows to have started crawling across the ground yet.

The first rule of business his mother ever imparted into him was to never like anybody. A maxim she pounded into him from the very moment they arrived in America, after he and Enzo were both laying bloody and beaten in the dust.

Liking people led to trusting them, which was a fool's errand. The start of ending up just as they had that day, when letting their guard down for just a moment got their asses kicked.

Liking people also led to expectations. People hoping to leverage something from them or ask for favors they didn't deserve.

People, in Sofia's opinion, were carnivores by nature. In one form or another, they were always trying to consume.

Knowing that, she believed that everyone was to be seen as a threat or an opportunity and had built her business as such. The fledgling start of something that Garcia took over long ago, building it into its current state.

"Tell you what I would like," Sofia says, drawing Garcia's attention back over her way. "Another show this evening. That guy last night didn't even try."

"Not tonight," Garcia replies. Calling to mind the incident with Miguel in the gym this morning, he adds, "Soon, but not quite yet."

"Good," Sofia says, her eating picking up speed, the knife and fork attacking the plate with aplomb. "The lawyer?"

"Not her," Garcia answers. "That one had to look legit. Enzo took care of it last night."

Grunting softly, Sofia forks more meat into her mouth. Her head tilted forward, she chews twice before asking, "And how is Enzo? Haven't seen him around much lately."

CHAPTER TWENTY-TWO

The sun isn't even fully below the horizon yet and already Enzo can hear the music emanating from the club. The low buzz of an electronic beat, paired with the concussive thump of the bass traveling along the pavement behind the place and up through the soles of his shoes. Pounding so visceral it passes into his ankles and up the length of his legs, making each step forward feel buoyant as he heads for the backdoor.

"Jesus Cristo," Hector mutters, walking a step to the left and a step behind Enzo. Space just enough to accommodate the plain black duffel bags held in either hand, the tops zipped closed, the straps bound tight with Velcro.

A positioning and load matched by Ramon on the opposite side.

A three-man arrowhead, making their last stop of the night. A weekly visit that has continued to swell in size over the course of the last year, matching the recent growth of the greater Austin area.

Californians fleeing the high cost of living along the coast, looking to head to a tax haven state, bringing along all their hippy proclivities and liberal ideologies with them. Young millennials, constantly seeking out the hottest new locales.

Scads of people in between, from tech workers relocated by their corporate overlords to illegal migrants just in from south of the border, hoping to find work and disappear into the burgeoning crowd.

All of it a new target market for Leo Garcia and his expanding interests. A two-part business model, helping people find refuge in the area so they can sell the product tucked away in the quartet of duffel bags to them.

Cattle that are milked until they are completely dry, at which point they are swapped out for new.

"If these *gringos* are going to play their shit so loud, at least make it worth listening to."

Snorting loudly, Ramon fires back, "Like you'd know what the hell good music is. The last concert you went to was a damn mariachi band."

"Screw you, *puto*! That was a fiftieth anniversary party, and those mariachis were their sons!"

Unable to help himself, Enzo snorts at the reply. A retort that was supposed to be some kind of defense, when in reality it only proves the point Ramon was trying to make. A tally on his score for the day, evening up from the shot at his expense while riding in the UTV earlier.

Another draw in the battle between the two men that has stretched back to their first days working together as a trio. A way to pass the time that the two only rarely let bleed into the work, largely because Enzo is always there to play referee, inserting himself whenever necessary.

Moments just such as this, knowing that otherwise Hector will continue to defend himself, the two as likely to stand in the parking lot all night insulting each other as they are to remember why they came and ever take the bags they are carrying inside.

"Alright, that's enough," Enzo says. "Last stop of the night, and then you two can sit and pick at each other all you want."

Letting the increasing pounding of the sound waves lead him in, Enzo goes directly for the rear entrance to a place called Brick by

Brick. A moniker that probably has some specific meaning to it, though Enzo has never heard the story and has never cared enough to ask. More bullshit from the rotating cast of businesses under Garcia's control, the number much too high to ever burden himself with all the details.

Part of the first iteration that Garcia began partnering with, the place is a combination lounge and music venue. Located along Sixth Avenue in the heart of Austin, at the time, the place was the hub of the burgeoning scene. A see-and-be-seen joint that every sorority booked for their mixers and every visiting businessman under the age of forty made a point to swing by so they could admire the view.

The proverbial It Spot for the better part of a decade, eventually ceding the title due only to the changing demographics of the area. An infusion of homelessness and the associated violence that pushed most of the respectable crowd a block over, taking over Fifth Avenue for a couple of years before the slow creep of crime caused it to migrate again, this time over to Fourth.

Its current location, though how long that will last, Enzo has no clue.

A changing landscape he can't be too upset about, most of those changes on account of Garcia's assorted actions, whether it be in moving people or product. Signs that their enterprises are well received, coupled with increased opportunities for expansion.

Job security Enzo appreciates, even if it does come with the occasional bit of gray morality.

Aiming directly for the plain metal door in the center of the establishment, Enzo steps forward and kicks at the base of it, the thump of contact echoing out over the growing throb of the music. A moment later it swings outward, the music becoming much louder as a black man with steroid-infused muscles and a plain black t-shirt tight enough to limit circulation appears.

Recognizing them all by sight, he moves to the side, extending an enormous limb to hold the door open.

"Enzo," he says, dipping the top of his shaved head in greeting.

"Brock," Enzo replies. "G around?"

"In his office," Brock answers, holding the door long enough for Ramon and Hector to pass through before offering, "you guys need a hand with those bags?"

"They're good," Enzo answers, cutting off any answers before his guys can unload their cargo onto the bouncer. "Thanks."

Saying nothing more, Enzo goes straight on down the narrow hallway extended before him. A passageway employing the same color scheme as the rear of the building, with black tile flooring and walls painted the same color, broken up only by framed posters and photos every few feet. Vintage shots of previous concerts or programs from shows long ago.

The assorted history of Brick by Brick's heyday, if it could even be called such a thing.

Wall décor Enzo has seen enough times to barely notice, passing by a pair of doors pulled shut before arriving at his destination. The third one in order, denoted by being cracked open, allowing bright light to spill out, striping the midnight hue of the hallway floor.

Pausing just long enough to bang his knuckles against the metal frame, Enzo steps inside, using the soundproofing of the room to provide a blessed reprieve from the pounding of the music pulsating from the front of the building. Relief from one building headache that is replaced by another, this one in the form of the man leaning against his desk as if expecting them. Backlit by a glowing aquarium taking up the entire back wall of the office, a leering smile is on his face.

Clear indication that his nightly imbibing has already commenced, not one person foolish enough to believe that the bottle he is never without is actually filled with water.

With red cheeks and shiny teeth, he peers at them through dark sunglasses and asks, "Enzo, my friend, how are you?"

"I'm good, G. And you?" Enzo replies.

"Good, good," G – his preferred title, short for Giovanni - answers. "Hector, Ramon, all is well? Can I get you guys anything?"

"All good," Hector replies.

"Good, thanks," Ramon mumbles.

"We're all set," Enzo adds, "just came by to make this week's swap."

"Ha!" G snaps, clapping his hands together for effect. "Always right to business, these guys."

Using his hips, G pushes himself up from the side of the desk. Crossing over the plush rug on the floor between them, he heads for the black leather sofa against the side wall and reaches for the closest of four bags matching those just carried inside. Tugging back the closest zipper, he gaps open the top, making sure Enzo can see the contents.

Cash money, representing another week's haul.

The end result of the bags of pills currently filling the bags they are dropping off. A veritable pharmaceutical buffet, ranging from club staples like MDMA all the way to the newest form of defilement coming north in the form of fentanyl.

Offerings all clearly parsed and identified, ready to be flooded to the masses starting in just a couple short hours.

"And here we are," G says, "ready and waiting for the wash."

Sliding the zipper closed, he steps to the side, motioning that the bags are all theirs to be taken away.

"Any problems this week?" Enzo asks, watching as Ramon and Hector go right for them, leaving their newest offerings where they lay.

"I don't know if I'd call it a problem," G replies, "but we've definitely been running low lately. Another night around here like last night, and we'd be completely out."

CHAPTER TWENTY-THREE

The process is the same one that Remington has performed at least once – often twice or more – a day for three years now. A sequence that was unnerving in those initial few months, what should seemingly be so simplistic rife with potential pitfalls. Little things that most people wouldn't consider, from the extreme chafing that can occur from getting things twisted to the problems presented by just a small pocket of air between the distal end of his limb and the neoprene sleeve encasing it.

Things he ardently worked to avoid in the beginning that have now become rote routine. Mindless exercises he can perform while perched on the side of the bed in the second-floor bedroom, giving up on sleep after just five hours.

A stretch of fitful rest pockmarked by tossing and turning, the Egyptian cotton sheets damp beneath him. Rest that would never fully come, his physical form plenty exhausted, but his mind refusing to ever turn off.

An ongoing slideshow of images, starting with his sister-in-law on the table at the morgue and running through the gouges carved into the tree and the ruts cut through the detritus lining the side of the country road. Visuals backdropped by the soundtrack of hearing the message she left for Cortland playing on loop.

The pained gasps as she sucked in her final breaths, sharing her love before telling them to go and find whoever was responsible.

A charge that by the fourth or fifth replay seemed to address him directly, telling him to do whatever he must. Help Cortland however he can, protecting him from both himself and whatever danger might be out there.

Orders growing more pronounced before eventually culminating with the battered form of Maylinn on that table opening her eyes. Rolling her head to Remington and making him promise that he will see this through.

A final request. His last opportunity to ever make good on all that she has done for him.

Three years ago – almost to the day – Remington was a Staff Sergeant in the Army. In the midst of his second tour overseas, he was riding in the middle transport in a three-vehicle convoy headed for Bagram. Extra security on a supply run that was made twice a day, the rote monotony of it what caused the driver in the lead truck to get lazy, missing the obvious signs of an IED in the road ahead. A circle of freshly overturned dirt signaling recent excavation that all who go on such runs are trained to spot, the man somehow thinking nothing of aiming the driver's side tires right over it.

A direct hit that ignited the makeshift mine buried underneath, sending the truck spiraling into the sky. A celestial projectile tossed back at the truck Remington was riding in, their driver having no choice but to snap the wheel to the side.

A knee jerk reaction that sent them into the low brush growing alongside the roadway, where another mine had been planted.

A planned sequence that worked to perfection, lifting and flinging their ride back into the one behind it.

A domino effect that wiped out the vast majority of the supplies intended to be delivered and decimated the men riding with them. A fifty-percent casualty rate that included Remington's left leg from the mid-calf down, his very survival only through the fortuitous positioning of a combat trauma surgeon who happened to be nearby.

Medical care that saved his life but effectively ended his time in uniform, setting him off on what was easily the most difficult eighteen-month stretch of his life.

A period he has no problem admitting he only made it through because of the house he now finds himself in, the very room where he sits given to him the day he first came back on crutches. The manifestation of a promise to take as long as needed and do whatever was necessary that he never imagined encompassing all that it did.

Debts that he will never be able to repay to Cortland.

Will never even get the chance to for Maylinn, the patience she showed during those first few months, when his PTSD was at its worst, and the legal aid she provided later in securing the benefits he was owed, far surpassing anything he would have ever expected.

Gestures afforded him that she never once mentioned – let alone asked for retribution. Kindness that still weighs on Remington, her turning in the dream and asking for his help the result of his own feeling that he owes her, not anything she would ever say on her own.

A marker he fully intended to find a way to make good on someday, even if he never would have imagined this to be the time or manner.

Snapping the top of the sleeve into place around his lower thigh, Remington takes up his prosthetic from where it leans against the bed beside him. The last thing done before laying down earlier, ready to be snatched up in an instant upon waking.

Fitting the cupped end of it over the bottom of his leg, he uses the elastic bands to secure it into position, winding them around his knee before cinching them tight with Velcro. Once it is in position, he tugs on his opposite shoe to make sure his height is balanced evenly before rising and heading out into the hall.

Five minutes later, after a quick trip to the bathroom to relieve himself and brush his teeth, he steps into the kitchen to find a close approximation of what he discovered upon first arriving this morning.

Two scenes more than sixteen hours apart, the only differences being that instead of resting on the floor in bloodstained clothes, Cortland is sitting at the kitchen table in a pair of gym shorts and a Texas Tech t-shirt.

Elbows balanced on the table before him, he sits in the semi-darkness with Shine on the floor at his side, the room completely silent as he stares straight ahead, waiting until Remington pulls out a chair at the head of the table before blinking himself alert.

"Couldn't sleep either?" Cortland asks.

Settling in to match his brother's pose, Remington considers telling Cortland about the dream he just had. The assorted thoughts and mental images that kept flashing by. The evoked feelings from being in the house.

Things that are all true, but right now his brother doesn't need to hear. More stuff for the tally of items to be gotten to at a later time, but not at this moment.

Not yet.

"The room is exactly the way I left it," Remington says instead.

"Yeah," Cortland replies. Pulling his left hand back from the table, he drops it by his side, letting his fingers graze the fur along Shine's back. "Maylinn always said you'd be back."

"Yeah?" Remington answers. Letting a wan smile play up, he adds, "Not a lot of faith in us at the auto shop, huh?"

"No, no, nothing like that," Cortland says. Giving Shine one last pat, he pulls his hand back, returning it to its original position.

A pose he holds for nearly a full minute before adding, "It's just, part of her taking on that new job was because we were thinking about starting a family soon. Fewer hours, easier commute."

Flipping his palms upward, he continues, "And she knew you'd want to be around a lot for that."

The first Remington has ever heard of such a thing beyond the occasional joking question around the dinner table, it hits him square in the solar plexus. A shot to the stomach, driving the air from his lungs as his head rolls forward, coming to rest on his outstretched forearms.

Another unexpected blow added to the sheer volume of the last day. An unending string of them already creating a potent mix of responses within, no doubt destroying his brother, no matter how well he might try to hide it.

More things that will never come to pass. Opportunities for all of them, ripped away.

The chance at family expansion, allowing Remington's circle to grow from two to three, instead of it being reduced back to but one.

"She's right," Remington whispers. "I would have. All the time." Rotating his focus back up to look at his brother, he adds, "Enough that you would have gotten so damn sick of having me here."

The line wasn't meant as a joke, but it is enough to cause Cortland to cough out a laugh. Reaching out, he rests a hand on Remington's wrist, giving it a shake to either side.

"Yeah, that's probably right."

CHAPTER TWENTY-FOUR

Barely did Cortland feel like eating, the thought of trying to force anything into his stomach enough to bring about a wave of nausea, though he did concede that his brother was right. Not only had he not consumed anything beyond a couple cups of coffee in the last twenty-four hours, he'd also actively been pushing fluids out in regular intervals. Sweat and tears that left him parched and light-headed, his legs beginning to feel weak beneath him.

A diminished state that a few bits of shallow sleep on the couch weren't able to stave off, his body in dire need of replenishment.

Acquiescing to his brother's suggestion, Cortland's first thought was to order pizza. A couple of plain cheese pies that would be about as bland as possible, posing no threat of turning his uneasy stomach. Bread and grease that would provide plenty of energy, as well as form a basis to allow rehydration to occur.

A suggestion that made it barely a couple of minutes before being shot down, Cortland's inability to think of a pizza place that wasn't his wife's favorite and Remington's insistence that they needed animal protein for strength causing them to decide on sub sandwiches. A trio of foot longs loaded with beef and chicken and cheese, more than sufficient to fill both of them and have plenty left over to toss to Shine on the floor of the back deck between them.

A meal eaten largely in silence, both of them working through the previous conversation and the events of the day. The visit to the morgue followed by the start of a covert investigation Cortland can't help but feel they are woefully unprepared for, though he isn't about to turn away from.

Not after the way the sheriff acted the previous night when asked about the presence of a second vehicle.

And damned sure not when doing so is the last words his wife will ever say to him.

Dinner now complete, Cortland has headed back inside and sits at the kitchen table. Eschewing his normal seat at the head of it, he rests in the same center chair along the far side as earlier, his back to the bank of windows behind him. On the opposite side, Remington paces back and forth, his gait emitting a beat that is just slightly off as he walks with his arms crossed, his brows twisted up in thought.

Open in front of Cortland is his laptop, an internet browser with a dozen or so active windows up on the screen. Portals into every major news station and publication in the area, along with a couple of national media outlets. The end results of Googling every possible permutation Cortland could think of, trying to determine if something like this might have happened before.

Attorneys who perished in traffic accidents. Deaths that were made to look like accidents. Professionals who might have died in ways that weren't fully explained.

More than an hour of digging that has rendered precious scant information, the search accomplishing little beyond making Cortland's head hurt. A direct result of eyes already swollen and puffy, forced to focus on the bright glare of the screen.

"I'm telling you, there's no record of anything like this happening in the area in the last year," Cortland says. "Couple of years, even."

Leaning back, he raises both hands to his face, pressing his palms against his cheeks. Rubbing briskly, he slides them back over his scalp, peeling his hair away from his brow.

"But there has been a spike in crime," Remington counters. "Right?"

"I mean, yeah," Cortland says, "but none of it fits. Homelessness. Drug overdoses. Hell, even a handful of wild animal attacks. Nothing like this."

Arms still bracing his torso, Remington continues to move. Passing back through Cortland's direct field of vision, he nods in agreement, adding, "That sure wasn't a wolf or a coyote I saw chasing her on the screen in her car earlier."

"Exactly," Cortland replies. "I doubt it was a homeless person or someone stoned out of their mind either."

Saying nothing to that, Remington continues his parade across the kitchen floor. Marching the length of the table, he continues on to the island, drawing up Shine's attention from her post on the floor, before pivoting on his prosthetic foot and heading back the opposite direction.

Steps that are all audible, his brother always in shoes to maintain an even height. A matching set of Asics that are changed out every few months, rarely swapped for alternative footwear, regardless of the occasion.

"No, this looks and feels personal," Remington says, his detached voice giving the impression he is more thinking out loud than addressing Cortland.

His features twisted up in thought, he continues his march back in the direction he just came from, drawing almost even with Cortland before stopping.

"Tell me about this new job."

CHAPTER TWENTY-FIVE

"Did you ever meet Maylinn's friend from law school, Beth Towner?" Cortland asks. His features aglow from the computer screen before him, he leans back in his seat. His fingers are laced together, balanced atop his head. "She was from here, but moved over to Baton Rouge with her husband-"

"Yeah, yeah, yeah," Remington says. Cutting his brother off, he extends a finger, pointing it across the table. "She's the one who stopped by with that big batch of beignets at Christmas? Ugly as a mud fence, but sweet as hell?"

"That's her," Cortland replies. "Anyway, not long after you left, Beth and her husband got divorced. She stuck it out and stayed over in Louisiana for a while, but eventually she started looking to head back this way.

"She knew Maylinn had been wanting to get out of Big Law for a while, so she reached out, asked if she'd be interested in hanging a shingle together."

Listening to his brother speak, Remington continues to move through the kitchen. Pacing that has now evolved into laps, easily done through the palatial open concept. Starting at the kitchen table, he wraps his way around the island and back between the loveseat and wall-mounted flatscreen serving as a second living room.

A loop that is almost fifteen yards in total, allowing him to keep moving forward without having to turn and restart every few steps. Redirection that he never much thought about before the injury, but is a major pain in the ass now that he wears a prosthetic.

Never before has Remington heard the expression about hanging a shingle, though it isn't hard to figure out. The legal equivalent of what he and Tyrell and Val did, opening up a shop and putting a sign on the side asking people to stop and give them a chance.

"What kind of stuff do they do there?" Remington asks.

"A lot of non-profit work," Cortland replies. "Immigration, environmental law, things like that. The kind of stuff she talked about back before going to law school, but kind of got pushed to the side by student loans and such."

During the year and a half that Remington called this house home, Maylinn was still living the Big Law life. Days that started at exactly six, with her hitting the door by seven without fail. Six days a week of that, never returning back before seven, usually closer to eight or nine. Twelve to fourteen hours a day, always beholden to something called billables.

A concept she tried to explain to Remington on more than one occasion, finally breaking through by explaining to him that while most workers are paid for their output, lawyers – especially corporate ones – are paid for their time. Hours are broken into six-minute increments, and the more of those that can be attributed directly to a particular case, the better.

A way of conducting business – and living life – that Remington couldn't much wrap his head around, the way she described it sounding like the definition of insanity. A slave to the clock in the truest form, which Maylinn eventually confessed was how she was starting to feel.

An admission she made while sitting on the back porch, each of them sharing what they were going through. Remington, getting used to his new carbon alloy leg and trying to find a way to sleep through the night. Maylinn, with her budding ulcer and the constant need to have her phone in her hand, in case a partner should ever call or email.

States of being they were both trying to work past, hopeful for better days on the horizon.

A path they had both managed to find, Remington's only hope that he was even a sliver as much help in her search as she was in his.

"Okay, let's start there," Remington replies. "Immigration law. As in...?"

"Not what you're thinking," Cortland says. "She wasn't prosecuting border jumpers or anything like that. Most of it was helping people renew their green cards or visas each year, making sure they filed any outstanding paperwork, that sort of thing.

"From what she said, the biggest hurdle for most of these people was the language barrier, not the fear of deportation."

Bobbing his head in understanding, Remington continues moving. Lifting his right thumb to his mouth, he gnaws on the edge of it, tasting the familiar tang of grease under his nail. An omnipresent substance, no matter how many times he scrubs his hands.

The most obvious thing on the short list Cortland gave him already crossed off, he moves on to the next in order. "Alright, environmental."

"Same thing," Cortland answers. "Lot of paperwork. Making sure new construction didn't infringe on wetlands, small businesses conducted the right impact assessments where necessary."

"No big oil or anything like that?"

Snorting softly, Cortland replies, "Not even close. From what she's told me, that's mostly handled over in Houston anyway."

"Strike two," Remington mutters. Continuing his untold lap, he glances sideways at his brother as he goes. "Anything else?"

"I mean, it's not like she discussed every single case with me," Cortland replies. "Confidentiality, and all that. I know she was starting to get into veteran's law, but I can't see this being about that either."

Pulling to a stop, Remington posts up at the corner of the table. Drawing the thumbnail from his mouth, the first hint of blood just barely present, he folds his arms back into place.

"No," Remington admits. "Not if what she was doing for them was anything like what she did for me."

Replying with nothing more than a shrug of his eyebrows, Cortland lowers his hands back to the keyboard. Light flickers across his features as he begins again, riffling through various screens. A transition Remington watches for a moment before letting his eyes glaze, his mind continuing to work.

All day, they had been playing catchup. The twin shocks of what happened and the message that was left had put their worldview on tilt, thrusting them into something they weren't expecting, and sure as hell weren't ready to begin. A starting point that was far from optimal, meaning they had to do the necessary legwork to get up to speed.

A baseline of understanding exactly what took place, from which they could begin probing.

A process they both had confessed just minutes before felt wrong, but had to be done. A duty owed to Maylinn, no matter the pain.

Of which, there was plenty.

Now that those essential first steps were over, a bit of rest had, some food ingested, it was time to begin moving forward. The time for excuses was past.

They needed to start making sense of something coming from far afield.

"What about her old firm?" Remington asks. "Any bad experiences that kind of sped up her decision to go? Any bigwigs who might have been worried about something she knew?"

Ceasing his search, Cortland's eyes widen. His mouth forms into a circle as he considers the idea a moment before eventually shaking his head to either side.

"No, nothing like that. Confidentiality or not, she would have told me about a scandal." Drawing his hands back into his lap, he adds, "Hell, when she left, they had a big farewell party, which was basically just an attempt to get her to stay."

"Still," Remington counters, "what I saw today? That was personal. Targeted."

CHAPTER TWENTY-SIX

Three sharp knocks sound out from the closed door on the opposite side of the office. A trio of contacts that puncture the quiet of the room, drawing Leo Garcia's gaze up from the ledger sitting open on his desk. Row after row of painstaking entries in black ink, outlining every dollar coming in through the various channels of his organization. Individual spreadsheets dedicated to each aspect of both the drug and human trafficking pipelines, breaking everything down into manageable chunks.

Means of ensuring that no matter how vast his empire might get, it never becomes unwieldy. Fissures aren't allowed to form, letting money slip by unnoticed.

And, most importantly, that he never trusts his vast fortune entirely to an accountant. Someone who hasn't done a thing to earn the money, but is given complete control over it.

Another of the many maxims imparted to him by his mother, the two of them having experienced the true definition of struggle. Lean times when not just dollars, but every cent too, was of paramount importance. The difference between them scraping together enough for dinner or going to sleep hungry.

A mindset they both have maintained even now that the fear of being famished has vanished. A refusal to fall into the same trap as so many others in their position, becoming comfortable with their new wealth. Affluence that can lead to largesse, keeping them from ever fully attaining all that is possible.

Weakness that can be exploited by others, whether it be competitors looking to move into their markets or employees trying to shave off a bit extra for themselves.

One of the final tasks Garcia attends to at the end of each day, he is aware that most in his position would see what he is doing as legwork they would never dare stoop to. Number crunching that eggheads with thick glasses and suspenders could be paid to handle for him.

Such a mindset being exactly why he insists on doing it. An unofficial copy that ensures he is completely abreast of everything under his control. Total mastery that can only be realized through having a working knowledge both of machinations and finances.

And that he has his own records for any discrepancies that arise. A way to check anyone who might dare try to take a nickel that is his, much like the man who was used as a demonstration for the Kleeses the night before.

"Come in, Enzo," Garcia says. Sliding the pair of reading glasses he wears only in these rare moments while studying the ledgers alone in his office from his nose, he drops them upside down on the desk. The hinges on his desk chair whine as he leans back, raising his right ankle to his left thigh.

Across the room, the door opens just wide enough for Enzo to slide through. Still dressed in the same jeans and snap-button shirt he was wearing earlier, he eases sideways through the doorway and closes it behind him, not making a sound until it is shut.

"Sir."

Same as he does every night, Garcia waves off the opening. A motion that is meant to show camaraderie, hinting that such formality is not required when it is just the two of them, beyond the prying ears of employees or associates.

Side by side, Garcia and Enzo have been together since the beginning. The start not just of the organization, but of their time together in the United States. Fellow travelers on the same migrant caravan north over the border, Enzo having jumped in to help Garcia when a pair of fellow travelers who had posed as friends throughout the trip tried to rob Sofia.

The solidification of her already healthy distrust – and disdain – for people.

The first time Garcia had ever been in a fight, he'd been on the losing end of things when Enzo came to his aid. A wiry teenager barely resembling the man taking a seat across from him now, Enzo had fought with a ferocity that immediately shifted the tide, helping them to battle to a draw, despite giving up a great deal in size and age.

A savage affair that left them both bloodied in the dirt afterward, the scar slicing down Enzo's face remaining to this day. A constant reminder of the favor that Garcia and his mother have felt forever indebted to, ensuring that Enzo has always been taken care of. A trusted ally during those first fledgling days of their business. The senior-most employee now that it has grown to the level it has.

Blind loyalty that has been repaid in kind.

And has been no small part of Garcia's trips to the gym each morning, ensuring that never again does he find himself in need of assistance.

"How'd it go?" Garcia asks once Enzo is seated in the padded leather chair across from him.

Running the fingers of his right hand back through the thick hair just starting to show hints of gray, Enzo replies, "I always feel a little greasy after I leave that damn place."

"Brick by Brick, or Giovanni's office?" Garcia asks.

"Yes," Enzo answers, "but mostly the latter."

Having had the same feeling on more than one occasion dating back years, Garcia nods in understanding. "Any problems?"

"No," Enzo replies. "We dropped the bags off with Milo, he says he can take it from there."

Leaning forward, he braces his elbows on his knees and adds, "G did have something interesting to share at the end I wanted to run by you, though."

Lifting his palm toward the ceiling, Garcia folds his fingers back toward himself, motioning for Enzo to continue.

"He was saying that demand has been going through the roof. Said they were almost out of product by the time we got there this evening."

Feeling his brows rise, Garcia purses his lips. Rotating his gaze away from Enzo, he looks to the bank of windows lining the side of the office, the darkness outside turning them into mirrors. A perfect rendering of the two of them across from each other, seated beneath a wide light fixture with more than a dozen bulbs.

"When you met with the sheriff earlier, did he say anything about the recent rise in OD's?" Garcia asks.

"Never mentioned it," Enzo replies. "Just the accident last night, and asked if there were any more animal attacks."

Grunting softly, Garcia nods. "I was just looking at the numbers a few minutes ago. Giovanni is already one of our biggest movers."

"He is," Enzo agrees, "but he showed me his stores. He wasn't lying. A little Molly, some of the prescription stuff, but otherwise he was bare."

If it was almost any of his other business affiliates, Garcia might be suspicious. A legit business like The Char Pit, or Soap n' Suds car wash chain, or even the handful of dry cleaners he acquired just last year, he might have to do a little deep diving to see what was going on. Why there suddenly seemed to be heightened demand, especially in the face of increased media scrutiny about recent drug-related deaths.

Coming from Brick by Brick though, he can't say he is terribly surprised. That particular enterprise, in that particular location, it is almost to be expected.

Proof that their synergistic approach to things is working.

"He say how much he wanted?" Garcia asks.

"Not an exact number," Enzo says, "but he seems to think he could easily go up ten percent a week."

Flicking his gaze down to the ledger before him, Garcia runs the numbers in his head. A bump like that might result in another junkie or two in the gutter, but it would also accumulate to quite a hefty increase on their annual bankroll.

A potential swap he would be foolish to pass up, especially when he can always just bring in more users whenever he wants.

"Call him and tell him we'll bump him up starting tomorrow," Garcia replies. "Take the guys down to the mine in the morning and get whatever you need."

"Will do," Enzo says. "Anything else?"

"Yeah, *madre* was asking about you this evening. You should stop by to visit her tomorrow."

———

"Twelve?" Wes Callum spat. Seated behind the battered metal desk in the back room of the barn repurposed into an office, the floor still spattered with grease and oil from its previous incarnation, Callum leaned forward, peering through eyes that were barely more than slits. Narrow gaps in a visage that had lived too hard for too long, his wrinkled skin taking on the texture of leather. Thick gray hair sprouted from every possible opening, lining his cheeks and jaw, hanging down across his forehead, and even framing his brows.

Lips peeled back over teeth stained by years of puffing on the unfiltered cigarette pushing smoke up into the air between them, he said, "I ordered fifteen."

In Cortland's periphery, he could see the pair of lackeys inside the office take a step forward. Younger versions of Callum, with the same hooked noses and squinted eyes, the only differences being less facial hair and a longer remaining walk on the road to skin cancer.

Fully expecting some sort of pushback before stepping out of the Charger, Cortland reached to his back pocket. Acutely aware of the stiffening of the men on either side of him, he carefully slid out the small ledger book and opened it to the bookmarked page. More than a dozen entries all clearly delineated, outlining every order ever placed by Callum.

Listings that told a story of stops and starts, his little enterprise popping up a handful of times before people lost interest or the cops discovered their newest location, only to be shut down again.

The first time he had called them in the better part of a year, the request for twelve jars was one of his largest orders ever. An escalation indicating he expected a large crowd, with plenty of room in the barn behind them to accommodate.

A spectacle Cortland had no interest in sticking around to see.

"I'm sorry," Cortland said. Thrusting the ledger out, he pointed to the final listing. "You can see here, it clearly says twelve, and grandpa checked each of these before we took off earlier."

Not so much as even looking at the offered evidence, Callum kept his ire aimed at Cortland. Deep lines formed around his eyes as his scowl grew more pronounced.

"I don't care what the hell that thing says. Your grandpa promised me fifteen jars, and that's what I'm going to get."

To either side, the two younger Callums took another step forward, the man on the right sliding his hand out from where it had been tucked behind a leg, revealing a length of pipe in hand. A makeshift weapon there was no doubt the other had to match.

Visible anxiousness that subsided slightly at the sound of jars rattling behind Cortland. A noise he would recognize anywhere, a jolt of relief passing through him as it grew closer.

"Here we are," Remington said as he stepped into the room, the requested twelve jars in hand. Filling eighty percent of a box, it was enough to cause the veins lining his arms to bulge, on plain display as he walked forward and balanced it on the edge of the desk.

Leaving it there, he glanced to either side, taking in the young men gathered in tight before sliding his gaze to Cortland.

"Problem?"

Jutting his chin forward, Cortland motioned to Callum on the far side of the desk. "It seems there's some discrepancy in the number that was requested. Grandpa has them down for twelve, but-"

"I ordered fifteen," Callum spat, practically flinging the words across the table. "And you're not leaving until I have fifteen."

To Cortland's left, he could see the second of the younger man rotate his arm forward as well, a wooden club gripped tight. Sinewy arm protruding from the side of the bib overalls he wore, he twisted it an inch to either side, preparing to strike.

"Fifteen," Cortland repeated, sweeping his gaze past the man and back to his brother. "Do we have three extra in the car?"

"Three?" Remington replied. "We don't have any extra, let alone three."

Taking a step forward, he grabbed up the closest jar from the box. Holding it up to the filmy glow of the lone bulb in a cage burning above, he shook the jar twice, revealing the clarity of the product.

"Are you guys sure you need that many, though? I mean, look how clear this is? No impurities or imperfections in this whatsoever."

Flicking his gaze to Cortland, he cut his gaze to the side. A silent signal toward the door before returning to the jar, twisting the top off and taking a deep inhalation.

"And I mean, just smell="

In one swift movement, he swung the jar forward, splashing the moonshine across the front of the desk. Distilled alcohol that spread fast across the bare metal, touching the tip of Callum's smoke still burning strong. Instant ignition, sending flames skyward in a whoosh.

The start of a blaze that caused all three Callums to jump back in unison, calling out in protest as Cortland and his brother both turned and bolted for the Charger.

CHAPTER TWENTY-SEVEN

Of all the people Cortland's wife used to work with during her law firm days, the various secretaries, associates, and even partners that he was forced to interact with at holiday parties and mixers over the years, only two names immediately came to mind when thinking about who to reach out to. A pair of people that worked closely enough with Maylinn to actually serve some purpose, and that Cortland knew sufficiently well to ask such questions without worrying about them immediately running out and informing someone else.

The start of a gossip chain that could easily lead back to whoever sent that black truck after his wife two nights before.

Perhaps even the driver themselves, working in disguise.

Warning flares that Cortland would rather not send up just yet, their investigation still far too early to be drawing any unwanted attention. That approach would be best saved as a last gasp should nothing else turn up anything useful. The proverbial Hail Mary, using themselves as bait to try and draw their opposition out.

A tact neither are too keen to pursue so soon, wanting to save self-sacrifice as more of a last resort.

The first person who came to mind was Maylinn's paralegal Kenzie Lyons. A new hire who came on at the start of Maylinn's third year, it was through dumb luck that they were assigned to work an early case together, each instantly recognizing a shared working style in the other. Compatibility in the face of a chaotic environment both immediately latched onto, collaborating on no less than a dozen cases in the ensuing years.

The only person Maylinn even considered trying to poach when she decided to leave, discussing it with both Cortland and Beth Towner a time or two before it was agreed that it would be an unfair position to put the young girl in. A choice between friendship and financial incentive they refused to ask her to make.

Of everyone in the world, Kenzie would have the best grasp of what Maylinn was working on before leaving. Inside knowledge on clients and litigation that could be invaluable.

And also highly illegal, Cortland refusing to put the young woman in such a position, using emotion to try and extract potentially confidential information. An assault not just on her financial security as before, but her career and even her freedom.

The second woman who came to mind was Eleanor Patrick. A shared secretary, working with Maylinn and a pair of other mid-level associates. A grandmotherly sort who wore cardigans and thick glasses and was reputed to know every clerk of court in the lower half of the country. A wiz with filings who never wavered in the face of deadlines and never snapped at opposing counsel shenanigans, no matter how egregious.

A kind soul who Maylinn always spoke of in glowing terms, Cortland seeing exactly why as he was welcomed into her home upon arrival. Still donning her trademark cardigan even in retirement, she'd met him at the door with a warm hug and the offer of baked goods, the air redolent with pumpkin and cinnamon.

Smells that under any other circumstances Cortland would have jumped at, the thought of food in the face of what was about to happen something he could not consider.

A move having proved prescient as he sits and stares at her now, the glasses slid from her nose and left to dangle on the chain around her neck so she can better access her eyes. A linen handkerchief gripped tight, she dabs at the torrents of tears streaming south over her cheeks, smearing the faint bits of eye makeup she wears.

A sight that Cortland can only watch in fleeting glimpses before feeling the warmth rise to his own cheeks. Emotion that has been given the better part of a day to rebuild, ready to be unleashed anew.

A daily struggle with no signs of slowing, the odds low that it will any time in the near future.

"I..." Eleanor whispers. "My god, I just talked to Maylinn last week. We were planning to have lunch next Friday, before the holiday rush really picked up and we all got too busy."

Raising a hand before her, she motions as if there is more to be said. Further explanation or future plans or whatever else, lost to silence as her voice deserts her, no sound making it past her lips.

The web of lines deepens around her eyes as her features contort, more tears rising to the surface, glassing her pupils from view.

"Yeah," Cortland says. "I remember her telling me she was looking forward to it. Alexander's, over on Vine, right?"

More fine lines appear as the corners of Eleanor's mouth turn upward in a smile. A reflexive response, decidedly at odds with the sorrow painting most of her face.

"That's right. Alexander's, same as always. I would get the French onion soup, and she would get the-"

"Bacon ranch panini," Cortland finishes, his own faint smile appearing.

The first hint of levity since those initial moments upon entering, well before news of what happened to Maylinn was shared. A bit of mirth that is nowhere near a full opening, but is likely the best he is going to get.

Raising his voice just slightly to be heard through the muted call he'd left streaming through his cellphone, he begins with, "Eleanor, I can't thank you enough for having me, but I have to confess, I wasn't entirely truthful in my request to stop by."

Motioning to his own face, only nominally less puffy than the woman across from him, he continues, "As you can tell, I haven't really slept in two nights now. Hour after hour of laying there, staring up at the ceiling, trying to make sense of this. Trying to understand how it could have happened. Why her? Why now?"

On the drive over this morning, he'd gone through a couple of different iterations. More direct approaches, either coming right out and asking if there was anything in Maylinn's work history that might have made her a target, or going with the same approach just used, but taking it much further.

Mentioning the skid marks. Hinting at what Remington said the night before in the kitchen about it all feeling very pointed and targeted.

Tactics they both decided against, hoping that this would do the job. The grieving husband clutching at something vague and amorphous, trying to achieve some modicum of understanding.

An approach he sells by opening his mouth a couple of times as if trying to continue before lifting his hands in a shrug, the words evading him.

Stopping there, he says nothing more, letting almost a full minute of dead air pass before finally Eleanor responds.

Reaching to her neck, she hooks a finger into the side of the thin gold chain hanging around it. Tugging it forward, she reveals a matching cross pendant, the base of it clutched between her thumb and forefinger.

"I'm not sure if Maylinn ever mentioned this," she says, "but I am a woman of faith. Have been my whole life. It was what got me through my husband being sick a while back, definitely got me through all those long years at the firm."

Curling up one corner of her mouth to let him know that was a joke, she adds, "Because of that, I understand what you're going through right now, trying to find something to make it make sense. Some reason why something like this would happen.

"This might not be what you want to hear, but the stuff we used to work on, it was nothing. Benign. Our clients were corporations. There were no real victims, only money changing hands."

Twisting the cross slightly to either side, she finishes with, "I'm so sorry, Cortland, I really am, but this was God's will. Nothing more."

CHAPTER TWENTY-EIGHT

Remington heard every word exchanged between his brother and Eleanor Patrick. The initial pleasantries as she greeted Cortland at the door and offered him cookies and cider. An old-school welcome in line with what was described on the way over, the gesture and the tone of her voice painting a very vivid depiction of the woman in Remington's mind.

What he would imagine a grandmother to look and sound like, if ever he had met one of his own.

After that, he'd sat and listened through the muted call from Cortland's cellphone to his own as news of Maylinn's demise was shared. The shock of it hitting her full and the fallout that ensued as Eleanor broke down and his brother willed himself not to do the same. A tidal wave he was just able to outrun, withstanding without succumbing to the emotion.

Release that Remington would not have faulted him for, plenty of feelings of his own arising as he heard the poor woman cry. The next step in his processing sequence, manifesting as anger. Rage that had him sitting with fists clenched, wishing so badly that he had something to aim it at. A bag to punch or a wrench to throw.

The driver of that damned black truck to take out into a field and annihilate.

Fifteen minutes after arriving, Remington had listened as the conversation shifted again. A move toward the reason for their visit, Cortland gently prodding around the edges of what types of things they used to work on together. An open-ended question discussed before arrival that the woman had picked up on, offering them an answer without supplying any real information.

Assurance that they were looking in the wrong place before offering him words of faith and sympathy.

A grandmother to the very end.

Lasting almost an hour in total, nearly as much time has passed since. A gap long enough to allow them to both sit in silence, stewing over things while in a booth at Whataburger. Burgers and fries that Remington barely tasted as he ruminated on what was said.

A tale of basic transactional law, not that different from what Cortland does. Numbers and figures on sheets that – like Eleanor herself said – don't have true victims.

Most people like to believe that money is the greatest motivator for evil, and on a certain level that is true. Corporate greed or government oversight, where the figures are truly astronomical. Sum totals that can shift the trajectory of an industry and change a person's fortunes for generations to come.

The sort of thing Remington has no doubt he played a part in during his days in uniform. The bludgeon used as proof that the threat of violence was real. The security blanket employed to ensure that oil or mineral resources were secured.

On a lower level, though, Remington has a hard time believing that someone would go to the trouble of killing over a few dollars. Transactional amounts that – like Eleanor just stated – weren't truly hurting anybody, more like putting things right. Correcting existing mistakes or slapping the hands of someone who might have tried to take more than their share.

Not the sort of thing to make someone follow her out into the country more than a year after the fact and run her off the road.

Sure as hell not the kind to go the extra step of trying to make it look like a mistake - and potentially even paying off the sheriff - over.

Eating largely in silence, not until both were finished and their wrappers wadded into the trash did they begin to speak, agreeing that the trip to see Eleanor was beneficial mostly as a means of clearing away a possibility. While they were no closer to finding an actual motive, they had at least removed one glaring possibility.

An addition by subtraction that would fast grow unnerving if it becomes a pattern, but for their first real conversation, was as beneficial as could be asked for. A firm conclusion making it that much easier for them to head on to their second meeting. A turn away from what Maylinn was doing in the past to how she was filling her time just a couple of days before.

A swap of the gleaming edifice of downtown skyscrapers to a street in the northern suburbs. Three lanes across, it is lined with buildings rising no higher than two stories, most of them made from brick a few decades ago and having faded with sun exposure since. Structures almost all bearing the same size and shape, differentiated by the signage along the road or the letters in gold plating affixed directly to the outside walls.

Office buildings of every possible type, interspersed with a few more recent constructions. Fast-food chains and gas stations and minimarts, serving the basic needs of the people and employees filling the various nearby spaces.

Businesses with windows universally filled with shades of orange, whether it be fandom for the local Longhorns or decorations for the fall season.

"There," Cortland says, pointing from the passenger seat of Tyrell's truck. A vehicle chosen with the intention of nobody in Austin recognizing it, should anybody happen to take an interest. The driver from the other night, or whoever might be employing them.

The very reason he was told to bring the unknown vehicle to begin with.

"On the corner."

Grunting in understanding, Remington lifts his foot from the gas. Bypassing turning into the attached parking lot, he sidles up to the curb in front of the place, passing his gaze across the front of the building. A quick look to see if there are any cameras present before turning his attention to the opposite side of the street.

"Closed until further notice," Cortland whispers, the sound of his voice pulling Remington's attention back that direction. Using the same finger, he taps at the glass, gesturing to the sign taped to the front door.

Another of a thousand tiny ripple effects starting to be felt by all.

"Beth will be the only one here," Cortland says. "You're welcome to come in."

Leaning forward a few inches, Remington considers the building once more before turning back in the opposite direction. A second sweep, taking in the trio of businesses crammed into the length of a single block.

"That's okay," he replies. "You go on ahead, I'm going to look into something else out here."

CHAPTER TWENTY-NINE

The face sitting directly across from Cortland is thirty years younger than the one he was staring at a couple of hours earlier. The hair is darker. There are fewer smile lines around her eyes. The parentheses framing her mouth are less pronounced.

But there is no mistaking the devastation marring Beth Towner's features as matching that of Eleanor Patrick.

Even his own, Cortland imagines, having actively avoided all mirrors and reflective surfaces for that very reason. Anguish he doesn't need to see staring back at him, acutely aware of it during every waking moment since arriving at the accident scene two nights before.

A constant stab he feels with every breath, the only reason he isn't leaking tears right now being that he released everything he had at home the night before. His body's own way of pacing, recognizing that no matter how close he might have come sitting across from Eleanor, it simply has no more to give right now.

Sitting in the padded chair behind her desk, Beth's cheeks are red and ruddy. Her hair hangs lank to her shoulders, brushing over bare skin, her traditional business attire swapped out for jeans and a tank top. Fashion choices to match the sign on the door, informing clients that the office will be closed for the foreseeable future.

One of a thousand different consequences of what happened to Maylinn. Manifestations of how far her reach was. How imbedded she was in the community.

The number of people who relied on her, none more than the two people sitting on either side of the desk. A pair who have known each other for the better part of a decade, but have never interacted without Maylinn as a touchstone. A mediator bringing the two sides together.

A shared contact whose absence now feels especially pronounced, each of them sitting in silence, fighting to process what has happened.

"You don't really think..." Beth begins. A sentence without a conclusion, her voice trails away as she lifts a hand, motioning to the space they now sit in.

A room that is decidedly a step down from the office Cortland used to visit at the firm downtown.

One of the first tasks Maylinn was given when accepting her previous job right out of law school was outfitting her office. Barely measuring a dozen feet in either direction, she was given a budget of ten thousand dollars and a stack of binders and magazines of approved furniture and fixtures. Pieces cut from the finest woods or employing the choicest leathers.

Everything done in dark shades of gray or cranberry or black, meant to match the overall aesthetic of the firm. A coordinated façade that exuded posh, catering to the highbrow market they were known for.

Businesses that had been in the community for decades, along with the infusion of new capital arriving each month.

Clients on the far opposite end of the spectrum from those Maylinn and Beth aimed their practice toward, as evidenced by the modest furnishings inside the office. A conscious swap of polished and clean for an environment made to feel inviting.

Separating Cortland and Beth is a desk of blonde wood, a few nicks and scratches visible in the top of it. Made from ash, it matches the bookshelf along the wall and the frames of the photos lining the top of it. Images depicting Beth's trio of dogs at home, all in various states of sleep or play.

In the corner, a plant hangs from the ceiling, flowered vines dipping over the side and perfuming the air.

"I've been here all morning," Beth says, the sound of her voice drawing Cortland's attention up from his lap. The first thing either has said since the initial back-and-forth, Beth already aware of what happened, but asking to hear the full story. "And I haven't done a single thing. I keep thinking of everything I should be doing, what I would be doing if this was just a regular Thursday, but..."

Intimately aware of the point she is trying to make, Cortland nods. "Last night, my brother and I were trying to order pizza, but couldn't because I couldn't think of a single place besides her favorite."

Blinking twice, Beth says, "Giardi's."

"Giardi's," Cortland murmurs, echoing the statement.

"Pepperoni and mushroom."

"Every time," Cortland whispers. "And can you imagine what would happen if I did call and tried to order something different? Had to explain to them what had happened?"

Her lips parting to reply, Beth makes it no further. Her blinking increases rapidly, her oversized eyelashes fluttering like hummingbird wings as she fights to keep herself from descending into tears again. A battle that wages for the better part of a minute before she manages to whisper, "I'm so sorry, Cort."

Leaving things there for a moment, she turns her gaze to the side. Drawing in a deep breath, she slowly releases, using it to keep herself together. A conscious pause to prevent another deluge before adding, "And I get it. I did the same thing this morning, trying to figure out how or why this could have happened."

Lifting a hand, she motions to the office they are sitting in, pointing out the same hand-me-down furnishings Cortland was just inspecting.

"I just...I mean, what we do here is important, but it isn't the kind of stuff someone would target us over."

Much like sitting down with Eleanor earlier, Cortland hadn't arrived expecting to find the proverbial smoking gun. The most obvious starting point for why anybody would have targeted Maylinn was her work. Outside of the house with him and Shine, it was where she spent the vast majority of her time.

It was a source of pride. No small part of her identity.

And absolutely the only thing in her life that might have conjured some bit of ire, whether intentional or not.

At the same time, as Eleanor mentioned and Beth seems to be intimating, it wasn't like she worked on high stakes criminal matters. In all the years she'd been practicing, she'd only been through a complete trial a couple of times. Most of the people she went up against were megalith corporations who would just as soon settle to keep things out of the papers.

"What kind of stuff was she working on?" Cortland asks. "I know you can't get into specifics, but..."

"That's just it," Beth says. "On Tuesday, before she left? A landlord-tenant dispute. The day before? An uncompensated care request to a hospital on behalf of a small child hit by a car."

Seeing where she is going with it, Cortland nods. The list seems much in line with most of what Maylinn used to describe. The types of things more likely to get her nominated for a civic award than targeted for assassination.

At the same time, Cortland has to agree with his brother's assessment. Whatever happened to her was on purpose. The circumstances of her crash, the ragged voicemail she left, simply doesn't support anything else.

And unless his wife had a secret life he knew nothing about, whatever reason there was had to begin inside this building.

Shoving out a slow breath, Cortland says, "Thank you for

meeting with me. I know I'm just clutching at straws here, but it beats trying to avoid the obvious right now, you know?"

"Yeah," Beth whispers. Nodding, she adds, "Believe me, I do."

Matching her nod, Cortland presses his lips together. Glancing to the wall beside them, he asks, "I don't suppose she happened to leave her cellphone or laptop here that night, did she?"

CHAPTER THIRTY

The minimart on the corner was a strikeout. The only two cameras on the outside were pointed along the sidewalk lining the front, hoping to get clear views of anyone entering or exiting. At most, a glimpse of license plates parked in the dozen spots lined up the length of the building.

Inside, there was but a single camera, this one turned to watch over the cash register from the back, monitoring all transactions while getting a full facial look at anyone across the counter.

Optimal placement for a bare bones budget that Remington couldn't begrudge, even if it did afford little help in what he was looking for. Angles that never made it as far as the road outside, let alone Maylinn's office across the street.

Going through the motions of grabbing a Gatorade, he'd considered asking the aging redhead behind the register if she might have noticed anything unusual in the last week or two before thinking better of it. Already forced to stand perpendicular to the road, every available moment she wasn't ringing someone up was spent staring down at her phone. Frantically tapping out text messages or quivering with muted chuckles from whatever she just read.

A witness that would hardly be useful in the best of circumstances, asking if she might have noticed a black pickup – in Texas – far from that.

Taking up his beverage and nodding his thanks, Remington had climbed back into the truck and driven the short distance down to the far end of the block to the filling station on the corner. A no-name establishment with a glowing awning out front, providing shade and shelter to a quartet of gas pumps, all currently servicing customers. Behind it stood a building split in two down the middle, the far end acting as a convenience store and cash register, the remainder as a service station providing basic auto care.

Oil and battery changes. Tune ups. Tire rotation.

The sorts of things Remington recognized right off, not requiring certified mechanics, but still able to be charged for at a premium fee.

Pulling into the parking lot for the establishment, Remington's first move was to again scope out the cameras for the place. Outside security that was beefed up from the minimart down the street on account of the working garage, providing oversight for the smattering of vehicles parked outside. Sedans and mid-sized SUVS, a couple of which looked like they'd been onsite for a few days.

Eschewing the use of old-school cameras, the station employed orbs attached directly to the building and underside of the overhead awning. Half-globes with darkened glass that extended like black warts from various places, more than a dozen in total visible on his pass through. Placement accounting for coverage not just of the entire grounds, but a decent chunk of the world beyond as well.

Visuals that could quite easily extend all the way to Maylinn's office a short distance away, depending on the exact arrangement.

A chance worth taking, prompting Remington to pull in next to a silver Subaru Outback on the far end of the cluster waiting to be serviced. Climbing out, he can hear the faint call of classic rock music drifting out, just barely audible beneath the sound of an engine being cranked again and again. Futile attempts lasting longer with each successive try, the engine refusing to turn over.

A problem Remington has seen more than his share of in the last couple of years, giving him the opening he needs. A means of establishing common ground before making his request.

"Oh man, that ignition switch is toast," Remington says, stepping over the crack delineating the lot from the garage floor. A transition from cracked asphalt to polished concrete, making for easier cleanup at the end of each day. A lack of friction for oil and grease to cling to, a simple hose more than sufficient to wash it clean.

Moving inside, the bright sun of outside falls away, taking much of the midday heat with it. A drop in temperature aided by the enormous fans mounted high in either corner, shoving a breeze down that is enough to tug at the tail of his shirt.

"That's what I tried to tell them," the man seated behind the wheel of an aging Lexus replies. The driver's door propped open, his left boot is planted on the ground, stained brown leather peeking out beneath a rolled pant leg.

"They keep insisting it's just the battery, though."

Giving the engine one more crank, he lets the ignition go for several seconds. More wasted effort that ends with the same result, the vehicle refusing to come to life.

An outcome Remington gets the impression has happened many times already, as evidenced by the exasperation painting the man's features.

"You can change that battery a hundred times," Remington replies. "Won't do a damn bit of good if the juice doesn't get where it needs to go."

"Exactly," the man says. Pulling himself up out of the front seat, his ascent stops just below Remington's chin. Dressed in the same blue work pants as the man at the salvage yard the day before, his uniform shirt has been stripped away, leaving only a sweaty undershirt that was originally white, but has since been stained in various places. Smudges of automotive and bodily fluids, giving the garment a dinghy hue.

Well into his forties, thick whiskers line his jaw. Bristly hairs of black and silver crisscross his forehead.

"Maybe I can get you to explain that to the owners. They sure as hell won't listen to me."

"Oh, I know that kind," Remington replies. Forcing a smile into place, he leans forward, extending the back of his hand toward the man. "I'm guessing they also didn't listen when somebody told them not to buy a damn Lexus."

"Ha!" the man bursts, his voice booming, reverberating over the sounds of the radio and the fans. "I heard that."

Shared humor, the universal language for auto workers the world over.

The exact connection Remington was hoping for, leading the man to extend his hand and say, "Name's Paxton. What can I do for ya?"

CHAPTER THIRTY-ONE

In the wan half-light of the mining shaft, the filmy glow from the string of bare yellow bulbs extended down into the earth catches the sweat resting across Ramon's face more than his features themselves. Thick strips of perspiration that shine along his cheeks and neck, a result of the last thirty minutes spent more than two stories below ground.

Exertion in the crowded, airless space that has outpaced any cool the earth packed tight around them might provide.

"We got everything?" Enzo asks.

Grunting softly, Ramon nods. "I'm good, but you might want to get us out of here before Hector starts having a panic attack over there."

"Go to hell, *puto*," Hector mutters from Enzo's opposite side. "You don't do heights, I don't do tight spaces."

"Maybe you would if you stopped eating so much-"

How the retort is meant to end, Enzo doesn't much care to hear. Another round in the endless banter between the two, the only reprieve from it being the rare moment when they are in the presence of Leo Garcia himself.

Blessed silence that Enzo can only long for at the moment as he operates the mechanical lift, using the whine of gears to drown them out for the next couple of minutes. The gnashing of metal that is more than half a century old, reverberating from the narrow space of the shaft as they climb upward.

An ascent toward the box of daylight above, growing steadily wider as they go.

Seventy years before, the shaft they currently traverse was used to haul men and silver up and down by the ton. A vein of ore that someone had stumbled upon by mistake and immediately set to make full use of, blasting a hole down more than thirty feet before drilling out a network of tunnels spread over a hundred yards in every direction. A spider's web of interconnected passageways that kept many families fed and provided various souvenirs and trinkets to a dozen businesses in places as far away as Dallas or New Orleans.

A booming enterprise that ended almost as quickly as it started, the vein lasting for almost twenty years before giving out, the deposit of precious metal completely tapped. Land that at one point was some of the richest in Texas turned virtually worthless overnight, the owner unable to do anything with it until eventually dying fifteen years later. The start of an intestate process that saw it pass through several disinterested heirs before eventually reverting back to the state, where it was later bought up by Garcia for pennies on the dollar.

A minor financial investment made not with any interest in mining futures, but in the very underground network Enzo and his colleagues now rise from. Deep caverns ideal for hiding things, such as the bundles of product that now fill every spare inch on the floor of the lift around them. Bricks wrapped in aluminum foil and bound tight with duct tape, protecting them from rodents or the off chance of a flash flood spilling down the mine shaft.

Precious cargo that is kept far removed from the mansion grounds, well beyond any prying eyes who might one day come snooping around. One of many drop sites in the greater Austin area, various holdings stretched from the epicenter of the city over a diameter more than a hundred miles across.

A meticulous attention to insulation, ensuring that any risk assumed is always on the part of one of Garcia's associates. People like Giovanni or the Kleeses or even the agricultural co-op that holds the title for this place.

Pawns that Garcia uses not just to keep his assorted enterprises separate, but to make certain nothing ever gets anywhere close to him.

Laughing Leo, doing what he does best.

Standing in the front corner of the rickety metal assemblage, Enzo keeps the knob atop the small lever on the control panel pointed forward. His gaze aimed upward, he watches as the square of light above grows ever larger. The air around them gets cooler, faint puffs of breeze traveling down the shaft, touching the sweat lining his own features.

At his side, he can hear Ramon continuing to make comments. Words that can't quite be deciphered, Enzo in no mood to ask him to repeat himself or – even worse – to talk louder. Unending barbs he lets slide by, keeping his focus on ground level coming steadily closer.

Their third and final climb of the day, this load earmarked for his pickup parked just inside the edge of the mine. Transport for enough additional product to fulfill whatever demand the city might need through the end of football and college finals season.

Keeping the operational lever pinned forward, Enzo raises them up the last few feet. A climb from the depths of the earth back to ground level, ending with a palpable shudder. A rattle of man and machine before sputtering to a halt, the narrow shaft they were in just giving way to the ground floor.

A cave stretching more than thirty feet across, serving as an entrance to the mine. Carved from the side of a towering foothill, it is held up by a series of supports and overhead beams, with plenty of space for the lift they are in and a few other remainder pieces of equipment. Drills and saws and even an old truck that hasn't moved in so long the tires have long since disintegrated.

Rusted pieces offset by the trio of gleaming pickups backed just shy of the lift. Three matching F-350's, specially modified with storage compartments built under the false bottoms of the beds.

Space for moving product in concealment, the silver and blue trucks to either side already loaded and sealed, leaving only Enzo's black model in the center to be filled. Resting with the metal liner of the bed tilted upward, it sits awaiting their deposit, struts on either side keeping it open.

A hungry mouth waiting to be fed, after which it is only a matter of sealing the bed into place and pulling shut the gate standing open across the entrance.

"Air. Thank God," Hector mutters, unlatching the metal chain enclosing the lift and stepping out onto firm ground.

"Yeah, yeah," Enzo replies, jumping in before Hector has a chance to set things off anew. "Let's just get this shit unloaded and get out of here, huh?"

CHAPTER THIRTY-TWO

The bus looks like something from a futuristic apocalyptic thriller. A vehicle taken directly from one of the *Mad Max* movies, or even the book of Revelations. A hell rig that was once used to transport school children, all paint and identifying features since stripped away, rendering it bare metal and rust. Most of the windows along either side have been shattered and busted out, leaving empty frames or jagged shards of glass.

Should a rare Texas rainstorm ever kick up, there is no chance the driver would be able to see a thing, the wipers – and even the sockets they attach to – also casualties to the ravages of time.

The only thing – outside of the two matching vehicles also en route to or from the border - in Leo Garcia's entire extended empire that isn't kept in pristine condition. A state of dereliction attributed both to the task it is meant to perform and the cargo it is hauling.

To drive straight from Austin to the Mexico border would take Garcia just shy of four hours. Two-hundred-and-thirty-five miles along paved freeways in the air-conditioned comfort of his Escalade.

For the bus pulling in before him, the trip is closer to eight hours. A full third of a day spent bouncing over backroads and dirt, starting from an outpost six miles in from the border. The endpoint of a march that for most of the people crammed inside the vehicle started more than a thousand miles to the south. A walking caravan beginning deep in the Central American panhandle, swelling with size as it passed through Honduras, Guatemala, Belize, before eventually traveling the full vertical length of Mexico.

A voyage that not all finish, the motley crowd unloading from the bus representing barely half of those who initially set out. A herd culled after a long winter, with the oldest and weakest stripped away, leaving only the strongest and most determined behind.

A fact Garcia cannot help but find difficult to imagine, sitting and staring at the rabble spilling onto the barren sand. A collection of protruding ribs and elbows, wrapped in dirty clothing and topped with hair in dire need of washing. The basis for a stench that emanates outward in waves, Garcia making it barely within twenty yards before pulling up.

Feet planted in the dirt and sand, he waits as the last person unloads from the bus. An ending marked by the driver spilling down behind them and making his way over, a duffel bag loaded to capacity slung over a shoulder. Heavy enough to cause his slight form to list to the side, he shuffles closer, kicking up plumes of dust that are immediately pulled away by the breeze.

Wind strong enough to also tug at the hair hanging just past his chin and the open tail of the Aloha shirt he wears.

"Mr. Garcia," the man says, knowing not to come too close, the residual odor of the cargo imbedded in him as well, clinging to all who venture inside the van. Instead, he moves at a diagonal, going to the closest of Garcia's guards.

Sliding the duffel from his shoulder, he lowers it to the ground before retreating a couple of steps.

The moment he is out of reach, the guard steps forward and pulls the zipper back to reveal an odd assortment of currencies. Bills and coins representing multiple countries that will be taken back to the warehouse and counted before being funneled through one of the many businesses.

Much like the people it originated with, by this time next week, it will be lost in the city.

"Tyson," Garcia replies. "Any problems?"

"Not with the trip."

Raising an eyebrow, Garcia asks, "Meaning?"

"Meaning we have two issues this time," Tyson answers. "One was a baby that was born two days ago, but the mother didn't have the money to cover it."

Pausing there, he rotates at the waist and extends a finger, pointing to a woman on the far-left end of the group. Clutching a dirty bundle to her chest, she makes a point of staring straight at the ground before her, lower mandible quivering as if she might burst into tears at any moment.

"And the other?" Garcia asks.

Twisting a bit further, Tyson motions to a young man standing in the center of the group. Chin raised above parallel, he stands with both hands balled into fists, staring directly back at them.

A look of defiance, almost daring them to come closer.

"That little shit in the middle there," Tyson says. "I wasn't going to let him on, but he claims he knows you."

Feeling his brows rise, Garcia flicks his gaze to the side. "Said he knows *me*?"

"What he said," Tyson replies. Turning back, he lifts his palms in a show of surrender and adds, "Even dropped your nickname."

His eyes widening in surprise, Garcia takes a couple of steps forward. Strides that move him well within the zone of stench, his self-preservation overridden by his business interests. Equal parts anger and curiosity that allow him to cut the gap between himself and rabble by half before the smell becomes too much, his eyes beginning to water as he comes to a halt.

Hands placed on either hip, he makes a show of scanning the group. A complete pass, taking in each of the new arrivals, many standing with their heads tilted down, gazes averted. Lank clothes and stringy hair blowing in the breeze, they say nothing, visibly tensed in the face of what may come next.

The end product of a journey far more effective in ensuring compliance than any show with the hyenas could ever be.

The lone outlier is the young man in the middle. Wearing stained jeans and a sleeveless shirt of indeterminate color, he waits with his arms still flexed. Veins and tendons stand out plainly beneath his skin, the outer layer practically shrink wrapped to his slight frame.

"The rules of your coming here were very clear," Garcia opens, causing several people to visibly flinch at the sound of his voice. "Every new arrival must pay. Doesn't matter when they got onboard or who they *think* they know."

Making a point of scowling at the two offending parties, he continues, "Up until you crossed the border, you were all on your own. You could have fallen down a canyon or drowned in a river and it wouldn't have meant shit to me.

"But once you all piled on that bus – *my* bus – you made a promise. And breaking that has consequences."

Off to his left, Garcia can hear the new mother let out a gasp. A pained cry that is there and gone in an instant, replaced by the low murmur of voices rising the length of the group. Concerned chatter that is too low to make out, comments being passed from one person to another. A game of telephone, skipping only the young man in the middle.

One of the offending parties.

The kid with the audacity to claim he knows Garcia personally.

"But I am a businessman, first and foremost," Garcia continues, running his focus once more down the length of the new arrivals, "so I will give you all one chance. One last opportunity to scrape together enough to buy your freeloading fellow passengers' safety."

Slowly, he rotates his focus, settling it on the defiant young man in the middle. Still unmoving, his entire body is clenched, as if expecting an attack at any moment.

A pointed stance, giving Garcia the faintest hint of an idea.

"Otherwise, I will show you all exactly how it is I got my nickname."

"Jesus Christ, can you slow down?!" Cortland hollered from the passenger seat, the words just barely audible over the sound of the wind rushing through the car and the pounding of his own pulse. Thrumming that settled into his ears, climbing with each twist and turn of the muddy path hugging the banks of the Scippo River.

A body of water barely large enough to even be classified as such, affectionately renamed by the locals decades before as Moonshine Creek.

Proper deference paid to the Alder family lineage and their unique skillset. Purveyors of a necessary product, vital to the local health and well-being stretching all the way back to the days of Prohibition.

A legacy of bootleggers and outlaws that Cortland still suspected his brother believed himself to be a part of, insistent on flying down the unpaved path as if the law was closing in behind them. Wailing sirens and flashing lights that existed only his mind, constantly pushing the accelerator down a bit further toward the floorboards.

Speed that today seemed more excessive than usual, spurred onward by the recent dustup with Wes Callum and his sons. A near miss that had both of their adrenaline up as they slid into the Charger and tore away.

"I'd hate to think we dodged a beating just to die out here now!"

"This is the same speed I always go," Remington called from the front seat. "And they're the ones who missed a beating!"

His left wrist draped over the steering wheel, Remington stared straight ahead, his gaze pinched. His standard pose whenever he was pissed. A warning sign for Cortland to push no further, his grip tightening on the handle affixed above the passenger side window. A point of contact to keep him from bouncing across the front seat, even as the vehicle swung in and out of turns.

A slalom run along the narrow track, with dense forest pushing in on one side and the ground giving way to the river on the other, leaving them with a margin of error that was preciously slim. Tight confines Remington seemed oblivious to, pushing through the last mile of their journey.

One final stretch hugging the banks of the river before their path mercifully started to drift inward. A gradual move away from the water's edge, meant to stay in a straight line, avoiding the elbow that jutted out into the water. A chunk of land encompassing a dozen acres in total that their great-great-grandfather first commandeered more than a century before.

The Alder family homestead, complete with a two-story farmhouse in the center, a freestanding garage with double doors to the side, and a boathouse extended just over the edge of the river out back. Three structures wedged tight into the forest, all constructed from materials harvested in the surrounding area.

Space enough for ten or twelve, home for the last decade to just Cortland, Remington, and their grandfather Garrison – known to most of the world simply as G. An unexpected living arrangement thrown together by the sudden passing of their parents, not without its bumps early on before leveling out into something resembling a peaceful existence.

Or, at the very least, a successful partnership.

Turning left off the two-track, Remington let the Charger roll forward, bringing it to a stop beside G's battered farm truck. Another remainder item passed down from previous generations that he'd never had the time or inclination to replace.

Hitting the horn twice, Remington climbed out, the door barely shut behind him as a gray and white border collie bounded forward to meet him. Less than a year old, all oversized paws and awkward energy, its wagging tail thumped against Remington's exposed shins.

"Hey, Shine," he whispered, bending forward and wrapping both hands around the soft fur of her neck.

A quick greeting that ended as abruptly as it started by their grandfather emerging from the boathouse nearby. Well into his sixties, his thick hair was snow white, matching the tuft of beard hanging from his chin. Dressed in a sweat-stained white Henley and a pair of thick suspenders, he looked warily at the two boys, clearly not appreciating being summoned from his work.

A job that - as they told the judge earlier - seemed to be never ending this time of year.

"What the hell happened now?"

CHAPTER THIRTY-THREE

Without Remington onsite, the job of controlling the radio inside the auto shop reverted back to Tyrell. An opening the man must have jumped at the moment he saw the taillights of his own truck fade into the night a couple of days before.

Most of the time, the dial is set to the local classic rock station. Agreed middle ground that suits both of their tastes, as well as many of their customers who pass through the door. A steady diet of Lynyrd Skynyrd, Marshall Tucker, and Led Zeppelin, interspersed with the occasional Jethro Tull, Steely Dan, or ZZ Top. Background noise for the assorted sounds of the shop, everything from bench grinders to air wrenches ringing out at least twelve hours a day.

A soundtrack Remington has grown accustomed to over the last couple of years, making the noise pollution that passes through the phone especially caustic. An auditory intrusion that causes him to wince, jerking the phone away from his face.

"Good God, what the hell is he listening to?"

Groaning loudly, Val replies, "I've been saying the same damn thing since you left. If I have to hear about one more two-step or broken heart or hunting dog, I'm going to kill myself."

Curled up behind the steering wheel of the truck, Remington shakes his head in derision. His gaze fixed on the front of his brother's house, he watches as Cortland winds his way up the sidewalk, heading for the door.

An early departure Remington told him to take, needing a couple of minutes to place this call. Contact he decided to spare his brother from not because of subject matter, but because of his state after the pair of meetings. Necessary stops on their investigation made worse by the emotion of having to tell two of Maylinn's closest friends and colleagues what happened to her.

Minor progress made at the expense of extreme emotional toll.

Even without yet knowing what Remington was able to uncover.

"Only black man I've ever known whose music of choice is old cowboy country," Remington mutters. "And hell, I'm from Texas."

"Yeah, well, I may have to join you there if this shit keeps up much longer."

Saying nothing more, Remington can hear Val put the phone down. A moment later, he can just make out her voice as she tells Tyrell he has a call, the sound of the same caustic music growing much louder for a moment, lasting until the phone is grabbed up again before falling away completely.

"Country Boy Auto," Tyrell answers, "how can we help ya?"

Even after the assorted meetings and findings of the morning, Remington can't help but grin. A response that is completely involuntary, followed by him replying, "You're about as country as my left foot, you know that, right?"

"Oh, come on," Tyrell replies, the words underscored by a chuckle, "at least give me the one that's still attached."

"Nope," Remington says. "The only thing country about you is your gawd-awful taste in music."

"I'll have you know that song you just heard is a classic," Tyrell fires back.

"That's what the owner of the Eldorado said the other night too,"

Remington retorts, "and we saw what kind of shit show it was up under that hood."

Conceding defeat with another burst of laughter, Tyrell switches gears, offering, "I take it things down in Texas aren't as bad as you feared when you tore out of here the other night?"

Any mirth existing just moments before fades. Levity that had crept up on Remington under the guise of hearing Val's voice and sharing a few jokes about the noise pollution filling their shop.

A different time and place that allowed him to put things at arm's length for a moment, the reality of the situation rushing back as he flicks his gaze to the front of the house. An imposing reminder of where he really is and why.

"Worse," Remington replies, his voice losing any pretense of joking. "A helluva lot worse."

"Oh, shit," Tyrell mutters, his own tone dropping to match Remington's. "Cort?"

"His wife," Remington replied. "Killed in a car accident that was definitely not an accident."

"Oh, shit," Tyrell repeats. His go-to response whenever processing new information, said no less than a handful of times every day. "You sure?"

Again, the frozen image from Maylinn's Tesla screen flashes across Remington's mind. A visual that lingers for a moment before being pushed away by the memory of her resting on the steel slab in the morgue. And the markings along the country road the day before.

A damning collection painting a vivid sequence of events.

All of it made more pronounced by what Remington just saw on the camera feed outside the auto shop across from Maylinn's office.

"Positive," Remington answers, "which is why I'm calling you now."

"You need us to come down?"

"Maybe," Remington concedes, "but not yet. I was actually calling to see if you could hook into the network, see if you can track down a truck."

Staying silent for a moment, Tyrell replies, "A truck?"

"Yeah," Remington replies. "I just saw an image of the rig that ran her off the road from a nearby security camera. Big ass Ram 1500."

"Ah," Tyrell whispers, the sound coming out as little more than an exhalation. "You figure they'll be looking to offload it?"

Barely a minute after swinging closed, the front door to the house opens again. Through it passes Shine, headed straight for the stairs, off to do her business, followed a moment later by Cortland.

Making it no further than the top step, he pauses and crosses his arms, alternating his gaze between Remington and Shine.

"I do," Remington says. "Or at the very least, chop it up and start scrapping the parts."

"Right," Tyrell says. "Right, right, right. Yeah, I can do that. I'll start in Austin and work my way out."

"Appreciate it. I'll send you over a picture as soon as we're done."

CHAPTER THIRTY-FOUR

"You go first," Remington says. A simple statement that isn't meant to be an order, even if it does admittedly sound like one. An outpouring of the angst he has been carrying since leaving the filling station a short time earlier despite the brief break with Tyrell, directly fueling his suggestion that they wait until home to discuss whatever they each found.

An option his brother jumped at, clearly needing a few minutes to get past another difficult conversation.

On the edge of the porch overlooking the backyard, Remington stands with his right shoulder pressed against one of the support poles holding up the roof above. Weight shifted to his right leg, he raises his opposite shoe a few inches from the ground, taking some of the pressure off the distal end of his left leg.

A practiced pose, done not out of fatigue – the amount of time spent on his feet today much less than usual – but anticipation of a long night ahead. The combination of what was just revealed and an almost certain inability to get any rest.

What he found on the security cameras at the station far surpassing the frozen image on the screen in Maylinn's Tesla.

Fifteen feet away, Shine works her way along the crisp line separating thick grass from mulch beds. Her head lowered to take in the various scents, she hops slowly along, shifting her weight between her remaining three limbs.

"Couple things," Cortland says, launching straight forth without objection. Seated on the edge of the porch by Remington's side, he speaks without glancing up.

Two brothers both locked on parallel tracks, watching Shine go about her business, even while their thoughts are elsewhere.

"First, Beth said pretty much the same exact thing Eleanor did," Cortland continues. "Swears that nothing they do rises anywhere near the type of thing someone would want to kill over. Like I said before, lot of nonprofit stuff. Housing disputes. Veteran affairs."

Grunting softly to clear his throat, Remington says, "Desperation can make people into savages."

"I said that too," Cortland replies, "but Beth seemed to think a lot of these people are the kind trying hard to be invisible. She can't imagine anyone doing something like this, if only for wanting to avoid the attention."

Bobbing his head, Remington can see how both sides could be right. As he just mentioned to Cortland, fear can make people do outrageous things. Stuff they normally wouldn't even consider, let alone follow through with.

Descended into a state of complete desperation, it isn't hard to imagine someone sitting in an oversized black truck and waiting for Maylinn to exit before following her out into the countryside.

At the same, what Beth said is just as likely. Having grown up in Texas, Remington has known his fair share of people whose immigration status isn't exactly legal. Folks who live and work and raise families without the slightest problem, provided they avoid anything that might bring an unwanted spotlight their way.

Conscious tiptoeing that keeps most from ever so much as jaywalking, let alone committing vehicular homicide.

"Was her laptop there?" Remington asks. "Cellphone?"

"No, and no," Cortland replies. "And Beth agreed that Maylinn took them both with her every night. Even on days when she was ahead of everything and didn't intend to work, she still took them home to avoid leaving them in the office.

"Too much sensitive information."

Turning his chin a few inches toward his brother, Remington asks, "Sensitive enough to...?"

"I asked Beth that too," Cortland replies. "Basically, got the same answer as before. She said there was stuff that could be damaging to their cases, might get their clients in trouble or embarrass them a little, but nothing like this."

From what Remington can tell, it sounds like the woman had made up her mind about things before their arrival. After first hearing about Maylinn's death, she had wanted so badly for it to just be a random accident, she had gone ahead and convinced herself of as much.

Self-preservation in the form of mental firewalls that were actually a detriment, making her incapable of considering the alternative.

"If they aren't there and they aren't here..." Remington prompts.

"I agree," Cortland says. "Whoever ran her off the road must have nabbed them."

"Or the sheriff before you got there," Remington adds. "From what you were describing, things were a little squirrelly there, too."

For a moment, Cortland lets that thought sit. Inhaling sharply, he works through it, Remington's focus going back to Shine, her trip along the mulch bed having ended, her attention now aimed across the open lawn.

"They were," Cortland agrees. "Though that seems more like a place to end, not begin."

To that, Remington can't argue. Much like the way Beth was describing many of their clients, the goal for the two of them and their investigation – if it could even be called that – is to keep it clandestine for as long as possible.

Going right after the sheriff is more of a last resort. A red flare hoping to draw someone in, once all other options have been exhausted.

"Anything else?"

"Beth couldn't give me specific client information, but she gave me a list of ongoing cases," Cortland says. "Stuff that Maylinn was working on that has already been filed, making it public record."

Glancing over, he adds, "No details whatsoever, but named parties, anyway. People we could go talk to if we really want to, but it seems like it might be a fool's errand."

Waiting long enough to make sure his brother is done, his gaze moving back to Shine in the yard before them, Remington reaches to his back pocket. Taking out his phone, he pulls up the photo he just sent to Tyrell. A snapshot of the monitors of the security cameras outside the auto shop, clearly showing a black Ram 1500 driving by.

Handing it over, he keeps his focus aimed outward, his vision blurring as he recalls sitting in front of the screens and seeing it for the first time less than an hour earlier. Recent enough that it is still fresh, his molars coming together as his right hand curls upward into a ball.

"That was taken at 6:04 Tuesday evening," Remington says. "From where the camera is positioned, I could clearly see Maylinn's Tesla pull out and head off at 6:03. One minute later, that asshole came rolling past."

Accepting the phone, Cortland pulls it close. Holding it within just an inch or two of his face, he studies the image for the better part of two minutes before saying, "Was he sitting in the parking lot with her?"

"No," Remington replies. "But based on the angle, I couldn't see where he was parked. Couldn't get a look at the license plate, either."

Bending his left leg at the knee, he keeps it held above the ground, feeling the weight of the prosthetic. "I called Tyrell and asked him to look through the used car network. See if anybody in the area is unloading a truck like that, either whole or in parts."

Grunting softly, Cortland says, "Looks like one guy behind the wheel."

"That's what I thought too," Remington replies. "Couldn't get much of a look at him, but in that truck, at that time..."

"Right," Cortland agrees. "Targeted."

"Mhm," Remington mutters, letting the reply hang as his brother continues studying the photo before asking, "Still think it sounds like a fool's errand?"

CHAPTER THIRTY-FIVE

Staring at the full list of open court cases Maylinn was involved with, there was no way to put them in any sort of rank order. Cortland had tried to, spending a few minutes digging around on Google, only to confirm much of what Beth said earlier about the work they do. Litigation on behalf of people who tried everything short of it to reach resolution against adversaries who lorded whatever little bit of leverage they might have over them.

A veritable Who's Who listing of Austin area scumbags. Government bureaucrats and slumlords and unscrupulous businessmen, hellbent on getting ahead by stepping on those they feel beneath them.

A cluster of names and stories that managed to do the impossible, inciting an emotion beyond just anguish in Cortland for the first time in two days. Small embers of disgust and animosity that he allowed to fester for a few minutes before giving up on it and announcing that they would start with the most recent matter Maylinn was working on. The very last case she visited on Tuesday afternoon before closing up and heading home, never to return.

"So you're looking to rent, huh?" the man seated behind the desk in the small office on the first floor of the Shady Glen apartment complex says. A carveout that would normally be another apartment, set aside as an administrative suite.

One of more than a hundred matching units split between a trio of buildings, all standing two stories tall, with doors facing outward on both sides. Lined up next to one another, they seem to have sprouted directly out of the asphalt, the only vegetation to be seen the sprays of weeds poking up through cracks and potholes.

Landscaping on par with the rest of the place, the structures looking to have been erected in the sixties or seventies without a single repair made in the time since. Decay easily evident on the short walk from the parking lot to the office, on display via faded paint and crumbling stucco and rusted stairwell supports.

A spot that the health department would be well served to visit, it coming as little surprise that Maylinn was asked to get involved.

A first impression made no better after stepping inside the office into a den of arrested development, the space more suited to a teenager's bedroom than a working office, the main difference being the massive remainder desk serving as a centerpiece rather than a decrepit waterbed.

On the walls are hosts of posters for musical groups last popular in the nineties and comic book covers depicting superheroes Cortland has never heard of. Bright colors and shapes that are stapled to the walls at odd angles, filling most of the available space. Wallpaper hinting at extreme structural damage underneath, or a massive detestation for the eggshell paint.

Under them are metal shelving units rising to waist height. Abutted tight to one another, every last one is loaded with items, ranging from those same comic books to aquariums of various sizes. Holding cells for fish and assorted reptiles, requiring the air inside the office to be warm and humid to a level bordering on uncomfortable.

Underfoot, a zebra-print rug covers much of the floor, again begging the question as to whether it is a matter of choice or a means of camouflage. Options that could go either way, based on the figure sitting opposite Cortland and his brother. A guy who introduced himself as Manny and looks like he is about five states east of where he should be given his wardrobe choices of flip flops and board shorts.

A pair of sunglasses with neon orange frames rests beneath a thatch of blonde curls, despite most of the light inside the room being provided by a handful of lava lamps.

"I am," Cortland replies. "I just moved down from Tennessee and asked my brother to take me around to look at some places."

The story is a pared down version of what they discussed on the way over. A ruse backstopped by again taking Tyrell's pickup and included Cortland posing as a cosigner and all the rest, cast aside on the fly after seeing the guy sitting before them.

Superfluous information there is no point in adding, it likely to only confuse the young man already having a difficult enough time mastering basic English.

"Cool," Manny says, bobbing his head forcefully enough to cause the chair he sits in to rock forward. "Cool, cool, cool."

"The place looks great from the outside," Cortland adds, "but we did want to ask about a report we saw about the place going through some legal proceedings regarding mold on the premises?"

"Oh, that," Manny replies. Unlacing his fingers, he waves a hand across himself, dismissing the question. "We get those come through here from time to time. People looking for a quick buck, saying they've got mold, or there's faulty wiring, or they slipped and fell.

"It's nothing. Another freeloader trying to force a settlement." Peering through his gaudy sunglasses, he glances to each of them in order. "I'd say it's amazing that they even get people to bring these things, but you know how lawyers can be, am I right?"

Lips spread wide to reveal two rows of stained teeth, he again looks from Cortland to Remington and back, searching for validation. Agreement to the barb he just tossed out there, trying to use it as a basis for some sort of shared kinship. The start of a business relationship that will never happen.

Is more likely to end up getting his ass kicked.

Badly.

"I noticed on the way in there's a VW bus parked out front," Remington says, bypassing the comment entirely.

Even attempting to force his voice to remain neutral, Cortland can plainly hear the strain in his brother's tone. Desires such as his own, wanting to fly across the desk and make the man take back what was just said.

With the added benefit of releasing some of the underlying angst they are both carrying.

"That yours?" Remington asks.

"Oh, yeah," Manny says, his previous grin returning to full luminosity. Rocking himself forward in his seat, he reaches out and snatches up a framed photo from the desk beside his computer. Flipping it around, he holds it up for them to see, the same lime green van they passed by when entering stretched across it. "That's my baby, The Love Machine. Took me years to save up enough for her, doubt I'll ever drive another car again."

CHAPTER THIRTY-SIX

The top rail of the metal truck bed is hot to the touch. Hours of sitting in the Texas sunshine has turned it into a cooktop, the only things making it bearable being the cuffed sleeves of Cortland's button down providing a thin barrier and the fact that it is early November.

During the summer months, even attempting such a pose, standing along the side of the vehicle with his forearms braced against it, would be asking for severe burns. The old adage about it being hot enough outside to cook an egg, applied to human flesh. Charred skin and blistering almost immediately, made worse with each progressive second.

Aware of the warmth passing through his shirt, Cortland puts it out of mind enough to focus on the man across from him. A massive figure with a matching pose, a pair of thick arms with sleeves of monochromatic ink snaking out from beneath his tank top, reaching all the way to his wrists. Artwork barely obscuring the network of veins and cabled muscles underlying it.

Hair buzzed almost to the skin, the sun has stained the underlying scalp – and the rest of his features – a deep olive hue. A hooked nose protrudes from between sharp cheekbones and dark eyes.

"Where'd you serve?" Remington asks. Lifting his chin, he motions to the network of symbols etched into the man's forearms.

Rolling his wrist outward, the man named Linc Brady exposes the full muscle belly of his forearm. A meaty limb almost twice as broad as Cortland's, providing plenty of space for the central image. A bulldog with muscled arms to match Brady's in an olive-green uniform, with a cigar protruding from his mouth and the letters USMC in block beneath.

"Started out in Pendleton for ITB," Brady replies. "After that, two tours each in the brown and green. You?"

Rotating his arm up at the elbow, Remington points to his own military record printed along the outside of his ulna bone. "Sill, and then Hood. Was in round two in the sandbox when I lost my foot."

"Sorry to hear that," Brady replies, dropping his hands back into their previous position.

"All good," Remington answers. "I got to come home, that's a lot more than others can say."

"Amen to that, brother," Brady replies.

"You miss it?" Remington asks.

"Part of it, I miss every day," Brady says. "Others, I hope to never see or hear of again."

"Amen to that," Remington echoes, parroting the man's own words back at him. A conversation Cortland takes to be building rapport, even as it leaves him standing on the outside for a few minutes.

Coded speak he is not privy to, and knows better than to ask, waiting until Brady says, "What can I do for you fellas?"

The next name lower on the list handed over by Beth Towner earlier, Maylinn had just recently filed suit on Brady's behalf against a company called Electronic City. A big box store rivaling Best Buy or the old Radio Shack chain that Cortland has seen around a few times, but never been inside.

Given no more information from the simple list he was handed, it didn't take more than a few moments after pulling up in front of Brady's home for Cortland to piece things together. A narrative that practically wrote itself, as evidenced by the trailer currently attached to the truck they are leaning against, the bed of it loaded with lawn equipment of every sort. Riding and push mowers, alongside a hedge trimmer, weed eater, and powered blower.

Machinery dappled with sprays of mud and dried grass clippings that does the heavy lifting, the rest finished by the handful of rakes and brooms filling the truck bed between them.

"You'll have to forgive us for coming to your house like this," Cortland says, "but we wanted to talk to you for a minute about a case you recently filed against Electronic City."

Hearing the words out loud, the unintended message they convey, he instantly raises his hands. A means of appeasement that gets no further as a sour look crosses Brady's face and he pushes himself back from the edge of the truck.

"Who sent you?" Brady snaps. "EC? That damned crook of an attorney of theirs?"

"Actually, your attorney is why we're here," Remington says, raising his hands a few inches as well.

Ceasing his retreat, a divot forms between Brady's brows. His gaze flicks between the two of them, trying to assess whether he is being led on, before he asks, "You know Maylinn?"

"We did," Cortland replies. "She was my wife, his sister-in-law."

"She was killed in a car accident two nights ago," Remington adds. "Or so they say."

There is no effort to hide the underlying implication. An approach much more straightforward than would probably be attempted with anybody else on the list, given the man's profession and his shared history with Remington.

A forthright explanation of what happened that hits Brady square, again switching his focus between the two of them as he returns to the side of the truck. Reassuming his previous position, he lowers his gaze to the tangle of hand tools between them and mutters, "Jesus, I'm sorry guys. She was a good egg. Was really making their life hell."

Hearing the words out loud, visibly registering what was just said, he jerks his attention back up. "Shit, you don't think...?"

"We don't know," Remington says. "We know for a fact somebody did it and went out of their way to hide it, so we're just kind of going around, talking to people on the QT."

Nodding in understanding – both at what they are doing and the need to keep it quiet – Brady shifts his focus past them. Staring along the string of houses lining either side of the street, his eyes glass. He retreats within himself, processing what was shared, considering what was asked, before eventually giving his head a shake. A quick turn to clear away whatever debate he was locked in, his eyes blinking rapidly as he returns to the present moment.

"I really wish I could help you out on this," he says. "I do. She was a nice lady, and she was really going out of her way to help me.

"But I can't see this being tied to that at all. She was just trying to help me recover a few months of unpaid landscaping work. Couple grand at most."

Stopping for a moment, he lifts his eyebrows before adding, "And trust me, if you go and talk to those guys, you'll see pretty quick that they aren't the type."

CHAPTER THIRTY-SEVEN

Even at four o'clock in the afternoon, the place is already bedecked for the night ahead. Blue and silver streamers have been threaded through the rafters above. Balloons of the same colors are affixed to every support post and horizontal surface throughout the place. Décor in line with the Dallas Cowboys, brought out in anticipation of a Thursday night tilt against the Green Bay Packers.

A game Enzo could not give a shit about, aware of it only because of Hector and Ramon's constant prattling earlier. The rare topic that the two can actually agree on. A safe space for them to retreat into once they know they have reached the end of their tether, having worn through whatever patience Enzo might have.

Reserves that earlier were even smaller than usual, given the extreme warmth and narrow confines they were forced to work in. A retrieval run that was for the same reason he now finds himself inside the bar and grille known as The Lone Star.

A not-so-clever allusion both to the state of Texas, and to the team they make no secret of supporting.

"Dammit, where are my tall boys?!" a man dressed in jeans and a blue Cowboys jersey yells from behind the bar. "God Almighty, people are going to get off work any minute now, and you know they're coming right over to start in before kickoff."

Standing on the corner of the raised platform comprising the base of the bar, his height still stops several inches short of Enzo's. A lack of vertical stature that is made up for with girth, the bottom half of the jersey pulled tight across his stomach, causing the numbers 2 and 1 to stretch outward away from each other.

The name Elliott is spelled out across his back, though Enzo knows him to actually be Chuck West, owner and operator of The Lone Star.

A business that would have closed years ago if not for the sudden and unexpected aid provided by Leo Garcia.

"Sorry, Mr. West," a young lady who barely looks old enough to serve alcohol replies. Dressed in her own version of team-appropriate regalia, her faded Cowboys t-shirt has been cut off at the ribs. A deep trench has been carved into the neckline. Blue stars festoon either cheek.

Trying to balance herself on a pair of cowboy boots with a three-inch heel, she shuffles along behind the bar, testing the limits of her pushup bra.

"I'll get those out right now."

"Damn right, you will," West barks. One fire extinguished, allowing him to move onto the next. A laundry list that Enzo imagines to be as long as the man's grocery receipt, his face glowing bright red as he spins back in the opposite direction, ready to issue his next orders.

Commands that make it no further than his gaze landing on Enzo before dissipating, his brows rising in surprise.

"Enzo. Hey there, didn't see you come in."

"Chuck," Enzo says, dipping the top of his head forward in greeting. "Bad time?"

"Wouldn't be if people did their damn jobs around here."

Stepping down from the raised platform, West casts a glance over his shoulder. One final withering glare that goes unnoticed, the young girl behind the bar already busy with her assigned task. Grabbing bottles of beer in either hand, she smashes the bottoms down into the ice filling the bins behind the bar, driving them like railroad spikes into the slush.

Leaving her to it, West marches straight for Enzo. Extending his fleshy palm before him, he pumps Enzo's hand twice, leaving a damp residue behind as he releases and motions him on toward the back.

"Come on up, something I need to talk to you about."

Falling in behind the man, Enzo winds his way through the place that – as yet – has no more than a handful of patrons. A couple of pairs with food in front of them, opting for a very late lunch or very early dinner. A few singles have already posted up with beers, ending a bad day at work or securing a spot for optimal viewing of tonight's game.

Folks who barely glance over at West and Enzo slipping by, cutting a diagonal through the tables of assorted heights and sizes. A world of silver and blue and wood bearing several layers of lacquer, reflecting the overhead lights and the sun streaming in through oversized windows lining the front.

Heading toward the corner, they slip past the restrooms before beginning to climb a narrow staircase, the yellow chain normally blocking it off unlatched on one side and left trailing down the stairs. West's own private access, his assorted grunts and groans making his growing difficulty with the passageway obvious. Audible efforts paired with his shoulders brushing the walls on either side, the various framed photos and posters that used to hang there likely removed for just that reason.

His weight swinging from side to side, he manages to clamber up the dozen stairs and descend a short hallway before entering an office overlooking the floor below. Made from the same light wood as the main level, it is separated from the noise by a bank of windows with curtains left open for the time being, allowing him to keep watch from on high.

"Sorry again about that," West says. Motioning to a brown leather sofa with a Cowboys throw draped across the back, he adds, "Have a seat. Can I get you anything? Water? Beer?"

Glancing over to the offered couch, Enzo remains in place, standing just inside the door. Watching as West goes for the personalized fridge with a clear glass door behind his desk, he waits for the man to pull out a bottle of Coke and pop the top off, letting the metal cap fall to the floor.

Dropping sideways into his rolling desk chair, he upends his beverage, leaning back to expose several inches of stomach lined with stretch marks.

Only once he is done, sitting and panting lightly, does Enzo say, "No, I'm good, thanks. I won't be here but a minute."

"You sure?" West offers. "Welcome to stay for the game. The guys will have the grills up and going here soon if you're hungry."

Much like Giovanni the night before, the reception is not unusual, just as Enzo would expect if he happened by The Char Pit this evening. Southern hospitality taken to an extreme level, given who Enzo works for and the position he holds.

"No, really," Enzo says, holding his hands out before him. "I just wanted to stop by and ask how you're doing on supply these days?"

The bottle of Coke already halfway back to his mouth, West pauses. His eyes widen as he slowly lowers it back into position, sliding it up onto the edge of his desk.

"It's actually funny you should ask," he says. "And the something I wanted to talk to you about, because you're not the first this week to bring it up."

Taking a half step forward, Enzo folds his arms over his torso. "What do you mean?"

"Cops," West replies. "They were in here yesterday, sniffing around about the recent overdoses in the area."

The first he's heard of such a thing, red lights begin to flash across Enzo's mind. Indicators of impending trouble, whether it be from someone in their network having loose lips, or some new enterprising law enforcement officer poking around where they shouldn't.

A host of bad options that Leo Garcia will not be happy to hear about.

"Did they seem to have anything?" Enzo asks.

"Didn't sound like it, but it also didn't sound like they were going away anytime soon," West says. "To answer your question, my supply is piss poor. I'm burning through everything I've got and could honestly use more, but..."

Nodding slightly, Enzo says, "Better to lay low for a little while."

"That's what I was thinking," West replies. "At least, until we get an idea on what this is all about."

CHAPTER THIRTY-EIGHT

The lights inside Leo Garcia's training center are not nearly as bright as the midday sun earlier, but they are plenty sufficient to illuminate the full physique of the young man standing before him.

Or, rather, the complete lack thereof.

Malnourishment put on plain display, with every visible ridge along his torso and arms evident. Skin that looks to have been painted onto a skeleton, outlining the dips of his collarbones and the trenches carved between his abdominal muscles and his ribs, as well as a dozen or more prominent scars. A human anatomical chart made even more pronounced by his dark tan, his epidermis nearly matching the color of his hair and eyes.

The most positive thing Garcia can say about his body is at least it isn't marred by tattoos. Gang ink announcing affiliation to MS-13 or Barrio 18 or whatever the latest flavor of the week might be.

A walking billboard inviting both scrutiny and conflict, neither of which Garcia has the time for.

Standing more than fifteen feet away to avoid the stench rolling off him, Garcia lets his gaze travel the length of the young man and back. A slow sweep he does nothing to try and hide, wanting to see how the young man will respond to scrutiny. If he will stand there and scowl in defiance as he did earlier or if he will wither under a sharp gaze.

If he possesses the stones to look Garcia in the eye.

"What's your name?"

Garcia's first impulse after the little display at the unloading zone earlier was to tell his men to dispose of the young man. Right then and there, serving as an example to everyone who had just stepped out of the bus.

They had been brought to America not by their own money or perseverance, but through his benevolence. Kindness that he did not owe them and could rip away at any time.

Support that would only last so long as they did what was demanded of them, showing up with empty pockets being a transgression he will not allow. A cautionary tale about how the arriving group was able to scrape together enough to cover the baby, but not the young man before him, meaning they all must suffer.

An unforgivable error that Tyson would carry back to the border, making sure it travels the length of the caravan all the way to wherever the rabble starts to congregate.

A standing example to anybody who thinks they can get away with mentioning his nickname, as if that is some sort of secret password to gain free admittance. Already, Garcia has enough bodies to dispose of maintaining his empire in Austin. He does not need more added to it by people such as this young man thinking they are an exception.

The rules do not apply to them.

Seeing the set of the young man's jaw though, Garcia managed to tamp down such an immediate reaction. A response not steeped in any particular caring or kinship for the young man, but rather an opportunity.

A chance to take care of something that has been bugging him the last couple of days, and still deliver the show he promised his mother the night before.

"Aguilar," the kid replies.

"You speak English?"

Uncertainty is obvious on his features. Mental calculations that are made in real time, trying to decipher if each question posed is a trap.

As if Garcia would ever make it so easy as to allow this little pissant to figure him out.

"Yes," he replies, the word just as heavily accented as the pronunciation of his own name.

"How old are you?" Garcia asks. Extending the forefinger wrapped over the top of his cigar, he cautions, "And don't you dare lie to me."

Again, the mental calculations before he replies, "Nineteen."

Whether that is true, Garcia has no way of knowing, though he can admit that it is within the realm of possibility. An age range he would have allowed to climb all the way to twenty-one before calling bullshit, making nineteen just as likely as any other number to be true.

The penultimate question on a checklist that has nothing to do with getting to know the young man. Who he is, how old he might be, Garcia could not care less about. Just another dirty, stinking arrival who will end up dead or in prison within eight months.

Maybe if Garcia is lucky, a paying customer who will fill his nose and stomach with contraband substances, working off his debt in another manner.

What he is really trying to measure is how useful Aguilar might potentially be. If he may be worth bringing into the fold, starting him with a rake or broom and letting him work his way upward.

A long process that isn't worth the effort if the kid can't speak passable English or is covered in gang ink. The surest ways to draw attention, even in a place like Austin.

"And last one," Garcia says, "where you from?"

Casting his gaze to either side, Aguilar looks to assess the gathered crowd around him. A throng of people numbering more than a dozen, called in from their various tasks for this particular encounter. A mass pulled together while Garcia was en route back from the drop-off location, there and waiting as the Escalade pulled in.

"Tegucigalpa."

In an instant, the defiance that was displayed earlier makes sense, as does his telling a lie to gain entry onto the bus and the collection of healed wounds marring his skin. Growing up in the capital of Honduras without a gang affiliation means the kid must be tough as hell. A born fighter who was forced to constantly watch where he was and who he was with.

A daily struggle that probably made saying whatever he had to to gain entry into the States worth it.

Plenty more questions arise, though Garcia pushes them aside without voicing a single one. If the kid passes the test he is about to receive, there will be plenty of time for such things later.

If not, there is no point in wasting another moment on the conversation.

"Since nobody stepped forward earlier to pay your way, this is your one chance," Garcia says. "Your only shot at staying here and not ending up hyena shit next door. You understand me?"

Just as they did earlier in the day, Aguilar's hands ball up into fists. His chest rises as he draws in air. A natural defense mechanism stolen from the animal kingdom, meant to make himself look larger. Nostrils flaring, he inches backward, glancing to either side as if measuring the men around him.

"What do I have to do?" he asks.

Smirking softly at the show of bravado, Garcia pushes his gaze to the side. Ignoring the question, he passes his gaze over the men gathered inside, sweeping by the assortment of familiar faces. Men of various sizes and ages, many he remembers squaring off in the ring with himself at one point or another.

Guys dragged in from their work, their features stained with sweat and dirt.

One at a time, he makes eye contact with each, giving the impression of consideration, before eventually his focus lands on who he is looking for.

The man who wasn't smart enough to heed the bell the day before, left wondering for more than thirty hours what his fate might be.

"Miguel, you're up."

———

Despite being well into the backend of his sixties and carrying at least twenty extra pounds between the straps of his suspenders, Garrison moved with the ease of an athlete. Eschewing following the footpath all the way around to the front of the porch and climbing the trio of steps, he came at it straight from the side, hopping up with both feet.

An unceremonious entrance that jerked both Cortland and Remington's attention to the side, snapping their focus away from the microwave dinners balanced across their laps. Both gripping their forks tight, they tensed for but a moment, staring at the unexpected arrival, before slowly relaxing.

"Good Gawd. Ol' Callum must have really gotten to you two," G said. "Both wound tighter than a whore in church."

Pausing to smack the insoles of his boots against the corner post, he knocked away a fair bit of the mud that clung to them before crossing over and grabbing up Cortland's lemonade. Upending the bottom, he drank down several inches before pulling it away. Examining the contents for a moment, he returned it to the inverted wooden crate serving as a table and said, "Not the best thing I can think to put in a Mason jar, but it'll do I suppose."

Chuckling softly, Cortland added, "And it does come with the benefit of not having fuzzy vision for the rest of the night."

"Aw, hell," G replied, waving a hand to dismiss the comment. "My

vision's been blurry for fifteen years now. Drinking the good stuff is about all that clears it up these days."

Crossing past Cortland and Remington both seated in the pair of rockers framing the picture window from the living room behind them, G made his way over to the hanging porch swing on the opposite side. Boot heels scraping across the floor, he left narrow strips of mud in his wake, outlining his path.

Streaks he gave no mind to as he dropped himself down onto the swing, the rusted chain securing it to the bolts in the ceiling moaning slightly in protest. Faint squeals that continued as he rolled his feet from heel to toe, pushing himself forward and back a few inches at a time.

"Got a lot left to run tonight?" Remington asked, posing the question before sawing off a chunk of Salisbury steak and forking it into his mouth. One of two favorites, preferring to always go with the steak or fried chicken on nights when their grandfather was working late and they were left to their own devices for dinner.

A cumulative culinary skillset best suited to using a microwave and little else.

"All night," G answered. Lifting his right arm, he used the sleeve of his shirt to wipe sweat from his brow before adding, "The VA is having a get-together on Monday for the holiday. You know how those go."

Having been around long enough to know exactly what he was alluding to, both nodded in agreement.

"Does that mean no Smokehouse for you this year?" Cortland asked. "Sheriff Myles and Judge Mason were both asking after you earlier."

Dropping his arm back into place, G let his cheeks bunch. Quiet chuckles at the thought of his friends requesting his presence in public before saying, "No, I think you two will have to represent the Moonshine Creek Boys alone this year. Please tell the womenfolk I am sorry."

His turn to laugh, Cortland bobbed his head and replied, "I'm sure they will be crushed."

"Crushed, indeed," G answered.

A response that evoked another laugh from all three. A moment of levity that lingered the better part of a minute before Remington asked, "For real though, we were both thinking on maybe sitting this one out."

"Why?" G responded, his bushy white brows climbing up his forehead. "Because of what happened with Callum earlier?"

CHAPTER THIRTY-NINE

A plume of incense hits Cortland full in the face, engulfing him the instant he passes through the strings of beads hanging across the opening to the shop. Mixtures of various floral scents, he can pick up jasmine and plumeria, only because they were two of his wife's favorites. Smells she used to occasionally spray while cleaning and liked to grow on the back porch during the summer.

More of the thousand little reminders that have already come to him, certain to grow rapidly in the days and years ahead. Aromas that work wonderfully while standing alone, but when mixed together – along with no less than a handful of others he thankfully can't place – become a bit overwhelming. A concoction that causes his nostrils to burn and his eyes to water, forcing him to cough into a fist.

An ideal – if unintended – icebreaker, bringing about a chuckle from the woman manning the cash register just inside the door.

"Yeah, sorry about that," she says, drawing Cortland's attention over to see a middle-aged woman with red hair sprawling away from the crown of her head in waves. Long strands that reach clear to her shoulders before disappearing, giving way to a light purple shawl thrown over a multi-colored halter and matching skirt.

Silver earrings hang on either side of her face. A necklace fills the space left by a plunging neckline. Around either wrist are no less than a half dozen silver bangles, the implements clinking together as she motions to a round table nearby with glass jars of scented sticks piled within. Receptacles for various smells, ranging from those Cortland could identify on to patchouli and something called dragon's blood.

"Some kids were in here earlier trying out the new arrivals and got a little carried away. I had to turn the fan on after they left to get some of it cleared out."

Glancing from the table back to the woman, Cortland asks, "You mean it was worse?"

Smiling broadly, the woman nods. "Yeah, if you can believe that."

Matching her smile, Cortland gives a second look to the shop around him. A space filled with things like the beads and scents that greeted him, an assortment of items ranging from prayer cloths to massage oils lining the walls. A selection that he can see but a subset of, the design of the shop arranged in a pattern that seems to flow from one room to the next, a narrow walkway allowing him to see to and through the back door. An indirect route that wraps around tables and beneath dream catchers and potted plants hanging down.

All of it funneling him toward the Colorado River out back that the building hangs over, the rear end built atop a series of stanchions.

"Nice place you have here," Cortland says. "I assume you're Lady Fyre?"

The smile the woman wears grows larger, revealing two rows of dazzling white teeth. Extending her right arm before her, hand tilted down at the wrist, she says, "That's the name we put on the door because it draws curiosity. Real one is Freya Madisen. It's nice to meet you."

Stepping forward to close the gap between them, Cortland meets her grasp. "Cortland Alder. Nice to meet you as well."

Pumping her hand twice, Cortland starts to pull back, his hand trapped in her grip. A firm hold that is joined by her opposite hand as well, the warmth of both palms passing into either side of his hand.

Taking a step closer, the smile Freya wears fades. Sadness tinges her eyes as her features sag, adding what looks to be a decade to her features.

"Oh my," she whispers. "Such sorrow."

Moving closer still, she releases her left hand from the backside of his and moves it upward, clasping his forearm. "No, agony."

Her brows draw together until they form almost a single line. Moisture rises to her eyes as she stares at him, almost awestruck by whatever she seems to be drawing from him.

A connection that, for whatever reason, Cortland can't bring himself to pull away from.

"Alder," she whispers, repeating the name he just gave her.

"Cortland," he replies. "Husband of Maylinn. Or, rather, the widower of Maylinn."

Pulling both her hands back at once, Freya snaps them up to her face. Covering her mouth from either side, she stares at him with wide eyes, her features registering shock and grief simultaneously.

"No," she hisses. "I just talked to her-"

"On Tuesday," Cortland finishes. "Which is why I'm here."

Her gaze never wavers, fixed on Cortland as she moves to the side. A shift of just a couple of inches, allowing a clear sightline past his left shoulder. Room enough for her to call out, "Ashleigh!"

From somewhere in the back, a voice replies. A young female that Cortland doesn't bother turning to look at, keeping his focus on the woman before him.

"Yeah?" Ashleigh calls back.

"Can you watch the front? I need to step out back for a few minutes."

"Sure thing," the girl replies, the answer barely out before Freya turns and heads for the rear exit. The shawl and the tail of her skirt both flowing behind her, she winds her way through the space, navigating it as if she's done so untold times before. Deft movements under and around various things, opening a gap between herself and Cortland.

Distance enough that by the time he steps over the rear threshold and onto the thick planks comprising the back deck, she is already in position, leaning against the wooden rail encasing the space. Bypassing the host of wrought-iron chairs with padded cushions available, she stands amidst a series of willow branches hanging down. Thin tendrils deep in the throes of autumn color that seem to swallow her up as she stares out, watching the body of the Colorado roll slowly past.

Water that is shaded deep blue and turquoise, punctuated by the occasional white cap produced from rolling over exposed rocks.

"I have a feeling I know why you're here," she says. Sliding her focus away from the water, she turns her gaze toward him, her eyes rimmed with red. "But please tell me I'm wrong. That what happened has nothing to do with this."

Not sure exactly what she is referring to, Cortland asks, "With what, exactly?"

Extending a hand, Freya replies, "This. The river. Please tell me our fight for Mother Nature didn't end with her own sacrifice."

Still not sure exactly what she is referring to, Cortland takes another step forward, feeling the cool touch of air coming up off the water. One more, and the sound of the current rushing over rocks becomes louder.

"You were the plaintiff," he says, recalling what was printed on the sheet Beth Towner gave him. "And the defendant was-"

"Reseda Brothers Meat," Freya finishes. "Which, even though I'm a vegan, I don't begrudge them what they're doing. People need to eat, and they need jobs.

"What they're pumping into the river, though, that I can't condone."

His mind spinning to process what was just shared, the information already taking things much further than what he arrived with, Cortland covers the last few steps across the deck. Carving a path through the chairs strewn about, he presses himself against the rail and peers out, looking down the length of the river.

A waterway more than a hundred yards across, lined with structures ranging from small outposts like the one he is standing on to much larger facilities.

One of which, he imagines, is the site of the litigation his wife recently filed.

The first hint of something that could be the cause of what happened to her. A large company polluting the river and hoping to avoid a lawsuit or public scrutiny.

To quote Remington earlier, he's seen people do more over less.

"Was it ugly?" he asks.

"I use the river to make tonics," Freya replies. "So in that regard, yes. Very. As far as the litigation was going though, not at all. They've been nothing but civil. They've tried to get us thrown out over something called standing, and even offered to settle a time or two, but there've never been any threats that I'm aware of."

CHAPTER FORTY

The sight of the name splayed across Enzo's cellphone screen causes the right corner of his mouth to crease back in a smile. A half grin in response to the call he's been expecting, arriving like clockwork each time he performs a job such as the one a couple of nights before.

Self-adulation that has become something of a running joke, the man calling him now gifted with the easiest part of the entire process, but still always insisting on phoning to do a little tire pumping after the fact.

Gentle barbs to make sure Enzo is acutely aware of just how important he is to the entire operation.

Ribbing that would never happen in front of Leo Garcia – for a variety of reasons, chief among them being the boss's complete lack of humor, especially on matters of business – but Enzo doesn't mind enduring from an old friend.

"Aw hell," Enzo says in greeting. Switching the call to speaker, he drops it down upon his thigh, the volume up as high as it will go. "I should have known I'd be hearing from you."

"Yes," Victor Korneky replies, "you should have!"

His trademark nasal voice turned up to eleven, he practically yells into the phone. A sound of exasperation that makes Enzo's smile grow into a full grin, even before he adds, "That wasn't a truck you left me to get rid of the other day, that thing was a damn tank!"

Eliciting a chuckle, Enzo says nothing as he flicks his gaze to the rearview mirror. A reflexive check of the mirror whenever leaving the city, meant to ensure there isn't someone behind him. Some enterprising young officer or deputy who isn't yet on the payroll, trying to make a name for themselves. A business rival hoping to grab him for information.

One of the endless number of people they might have pissed off over the years, foolishly believing that whatever slight they endured was worth facing certain death – either from Garcia's security team, or another feeding for his pets from Hell.

Seeing nothing beyond the usual thinning crowd of evening drivers all looking to make it home in time for dinner, Enzo moves his gaze to the road ahead. A concrete ribbon extended out before him, painted gold by the setting sun moving steadily toward the horizon. Bright light causing him to squint against the glare, the mirrored lenses of his sunglasses no match for the solar intrusion.

"Does that mean you're calling to let me know it is done?" Enzo asks.

"It's done, but that's not why I'm calling."

Rocking back slightly in his seat, Enzo chuckles softly. "Alright, let's hear it. Tell me all about how much trouble it was and the mountains you had to move and the number of favors you called in getting one little truck disassembled and disappeared.

"At a premium price, no less."

Victor's turn to laugh, he lets out a squeal of glee that makes Enzo glad he switched the phone to speaker, the sound reverberating through the truck. Not unlike the call of the hyenas he was just thinking about, it is something akin to a wail, passing through the cab of his pickup before mercifully falling away.

"First of all," Victor says, still wheezing from his bout of laughter, "it was closer to a damn eighteen-wheeler than a little truck. Do *not* minimize what I do over here."

Lifting his hands from the steering wheel, Enzo continues to smile, muttering, "My apologies."

"Thank you," Victor returns. "And since you mentioned it, it *was* a lot of trouble, I *did* move a couple of mountains, and *more* than a few favors were called in."

Nodding along with the narrative, Enzo prompts, "All for a premium-"

"For a premium fee," Victor finishes. "Yes, you are correct. But again, that isn't why I'm calling you."

Flicking his focus from the road to the rearview mirror, Enzo makes sure that the lane beside him is clear. A last-second check before swinging himself off the highway and onto a smaller two-lane heading north.

A little detour he occasionally takes when he's carrying product to ensure nobody might be lying in wait, hoping to make a big score.

Garcia's paranoia passed directly onto him, erring on the side of caution.

"Okay, I'll bite my friend," Enzo says. "To what do I owe this pleasure?"

"I just got a call," Victor replies. "A most curious one, at that."

"A most curious call," Enzo repeats, lifting a hand and motioning it in a circle, hinting that it is time to move forward. "From?"

"From Memphis," Victor answers.

"Memphis...Tennessee?"

"Yes, but that's not the curious part. He was looking for – specifically - a Ram 1500."

Enzo's left hand tightens on the steering wheel as he glances to the rearview mirror again. As Victor himself just confirmed, there will be no finding that truck. That part doesn't concern Enzo.

The fact that anybody is asking at all does.

"What did you tell him?"

"Told him I didn't have anything, but that he might want to check with Tony," Victor says. "May be nothing, but I went ahead and offered to set it up for later this evening just in case you wanted to take a peek."

"We'll do that. Thanks, Victor."

"Hey, always happy to help, my friend. For a prem—"

"Premium fee, of course," Enzo finishes, though his voice lacks much of the mirth from just moments before. "Yeah, yeah."

Ending the call without another word, he alternates his focus between the road and the screen of his phone. Scrolling down through his recent log, he goes past a handful of entries before finding what he wants and hitting send.

A moment later, Hector is on the line.

"Yeah?"

"Got something for you."

"Sure thing. When?"

"Now."

CHAPTER FORTY-ONE

Remington could tell when his brother stepped out of Lady Fyre's that she'd had something to share. Information that he hadn't been able to hear over the phone, most sound drowned out by the rushing water of the river. Radio silence that left him antsy in the small parking lot out front.

Thumbs tapping at the wheel, more than once he'd considered ducking in to make sure everything was okay. The same thing that befell Maylinn wasn't now going after Cortland.

An internal debate that nearly had him step out of the truck before ultimately his brother exited. Walking fast, he came straight over and climbed in, unloading what he'd just found out before they even attempted to leave.

Information that wasn't quite the case cracker Remington was hoping for, but was a start. A bit of something far more promising than any of their previous visits on the day, the only downside being that it occurred after the close of traditional business hours.

A hard stop occurring before they really even got going.

A reluctant halt that had them going off in search of dinner when the phone rang, Tyrell calling to inform them that he had someone they should talk to and to be there in thirty minutes. A short gap that didn't leave them with much time, Remington making the mistake of asking if they should abandon their previous plans for barbecue in the name of doing something quick.

An error that was immediately pounced on, Cortland pointing out that anyone who would even consider such a trade short of starvation must have gone soft while living in Tennessee.

The beginning of a back-and-forth that carried them all the way to where Remington now finds himself, for the first time acting as the one inside while Cortland waits in the truck.

"Garrison," he says, extending a hand before him, borrowing his grandfather's name for the next few minutes.

"Anthony," a man with a pompadour hairstyle flecked with gray says while flashing a smile that reveals a pair of silver teeth. One each on the top and bottom, offset to either side to give a disorienting effect. Bling that could be either essential or cosmetic, meant to match the trio of necklaces around his neck and the rings on no less than three fingers.

A vibe he might have been able to pull off twenty years ago, but now that he is well past fifty, just seems like he is trying too hard.

"Call me Tony." Grabbing Remington's hand, he says, "I'm told you're new to the area, might be looking for something specific?"

"I am," Remington replies, leaning into the backstory Tyrell supplied before his arrival. A standard narrative of a recent transplant trying to avoid paying taxes in multiple states, instead waiting until relocating to pick up a new ride. "Just got a piece of land up north in Williamson, need something with a little more space and power than the Tundra out there."

Hooking a thumb to the side, he gestures to the pickup sitting on the edge of the concrete pad serving as a parking lot. A slab of asphalt with years of cracks threaded through it. Tendrils that have split as wide as a couple of inches in places, allowing chunks of rock to break away and weeds and thistles to poke up through.

An entrance to the Quonset hut that serves as the hub of the location. Seventies-era architecture and materials that were probably culled together from military surplus. An abundance of supplies that were produced in the wakes of the Korean and Vietnam Wars, suddenly flooded onto the civilian market once public sentiment demanded a ceasefire.

Stretched wide to either side of the main facility is chain link fencing covered in green mesh. Barriers that probably are transparent under the light of day, but now that the sun has all but disappeared, serve the purpose of keeping the inner workings of the place hidden from view.

A combination used car lot and junkyard, signage on the drive in announcing that they can fix or find damn near anything automotive.

The type of place Remington's own shop deals with frequently, overnighting in parts or making swaps on out-of-commission vehicles, it hardly a surprise Tyrell was able to make contact and set them up so quickly.

"I'm told you might have a Ram 1500 available?"

"Sure do," Tony replies. Motioning back over a shoulder, he gestures for Remington to follow him up through the heart of the Quonset hut. Despite the hour, the front doors on it have both been pushed out wide. Metal sheets slid along rollers, allowing a clear view to the inner workings of the building.

To the left, Remington can see a decent chunk of the square footage has been parsed off into an office. A couple of hundred square feet framed by steel and windows, filled with the requisite desk and file cabinets that most businesses have.

Just past it sits a kitchen, complete with a solid slab table and a stove and refrigerator installed around the same time as the building itself. Items from a different decade that both still look to be going strong, as evidenced by the pair of people currently using them. Guys in jumpsuits stained with grease, one stirring a pot while the other grabs beers.

The end of a long shift, or a break before returning back to it.

On the opposite side of the wide aisle cutting through the center of the building is a ping pong table, billiards table, and a trio of leather sofas grouped around a big screen TV. A full-on employee lounge that currently goes untouched, the screen dark and silent, reflecting Remington and Tony's progress as they pass.

"What part of Tennessee you from?"

His initial thought to keep up the ruse started with the use of the fake name, Remington opts against it. Lying a second time may expose them, whether it be from the county label across the bottom of Tyrell's license plate or depending on how his friend identified himself when calling down to set this meeting up.

Downsides far outweighing any gain to be had by continuing to obfuscate, leading Remington to say, "Just outside of Memphis. Place has been getting too damn crowded, so I decided to head this way."

Snorting loudly, Tony replies, "Not much better down here these days, though at least you get to keep avoiding paying state taxes, huh?"

"I heard that," Remington replies, keeping pace beside Tony as they cover the last of the place and pass through to the other side. An access point to a spread stretching wide in both directions, revealing a world completely hidden from the road.

Standing on the southern edge of a large gravel clearing, surrounding it are three other structures. A pair of block buildings with windows darkened and doors closed, their purposes Remington can only guess at, offset by the garage where the two men inside were probably working just moments before. A massive pole barn structure with roll top doors pushed open and rows of hydraulics lifts inside, easily visible from the bright light spilling out across the ground.

A setup Remington doesn't mind admitting dwarfs what he and Tyrell and Val have, the slightest tinge of jealousy kicking up within.

Filling the gaps between the buildings are rows of cars in various states of disrepair. Vehicles that look like crushed soda cans, all the way to fully intact automobiles that have sat for so long, they have given way to rust and weeds.

The source from which a faded red Ram 1500 has been pulled.

Sitting on the edge of the clearing, it rests facing the Quonset hut they just exited, pockets of rust visible along the hood and bumper.

"Well, what do you think?" Tony asks, raising a hand and motioning to the truck. "That what you have in mind?"

Nothing about the truck matches what Remington is looking for. A chance that was taken when he told Tyrell to be deliberately vague, not wanting to tip their hand too much, calling around to ask about anything too specific likely to have aroused suspicion.

Especially in a place where it seems even the sheriff could be on the take.

"Looks solid," Remington lies, putting a bit of space between himself and Tony to walk along the side, going through the motions of inspecting it. A continuation of the charade, should any information about the visit be passed on afterward.

"What year?"

"2012," Tony replies. "One-hundred-and-forty under the hood."

Nodding his approval, Remington continues his loop. A purposefully slow circumnavigation, taking in the bald tires and dented side panels. Forced interest in something he would never drive, even if Tony were to pay him for it.

Wasted time that he considers chalking up before deciding to make one last stab. A shot that may or may not work, the aftermath potentially telling them just as much.

"I don't suppose you've got any of these around here in black?"

CHAPTER FORTY-TWO

The pair of people standing by Leo Garcia's side atop the veranda overlooking the compound behind his mansion is markedly different than the group that gathered just a couple of nights before. Gone are Maribelle and Johnson Kleese, taking with them their garish outfits and their overblown hair and their exaggerated manner of interaction. Makeup that is too bold and heels that are too tall and laughter that is much, much too loud.

An evening Garcia would just as soon face the hyenas below than have to relive.

Taking their place this evening are two men as different from the Kleeses as possible. Enzo, standing on the far opposite end, in his dusty jeans and sweat-stained snap button shirt, a long day of going deep into the silver mine and then making the rounds with the goods acquired there plain on his personage.

A tired and dirty exterior that makes his joining Garcia's mother this evening out of the question, no matter what she asked the night before.

Filling the space between them is Aguilar, the victor of this afternoon's fracas in the gym. A battle that Garcia expected to be more contentious than it ended up being, severely underestimating the raw savagery the young man by his side was capable of. Carnal rage from a lifetime of clawing by, honed into a demeanor and raw fighting style that easily surpassed whatever training Miguel carried into the ring with him.

A spectacle that called to mind the old maxim of never bringing a knife to a gunfight, altered to warn a boxer to never climb in the ring with a fighter.

Or, in this case, a berserker, Miguel barely landing a few punches before Aguilar tore into him with a flurry of knees and elbows, claws and teeth, that very nearly ended tonight's demonstration before it began. A hyena in human form who had to be pulled off before destroying the show Garcia's mother was waiting for and ruining the message he is now here to impart.

"What you did today was..." Garcia begins, his opening timed out exactly as it was a couple of nights before. A speech serving as prelude, brought on right as the top lip of the setting sun rests on the horizon. "Impressive. Miguel has been trained. He's six years older and forty pounds heavier, and you beat the piss out of him simply by wanting it more."

Sliding his gaze to the side, Garcia checks the expression on Aguilar's face. A look to see if the praise will evoke pride or self-right-eousness or if it will slide off completely unnoticed. A final test that will have no bearing on how things go this evening, but will help inform next steps.

The post Aguilar is given and the people he is surrounded with.

His eyes pinched up to block the incoming glare of the setting sun, Aguilar gives no response at all. Gone is the open defiance he wore earlier, washed away in the bath he was told to take after this afternoon's brawl.

A thorough scrubbing that, when mixed with the clean clothes he is wearing, almost gives the impression of him being just another college student around town. A freshman or sophomore at UT, still gangly and in need of a few meals for sure, but hardly the starved and dirty vermin who stepped off the bus just hours before.

An outward visage that Garcia can use. A young boy rife for underestimation, there being no way anybody who wasn't there this afternoon can possibly look at Aguilar and imagine what he is capable of.

A rare commodity, not that different from Garcia or Enzo once upon a time.

"What you did before that, though," Garcia continues, "was stupid as hell. Not just getting on that damn bus without money, but using my name to pay for it. Pretending for even a second that you knew me, let alone that I would somehow cover what you were up to."

In his periphery, Garcia can see Aguilar's fingers work their way up the outside of his jeans. Talons curling up into balls, ready for combat.

His gaze remains fixed straight ahead, even as his breathing slows. Air clenched in his chest as he prepares to strike, probably weighing in his mind the best way to go at it. Which direction to lead with, and which of the two men he can outrun.

"Starting tomorrow, you will take Miguel's place on the grounds crew, and you will work off every dime you owe me. The full cost of the trip up here and the clothes on your back and even the food you eat between now and then.

"You will be on time every morning, you will keep your mouth shut, and if someone here tells you to eat shit, you will smile and swallow it down. Do you understand me?"

Rooted in place, his gaze fixed straight ahead, Aguilar nods. A short, terse gesture that makes Garcia want to reach out and smack the back of his head.

"That's not going to get it done," Garcia snaps instead, whatever goodwill he might have harbored after the fight earlier dissipated by the call Enzo received from Victor Korneky. The start of something that should be over with, triggering a headache even larger than the one they were hoping to get rid of originally.

A festering problem that could easily become worse, something Garcia has always prided himself on avoiding.

Bullshit mistakes that drag down his competitors, but never him.

"Do you understand me?" Garcia repeats.

"I understand."

"Good," Garcia says, watching as a lone figure appears in the compound below. Still stripped bare to the waist from the fight earlier, dried blood can be seen dotting his pants. Dark splotches of early bruising mars his ribcage.

Wounds that would look atrocious by morning, if he were to live that long.

Staggering sideways, he doesn't make the same mistake as the man a couple nights before. Having stood in the very spot and watched the show himself, he knows better than to even try, instead putting his sights on the closest tree. A listing gait with clear intentions that will do no good against the leaping abilities of the hyenas, though will make for a far better show than the last.

"If you don't," Garcia says, "you will get the same fate as Miguel down there."

Folds of skin appear around Aguilar's eyes as he stares on, trying to comprehend what he is seeing. "Which is?"

"Watch."

CHAPTER FORTY-THREE

The smell was there to greet them the instant they stepped out of the truck. An aroma that hung in a cloud about the place, engulfing it in a scent that Cortland can only describe as heavenly. An instant cure to anyone who might be considering a life as a vegetarian or vegan, a single hit on the intoxicating smell enough to make them cast aside such thoughts and go running to the counter.

Pretty much exactly what Cortland and his brother did, abandoning their previous discussion for the few minutes it took them to cross the parking lot and head inside, only to be greeted by an escalation of smells. The original baseline of charred animal flesh and woodsmoke pouring from the exhaust pipes along the side of the building, flagging down passing motorists in a manner of modern siren song, mixed with baked cornbread and fresh cobbler and in-house barbecue sauce.

An olfactory cornucopia that pushed all else from mind as they ordered and collected their meals, both starting in on their food before saying a word.

"Tell me something," Remington offers as an icebreaker. Saying no more, he waits as Cortland finishes the bite he is working on and brushes a paper towel across his face before continuing.

"Why in the hell would a place that can do this," he asks, waving a hand at his tray for emphasis, "advertise themselves as the worst barbecue in Texas?"

After the events of the afternoon, Cortland wasn't sure where the opening to his brother's statement was headed. Any of a number of directions stemming from the various meetings they'd had.

A lot of sorrow and unanswered questions adding up to precious little they can actually use. A sum total that Cortland can't deny is starting to get frustrating as hell, even for him.

There no telling what it must be doing to his brother, never exactly known for his patience.

"That's Rudy's for you," Cortland says, adding a small chuckle. A rare moment of levity that was unexpected, but he is not about to turn away. "Self-deprecation works every time."

"No," Remington replies. Twisting his head to either side, he props his elbows on the table, preparing to go back in for more. "Killer brisket works every time. Self-deprecation is just something to put up with while eating."

Sawing off another chunk, he stabs it with the end of his fork. Holding it up between them, he inspects the glistening fat cap along the top edge and asks, "Why didn't you bring me here before?"

Barely is the question out before he shoves down the hunk of meat, chewing only twice before swallowing. A wad of beef and fat that Cortland can see traveling the length of his throat, evoking another chuckle before replying, "Because you never left the house before."

His plastic fork still extended before him, Remington jabs at the air between them. The start of a return quip that makes it no further, the words he is looking for evading him. A crushing victory that refuses to find him, ending with him raising his brows in resignation and replying, "Maybe not, but I just saw some people taking theirs to go. You could have done that."

"Maylinn would have never allowed it," Cortland answers. "You know that. She barely let us bring home takeout pizza. Certain foods are to be-"

"Eaten fresh or not at all," Remington finishes, rattling off the mantra they've both heard her say a hundred times before. A firm stance she had against spending too much on food not to eat it at its absolute best.

Lingering frugality that she could occasionally push aside for household items or for her Tesla, but still clung to on a daily basis. Business suits that were purchased from Nordstrom Rack and a preference for cooking at home.

Idiosyncrasies that were but a tiny part of her charm.

"Besides, you live in Memphis now," Cortland says, steering the conversation – and his thoughts – back toward safer ground, the last thing he or the other customers need being for him to break down again, his last spell now the better part of a day past, and well overdue. Crying that at some point might well pull his eyes from his sockets, his tear ducts only able to take so much abuse. "Don't tell me you're not getting good barbecue on the reg."

"Pork barbecue," Remington fires back. "Completely different thing."

"Oh, really?" Cortland answers. "Enlighten me."

Dropping the fork he was loading with okra and potato salad down onto his tray, Remington balances both forearms across the edge of the table. Lacing his fingers, he stares back, a diatribe ready to be unleashed.

"Uh-oh, he means business," Cortland mutters.

"Damn right I do," Remington answers. "On barbecue, and a few other things too, since we're here."

Dropping his fork as well, Cortland raises his arms to match his brother's pose. A stance to brace himself, preparing for an onslaught. An outpouring akin to a desert cloudburst, not arriving often, but when they do are sure to unleash a deluge.

"First, yes, we have barbecue in Memphis, but like I said, it's different. If baby backs or pulled pork is your thing, you are in heaven. You like every seasoning on the planet on the outside? Mustard and vinegar in your sauce?

"By all means, pony up."

"But..." Cortland prompts.

"*But,*" Remington echoes, "if you happen to prefer cow, and believe that salt and pepper are the only way to dress it-"

"The way, oh, say, you might?" Cortland inserts.

"The way anybody who grew up in Texas should," Remington corrects, "then there is really no comparison."

Still gaining speed, he continues, "Just like, no matter how many damn Alabama or Georgia fans I have to listen to about the SEC, there is nothing like football down here either. Packed stadiums every Friday night, the Longhorns and Sooners in Dallas every October," waving a hand to the screens above, he adds, "even the damn Cowboys.

"What they have over there is a hot streak. This...this is tradition."

Warmth rises to Cortland's face as his cheeks bunch. The start of suppressed laughter that causes his shoulders to quiver, it having been far too long since he heard one of his brother's patented rants. Stored thoughts and energy that eventually reach max capacity before the dam breaks, and it all comes out.

"I can see you've put a lot of thought into this," Cortland offers.

"Damn right," Remington says. "Going on two years now, I've been hearing all the barbs. Beef ribs aren't as tender. Texas has become a basketball state. On and on and on."

Shaking his head in disgust, Remington reaches for his fork. Casting a sideways glance to the door, he pauses with his fingers poised above the utensil, his eyes narrowing as he stares out.

Whatever thought he was just having fades, a single muscle twitching in his cheek as he begins to rise from his seat.

Unsubtle messaging that Cortland picks up on, turning to check the door as well.

"What?" he asks.

"I'm not sure," Cortland says, sliding out from the bench seat he is resting on. "But go ahead and get that extra meat you were talking about for Shine. I'll be back."

CHAPTER FORTY-FOUR

The mistake whoever the hell is behind the wheel of the silver Ford F-350 made was in staying on the move. Continuing to rove by, keeping a vigil on Remington and Cortland even after following them from Tony's garage to Rudy's BBQ. An error in judgment that they have probably made a hundred times before, believing that even in a truck so large and gaudy, they are much less likely to be noticed swinging by every so often. Periodic checks to maintain position while ensuring that once movement begins again, they can easily swing in behind.

A bird in flight, and all that shit.

A rookie move that was the entire reason Remington even noticed the oversized machine rolling past. A chance glance up while the front door was standing open, removing the reflective glare of the glass for just an instant. A quick moment in which he was able to spot the vehicle with the windows tinted dark sliding past.

If the driver knew the first damn thing about what they were doing, they would have posted up somewhere nearby and waited them out. With the sun gone from the sky and most of the businesses around closed for the evening, there would have been plenty of places for it to pull in and kill the lights, waiting until they were done before following.

A mistake proving that this is someone who either doesn't know what they are doing or doesn't particularly care if they are seen. Is maybe even trying to get spotted, hoping to draw them out or make a statement that whoever attacked Maylinn is now on to them too.

A possibility Remington can't pretend he doesn't find at least a little intriguing after the events of the day. A whirlwind of meetings and interviews that have worn them both down, providing nothing in return but a whole lot of frustration. Growing acrimony that right now Remington has aimed at the roving F-350 as he slides into the front seat of Tyrell's Tundra and turns over the engine. Checking the rearview for only a second to make sure there is no one behind him, he drops the gearshift and reverses out.

Pausing just long enough to scan the road ahead, making sure that the truck hasn't already come around for its next pass, he leans on the gas, spewing dirt and gravel out behind him. Shooting out across the front of the building, he passes through the light on the corner, remaining on the same street as Rudy's before making a turn a block later.

Following the same pattern, he proceeds forward another couple of blocks before turning right again.

The start of a spiral, slowly working his way outward. His backside pressed deep into the well of the seat, he leans forward, peering over the steering wheel. With his foot pressing lightly on the gas, he goes just fast enough not to draw notice, his gaze swinging to either side.

A constant sweep of every business and parking lot he sees, whether they be open or long closed for the day. Slanted stalls along the front of gas stations or minimarts. Chunks of paved asphalt extended from the sides of bank branches and restaurants.

A constant vigil, seeing and dismissing every large vehicle he sees.

An ongoing search, hoping to spot that same damned pickup.

At what point the driver first caught up to them, Remington can't be certain. He doesn't remember spotting it while sitting outside of Lady Fyre's, but once Cortland came out and started sharing what he'd learned, Remington's attention had admittedly waned. Focus that turned to what was being told, rather than the world around them.

The start of a pattern, extending after hearing from Tyrell and making the trip out to Tony's. One thing after another demanding his attention, each examined exhaustively before finally being pushed aside by the promise of food and rest.

The hope that they might be able to tamp down the growing agitation, making for clearer thinking come morning.

An acceptance not of defeat, but that there was going to be precious little more they could accomplish this evening.

A fleeting moment of clarity, during which he first spotted the enormous rig in his rearview. One lane to the side and three car lengths back, it had followed them for three blocks before making a right and disappearing.

Only to then pop back up a half mile later.

And, most recently, outside of Rudy's.

Three separate sightings that are too much to be coincidence in a vehicle that is too unique to be mistaken for something else.

"Come on," Remington mutters. "Show yourself, dammit."

Flipping the turn signal upward, he makes another right. His third turn since leaving, bringing him back toward his starting position. The beginning of another loop, this time a block further wide, swinging back in the opposite direction.

A change of heading that will hopefully catch the F-350 by surprise.

Get them to reveal themselves before even realizing it.

———

There was little to match the concentrated pandemonium inside The Smokehouse with the scene that Cortland and Remington visited just six hours earlier. Gone were the empty tables, where one could sit down and have a normal conversation. Missing were the clear lines of sight from the front to the back door, allowing plenty of natural light to spill in. Vanished even was the faint breeze that passed through, aided heavily by the fans turning lazily overhead.

In their place was a concentrated throng of humanity. People in various states of inebriation, sweating profusely but refusing to step away from the party in progress. Raucous laughter and suggestive dancing, all backdropped by Ketchum's kitchen staff playing DJ from somewhere in the back.

About the only things Cortland could rightly identify as remaining were the slight scent of wood smoke in the air and the attire Bill Ketchum was wearing. Togs given all evening to continue soaking up the smells of the wood pit out back and his own perspiration, the garments now saturated with both.

A pungent miasma of scents that rolled from the man in undulating waves as he sidled up between Cortland and Remington, throwing his arms across their shoulders.

A stance that wasn't the easiest for him to maintain given their respective height disparities, leaving the poor man standing with his hands raised high like a biker on a chopper motorcycle.

"You damn Moonshine Creek Boys," *he muttered, his tongue thick with the product they dropped off that afternoon, his fleshy features tinged pink to match.* "You all do know how to throw a party."

"Hey," *Remington replied, extending a bottle of Dr. Pepper out before him. Strict adherence to their grandpa's rule of never sampling the goods in public.*

And sure as hell never driving afterward.

"This is your party. We're just glad to be invited."

"Invited?" *Ketchum repeated, shifting his weight toward Cortland so he could peer up at his brother.* "Hell, you boys are family. Not going to be the same around here without you next year."

Peering over the top of Ketchum's head, Cortland cast his brother a sideways glance. A look Remington matched before they both turned away, each taking a pull from their beverage.

Neither wanted to be the one to correct the man – in his own place, at his own party, no less – though he was only half right in his assessment. The backend of it, when commenting that things wouldn't be the same starting in just a few short months. A topic they'd both already discussed at length, each openly wondering if they were doing the right thing by Cortland accepting a scholarship to Texas Tech in Lubbock and Remington joining up with the military.

Conversations deep into the night that G had caught wind of and shut down immediately, even going so far as to tell them they were no longer welcome as of September 1st, just to ensure they did go.

A hollow threat they both knew wasn't true, largely because of the part of the statement Ketchum got wrong. A comment steeped in good intentions, though to them family was but three people.

The Moonshine Creek Boys.

"What do we think?" Ketchum asked, mercifully sliding his hands from their shoulders and slapping them each on the back. "Can we beat last year?"

"Last year?" Cortland asked, his brows rising. "I don't know, has anybody seen Jim Montgomery?"

Letting out a thunderous laugh, Ketchum was still bent forward at the waist as Sheriff Myles elbowed his way forward. His uniform shirt completely abandoned, his white undershirt was soaked with sweat, his hair matted to his forehead.

Appearance hinting he'd been having a good time, decidedly at odds with the expression on his face.

"Sheriff!" Ketchum exclaimed, missing on the obvious cues before him. "We were just talking about you and your illustrious opponent from last year."

Saying nothing to that, Myles instead cut his gaze from Cortland to Remington and back. Mouth pulled into a tight line, he said, "Boys, the station just called. There's been an incident."

CHAPTER FORTY-FIVE

District Attorney Kennedy Banks stands before the small conglomerate of local news media, gripping either side of the podium so tight the whites of his knuckles can be seen plainly onscreen. A classic power pose, allowing him to clench his entire upper body tight, his biceps and deltoids threatening to burst through the suit coat he wears.

Strain provided not by any great amount of musculature, but from buying his business attire off the children's rack. Matching charcoal threads that Leo Garcia would imagine to be baggy even for Aguilar, on the brink of crossing from malnourishment into starvation.

Flexing his upper body as tight as he can, Banks tries to offset the strain by forcing a solemn expression onto his features. A look of sorrow and remorse, decidedly at odds with the megawatt grin he donned in that same exact pose barely a week earlier. Confirmation of his reelection, financed in no small part by Garcia's generous cash donations.

Bundled stacks like those at Milo's office the day before, piled high and wrapped in cellophane. Non-sequential notes grabbed up from the establishments lining the numbered avenues downtown, equal amounts spliced away from the hauls gathered at every bar and restaurant in the area.

Monies earned from the avarice and excess of others. Young students and tired tech workers and haggard divorcees, all looking for their particular fix.

A product that has played a prominent role in Banks getting where he is, his original placement on the ballot and his pair of reelections made entirely possible through Garcia's empire. A small down payment in the name of ensuring that the man continues to look the other way on anything they tell him to.

Making his little performance this morning all the more infuriating. An impromptu press conference that was neither vetted nor approved, on a matter that the man knows to leave well enough alone.

Especially now, when there is enough direct attention being paid to the matter.

Standing in the center of his mother's room on the top floor of the mansion, Garcia watches with his arms crossed. A pose he assumed after being summoned upstairs, barely making it through the door before his mother grabbed the remote and jacked the volume on her television. A none-too-subtle hint as to why she had called out for him, bellowing down from her perch until he was forced off the phone and out of his office, sprinting up the stairs.

A run fueled by annoyance, most of it bleeding away the moment he saw the screen and heard the first few sentences Banks uttered.

What anger remained made an abrupt turn, redirecting from his mother's pushy insistence to the egregious overstep now taking place. Irritation that rises with each passing moment, his arms tightening over his torso as he stands and watches.

"Just last night I was awoken by APD calling to tell me that two more young people had just been lost to overdoses. Juniors in the engineering department at The University of Texas, both with bright futures ahead of them. Their entire lives yet to be lived, with the vast promise of societal contributions.

"Outcomes that neither they nor any of us will ever come to realize after a night out celebrating with friends. A birthday party that ended with a trip to the emergency room, and after that, a final visit to the Travis County morgue."

Maintaining his death grip on the podium, Banks pauses there. A dramatic break as he looks around the room, peering into every last camera before him. A move learned while performing in front of juries, made to appear as if he is looking every last viewer directly in the eye.

A doleful stare that Garcia wishes nothing more than to reach through the television and knock right off the man. A hard left followed by a vicious uppercut, just two punches all that would be needed to leave the man broken and bleeding on the floor.

Another pretty boy in a suit taught what justice really looks like.

"After I got that call, I stayed up the rest of the night thinking about what had been shared. Not just last night, but on far too many nights in the last few months. Young lives cut short in such a horrific manner.

"The black mark that this scourge has become on our beautiful and vibrant city."

Working toward his big finish, some new initiative or proposed task force that was sure as hell never mentioned to Garcia, he pushes himself upright. Folding his arms, he poses as if some sort of self-styled superhero, cocking his head to either side, making sure the assembled photographers get a clear shot of his coiffed hair and chiseled chin.

More targets for the imaginary boxing match still playing out in Garcia's head.

"And so I made the decision, right there laying awake in bed last night, that first thing this morning, I would be starting an initiative to investigate – and prosecute – all sellers, suppliers, and users of these harmful narcotics in our community."

Having heard enough, Garcia's mother thrusts the remote control out a second time. Going beyond merely muting it, she shuts the television off, the screen cutting to black.

In the absence of it, sound filters in through the open windows. Lawn equipment and sprinkler heads outside, signaling the start of another day around the estate.

"I never did like his ass," Sofia mutters.

To that, Garcia says nothing. He doesn't bother to mention that his mother never likes anybody. Sure as hell doesn't bring up what Enzo shared the night before on the veranda after watching the midweek feeding about cops stopping by The Lone Star for a visit with Chuck West.

"Did you know about this?" Sofia asks.

Still rooted in place, Garcia tracks his gaze her direction, shaking his head just a few millimeters to either side. "No.

"No," she repeats, her lips twisting up as if tasting something sour. "At least tell me you don't intend to let this shit stand?"

CHAPTER FORTY-SIX

Enzo has spent enough time with Leo Garcia over the years to know when something is wrong. Minor irritations or lingering aggravations that the man is pretty good at masking from the outside world, using the deepening lines on his face or the expanding ring of hair encircling his mouth to obscure his true feelings. A mask that he was incapable of producing as a younger man, forced to learn to do so as he ascended to the head of a burgeoning business before mastering it once it truly began to build into an empire.

A skill acquired through both necessity and repetition, his mother hammering home a thousand times over how the figurehead of a business cannot let the outside world know what he is thinking. No matter the test or the opponent, they must be able to wall off anybody who isn't in the inner ring.

Placement Enzo has enjoyed for long enough that he can tell something is irking his friend and boss.

Just as surely, he knows not to directly ask, lest that ire be aimed his way.

"I heard back from Hector last night," Enzo offers instead. A bit of good news in the face of some unknown negativity. "Doesn't sound like it is anything to worry about. The guy was some roughneck type. Sleeve of tattoos, missing part of a leg."

His gaze aimed down at the concrete walk stretched out in front of them, Garcia doesn't bother to look Enzo's way. His expression doesn't alter in the slightest, a deep divot remaining between his bushy brows.

"You ever seen him before?" Garcia asks.

"Not me," Enzo replies. "Hector said the guy was driving a truck with Tennessee license plates, doesn't sound like he's from around here."

A small grunt is Garcia's only immediate response. A derisive sound from deep in his throat as they continue forward, sweeping around the side of the concrete wall lining the enclosure behind the mansion. A trek that normally is made on a golf cart – the path specifically laid wide enough to accommodate motorized vehicles – though this morning Garcia opted to walk.

The first sign that something was wrong, the man known for his ferocity in the gym, but having little time for such matters once the workday begins.

"Did the man buy the truck?" Garcia asks.

"Doesn't sound like it," Enzo replies. "He stopped by, took a look at it, and then was on his way a short time later. Stayed maybe fifteen minutes, then went to get barbecue."

"Hm," Garcia says. Positioned on the inside of the path, he swings in close to the shrubs lining the base of the wall, hugging it tight as he makes the corner. Walking in a pace that is much quicker than his usual gait, he lifts his focus, aiming it on the small outbuilding affixed directly to the side of the compound.

One of only two access points to the inside, one being the small holding chamber that Miguel made use of last night. An entrance for those about to become part of the evening show.

The other is the one before them. A combination of storage space for the UTVs and equipment needed on the inside, along with a hold pen for nights when there is a hunt or when the hyenas need to be fed or cared for directly.

No larger than a small horse stable, it is made of the same block and stucco as the outer wall, a wooden door with an arched top placed directly in front of them. One option for the path they are on, the other being to circle wide again, continuing on around.

A choice Enzo has a feeling isn't really one, Garcia having a tendency to end up one of two places when he is angry.

The gym, if it can be dealt with quickly and easily, and the holding pin, when something more is needed.

"From what I'm hearing," Garcia says, "it sounds like the man was looking for a particular vehicle, and when he showed up and saw that wasn't it, he moved on pretty fast."

"Could be," Enzo concedes. "But a guy we've never seen in a truck with out-of-state plates? Seems like a stretch."

Flicking a glance his direction, Garcia says, "More like a coincidence, and you know how we feel about those."

Of the various catchphrases Garcia has co-opted over the years, none have arisen as often as the same tired line about not believing in coincidences. A cliché taken to another level, Enzo having to force himself not to roll his eyes.

"True enough," he replies instead. "I talked to Victor last night, and the truck from the accident is long gone. Cut down into a thousand different parts and sent bouncing to garages all over the country needing them for repairs.

"No way in hell he ever finds that thing, no matter how many junkyards he goes to."

Reaching the split in the path, Garcia does what Enzo suspected. Moving straight ahead, he goes for the wooden door, grasping the wrought iron handle before pausing. Making no effort to push inside, a clear indicator that from this point forward he will be continuing on alone, he says, "It's not the truck that concerns me, it's the attention."

"Right," Enzo replies. "How would you like me to proceed?"

Opening his mouth to begin responding, Garcia stops before any sound comes out. His focus traces back down the path they just walked, climbing up the side of the mansion at the end of it.

The skin around his eyes tightens, hinting at more of the irritation Enzo has sensed since arriving.

"There were two more overdoses last night," Garcia says, ignoring the last question entirely.

A reply that wasn't what Enzo expected, he takes a moment to process before saying, "I heard."

"Hm," Garcia grunts, moving his gaze back to Enzo. "Did you also hear that little speech from our friend the district attorney this morning?"

"Banks?" Enzo replies, confusion passing over his features. "About what?"

"About shit he really shouldn't be talking about," Garcia replies. Depressing the spoon on the door's latch, he cracks it open, allowing the faint smells of feed and hay to seep out. "Call down there and set up a meeting."

"Will do," Enzo replies. "When do you want it?"

"Now."

CHAPTER FORTY-SEVEN

A pair of competing scents fills the open kitchen on the first floor of Cortland's home. One smell he is used to permeating the air each morning, and the other is a new one he brought home the night before.

Dark roast coffee courtesy of the family-sized Keurig resting on the counter by Cortland's side. A machine preprogrammed to begin brewing at exactly seven each morning, meant to be ready when Cortland comes down from the bedroom. Liquid energy he can grab along with his shoulder bag from the chair by the table and his lunch from the fridge before heading off to work, his last task before leaving to swap out the container resting under the dispenser and begin the process a second time.

An exact order to match for Maylinn, allowing her to grab it and her lunch as well.

A recent reversal of the morning routine that has existed for years. Daily work schedules that require both to be in the office by eight, Maylinn's reduced commute and court load allowing her to leave a little later.

An inversion she was all too happy about, often gloating of the extra twenty minutes she was afforded in bed each morning. Time that Cortland always threatened to take from her by being as noisy as possible, but could never bring himself to follow through on.

Precious rest that he wishes now he had robbed her of every single morning, if only to have had that many more minutes with her. An accumulation of hours of hearing her voice and drawing in her scent. Feeling the touch of her fingertips.

Memories that can never be recreated.

The sort of thing that so many people error in taking for granted, many falling to the same trap as him and not realizing it until after the fact.

The second smell filling the kitchen this morning is the remainder of the brisket from Rudy's the night before. Slabs of beef that Shine would have gladly gobbled up with her first helping, withheld only to keep her from getting sick.

Gluttony that Cortland would not have begrudged her, very nearly doing the same thing himself.

Cut into small pieces, the leftovers have been split between Shine's silver bowl on the floor and the Styrofoam container they were given at the restaurant. A slow doling out that is meant to keep her from inhaling it all directly. A solid plan Cortland was hoping would mean they could share breakfast together – hers of beef, his of liquid caffeine - though given how fast the first half vanished, realizes isn't likely. Wishful thinking he can't help but chuckle at as she sits at his feet, her haunches lowered to the floor, her upper body balanced on one paw.

Ears pinned back, her pink tongue flicks across her nose as she stares up at him, letting it be known that she is aware he is holding out on her.

A sight that evokes a small laugh as he places his coffee cup down and bends forward, sliding either hand over her face and down her neck. Lowering his forehead to hers, he stands locked in place for a moment, drawing on her energy, before rotating his chin forward and kissing the top of her head.

"Okay, girl, you can have the rest now."

Snatching up the empty bowl from the floor by her side, he upends the container from Rudy's into it, barely getting it back into place before she descends on it a second time. A flurry of jowls and snorts and teeth gnashing that pulls a chuckle from him, the sound still hanging in the air as Remington asks, "What's all this laughter I'm hearing in here? You guys wait until I'm gone to start having fun?"

Taking his coffee mug up from the counter, Cortland resumes his previous stance. Legs crossed at the ankles, he folds his left arm over his torso, his right elbow braced against it.

"I don't know about *us guys*, but Shine is sure enjoying herself this morning."

Dressed in a pair of gym shorts and a plain black tank top, faint wrinkle lines still visible on his face, Remington stops to assess what was just shared. A quick glance between Shine shoving her bowl across the floor and the empty packaging resting on the container.

A scene that causes him to shake his head as he loops out around the island, the usual uneven gait a bit more pronounced. The rigidity of his prosthetic, coupled with the stiffness of early morning.

The soles of his shoes shuffling across the hardwood, he circles around the island and pulls up in front of the Keurig, grabbing the second cup from beneath it. A fresh mug that most mornings would already be filling Maylinn's travel thermos, brewed unintentionally. Pure habit that will have to be unlearned, Cortland simply not having the strength for it just yet.

Grasping it in both hands, Remington drinks deeply, taking down several gulps before pulling it back and exhaling loudly. "Ah man, I needed that. Thank you."

The rim of the mug still just inches from his mouth, he turns to the side, watching as Shine pins her bowl into a corner, trying to pull every last molecule from within.

"Be lucky you were already done when I got down here, or I'd be having those leftovers to go with this."

Snorting softly, Cortland asks, "Another rough night, huh?"

"Not rough," Remington replies. Lifting the cup, he takes another drink before shifting his body to the side to lean against the island. "Just, short."

"Couldn't sleep?"

"Didn't try," Remington answers. Tilting his head back, he gestures down the hall toward the living room, adding, "After my search outside of Rudy's turned up nothing, I half expected them to make another run at us. Spent most the night in there on the couch."

How someone following them would have been possible, Cortland doesn't pretend to know. After Remington picked him up outside of Rudy's, he'd put on a clinic in evasive driving. A long and meandering route with repeated stops and backtracking, no sign of the Ford ever showing up again.

Losing any appetite for the acidic brew, Cortland places it down on the counter beside him. "You expected them to show up here?"

"Hell, I don't know what to expect," Remington replies. "All I know is, that tail showing up when it did, where it did, was not by mistake."

CHAPTER FORTY-EIGHT

Tony was just the right mix of slick and charming that Remington could see him putting the tail on them the night before. The kind of guy who was used to dealing with illicit characters, getting his hands on merchandise that was acquired through less-than-legal means or making deals strictly in cash, without the burden of paperwork. Someone who could absolutely make a certain vehicle disappear after the fact if need be.

The most likely candidate of everyone they spoke to the day before to have called in someone to follow them, if not for the fact that the timing didn't work.

Tyrell put them in contact, setting the meet for just thirty minutes later. A brief window during which Remington didn't notice anybody – distracted though he might have been.

Nobody was in the parking lot when they arrived. Cortland didn't see anybody as he waited in the truck.

After that, Remington was barely inside the place for more than ten or fifteen minutes. A quick conversation during which Tony was surprisingly forthright, not truly turning into the proverbial used car salesman until it looked like Remington was going to walk.

An about-face that wasn't so abrupt as to be out of the norm, Remington having seen far worse from many of the people who come through his shop, looking to patch something together with fishing line and duct tape. Just enough to get the vehicles up and running so they can sell it, foisting existing problems onto someone else.

If Tony was involved, the logistics simply didn't work. If he wasn't, there would have been no reason to have them followed, the exchange pleasant enough, ending with the promise that Remington would probably be back today.

A frontrunner that was shot down as fast as it showed up, leaving Remington and Cortland to go back to the list of cases they were digging into the previous afternoon. A total of more than two dozen, cut to just three before somebody made contact and sent the tail their way.

A trio of possibilities representing the best place to start anew. Bushes to keep kicking, hoping that the Ford will show itself again, this time coming at things from the opposite side. Conversations with the other named participants in the matters to see what else can be unearthed.

Data that might help them actually get out ahead of things for a change.

Of the three options, the clear candidate on where to begin is the rundown apartment complex and its equally downtrodden manager. Manny, who came across as more of a stoned slacker than a skeeze for most of their meeting before very nearly getting his ass kicked with a couple of snide remarks about lawyers at the end.

A guy clearly not used to interacting with women or people smarter than him and unable to handle someone who was both.

The client who Maylinn was representing against Manny and the Shady Glen apartment complex is a woman named Louisa Gonzalez. A name they bypassed reaching out to directly the day before because it was easier to show up at the apartment complex and put together a quick ruse to get what they needed. A mission that was more about elimination than confirmation, this impending second pass making it a little more important that they take a closer look.

A conversation with the client herself that, unfortunately for the time being, will have to wait. Louisa seems nice enough – or so Remington surmises after having heard her and Cortland speak on the phone – but is currently at work, unable to get away until noon.

From there, she has a narrow window of no more than ninety minutes before she is off again, no doubt to a second job, the sight of the Shady Glen complex depicting a scenario that is fairly easy to unravel. A woman working multiple minimum wage jobs, staying there only because she can't afford to be elsewhere.

All she asks in return is a little clean air to breathe.

A simple enough request that almost makes Remington want to go back for another little talk with Manny on behalf of Louisa and Maylinn both, this one not nearly as pleasant as the day before.

Amped on coffee and having some time to kill before Louisa is available, the decision was made to instead start with the second name on their list. The defendant in the case brought by Linc Brady for the matter of months of lawn maintenance that was never paid for.

Another task that is more about shooting down nonstarters than truly searching out a culprit, among the many reasons for their low expectations being Brady's own assessment that what happened to Maylinn was far beyond the purview of these people. White collar sorts who might withhold monies or threaten legal action, but are unlikely to ever turn to violence.

A projection Remington couldn't help but agree with in the moment, such a view becoming more solidified as they pull into the backend of a parking lot sitting just off the freeway. A massive chunk of asphalt lined out to hold more than two hundred vehicles, this morning hosting only a small fraction of that. Twenty or thirty in total scattered across the many rows, most with people striding quickly to or from the front door.

People looking as if they might break into a sprint at any moment, drawn by the massive banner announcing the place as Going Out Of Business hanging between the pillars framing the entrance.

A poor omen for the day ahead.

"Well," Remington can't help but mutter, "at least the landscaping looks good."

CHAPTER FORTY-NINE

Cortland cannot deny that his brother was right about the landscaping. Yard work and detailing that hasn't been touched up in a few weeks, but was pristine enough before that to have endured during the deep autumn months. Flowers still in bloom planted amid mulch beds void of weeds, their edges perfectly sculpted to match the contours of the parking lot and sidewalks. Framing for grass that at one point was probably mowed to resemble a putting green, now grown out to something closer to rough.

Not shaggy by any stretch, but enough that the ruts of mower tires have since disappeared.

Coupled with the banner hanging across the entrance and the arched sign above it, it gave the place enough of a professional veneer to seem presentable. A false façade, hiding what is truly going on within.

A sight Cortland was not walking in expecting, barely able to register the full breadth of it as he stands just inside the door. His eyes wide, he exhales slowly, matched by a low whistle from Remington beside him.

"Well, now, this is something," his brother mutters.

As good a term as any Cortland can conjure, he simply bobs his head in agreement.

No matter how calm the parking lot and exterior of the enormous warehouse might have seemed, the inside looks like a cross between a flea market and a mob looting. The worst Black Friday sale imaginable, coupled with an old game show where contestants were told they could keep anything that ended up in their carts.

Arranged in the same general layout as most big box stores, the place is essentially one open space. A giant warehouse with concrete block walls painted white and corrugated metal roofing above, dozens of light fixtures with halogen bulbs hanging down to give the place an ethereal glow.

Lighting that illuminates rows of red metal shelving and columns of the same material rising in intervals, signs affixed to them announcing various product types. Everything from computers to stereos to televisions, along with every conceivable accessory.

Or so Cortland would imagine that is how it was intended to look, most of the store now bare. What does remain is being actively plundered by an odd assortment of clientele, young punks with tufts of curls facing off with older couples fighting for the last remote control bearing oversized numerals.

A product siege that both makes Cortland want to step in to help, while at the same time remaining far, far removed.

"Excuse me," Remington says, snapping Cortland's attention over in time to see an employee go rushing by. A pudgy twenty-something in ill-fitting khakis and a red polo tucked in way too tight who barely glances their way as he goes, his features nothing short of terrified.

A guy who looks like his plan for the day is to just keep making laps, avoiding actual human interaction at whatever cost.

"Well, that was helpful."

"Yup," Cortland agrees.

"I was just going to ask him where to find the manager."

Again lowering his chin in a nod, Cortland gives the scene a second pass. Another scan of the chaos, this time taking care to look past the rushing throng of people in search of more red polos. Anyone standing stationary who may look like they are in charge, or can at least direct them to someone who is.

A search that lasts the better part of a minute, Cortland making it almost clear through his one-hundred-eighty-degree pass before his focus lands on the bank of cash registers along the side wall. A half dozen checkouts that this morning are being manned by just two people.

One, a young girl with thick glasses and a ponytail wearing the same expression as the plump bastard who just went running by.

The other, a guy with short receding hair and a budding paunch, a trio of lanyards swinging from his neck as he moves about.

"Register four?" Cortland asks, waiting as his brother swings his attention that direction before nodding in agreement.

"As good a place as any."

Turning away from the consumer carnage playing out on the warehouse floor, together they head straight for the checkout line, falling in behind a college-aged young man gripping a flatscreen computer monitor as if he would be willing to fight to protect it and a middle-aged woman juggling two carts and a toddler, bare legs swinging free from the raised seat on the front end.

A harried scene that nearly causes the girl with glasses to burst into tears as the woman pulls up and begins unloading goods onto the counter. A host of items that sparks something forgotten for the young man in front of them, causing him to turn around as if about to ask if they can save his spot before thinking better of it and taking off without a word.

A clearing of the path that leaves the man Cortland assumes to be the manager open for them just a moment later. Visibly panting, he leans forward with both palms planted on the counter, filling the gap between piles of boxed merchandise. The trio of lanyards hang down before him, one of them identifying him as Kip, the floor manager.

Nowhere near the top of the totem pole, but likely as close as they're going to get, anybody with any real cache having fled the scene long ago.

Twisting his gaze upward, Kip checks for signs of goods before saying, "I'm sorry, gentlemen, but we're no longer selling gift cards at this location."

A cleft forms between Cortland's brows as he glances to his brother. Seeing the same expression on Remington's face, he says, "We're not here about a gift card."

"I also can't accept any returns," Kip says, rattling the information off as if he's done it a thousand times in recent days. "All sales are final."

"Yeah, we're not here about that either," Cortland says. "We actually wanted to talk to you about an ongoing legal matter that you have outstanding."

"Le-" he begins, cutting himself off as his eyes flick between the two of them. Pushing himself upright, he retreats a step or so, allowing for a bit of space. His gaze moves to the side, seeking aid from the girl in thick glasses doing her best to finish the woman with multiple carts and a now-screaming child.

"Look, guys," he mutters, "I'm not sure exactly what you're referring to, but those are matters for our lawyers, which-"

"Linc Brady," Remington inserts, stopping the man before he can lob out some canned response. A sidestep of any responsibility, or even another barb about lawyers like Manny the day before.

"Oh," Kip says. "Linc."

"Yes," Cortland says, "Linc." Placing a hand down on the counter, he leans in a few inches. Casting a glance in either direction, he lowers his voice and adds, "Look, we work with Maylinn Alder, and we're not here to cause trouble. We can see what's happening here, and we know that once these doors close, any chance of getting Linc the money he is owed is gone."

The little bit of interaction with Kip has already confirmed what Brady said the day before, and the initial impression upon entering the parking lot. The people running Electronic City might be many things – including shitty businessmen – but they aren't killers.

Any time spent on that path is just wasted effort.

What they can do is try to secure a good man some of what he has coming to him. Salvage something of use from an ugly situation and then depart, hoping that one of their other meetings later in the day will produce results.

New information, or a return visit from the Ford, either one.

Fixed in position, his arms hanging by his sides, Kip draws in deep breaths. His ill-fitting polo visibly rises and falls as he weighs what was just shared.

Once more, he flicks a quick look in either direction before sliding forward and hitting a single button on the register. Sliding the drawer out, he grabs up a thin stack of bills, not even bothering to count them before folding them into a small wad.

Twisting to the side, he reaches for the stack of boxes to his left. Laptop computers on sale at sixty percent off, the usual security sensors already removed, making them ready for transport.

Grabbing up the closest one, he slides the stack of cash in under it and sticks them both into a plastic sack.

Not the smoothest thing Cortland has ever witnessed, though given the frenetic movement going on around them, he doubts anybody noticed.

"Tell Linc, I'm sorry. He deserves better than this, but it's out of my hands. This is the best I can do."

CHAPTER FIFTY

If the uniform Louisa Gonzalez is wearing doesn't hint at the job she performs and the schedule she keeps, the dark circles underscoring her eyes do. Indicators that it has probably been ages since she was able to sleep through the night, years of exhaustion leaving her aged far beyond her years. Fine lines and stray gray hairs hinting at a woman in her late forties, rather than one just past thirty.

A single mother of two, piecing together part-time jobs like the waitressing or maid staff that she just came from, those the only two things Cortland can imagine still requiring their employees to don zip-up rayon outfits. The first of multiple shifts she will likely endure today, this a rare break for her to change and eat, maybe grab the kids off the bus before heading out again.

A harrowing story pieced together while sitting across from the woman on a picnic table not far from the Shady Glen apartment complex. A neutral site Louisa suggested, probably close to where she now calls home. A new place nearby that wouldn't require a large departure from routine, allowing the kids to remain at the same school and her to continue working the same jobs.

Now just without the burden of breathing in mold while trying to sleep every night.

"Good afternoon, Ms. Gonzalez," Cortland says. Seated directly across from her, his elbows rest on the table, his fingers laced.

A few feet away, Remington leans against the corner pole holding up the roof above them. A standard public park shelter house, currently going unused, but no doubt a hub of activity at various other points throughout the week. A gathering place for pet owners in the evenings. A spot for families to conduct birthday parties for little ones on weekend afternoons.

His eyes hidden behind sunglasses, he appears to be staring straight out, though Cortland is aware his gaze is always moving, searching for that same truck he spotted the night before. A constant vigil that will continue until this is over.

A new point of focus for him to fixate on, replacing the image from Maylinn's Tesla screen or the photo lifted from the auto shop cameras in his mind.

"Thank you for meeting with us. I promise, this won't take long."

Shooting a quick glance over to Remington, Louisa nods before bringing her attention back to Cortland. "I'm very sorry about your wife. She was a nice lady. A good person."

Cortland's turn to nod, he dips his chin slightly, his focus never leaving Louisa. "Thank you. I happen to know for a fact she was really enjoying her new job, working with people like yourself."

Her hands folded in her lap, Louisa slides her gaze to the side, her shoulders twisting a bit as well. A defensive posture, not out of fear, but embarrassment. Self-consciousness that tinges her cheeks red, her teeth slipping out over her bottom lip.

"I really don't know how much help I can be," she offers. "The case she was helping me with was pretty simple. Our air conditioning broke a couple months ago, and when the repairman came, he said the air ducts were completely full of mold."

Again, she shoots a quick look over to Remington, her confidence rising as she moves back onto neutral ground, explaining what she and Maylinn were working on.

"He cleaned it out, but figured the whole building must have it. I've got two young children – first and third grade – so naturally, I was worried."

"Was Shady Glen aware of this? Before you called Maylinn?"

"Of course," Louisa replies. "I talked to a couple of neighbors, and they said they'd all lodged complaints as well, but that the owner shot them down."

A small snort slides out of Remington, pausing the narrative, pulling over the attention of both Cortland and Louisa. A break in the conversation that was unintended, Remington forcing a smile into place and offering, "Sorry. We met Manny yesterday. Isn't exactly surprising he didn't take your complaints seriously."

A thin smile rises to match Remington's. The corners of either end of Louisa's mouth curl upward, catching a stray hair pushed across her face by the breeze.

Lifting a hand lined with chipped fingernails to move it away, she says, "Oh, I don't mean Manny. Yeah, he's a little goofy, and he's hit on every woman that lives there, but he's harmless. He just collects money and handles applications.

"I mean the actual owners."

This time, Remington remains silent, though Cortland sees him turn his head a few inches to the side. A shift to allow him to hear better, even as he remains fixed in position.

"Which is who?" Cortland asks.

"Some people based in Houston," Louisa says. "Real estate developers that Maylinn said own lots of places like this throughout Austin, San Antonio, even Corpus Christi."

Cortland's initial impression of Manny was that he was a classic stoner, floating through life, though it would be more than possible that he had relayed news of their previous meeting up the ladder without even meaning to. A mention as casual as his quip about lawyers, referencing that someone had asked about the mold.

The start of a sequence that would have given someone enough time to put a tail on them later in the day.

"Have you ever met them?" Cortland asks.

"No," Louisa says. Shaking her head, she adds, "I only knew about them because a couple of other people have had the same issue and told me to reach out. They told me there were plenty of lawyers who would help me for cheap, and that the owners would settle to keep it quiet."

Offering a half smile, she shrugs her shoulders and adds, "I needed the money, so I figured it was worth a shot."

A few feet away, Remington turns back toward the road, shaking his head to either side.

The embodiment of the same feeling Cortland has, one more potential lead, extinguished as fast as it arose.

"And how was that going?" Cortland asks, even though he already knows the answer.

Expectation that is confirmed by Louisa nodding and saying, "They've already agreed to pay, we were just debating on how much."

————

Unlike their previous trip along the mud and gravel lane leading back to their place, Cortland felt like the Charger was spinning in quicksand. Forced to a manageable rate of speed by Sheriff Myles's cruiser in front of them, they barely cleared forty miles an hour, making the drive seem nothing short of interminable. Minutes stretched to hours while leaning forward in the front seat, trying to peer past the wigwag lights striping the forest blue and red around them.

A predominate color scheme highlighting every tree and bush along the way. A bright glare that remained behind his eyelids each time Cortland blinked, making what they finally arrived to find a full fifteen minutes after sprinting out of The Smokehouse and jumping into the Charger that much more jarring.

A sight they would have been able to easily see for miles away, if not for Myles's demand that they wait for him, letting him and his deputies clear a path.

Something that neither Cortland nor his brother would have allowed had they any idea of this.

The only description the sheriff had given when he elbowed his way through the drunken crowd and said he needed to speak to them was that there had been an incident. Something with their grandfather that Cortland took to mean he had fallen. Or he was experiencing chest pains. Maybe even there had been a problem with the still and he had been injured.

Things that had never happened before, but wouldn't be completely impossible.

Never did he imagine they'd pull up to find the boathouse behind their home a raging inferno. A bonfire nested deep in the woods, flinging flames high above the treetops, threatening to engulf the entire forest.

A bright and yellow flare rising above a handful of first responders. Fire trucks and ambulances and more cruisers.

Easily, every available emergency unit in the county.

A sight that ripped all air from Cortland's lungs, his entire chest clenching as sweat poured across his features. A product of his body's physiology spiking, making him almost feel the extreme heat pulsating from the blaze.

Shooting out a hand to the side, he clamped his fingers around his brother's shoulder. Skin just as slick with sweat as his own, the underlying muscles bunching and flexing as he yelled, "Hang on!" and jerked the wheel to the left, abandoning the lane and sending them caroming through the front yard, dodging trees and saplings along the way.

A zigzag path that got them just shy of the porch where they had sat with G not four hours earlier and had dinner, both hitting the ground at a sprint.

"Where is he?!" Cortland screamed at the first person he saw. A

deputy he vaguely recognized from seeing around town but didn't know by name.

A man who seemed stunned by their sudden appearance and the question, replying with nothing more than upturned hands.

A lack of usefulness that Cortland left standing on the front walk, barking the same question at a pair of EMT's standing along the front bumper of their ambulance. People who responded with wide eyes and sagging jaws, leaving Cortland to continue running, Remington close on his heels.

A hard charge around the side of the house, making it no further before being turned back by twin walls. Uniformed personnel blocking them from going any closer, paired with the invisible barricade of extreme heat. Temperatures hot enough to scorch leaves from the trees and char the boards lining the back of the house.

"G!" Remington screamed, bellowing at the blaze burning nearby, even as a pair of men tried to wrestle him back. Tears and sweat streaking his soot-stained face, he continued, "Garrison!?"

Efforts matched by Cortland just a few feet away, fighting the same battle. Ceaseless flailing against a trio of men, trying to get to the boathouse before them.

"G!! Shine?!"

CHAPTER FIFTY-ONE

Most of the time, Leo Garcia chooses to remain out of public view. While he might take a firm hand in controlling the day-to-day operations of his business, he doesn't need the constant adulation of the masses to affirm his place as a leader or as a man. No red-carpet events in a sports car, arriving in front of flashbulbs with scantily clad ladies on his arm. No black-tie galas, rubbing shoulders with so-called titans in the burgeoning market.

Public spectacle that many lesser individuals might require, needing it as much as food or water for them to get through each day. Sustenance that Garcia receives aplenty from his morning trips to the gym and his weekly climbs inside the ring, finding far more gratification from strapping on the gloves and taking the occasional jab to the face than can ever be provided by cameras and applause.

Scheduled reminders of how the world really works. What is required to get ahead. How fast it can be taken away if he were to stop and admire himself or his accomplishments for even a moment.

Another reason why he is where he is. One more maxim imparted from his mother, the two of them ascending while others kept stopping to enjoy the view, never to return to climbing.

Mistakes for weaker spirits that he never intends to make, most of his forays away from the compound for very specific reasons. Sojourns like the last couple days, when he shows up unannounced at The Char Pit or is there to greet the arriving immigrants at the drop point.

Moments intended not to garner reverie, but recognition. Statements to remind others who he is and what he is capable of.

Outings of a different manner in practice, though underscored by the same intent as this one. A show of force that today he makes no effort to hide climbing the stone front steps to the Travis County office complex. One of the original buildings in the downtown square, first constructed more than a hundred years ago, comprised of stone and brick. A solid, stoic edifice, meant to evoke the importance of the work that goes on inside.

A façade Garcia can appreciate, here to impart much the same.

If not with an extra pointed tone, just to be sure.

Serving as the lead for the group, Garcia is the first to pass through the front doors to the facility. A step behind comes Enzo, the two of them flanked on either side by Garcia's security team. A group bypassing their usual two-and-two formation for a solid line. All four dressed in black suits, Garcia has gone the extra step of swapping out his usual light-colored dress shirt for more black.

Midnight hues that match the color of his hair and the sunglasses resting on the bridge of his nose. A silent message sent and received long before he ever opens his mouth, as evidenced by the stare of the woman passing through the main foyer. Exiting one of the offices to his right, her lower mandible sags open, her pace increasing. Square heels that thump against the official county insignia inlaid on the floor, the sound reverberating through the circular space rising to the rounded globe window above.

"Which one?" Garcia asks, turning his chin toward Enzo. A simple question that is responded to with an outstretched finger, gesturing to the open doorway directly across from them. Wooden doors rising almost ten feet in height propped open, flags for the state of Texas and the United States flanking it.

Accepting the information in silence, Garcia strides across the foyer, his team fanning out to either side. Like a gaggle of geese, they form an inverted V through the center of the building, stepping into the outer office of Kennedy Banks less than five minutes after exiting the Escalade.

An arrival that is received much the same as their initial entrance into the building, the receptionist behind her desk stares up at them with wide eyes. A late lunch resting on the blotter before her, she pauses with a forkful of salad halfway to her mouth. All color drains from her features as she glances to each of the men in turn, making it all the way through the group before returning to Garcia.

"Can I help you gentlemen?"

"We are here to see the district attorney."

Her entire body goes rigid, seeming to shrink back into the cardigan sweater she wears. Without any blood in her cheeks, she looks completely monochromatic, white blonde hair matching her pale attire.

A stark contrast to the wall of black before her, only a narrow chunk of wood lined with photographs of children and kittens separating them.

A dichotomy she seems acutely aware of as she asks, "Is Mr. Banks expecting you?"

"Yes. Get him out here now, please."

"Certainly," the woman says, grabbing for the phone on her desk. Raising it to her face, she presses a single button and mutters a few quick words, the receiver barely back in its cradle before the door behind her bursts open.

Through it passes Kennedy Banks, the hair and suit and all the rest that Garcia watched on television this morning still in place. A manicured look that has withstood the day's activities without so much as a wrinkle or a hair displaced, appearing just as ridiculous now as when Garcia first saw him several hours earlier on the screen in his mother's room.

Hands already raised before him, Banks says, "Mr. Garcia, gentlemen, so good to see you. I was actually going to call you this afternoon, but you beat me to it."

Pairing the greeting with an oversized smile, it is clear the man is in damage control mode. A child who has overstepped and is trying to put on a happy face in front of angry parents, hoping to avoid discipline.

Cheap psychology that might play in front of a jury, or even a bevy of reporters, but Garcia is not about to let slide so easily.

Remaining silent, Garcia merely stares at the man. A hardened glare behind dark lenses, his hands clasped before him. A rigid post the men with him match, watching as the smile on Banks's face wilts. Any hope he might have had at spinning the situation crumbles, taking much of the color from his features.

"Please, come in," he says, sliding to the side and motioning them into the room.

An invitation Garcia lets sit for a moment, staying where he is, before slowly marching through. Not once looking at the man, he steps over the threshold into the office and slides the glasses from his nose, taking in the expected clutter that fills the space.

Bookcases lined with volumes that haven't been opened in years. Boxes of paperwork that Banks himself will never touch, waiting to unload it on the first staff underling foolish enough to come close.

Photographs and diplomas and such hanging on the walls.

"I think we have enough space for everyone," Banks says, bringing up the rear of the procession and pulling the doors closed behind them. "If not, I can go next door and grab some more seats."

"No need," Garcia says. Tucking his sunglasses into the breast pocket of his suit coat, he says, "This won't take but a minute."

A red sheen can be seen covering Banks's forehead as he moves around to the backside of his desk. Blood rushing to the surface that has already produced small droplets of sweat the length of his brow.

Obvious signs of nerves, at odds with the plastic smile fixed into place.

"Mr. Garcia, I know what you must be thinking, and I can tell you - I can promise you - this morning was not what it seemed. Political theatrics, nothing more."

Choosing to remain standing as well, he positions himself behind the high back of his rolling leather desk chair. An additional bit of space between the two sides that he grabs with both hands, clutching it as tightly as he did the podium earlier.

"After those two kids were found last night, the mayor called and said we had to do something. Coming so close on the heels of the election, we couldn't have the people turning on us already.

"But I can assure you, this is another working group that will go nowhere. Nothing more. Nothing for you to worry about."

No doubt having rehearsed the little speech before their arrival, it probably took him longer to get through on his prior runs. Practice efforts standing in front of a mirror with his chest puffed out and his TV voice on, taking care to use all the proper inflections and pauses.

Performative crap that went out the window the instant he was faced with the thought of actual consequences, the man practically sprinting through it. Words that come out as little more than a jumble before he falls silent, still clinging to the chair before him like he may try to wield it as a club if he needs to.

Garcia doubting very much the scrawny bastard can even lift the thing.

"Just so I have this straight," Garcia says, deliberately keeping his voice low, his diction even. "This morning, you have a press conference to assuage the voters just days after an election, without informing the man responsible for you winning?"

Across the room, Banks begins to respond. An answer Garcia has no interest in hearing, silencing him with a raised finger.

"I then have to call and ask you to meet," he continues, "at which point, you open by telling me what I am thinking and what I need to worry about?"

Again, Banks attempts to launch a response. Effort that this time is cut short by Enzo clearing his throat, drawing Banks's attention before shaking his head to either side.

A warning that Banks heeds, falling silent as Garcia turns and takes two steps toward the wall. Sliding past his security guards, he approaches one of the framed photographs he saw upon entry. A staged shot of Banks and his wife kneeling in the grass, their two young daughters and a fluffy white dog all piled together in front of them.

Matching blue sweaters and blonde hair and missing teeth all around.

A classic shot of Americana that probably does well on the campaign trail and at fundraiser events, today meant to serve a very different purpose.

"Allow me to tell you what I am actually thinking and worried about, Mr. Banks," Garcia says. Positioning himself in front of the photo, he uses the reflection on the front of it to clock the district attorney across the room, his mouth and eyes all widened into congruent circles as he stares on.

"I am thinking that what happened today was an unfortunate incident. I am thinking that the working group you were talking about better never see the light of day. I am thinking that this better be the last conversation we ever have on the matter – or anything like it – ever again."

Shifting his weight from one foot to the other, Garcia turns to stare at the man across the room. The skinny prick with the photogenic smile who was handpicked years ago, and can be cast aside just as easily.

"Because if it does, I am worried about what might happen to that pretty woman, and those two beautiful little girls, and even that cute dog you have there. I'm worried they may not fare so well when staring down a pack of hyenas."

CHAPTER FIFTY-TWO

Cortland's sleeves have been rolled back down to the wrists and buttoned tight, his left sleeve resting against the silver watch that is almost always covering his wrist. A blue sports coat has been grabbed from the dry cleaning stowed in the rear of his SUV and thrown on over it. Paired with the jeans and sneakers he was already wearing, it is a look his wife used to jokingly refer to as *associate professorial*. A mash of casual and professional seen with increasing frequency around Austin. An explosion stemming not just from the largest university in the state, but also the recent relocation of tech companies from around the country.

A younger generation armed with too much money and not a single clue what to really do with it.

A bit too much for the lingering late afternoon warmth outside, the outfit feels woefully inept for the interior of the Reseda Brothers Meat Processing facility. The named defendant for the third case on the list that Beth Towner handed over, the first two stops turning up just as much as the three the day before. A sum total that looked momentarily promising in talking to Louisa before being shot down, leaving only this last visit to make any kind of actual headway.

After that, they'll be forced to retreat and regroup, trying to simultaneously figure out who targeted Maylinn, and who put the silver pickup on them the night before.

"Sorry about keeping you waiting," Lance Reseda says, one half of the eponymous brothers stamped onto every surface both inside and out. The cause of the contamination Freya Madisen alluded to the day before, the source not hard to spot as they stride along the bare concrete corridor outlined in red paint around the edge of a warehouse standing two stories in height and stretched out the better part of a football field in either direction. The final bit of safe space where a person can exist without needing safety glasses and a hardhat.

Protective equipment that every other person in sight is donning as they go about their work, taking up assigned stations at various spots around the assortment of equipment covering the interior. Dressed in white canvas coveralls and gloves, they systematically go through the paces of breaking down bovine carcasses, parsing a fully grown cow into edible chunks within minutes.

A process both macabre and mesmerizing, filled with the squeals of power saws and sprays of bone dust and blood spatter. A scene that any of the numerous aspiring horror film auteurs in the area would love to gain access to.

A sight likely to cause Lady Fyre and her clientele to run shrieking in terror.

"We're coming up on shift change, which is the craziest time of day around here."

Much better equipped for the chilled temperature inside the facility, Reseda dons a fleece pullover and a puffy thermal vest. A heavy smear of whiskers lines his chin, equally mixed between brown and gray. Same for the hair atop his head, parted down the middle and left across the tips of his ears.

Walking fast enough to cause it to rise and fall with each step, he moves them toward the center of the facility before taking a quick right. Passing through a set of double doors, most of the chill and noise from the factory floor falls away, though the color scheme remains the same. White tile floors and painted walls, lined with photographs in simple black frames.

Images in black and white of company milestones starting decades earlier and moving steadily forward. The transition of a family business through the generations, the man beside Cortland not showing up until the last few photos.

Much younger at that point, he can be seen with another man bearing blonde hair shorn into a flattop, both of them smiling in a series of images that have clearly been staged. Shots of them accepting awards or donning jumpsuits and working the floor, surrounded by employees with forced smiles.

The same sort of thing Cortland walks past every day when going to his office at the accounting firm and Maylinn likely did as well at her law practice, owners the world over trying to prove that they're just like everybody else.

The mountains of evidence to the contrary be damned.

"Here we are," Reseda says, making one last turn into a corner office that is at least as large as the kitchen, dining, and sitting areas in Cortland's home. Space enough for a palatial desk and visitor chairs, as well as a leather sofa along the wall and a ceramic statue of a smiling calf in the corner.

An odd choice in décor, given the business they are in, though admittedly better than the photos lining the hall.

"Have a seat," Reseda adds, gesturing to one of the chairs as he swings around to the far side of his desk. Leaving his puffy vest on, he drops down into a rolling chair, his momentum carrying him a few inches.

"Thank you for meeting with me," Cortland says. "Especially on short notice, and during your busiest time of the day."

"Ah, not a problem," Reseda says, lifting a hand to wave away the comment. "It's the busiest time on the floor, but for me, the bustle is first thing in the morning. New arrivals, six days a week."

Left deliberately vague, Cortland doesn't bother pressing on what exactly is arriving, having just seen more than a few of them on his march in. Creatures that were alive only days before, soon to be hitting supermarket shelves throughout the area.

A daily process that the man probably gets through by using tricks just such as that, employing vague terms to avoid the obvious.

"What can I do for you?" Reseda asks.

"Well," Cortland begins, before pulling up. Bringing his brows together, he tries to exhibit some form of uncertainty, despite every desire to push straight ahead with why he is here and what he wants.

Days of tap dancing with little result that have him wanting to charge straight ahead, the growing frustration and the desire to get back to grieving his wife both rising with each passing hour.

"This is a little tricky, I understand, but I am a CPA with Cooley and Piper, and have been tasked with doing an assessment for a possible acquisition just downriver. Of course, that includes looking into any impending legal action that may encompass the property or its boundaries..."

"And you discovered the lawsuit that was filed not long ago," Reseda says, filling things in as a smile crosses his features. Glancing away, he chuckles softly, before turning back to Cortland and asking, "Tell me, have you happened to stop by and visit *Lady Fyre* yet?"

Raising his middle and index fingers on either hand, he uses them to make air quotes around the name, his grin growing larger.

"I did," Cortland replies. "I spoke to Ms. Madisen yesterday."

"Enchanting, no doubt," Reseda inserts, his tone and his expression both making it clear he finds the entire thing amusing. The woman, and her lawsuit, and everything else associated with the matter.

Candor that already prepares Cortland for this to be another worthless stop, nobody with something to hide ever acting so cavalier.

"It was...interesting," Cortland concedes, recalling the cloud of fragrances he walked into and the assorted offerings inside the shop. Items it would be easy for most to scoff at, any thought of doing so himself turned away after his conversation with the woman.

The show of genuine concern she had after shaking his hand, and the heartfelt sentiments offered to his wife.

"Yeah, that's one word for it," Reseda says. "And I get it, you've got a job to do, so you have to be evenhanded about all this, but what you saw yesterday is pretty much all there is.

"Some granola-chewing, hippie, vegan nut that doesn't like what we do here, and somehow convinced an attorney just like her to file a suit against us. Nothing more."

CHAPTER FIFTY-THREE

How in the hell Cortland was able to keep his cool after that asshole inside the meat processing plant took a shot at his wife, Remington has no idea. The instant he heard the comment come in over the speakerphone, he'd immediately let out a string of expletives, balling his left fist and pounding it into the empty driver's seat beside him. Turning his arm into a makeshift mallet, he'd snapped it straight down, using the entire side of his hand and forearm as a bludgeon.

One shot after another, continuing until the muscles in his shoulder started to burn from exertion.

The only possible thing he could think to do that would prevent him from jumping out of the truck and go rummaging in the backend of the SUV for a toolbox. Grabbing up the biggest wrench he could find, he would storm directly through the front door of the small addition on the front of the facility, searching out every room inside until finding his brother and the asshole he knows only by sound.

And then really going to work on the prick, not stopping until the processing floor had a few new additions to be sent out with the next load.

Now more than fifteen minutes later, he can still feel the anger hurtling through his system. Rage that has been building since first seeing the frozen image on Maylinn's Tesla screen and growing steadily since.

Vitriol that, for the first time since his arrival, he can also sense coming from the passenger seat beside him. An escalation from the few stilted words Cortland said in response to the quip, holding back his own immediate response in the name of staying the course. Continuing the task that was given to them by his wife.

Self-discipline that Remington always said would have made Cortland an ideal soldier, if only he had the temperament for it.

"Where'm I headed?" Remington asks, having installed himself behind the steering wheel. A relocation meant to let his brother cool down after that comment, knowing how pissed he must be, even if he doesn't show it.

The first words either have said since leaving the meat plant a quarter hour earlier, his main goal – beyond stepping inside for a little chat of his own – is to get them far away. A removal from the premises, both to keep from being spotted lingering outside, and to remove the temptation to go digging through the toolbox.

"Any sign of the silver pickup?" Cortland asks.

Casting a quick glance to the rearview mirror, Remington sees nothing but the same collection of sedans and minivans that have been clogging the roads for most of the day. Nine-to-five workers starting to spill out of their offices, rushing to get home and get their weekend started. Students from nearby UT, getting on the road for a couple days or headed down to the numbered streets to start their revelries early.

A college town without the usual weekend bustle of a home football game, but still with plenty of merriment ahead.

Ample traffic making the hulking rig from the night before easier to spot, if only it would show. A total absence that almost has Remington wishing they'd taken Tyrell's truck again, choosing to leave it at home for the sole purpose of not wanting to make things too easy for whoever might be tailing them.

A new vehicle that will turn the tables in their favor, making it clear when the tail shows up a second time who must have been the one to call it in.

A plan that seems to be backfiring, either working too well or the driver having lost interest and given up, much the way he seemed to last night.

An option Remington can't quite buy into, the effort took to look at them the first time too great to simply abandon.

"No," Remington replies.

"Shit," Cortland answers. Running his hands down the front of his jeans, he glances to the clock on the dash and says, "Almost quitting time on Friday afternoon. We didn't get jack shit today. No sign of our tail, and nothing new from the people we talked to."

Shoving out a sigh through his nose, he contemplates the statement a moment before rotating his gaze on over to Remington. "Swing by Brady's and drop this stuff off, then go back to the drawing board? Cut our losses for the day?"

After the conversation with Reseda, Remington had nearly forgotten about everything prior. Complete rage blacking out the visit to Electronic City, that being the closest thing to a win they've achieved since he arrived.

A pyrrhic victory that they might as well salvage what they can from.

"Sounds good," Remington says. "Barton Creek, right?"

"Yeah," Cortland mutters, the word barely out before he snaps himself forward and mashes both palms into the dash. His own version of what Remington was doing earlier, unloading on it a handful of times. Shots hard enough to make the gauges above the steering wheel shake, momentarily losing focus with each impact.

A half dozen in order, ending with Cortland flinging himself back in his seat. Folding his arms over his torso, he turns to stare out the passenger window.

An explosion over as fast as it began.

"This isn't adding up, Rem. We're missing something, dammit."

CHAPTER FIFTY-FOUR

No matter how excellent the enchiladas prepared by the kitchen staff, Enzo takes care not to scrape his plate clean. A conscious bypass of wiping up every delicious morsel of his dinner in exchange for not incurring the wrath of Sofia Garcia. A woman who is as close to a mother as he has, having been by his side for more than thirty years now. A lady of diminutive stature and waning oxygen capacity who still packs all of the combustible energy of dynamite, needing only the slightest spark to set it loose.

Something such as the sound of silverware scraping against dishes, the noise one of her personal pet peeves. A trigger that Enzo knows is steeped in much more than just the shrill squeak, taking her back to days when eating was done from her hands or the floor.

A time Enzo himself can also remember, having been present on many of those nights. Times when they were all new to the Country and banding together, pooling their resources to scrape by the best they could.

The start of their own little pack, marauding and scavenging like the hyenas Sofia and her son both now love so much.

"You get enough to eat?" Sofia asks. Seated in one of the two other padded chairs around the small circular table occupying the corner of her suite, she has a blanket wrapped around her legs despite the sun being just barely below the horizon, the temperature outside still above seventy.

The sole concession – outside of her omnipresent oxygen tank - made for her age or condition, otherwise she looks just as she has for the last decade, if not two. Always dressed for dinner, she wears a blouse with a high collar, the sleeves fastened at the wrist. Her graying hair is pulled back, held in place with a clasp at the crown of her skull.

Light from the chandelier above crosses her face at an angle, illuminating a web of fine lines around her eyes that are far less pronounced than Enzo's, despite their difference in age.

"Oh, yes, Ms. Garcia," Enzo replies. "Those ladies sure do know how to put on a spread."

"*Ms. Garcia*," Sofia replies, letting her tone and her expression both display her distaste for the term. The beginning of a back-and-forth they have been through many times before, Enzo continuing to address her as such not to needle her, but as a sign of respect.

A starting point from which she can tell him to call her by name, but he never wants to assume.

So easily, he could have ended up in a different caravan coming up north over the border. Had he a few extra dollars to pull together, he might have opted for the more direct route. If the old man whose seat he took hadn't dropped dead from a heart attack after plodding through the desert heat, he may have been on a different bus. Should the men who attacked Sofia and her son not thought them easy targets, he may never have jumped in.

Hell, if his sister hadn't been shot in the streets just a week before, he might not have made the trip at all.

Any of a hundred different things that could have derailed his path, meaning he and the Garcias never would have met. A chance encounter that has come to define him, granting him not just some form of family, but stability. A real job and a place to live and the future possibility of finding someone for himself, should he ever so desire.

Options that he holds no illusions about existing if not for that fateful day. A hellacious scrap with Leo by his side that he still bears a scar from, seeing it streaking down his cheek each time he looks in the mirror.

A defining characteristic, in every way.

"How many times do we have to go through this?" Sofia asks. "I have a damn name. Use it."

Feeling his cheeks bunch with muted chuckles, Enzo nods. "Yes, ma'am."

"Huh? What was that?" Sofia snaps, lifting her chin to peer down her nose at him, despite their height disparity.

The smile grows into a full grin, Enzo exposing his entire top row of teeth. "Yes, Sofia."

Maintaining her pose – as much to savor her victory as make a point, Enzo suspects – for another moment, slowly she drops her chin. Examining the remnants of her dinner on the plate atop the table, she pushes it away, her focus moving to the window beside them.

Another resplendent Texas sunset, this one containing more purple and pink than in previous days. Splashes of color that the woman seems to barely notice, her attention on the compound below.

A chunk of enclosed woods shrouded in shadow, the pack that calls it home no doubt about to begin darting through the shadows in search of dinner.

A meal that, sadly for Sofia, will be nothing more than a goat. A fattened offering ready for sacrifice, to be released with the setting of the sun.

"You guys go pay that crooked district attorney a visit this afternoon?" Sofia asks.

A question that comes as no surprise as her gaze is fixed on the compound below, the woman probably already envisioning looking down to see the spindly guy in the suit running for his life. Exasperation painting his features, making him look even more terrified than in his office earlier.

"Yes, Sofia," Enzo replies.

Dipping her chin in approval, Sofia asks, "Was the message received?"

"Oh, yes," Enzo answers, it easy to imagine what her son said earlier having come directly from his mother. A monologue she gave him the gist of, Leo later refitting it to use the very words Banks tried to employ in placating him.

A masterful performance that nearly made Enzo smile in the moment, and again at the sight of the secretary on their way out.

"Very much so."

"Good," Sofia says, "and..."

Wherever else the sentence is meant to go, Enzo doesn't find out. Her voice fading away, he follows her gaze to see her son standing at the end of the short corridor leading from her door, the same agitation he was wearing on their walk this morning back on his features. Hands both buried in the pockets of his slacks, he dips his head in greeting and says, "Sorry to interrupt *madre*, but I need to steal Enzo from you.

"We have an issue."

CHAPTER FIFTY-FIVE

Linc Brady was doing exactly what most people in Texas between the ages of ten and seventy do on a Friday night in the fall. Dressed in a blue long-sleeve t-shirt with a red W stamped across it in support of nearby Westlake High School, he was crossing his front lawn when he saw Remington and Cortland pull up. Abandoning his path, he met them just off the curb, accepting the offered cash and laptop with equal parts surprise and appreciation.

Payment that wasn't the full extent of what was owed, and not in the form expected, but after hearing about the scene at Electronic City, agreed it was probably the best he could hope for. Monies enough to at least cover his expenses, and a new device that his family could definitely get use out of.

Leaving the conversation at that, Remington and Cortland had headed back home, stopping by just long enough to pick up Shine before taking off again to do the same thing as Brady and his family. A sidestep away from the packed couple of days they'd just been through and the temptation of sitting at home, stewing in silence or rehashing through things time and again.

A momentary reprieve they both knew they needed, the mountain of grief and frustration of the last couple of days peaking with the comment from Lance Reseda. A barb that didn't even name Maylinn directly, but still set them both on edge, each barely able to contain their respective responses before getting out of there.

Reactions that would have made them feel better momentarily, but would have decimated their ongoing investigation. Short-lived gratification at the expense of what they are really trying to accomplish.

Letting down Maylinn something neither will allow, conceding to taking a couple of minutes to distract themselves for the evening if it means better serving her dying wish.

Something that has to be done before they can even consider laying her to rest or saying farewell properly.

Bypassing the enormous stadium and crowd of the Westlake game where Brady and his family were headed, Cortland had steered them to a much smaller school closer to his house. Drawing from a district comprised of mainly small cul-de-sacs and family farms, the entire student body was somewhere around five hundred. A minuscule number compared to most of the bigger schools in the state, able to cobble together a few dozen players in blue and gold uniforms.

A smattering that barely stretches between the forties on the sideline, matched by roughly the same number across from them in white trimmed with black and purple.

Not that anybody in attendance seems to notice, all of the other requisite trimmings out in force. Pockets of cheerleaders do their best to whip up the respective crowds, their shouting heard during the brief respites between offerings from the marching bands and chanting from the stadium bleachers. Full support from both communities that fills the wooden seats and spills down the sidelines, sending Cortland, Remington, and Shine all the way down to the ten-yard line.

A post in the corner where they can lean with their elbows braced against the fence encircling the field, hot dogs wrapped in foil in either hand. Two each for the both of them, along with a pair for

Shine as well. Rations that are torn off and dropped down to her sitting patiently between them, her muzzle rotating from one to the other, waiting for the next morsel to fall her way.

A process that lingers for more than a quarter, the two teams switching ends of the field and starting anew, before Remington asks, "Is it working?"

Looking up from the last chunk of his hot dog dinner, the frank slathered in mustard and relish, Cortland asks, "What's that?"

Flicking a finger out, Remington wags it at the field before them. "This. Is it working?"

"You know," Cortland begins, a half-eaten hot dog extended before him. Pausing, he watches as the home side takes a pitch around the end for twelve, picking up a first down and a host of cheers from the crowd. "He kind of had me going in there. Parading me through the warehouse, letting me see all the pictures of the family growing the business over time.

"I almost bought into it. Even his amused reaction made me think the whole thing was a misunderstanding. A difference of politics or life choices that had maybe gotten a little carried away."

"And then he went on that tangent about the lawsuit just being a bunch of hippy-dippy crap," Remington says. "I know. I thought the same exact thing sitting and listening to it. Kind of like, 'Where the hell did that come from?'"

In the immediate aftermath, it was all Cortland could do to get past the anger. Simmering rage over the comments belittling Maylinn, even if that wasn't the intent.

Now given a couple of hours to ruminate, really analyze what was shared, he can see the same thing. A candid statement from left field that might have been an accident in delivery, but not intent.

"Yeah," Cortland agrees. "One of those things that you only say out loud around your friends, but never in mixed company."

———

Remington's eyes felt like there was sandpaper affixed to the backs of his lids. Sheets of heavy grit that scraped across the lenses each time he blinked. A combination of the sting of sweat and the burn of smoke, only occasionally benefitting from the salve of his own tears. A light veneer that would rise to the surface each time he let himself think about G before he forced it away.

A firm stance against letting anyone see him cry that his brother didn't share in. Hunched in a padded chair nearby, Cortland leaned forward at the waist, his elbows on his knees. Head in his hands, he ran his fingers back through his hair, occasionally letting out the smallest sniffle.

Sounds acting as precursor for the stray tear that ran the length of his nose before falling to the floor.

The start of what Remington imagined to be an outpouring that would come soon enough, his twin doing his best to keep it together for the time being.

Standing with his shoulder pressed against the cool metal of a pole framing the front window, Remington stared at the grille of the Charger parked just outside. The bumper and hood aglow from the residual light spilling out, the rest was increasingly shaded as it extended out into the darkness.

A lone vehicle present at such an hour on a holiday weekend. A blessed bit of reprieve from the crowds of both The Smokehouse and even their own home earlier, only the aging secretary making a point of busying herself elsewhere there to see them in such a state.

"Misters Alder?" a voice asked, snapping the silence of the waiting room. A sound that pulled Remington's focus to the side, landing just long enough to register the man in a pair of green scrubs exiting through the stainless-steel doors on the far side of the room.

Using his elbow to lever himself away from the wall, he joined with Cortland rising from his chair, the both of them meeting the man halfway across the floor.

"Is she...?" Cortland asked, the impending possibility of another lost life making him jump right to the punchline.

"Shine will be okay," the veterinarian replied, tugging away the paper mask hanging around his neck. "Though, unfortunately we weren't able to save her leg."

Lifting his focus toward the ceiling, Remington let out a long exhalation through his nose. An audible release to match the sniffle from his brother beside him.

Unspoken responses the vet continued past, adding, "With her being so young, her bones still developing, there simply wasn't enough there for us to work with. Given the amount of blunt force trauma she sustained, it was reduced to splinters.

"She never would have been able to put weight on it. It would have just been an infection waiting to happen."

The man didn't say exactly what happened, though just a single word told Remington everything he needed to know. A full explanation of what he suspected from the moment Cortland's calls for her were answered by a pained bark emitted from under the porch.

A cry for aid that found her curled on her side, her front leg hanging by little more than the skin and fur encasing it. An injury that couldn't happen on its own, or even during the chaos of a fire.

The sort of thing that could only be caused by trauma. A direct blow from something like the pipe or bat Callum's sons were carrying earlier.

Retribution to match the blaze that engulfed the boatshed.

"And the burns?" Remington asked.

"Mostly superficial," the vet answered. "I'd like to keep her here for a few days for observation and to jumpstart her care. After that, I can prescribe ointments for those and her surgery scar that you guys can apply a couple times a day."

Glancing between them, he added, "It'll take time, but within a few weeks, she should be up and about again."

Drawing in another breath, Remington allowed his chest to fill, his shoulders rising, before slowly pushing it out. A conscious attempt to try and tamp down the assorted feelings he was experiencing, from the loss of their grandfather to the desire to go back to that same damn barn in the woods and finish what they started with the Callums earlier.

Thoughts he couldn't allow himself to entertain just yet, for myriad reasons.

"Thank you, doctor," Remington said, extending his hand before him.

A shake the vet met, mumbling something that sounded like, "Of course," before moving to Cortland beside him.

A shake that wasn't nearly as firm, followed by Cortland asking, "Can we see her?"

"She's still asleep," the man replied, "but you can come back as soon as you're done out here."

Lifting his chin, he motioned to the window behind them, the brothers both turning in unison to see Sheriff Myles pull in beside the Charger and begin to climb out.

CHAPTER FIFTY-SIX

Metal screens have been installed in lieu of windows on either side of the UTV. Protective shields that are normally left open, put specially into place on this one machine for nights just such as this. Times when Leo Garcia is pissed to the degree that a few rounds on the heavy bag in the gym or even a couple of miles on the treadmill he loathes won't begin to push it away. Simmering rage that makes standing still impossible, let alone trying to pour over the spreadsheets in his office or find rest.

Hostility that has been sitting at the forefront of his mind since he received a phone call more than three hours earlier. A check in from one of his older business associates that Garcia was barely able to get through before sprinting up the stairs and interrupting the dinner between his mother and Enzo. A stoppage to the affairs that Enzo would never dare question and Sofia did only until hearing the reason behind it before agreeing that he did the right thing.

A rare moment of praise that was immediately tempered by pointing out that it never should have happened to begin with.

A misstep by Garcia – and those under him – that he better hope they don't all end up paying for.

The absolute last thing Garcia needed to hear in that moment, he had left her in her room, heading back downstairs just long enough to ensure that Enzo and his small crew were off before stepping outside. His second stroll of the day, this one not with the intention of going around the enclosed space abutting the back of his home, but into it.

During the light of day, Garcia has been inside the enclosure plenty of times without need for the barricaded UTV. Moments on foot or a four-wheeler when he was content that the stun baton he was carrying was sufficient, his own vision and the tendency of the hyenas to be less active during the day enough to ensure his safety.

And if those things weren't, the crew of security alongside him could do the rest.

A litany of protections that tonight he is without, leaving without a word to anyone and climbing into the specially designed UTV for this purpose. The want, the need, to get close to the pack on his own.

Smell their breath. See the flash of their eyes in his headlamps. Hear their laugh.

Feel them circling around him, tightening the noose on his position.

Sitting in his office the night before and listening to the situation explained, Garcia had known then that it wasn't as simple as Enzo wanted to believe. A fallacious faith in his own abilities that refused to admit that he might have made a mistake. Perhaps he had been spotted by the woman he was tailing, either that night or in the weeks of observation before.

The start of something that Garcia should have squelched right in that moment, telling the man to go join Hector and take care of the problem. A potential issue that it was better to eliminate than let fester, it far preferable to kill off an innocent than to let a hostile walk free.

A mistake on his part that soon trickled down, Hector easily falling for the out-of-state license plates and Enzo so willingly grasping at the offered theory.

Errors compounded this morning by the sudden insertion of

Kennedy Banks and his little task force. A landmine demanding their attention, pulling them away from this issue just as they were on the verge of snuffing it out.

A dramatic swing from having no problems, the business in its best place ever after the acquisition of The Char Pit, to now having two.

Dropping the UTV into low gear, Garcia mashes down on the gas. Fuel intake not intended to send him hurtling across the enclosure, but to rev the engine. A homing signal, making sure the hyenas know where he is.

A distress cry, wanting to pull them in. Arouse their suspicion.

Bring them within striking distance.

His left hand draped over the top of the steering wheel, Garcia reaches out with his right and grabs up the stun baton. Sliding his fingers around the base of it, he seats it firmly against his palm, the pad of his thumb resting over the button on the end.

A trigger he can't help but press a couple of times, sending the flicker of sparks from the electrodes on the end. White-blue light that flashes, bringing with it the faint whiff of hot metal. A precursor to the scent of charred flesh that he almost aches for as he presses on the gas again. And then a third time.

Enough to send the front end of the UTV bucking through the ruts carved into the path, baked solid by the Texas sun.

Much like the orders he gave Enzo upon departing earlier, Garcia isn't in the mood for quiet. There are times and places for such an approach, tonight definitely not providing either.

Tonight is about sending a message to anyone who gets in his way, whether it be man, or beast.

CHAPTER FIFTY-SEVEN

Enzo knows that the only thing that kept Leo Garcia from exploding in his mother's room earlier was the presence of Sofia in the corner. Two-hundred-and-forty pounds of bubbling rage, standing and seething like a damned bull, ready to explode at the first available target. Hostility well beyond what Enzo witnessed earlier in the day, when the man was merely annoyed. Ire that was easily remedied, calling for an immediate sit down with the district attorney, during which threats were made and his ass was summarily kissed, assurances relayed that no harm would come to Garcia or his business.

Promises that there is no way of making now, the news that was received shortly after arriving back from the city infinitely worse than whatever little task force might be coming together. Information that not only was someone poking into their affairs, but it was regarding something they'd gone out of their way to keep hidden. A tangential matter that could paint a much more direct correlation and have infinitely larger repercussions than a few drunken college kids mixing drugs and alcohol and ending up drowning in their own vomit.

A matter of removal that is not the case in this instance, there likely little that could be done to shield them should the right people get on their trail.

Facts all that were enough to have Garcia fuming, that same vitriol now hurtling through Enzo. Hatred that has steadily built in the hours since, arguably taken even higher by the fact that no small part of all this is his fault. Steps that he thought had been taken nights before to protect them from any future blowback, and the later foolish belief in what Hector relayed about the guy in town looking for a Ram 1500 being nothing to worry about.

A coincidence he never should have accepted.

Especially after Garcia himself said as much.

"What's the plan?" Ramon asks from the rear bench seat in Enzo's truck. Having long since abandoned his spot between the two front captain's chairs, a hand on either shoulder to see out through the windshield, he has retreated back to the rear of the cab.

The loser of an impromptu game of rock-paper-scissors, he sits behind Hector in the front seat. The two men that Enzo never works without, especially on matters such as this. Guys who may have their peccadilloes, endlessly bantering with one another or tossing out a smart ass comment in the worst of situations, but know when to keep their damn mouths shut and handle business.

Joining them tonight is a fourth team member. An addition made at the last moment, meant not to serve as additional firepower, but as a driver. A means of ensuring a quick escape for the three of them, should anything go sideways in what they are about to do.

A man named Cesar who is barely in his mid-twenties, with thick hair that is so black it shines blue hanging across his forehead. The son of a longtime groundskeeper, he has grown up around the operation, taking on an active role himself more than a decade ago.

An extra set of hands to help his father feed their growing family that has served both sides, the young man showing promise enough to be included tonight. His first such outing, a success thus far for the simple fact that he's known better than to utter a word.

A potential distraction Enzo has been glad to be free of, his mind left to stew on what has taken place, and what they are going to do about it.

There is zero doubt that the man who Garcia described earlier is Cortland Alder. Not only was the physical description an exact match, but also the backstory that he handed over to Lance Reseda, later relayed on. A tale about doing background research for an upcoming acquisition on behalf of Cooley and Piper, the damned accounting firm where he works.

A ruse that is all but a middle finger, showing them that not only is he onto them, but he doesn't care enough to even mask what he is doing. An open dare calling them out.

A direct slight made worse by driving past his home a few minutes ago to spy the same truck with Tennessee license plates that Hector spent most of last night tailing sitting in the driveway.

Something they should have already eliminated, instead of letting whatever personal crusade Alder is now on go another day.

"We're going to drive by every fifteen minutes until we see the lights in the house go out," Enzo says. Words that draw over Hector's gaze in the passenger seat, the shadow of Cesar's dark hair shifting in the rearview mirror. "Then we're going to come right back here. The three of us are going to slip down and get rid of Alder and whoever he has staying with him.

"Cesar back there will move into the driver's seat, come get us and help us move the bodies when we're done."

CHAPTER FIFTY-EIGHT

The last light in the house went off twenty-five minutes ago, leaving only the pale glow of the security lamp overhanging the driveway to illuminate the interior. A thin bit of halogen light that passes across the front porch and through the living room windows, making shapes visible, but providing no detail. Minutiae Remington doesn't need as he sits on the sofa, the oversized cushions cocooned around him. Enormous pillows that allow him to sit at an angle, rotating his gaze between the various windows lining the room, watching both the driveway and the side yard.

The two most likely points of approach, should anybody come stealing upon them in the dead of night. A sneak attack he would have thought coming last night after spotting the tail outside of Rudy's, almost certain that it is en route now.

Another day of poking into things that was sure to be noticed by whoever is behind this, any uncertainty wiped away by the comment made by that prick Lance Reseda. An unprovoked barb that Cortland was right about, only coming up in such a manner if having been discussed multiple times before. The sort of thing one doesn't simply throw out to a stranger unless they have gone over it enough times to have forgotten it isn't public knowledge.

A sure avenue to be considered moving forward.

Another possible source of information to have gotten back to the person pulling the strings. The cause of the certainty Remington feels that tonight is the night, even if it doesn't explain how they were noticed the night before.

That, more than anything, what has been nagging Remington all day.

A question he has just begun to unravel, sitting alone in the dark, watching and thinking, before deciding to pick up the phone. Not wanting to destroy his night vision by holding the device up to his cheek, he sits with it flipped upside down on his lap, the volume lowered to just barely audible.

Sound sufficient to have raised Shine's ears atop her head as she sits curled on the floor by his feet, her eyes flashing like moist discs as she looks around, searching for the source.

"Hey man, how's it going over there?" Tyrell asks. Unlike their last conversation, there is no sound of atrocious music to be heard in the background. None of the usual accompaniment of tools clanging or equipment running.

Long after the workday is over, he and Val have retired back home. Two people with mismatched schedules, her likely to have gone to bed hours ago despite it being Friday night, intent to get an early start with a hike or trip to the gym in the morning, while Tyrell sits up watching bad television and whiling away the hours.

A teenager's schedule that Remington has given him enough shit for over the years, this hardly the time for doing it again.

"It's going," Remington replies out of habit before adjusting his response to say, "Sort of."

"That's never good," Tyrell answers. "Getting worse?"

"No," Remington concedes, "but not much better either, which is why I'm calling. I finally figured out what's been nagging at me all day."

Rotating his gaze in either direction, he checks the windows again. Another round in his ongoing vigil, ensuring that nobody sneaks up, even while he is on the phone.

Seeing nothing but the same collection of trees and shadows, he continues, "Yesterday, when I called and asked you about that Ram 1500, how did you end up with Tony? You know him, call him directly?"

"Naw, never heard of the guy before," Tyrell responds. "I actually called and talked to a cat named Victor. The OG of spare parts and such in that area. Called him up and told him what I was looking for, he said he'd get back to me.

"Maybe an hour later, he called and said the meeting with Tony was set."

Running the math in his head, Remington can feel things starting to align. A timeframe that finally makes a bit of sense, beginning to satisfy that feeling he's been carrying all day.

"What time did you first call Victor?" Remington asks.

"I don't know exactly," Tyrell says. "I was on the landline at the shop, so I don't have a log, but probably between four and five. Right after you called me."

An initial contact between four and five would give Victor plenty of time to reach out to whoever was sitting behind the wheel of the actual Ram 1500. A vehicle that likely no longer exists, broken down into pieces and funneled through places like his, and Tony's, and whoever else is in the area.

A goose chase that not only saw Remington waste time pursuing it, but even put them on Maylinn's killer's radar in the process.

Once Victor had reached out and spread the word, he'd lingered a few minutes, buying a bit of extra time, before setting the meeting up later. Plenty of time for the silver pickup to be in position, merely waiting for Remington to arrive.

Putting the timeframe together in his mind, Remington clenches his teeth tight. Turning his head to the side, he mumbles a series of expletives and self-flagellation.

The reason that nobody surfaced today, despite their revisiting the same three cases, was because the tail didn't originate with them. It likely started with Remington's side search, whatever they happened to kick up at Reseda's this afternoon more coincidence than causation.

A second contact that for sure has a target painted on them now. Multiple touches meaning someone is well aware of their presence, and he and his brother still have no clue who they might be.

A disadvantaged position that has gotten even worse.

A fact Remington is still in the middle of working out when Shine rises from the floor beside him. Snapping up onto three feet, she stretches her body into a line, everything from tail to muzzle drawn tight, her ears pinned flat to her skull.

Sliding forward to the edge of the couch, Remington places a hand along her spine. Feeling the underlying muscle clenched tight, bits of adrenaline start to seep into his bloodstream as he scans the windows in order, not yet seeing a thing.

"Ty, I'm going to have to call you back."

CHAPTER FIFTY-NINE

Remington gave no outward indication that he wasn't also going to bed when Cortland bade him goodnight an unknown amount of time earlier. He didn't mention wanting to stay up and watch the end of the college game that was on ESPN or needing to make a few phone calls. Never said he needed to shower up or wanted to do some reading or thinking before turning in.

Sure as hell didn't say he was going to sit vigil again tonight, guarding the place like he was still back in the Army, posted up in the desert somewhere with a rifle and a pair of night-vision goggles.

Somehow, though, Cortland just knew. Perhaps not overtly – just like he wasn't completely certain that Remington would do the same thing last night – but on a subconscious level. A niggling feeling in the back of his mind that refused to let him completely rest either, no matter how badly he needs it. Exhaustion of a physical sort to now match the days of emotional trauma, capable of being healed only through the tonics of time and sleep.

Instead, his body settled more into a state of hibernation. A computer with the screen turned off but the inner workings still moving at full speed, only the slightest shake needed to bring it back to life.

Or, in this instance, the light pressure of Remington's hand settling over his mouth.

Popping his eyes open in the darkness of the bedroom, Cortland sees the silhouette of his brother above him. A stark outline that includes the extended barrel of a gun in his right hand, his left retreating back from Cortland's face to hold a finger to his lips.

A silent message Cortland responds to with a nod, watching as his brother uses the same hand to hold up three fingers, motioning to the front and side of the house.

Another quiet missive Cortland answers in the same way, any grog of slumber dissipating in an instant. In its place, he feels a hit of adrenaline seep into his bloodstream, his pulse picking up as he jerks back the comforter and swings his feet to the floor.

"How long do we have?" he whispers.

"Minute. Two at most," Remington answers. "You have a gun up here?"

Cortland knows his brother has to ask the question, the same as he knows that Remington is already aware of the answer. A stark moratorium on weapons that was one of the very few hard-fast rules that Maylinn had. A matter of some dissension between her and Remington when he first moved back and was in the worst of his PTSD, sitting up for nights on end, a chef's knife clutched in his hand.

A rule against firearms that has extended to this very moment, the gun now gripped in Remington's hand the only one Cortland has ever seen inside his house.

Giving a quick shake of his head, Cortland slips past his brother to the closet behind him. Easing open the sliding door, he reaches into the corner and grasps the smooth wooden handle of the Louisville Slugger kept tucked away there. A solid piece of Kentucky Ash sanded down and covered in varnish, weighing just over two pounds in total.

"This do?"

Flicking his gaze between the bat and Cortland, it is clear there are a host of comments Remington wants to make. Smart retorts about the weapon or angry admonishments about not taking protective measures after what happened a couple nights before.

"It'll have to." Turning toward the door, he takes the gun in both hands before him. Extending it to arm's length, he crosses his right foot over his left, headed for the hallway. "Stay behind me. Keep low, out of sight."

"Got it," Cortland mutters, falling in on his brother's heels. Walking heel-to-toe, he follows him the length of the runner covering the hardwood floor, their steps silent against the padded rug.

Downstairs, he can hear nothing beyond the faint call of the breeze pushing through the screens. The sole sound penetrating the oppressive quiet, the air seeming to grow thicker with each breath.

His pulse thumping, sweat forms along his brow and underarms. He can feel the grit of sawdust against his palms as he rotates his hands around the base of the bat.

"Shine?" Cortland whispers.

"Bathroom," Remington hisses.

Saying nothing more, he slows his pace, stepping from the edge of the rug onto the top stair. Leading with his prosthetic, he places it carefully down before bringing his right foot in behind it, lowering himself to the next step down.

A decrease in height of several inches, the front tip of the gun swinging across the living room coming slowly into view. A descent that Cortland has made a thousand times before, though never has he looked at it in this manner. A space revealing itself bit by bit, each step down heightening the tension he feels.

His pulse thrums through his temples. Tension runs the length of his shoulders and biceps as he clutches the bat tight.

Sweat runs over his scalp, stinging his eyes.

More than a dozen stairs in total takes them from the second floor down to the main level. A journey with barely a sound, the hardwood underfoot remaining mercifully quiet. No moans or creaks to give away their position as they step across the foyer and into the open doorway, Remington jerking to a stop so abruptly Cortland nearly mashes into him.

Raising the gun to parallel, he presses his chin to his shoulder and whispers, "I start firing, you haul ass to the kitchen. You got me?"

His heart thumping so hard it practically makes his chest ache, Cortland peers past his brother to the rounded shape of a shadow crossing by the front window. A silhouette matching that of Remington in his bedroom just minutes before, with a gun in hand, the barrel pointed skyward.

Inching forward, the intruder moves until reaching the center of the glass pane, their full torso framed in the center, before Remington begins to unload. A trio of shots that easily penetrate the glass, the target grunting as they disappear from sight.

All the signal Cortland needs as he wheels on the ball of his foot and does as told, sprinting toward the rear of the house.

A run that is still underway, his sights set on the protection of the island in the kitchen, when all hell breaks loose, bullets peppering the house from multiple sides, chewing through glass and furniture alike.

CHAPTER SIXTY

The truck with the Tennessee license plate sitting in the driveway should have told Enzo this wasn't going to be as simple as it seemed. While his previous research on the Asian lawyer and her accountant husband might have made them look like easy marks, they weren't alone. They had someone with them that Hector identified as looking formidable, with some size and ink and the damn truck to hint that he was cut from a different cloth than the other two.

A family member called in for assistance, or a professional hired to look into things.

More mistakes Enzo can't bother dwelling on at the moment, his full focus put on the bullets spewing out from the windows lining the front and side of the house. Rounds that seem to be coming from a single location, firing off a pair in one direction before turning the opposite way.

Suppression fire, hoping to keep them on their heels before they get too close.

A means of taking their own perceived advantage of surprise and turning it back on them.

"He's down!" Ramon calls, his voice barely discernible beyond the echoing retort of automatic fire. "Sonsabitches shot Hector!"

Having sent the others straight at the front of the place, Enzo is tucked at the base of an oak tree in the side yard. A tree that has been around for decades, not quite thick enough to hide him completely, but plenty sufficient to keep him largely out of sight.

A shield that has already taken one bullet on his behalf, the dull thud of impact still echoing in his ears.

"How bad?" Enzo replies, keeping his voice as low as possible, hoping not to give away their exact positions.

"Bad!" Ramon replies. Having no such worries, he practically screams, adding, "I can't get close, but he's not moving. Shitload of blood!"

Jerking his attention away from Ramon, Enzo shifts his focus back to the house. His teeth come together, his entire jaw flexing in anger both at his own errors and at the actions of the person firing from inside.

The accountant himself or whoever he called for help doesn't matter, both targets to be eliminated.

Knees flexed, Enzo stands with his shoulder braced against the tree. Facing back toward the road, he listens carefully to the ongoing report of gunshots ringing out. The same pattern of two and two in either direction, accompanied by the tinkling of glass shards falling away from the windows or the thud of rounds slamming into trees or the supports lining the front porch.

Clear sounds that make for easy counting, Enzo zeroing his focus in on the climbing number.

Based on sound and impact, he would bet money that the man inside is firing a nine-millimeter. A basic Glock or Beretta like he is carrying, capable of carrying anywhere from fifteen to eighteen rounds before having to be reloaded, depending on the exact model and magazine size.

A window too broad to try and pinpoint exactly, the potential of miscounting, expecting the shooter to be reloading and stepping out into active fire too great. The shots to Hector proves that the man has some proficiency, and the willingness to use it.

A combination meaning that Enzo needs an alternate means of approach. A form of distraction that will give him the opening he needs to cover the fifteen yards between himself and the windows lining the side of the house. Panes of glass turned into gaping maws, with only a few remaining shards left to bar his entry.

An end goal there is no way Enzo is leaving without achieving. Not after seeing the way Leo Garcia came storming into his mother's room earlier, practically quivering with rage.

Sure as hell not while knowing that he is the cause of that anger, a series of miscues taking a simple matter and turning it into this. The elimination of an attorney, escalated into a gunfight along a country road, one longtime employee already shot and bleeding out.

A shit show that Enzo will allow to get no worse, the entire Alder family – and whoever they have with them – ending now.

"Ramon," Enzo hisses, extending his neck just a couple of inches, attempting to better help fling the words between them. "Ramon?"

"Still here," Ramon replies, timing his answer between the ongoing rounds punctuating the air. "He's not that good."

Holding off on an immediate response, Enzo counts two more shots. A pair bringing the total up above a dozen, meaning a reload has to be coming soon. A narrow window that might just give him the split second needed.

"On my count, I want you to fire back with everything you have," Enzo calls, keeping his voice only just loud enough to be heard, what they are about to do plenty difficult without being foolish.

Even if the shooter is probably hearing nothing but a dull ringing in his ears after rattling off so many shots in a row.

"Both sides of the front window, back and forth."

The instructions are just barely out before being swallowed by the report of the next rounds. Shot aimed Enzo's direction, one ripping through the leaves of a nearby tree, the other whistling past before disappearing into the distance.

Fourteen, at least, by Enzo's count.

And the moment in which the shooter is about to rotate back the opposite direction.

"Now!" Enzo calls, pivoting out from around the base of the tree. Shoving off the ball of his foot, he charges straight ahead across the clipped grass, making it but a single stride before Ramon does as instructed. The bark of a second gun calls out, eschewing their opponent's pattern of firing two at a time, opting for a complete onslaught. One shot after another, tugging back as fast as the firing mechanism in the gun can reset.

An all-out barrage, pounding the front of the house, beating the gun inside into silence.

The unknown shooter sent diving for cover, giving Enzo the opening he needs to bound across the side yard, covering the gap in less than a dozen long strides. Paced as fast as the jeans and boots he is wearing will allow, the Beretta is gripped tight in his hand.

Arms bent at ninety-degrees, he grits his teeth, his breath clenched as he focuses on the second window in from the corner. The one positioned deeper in the house, with the majority of the glass already stripped away.

An opening with only a few small pieces remaining. Misshapen triangles that protrude toward the center like jagged shark's teeth, sure to tear into him as he makes his way through.

Hits he is willing to take to make this bullshit go away.

A mess that was supposed to be over days ago, ending now.

His jaw clenched, Enzo peels his lips back. A grunt rises from deep in his chest as he hits top speed, fully exposed in the open for but a moment as the last of Ramon's magazine gives out.

One last stride without the benefit of cover fire before he plants his right foot on the landscape timber framing the mulch bed lining the house and hurls himself forward. A headlong dive through the open window with arms extended.

A damned Hispanic Superman with a Beretta as his weapon of choice, orange blossoms igniting from the tip as he squeezes off two rounds while hanging suspended in the air. Bullets that precede him into the opening, passing through unscathed before mashing into the wall on the far side of the room.

A fate Enzo isn't so lucky to share, feeling the sharp edges of no less than two chunks of glass pierce his skin. Wicked gouges carved into his left shoulder and right leg, drawing blood. Warmth he can feel spread across his skin, kept from streaming freely only by the clothing he wears.

A natural adhesive causing his shirt and jeans to stick to him, even as he hits the hardwood floor and rolls to the side.

A whirling cyclone of blood and glass shards that makes it through one complete revolution before stopping abruptly. A jarring impact not against the hard back of a sofa or table, but against human flesh.

The shooter, sent sprawling to the ground by Ramon's return fire. A mound of musculature wrapped in olive skin and decorated with heavy tattooing.

The new addition from Tennessee who Hector spotted the night before. A man who looks strikingly like the accountant, differentiated only by his hair and the ink covering his left arm.

No doubt, a missing limb, should Enzo's gaze make it that far.

Just as surprised by the unexpected collision as Enzo, the two of them stare at each other with wide eyes. A millisecond to allow for recognition to set in before descending upon one another.

A melee of knees and fists and elbows that sends their respective weapons skittering across the floor.

Carnal warfare, marked by sweat and blood and bare skin.

CHAPTER SIXTY-ONE

The Hispanic man with a heavy shadow of a beard has clearly been in more than his share of scraps. Years of hand-to-hand combat that have honed a style that is nothing like the way Remington was taught to fight in the military, this something more akin to brawling. A reliance on overwhelming an opponent, using sheer force of will and relentlessness to get the upper hand.

An approach that Remington can imagine works on the vast majority of people the man goes up against. Those who haven't been formally taught or have reason to harbor fear.

Disadvantaged positions that assholes like this rely on, and when they don't have them or can't attain them, they do something like force a young attorney into a tree along the side of the road.

Standing in the open center of the living room, Remington circles to his right. His dominant side by birth, made more so by the loss of his lower limb. An unconscious tendency to put the majority of his weight on his right leg, using the left to provide balance, nudging him in a slow circle.

Fists raised before him, a veneer of sweat covers his bare arms. Baseline moisture allowing the blood released from the series of cuts caused by the man slamming into him earlier, pinning bits of window glass between them, to run freely. Streaks of crimson that stripe his biceps, dripping from the tips of his elbows.

Three feet away, his opponent's snap-button shirt has been pulled open almost to the navel, revealing a flat stomach liberally splashed with dark hair. Tendrils of blood curl down from the corner of his mouth and the opposite nostril, tracing the scar on his face before hitting his exposed chest.

Resulting wounds from their initial fracas on the floor. An unexpected and impromptu scrum serving as the first act in their battle.

Dark stains mar the leg of his jeans and his left shoulder. More injuries, these sustained on his suicide dive through the side window.

Scarred knuckles are balled into fists before him, neither man making a move for the guns that were sent tumbling earlier. A mutual recognition of the threat the other one shows. Shared despisal for one another, both having taken someone away from the other. A scoreboard that stands at one to one, even if Remington feels that they are nowhere near even.

A nameless stooge brought along as a bit of muscle, as compared to his sister-in-law. One of just the few real vestiges of family he has ever known. A woman who went out of her way to care for him, helping to bring him back from the brink.

A kind soul who deserved far better than she received, whatever the reason behind her demise might be.

Somewhere behind him, Remington can hear Cortland and the other intruder engaged in an altercation. Men who both came rushing in from opposite directions, now engaged in combat of a different kind.

Cortland, still armed with his bat.

His opponent having picked up a weapon of his own.

Dueling bludgeons Remington can hear smashing into one another, offset by the growls and barks of Shine still locked in the bathroom. Signals that, for now, he can put his focus forward. He can start to unleash the animosity he feels, aiming it at the man across from him.

Given the size advantage he has, the prosthetic limb that takes away some of his mobility, Remington knows that the man across from him is expecting him to come straight ahead. A show of power, making this a match of mass against mass. Close combat, precluding the need for nimble movement or fleet footwork.

Assumptions Remington plans to use against him, ceasing his circle right and raising his weight up onto his toes. Two quick pulses, bracing himself, before feigning a forward lurch. A headlong tackle that gets no further than a single step, causing the man to jerk back.

His hands lower, moving to protect his midsection. Reflexive movements, done without thought.

Another sign of his lack of training, allowing nothing but instinct to take over. Learned behavior that this time isn't just wrong, but exactly what Remington wants him to do.

The instant Remington sees the man's hands drop toward his waistline, his hips pitching backward, bringing the bridge of his nose closer, he unleashes a wicked right hook. A shot unfurling from the shoulder, using the prosthetic leg as a pivot point to maximize centrifugal force.

Whipping his arm across his body, he lets his right arm unspool behind him, his massive paw curling into a bludgeon. A crushing blow that the man recognizes in real time, his eyes and mouth all forming into circles. Indicators of a known mistake as he jerks backward, spinning his head up and back in the opposite direction.

The best that can be hoped for in terms of a defensive position, catching the point of Remington's knuckle along his left cheekbone. Splitting the skin as he continues to twirl in the opposite direction, blood spatter spills to the floor.

A choreographed pirouette, just milliseconds from being a knockout shot. A spin he leans into, twirling his body around and coming back with a shot of his own. A hard overhand right from an angle too low for Remington to drop beneath, instead pushing right into it. Balling his left arm against his torso, he takes the full shot in the meat of his deltoid, the impact traveling through his entire core.

A jolt that he will no doubt feel later, once the adrenaline and anger have subsided.

One that, for now, he pushes past, driving his right hand straight ahead. An underhand shot delivered like a piston to the man's stomach, mashing into his midsection. Contact that pushes his hips back a couple of inches, providing just enough space for Remington to jerk both hands up in front of them, using them to deliver an open-handed shove.

Two flat palms into the man's chest plates, the difference in size and strength between them finally coming to Remington's advantage. Sheer power that pushes the man back into the sofa behind him, the arm of it clipping him behind the knees, sending him tumbling to the floor.

A backward sprawl flipping him end over end, his boots flashing past Remington's face as he disappears over the edge of the couch. Flailing feet and limbs that end with a thunderous crash as he spills onto the narrow runner table backed up against it, the sound of splintered wood and shattered glass filling the air.

An unceremonious crash that sends detritus across the floor, calling for Remington to follow. The sound of an opening he allows to pull him forward a single step before making himself stop.

For as much as he would love nothing more than to go diving over the sofa and finish what they started earlier, unleashing an onslaught of punches and forearm shots to the man until he stops moving, he has to be prudent. There is no doubt this bastard deserves to die. As does his partner. And the man on the front porch in the slim chance he is still breathing.

And they will.

But he can't be stupid about it.

Jamming his foot into the floor, Remington can feel his weight mash the distal end of his leg into the cup of his prosthetic. A jolt felt clear into his spine as he turns back the other direction, his gaze sweeping the floor out wide of the sofa.

Floorboards dappled with droplets of sweat and blood and the assorted debris of battle, all striped with the shadows of Cortland and the other man still locked in a fight in the kitchen. A multi-colored backdrop that his focus dances across, sighting in on what he wants lying against the foot of the closest dining room chair.

Shoving off the side of his prosthetic foot, Remington pushes himself to the right. A single long bound covering several feet, his weight landing square on his right foot. Knee flexed, he bends and scoops up his opponent's Beretta, barely getting it to shoulder height before his brother calls out, "Rem!"

Using the tip of the gun to lead the way, Remington rotates to his right, swinging the gun through a full arc. One hundred and eighty degrees in the opposite direction, letting him sight in on the full back of the fourth man in the house. Wearing jeans and a sweat-stained flannel to match his partner, he stands with his arm cocked high above his head, a knife in hand.

Stainless-steel with a wooden handle, grabbed from the block on the counter. An implement of death he prepares to drive down at Cortland bent back over the middle island, the Louisville Slugger balanced between both palms, acting as a barricade.

A sight Remington only needs to register before acting.

Three times in order, he pulls back on the trigger. Shots that strike center mass, forming a misshapen triangle across the man's back. A trio of distinct impacts that open deep gouges in his flesh, causing his body to jerk with spastic movements.

Sprays of blood hit the floor, followed by the knife sliding from his grasp.

Kill shots Remington barely has time to confirm, his focus still on ensuring the threat to his brother is gone, when a sharp blow strikes the bottom half of his left leg. A vicious swing that wrenches his prosthetic out of position, sending him tumbling to the floor.

A fall every bit as clumsy as his opponent spilling over the couch just moments before, his full weight coming down flat on his back. A freefall that mashes his teeth together, his vision blurring for just an instant.

Time enough to allow his attacker to reverse course, the last glimpse Remington gets of the man are his boots as he dives back through the window and out into the night.

———

The local funeral home offered to have the services free of charge. A final hat tip to a longstanding member of the community, complete with a casket and flowers paid for by friends and neighbors.

Kindness that Remington and Cortland both appreciated, but could not allow.

One, because G would have never stood for a thing, no matter how much charity he had given out in free moonshine over the years.

And two, because the thought of having a major event and having to stand in front of the entire town made their skin crawl.

Opting instead to cut a deal in private with the crematory in the neighboring town, the two of them had instead decided to go with a modest urn that was cradled under Cortland's left arm. By his side stood Remington, Shine tucked up against his chest, her body visibly trembling at being back at the site of what took place just a couple of weeks before.

A place the brothers themselves had been only a couple of times themselves, attempting to return a couple of nights later before giving up on it and grabbing a few bags of belongings instead. Relocation away from the charred remnants of the boathouse out back and the smells of woodsmoke and burnt flesh hanging in the air.

Omnipresent reminders of what took place.

A darkened hellscape they were both aware of in their periphery even now, well after the fact. An eyesore there was no avoiding as they stood a hundred yards on down the bank from the place where their grandpa had been born and spent his entire life, up to and including his final moments.

The same place where they had arrived a decade before with the passing of their parents, officially becoming Moonshine Creek Boys themselves, calling it home every day since.

As close a spot as they could find that wasn't ravaged in some way by the fire, whether it be burnt limbs or singed grass or even that stomach-turning smell. A place where if they stood and faced the right direction, were blessed with the wind blowing the right way, they could forget any of it had ever occurred at all.

A spot for eternal sleep tucked amidst the oak and sycamore trees lining the riverbed, their dense foliage providing plenty of shade to sit and watch the water gently roll by.

A grave the two of them would dig together, once the last of the two dozen or so people behind them had left. Those gathered for a small, invitation-only funeral that was more or less foisted upon them by certain members of the community.

Bill Ketchum and Judge Mason and a handful more who had known G going way back, insistent on being given the opportunity to wish him well.

Reasoning neither Cortland nor his brother had quite agreed with, though didn't have the strength to push back on.

"How you boys holding up?" a voice asked. Cutting through the silence, both turned to see Sheriff Myles approaching, his usual uniform swapped out for an ill-fitting suit. Black coat and trousers with a matching tie that was probably last worn around the time he and G were the boys' age.

More than a dozen responses immediately came to Cortland's mind. Everything from weariness to smart remarks, no doubt matched by his brother beside him.

Comments he managed to push away, stating, "It's never easy."

"No," Myles agreed, coming to a stop between them. "It never is."

Fixing his gaze on the water drifting slowly past, he stared straight out for a moment, refracted light passing over the droplets of sweat lining his brow. A pose of deep contemplation before adding, "I just wanted to let you guys know, just because we haven't got anything to stick yet, we're going to keep at this thing.

"Callums or somebody else doesn't matter, we'll get the people who did this."

Blinking himself back into the moment, he glanced to either side, looking at them both in turn. "You guys are staying over at The Buckhorn, right?"

Knowing his brother wasn't about to say a word, Cortland nodded. "Yeah."

"For now, or until it's time to take off?"

Picking up on the obvious insinuation, Cortland answered, "For the rest of the summer."

"Good," Myles answered, turning to glance at him before starting to head back the opposite direction. "I'll come find you there as soon as we know anything."

CHAPTER SIXTY-TWO

Enzo steps out into the center of the driveway and raises a hand, flagging down the driver sitting beside Leo Garcia in the front of the Escalade. Giving nothing more than a flick of his fingers, he immediately retreats to the side of the concrete opening. Pressing the back of his fist to his lip, he keeps his gaze averted, staring directly down at the asphalt, even as the Escalade rolls by him and comes to a stop in the middle of the drive.

His classic posture for the rare instances when he has gotten his ass kicked. Embarrassment, tinged with anger and humiliation.

A pose Garcia has not seen his friend exhibit many times over the years, most of those handed out by Garcia himself.

Forty-five minutes ago, Garcia was in the enclosure out behind his mansion. Standing in the front of the UTV, his body was extended up through the open top. A stun baton was in hand as he practically willed the hyenas circling the vehicle to come closer.

A blurred line between predator and prey, both sides looking to unleash on the other. Savage desire that was within moments of becoming realized, interrupted only by the shrill whine of Garcia's phone erupting.

A quick insertion of the modern into a scene ripped from the ages, shattering the illusion of the face off. A harsh cry of technology that sent the animals bounding off into the night, the auditory intrusion bringing about one last cry of their own in farewell.

The trademark cackling laugh, so beautiful just a couple of nights before, resonating this time with mocking cruelty, as if they knew who was calling and the news he was about to impart. Information Garcia is still processing, needing to come here and see things for himself before deciding on a course of action.

Hitting the window button on his door, Garcia lowers the piece of tinted glass separating him from the outside world. As he does so, the cool feel of the autumn air touches his skin, the temperature continuing to drop as they work deeper into the night.

Up close, without the veil of the darkened glass, he can see the full relief of what has Enzo standing with his head hung in shame. Injuries that he has seen approached only once before, on the very day he first met the man, then nothing but a child. A half-starved and angry boy who practically invited the abuse, flinging himself headlong into battle.

An ignorant youth who didn't know any other way, something that Garcia cannot imagine happened here tonight.

A gash creases Enzo's left cheek, the area around it already beginning to swell, making his features appear tilted to the side. No doubt there is bruising as well, hidden by the night and the dark streaks of dried blood that streak south, matting the side of his beard.

Stains that are matched by tendrils snaking down from his lip and nose as well, all three contributing to the host of droplets dappling his shirt torn open and hanging to the side. A garment that is nothing short of ragged, the left sleeve also ripped and bloody to match his right pant leg.

His gaze twisted into a scowl, he stares down at the ground, visibly avoiding Garcia's gaze, before slowly rolling his focus up to match it. Features burning with animosity, he spits at the ground between them, the saliva tinged red with blood.

"Where are they?" Garcia asks, bypassing any direct questions about what happened to him. Inquiries that will only spawn excuses or reckless behavior, neither of which he is in the mood for.

Enzo got his ass kicked. He doesn't need to have it pointed out to him.

"Up at the house," Enzo replies. "I left them where they lay until you got here."

Quite possibly the first thing he has done right in days, Garcia slides his focus over to the driver. Nodding once, he waits for the man to put the vehicle in park before pushing open the door and climbing out. Circling past the wad of spittle on the ground between them, he comes up on Enzo's opposite side, the two heading together for the house at the end of the drive.

A classic two-story that Garcia would never stoop to spend a night in, but can see the appeal for a low-level attorney and an accountant. People with wrongly calibrated notions of success, who probably think a couple of acres and an extra bedroom means they have made it.

The American dream, as if people like them can ever have the first damn idea what that really means.

"How many?" Garcia asks.

"Two," Enzo says. "And a dog. All three were gone by the time I got back."

Making it as far as halfway up the driveway, Enzo veers off to the side. A more direct path across the front lawn that Garcia follows, presumably retracing their steps from earlier. Padding across soft grass, they pass by a fall display in the corner between the driveway and front walk before pausing just off the edge of an extended porch.

Wood stained dark and lined with rocking chairs, now with the additional decoration of Hector sprawled flat on his back. A pair of crimson stains imbedded in his chest, rivulets of blood run along the cracks in the floorboards beneath him. Streaks already drying black, disappearing over the edge and into the mulch bed below.

A death that wasn't so much savage as stupid, it not taking more than a moment for Garcia to determine how it came to pass. Thinking anybody inside was asleep, Hector had gotten too close to the windows, putting himself on plain display.

The first shots fired, with fragments of broken glass splayed across him to prove it.

A death that will be felt by the organization. A trusted employee who Garcia would gladly trade any handful of men from his security or landscaping crews to have back.

A loss firmly attributed both to this messy situation and Enzo's errors. Mistakes a few days ago, and even larger ones here tonight.

Facts that the man seems well aware of, his head continuing to hang as he pushes forward across the deck, passing by Cesar before stepping into the house. A silent lead that Garcia follows, his feet crunching over chunks of broken glass.

Inside, the house is much in line with what he'd expected upon arrival. Hardwood floors and rustic décor and all the other touches that people without any real money try to do to convince themselves otherwise. Fixtures that have been aged to look expensive and color schemes that try to make rooms appear bigger than they are.

Probably clean and tidy just hours before, it now bears out the full extent of what took place. A visual explaining both the broken windows out front and the injuries marring Enzo's entire body.

Crossing through the main living area for the place, Garcia takes in the divots gouged into the walls. Bullet holes chewed into sheetrock, chunks of it and the accompanying dust settling on the floor and nearby horizontal surfaces.

The couch in the center of the room has been knocked off center, pillows strewn on the floor. The mashed remains of an end table and assorted knickknacks litter the ground behind it.

Streaks of blood mar both fabric and flooring.

A scene depicting quite a fight, culminating with Ramon resting face down in the back of the room. Head turned to the side, his mouth gapes, unseeing eyes staring straight ahead.

The same as the death of Hector, it isn't difficult to envision how things went. Fighting two to a side, whoever Enzo had been paired off with got the better of him, sending him over the couch and crashing through the table.

The reason for the deep slashes to his leg and arm.

An opening allowing his opponent to pick up his weapon and shoot Ramon in the back from across the room.

Another loss that will reverberate through the organization, completely annihilating the crew set aside for special projects. Jobs like going into the mines to pick up new product or handling cash deliveries to and from Milo's.

Men who spent years earning Garcia's trust, neither of whom can be replaced on a whim.

Feet planted in the center of the living room, Garcia makes no effort to go any closer. It is apparent that Ramon is dead, his eyes already cloudy, the bloodstains on his back and the floor around him beginning to congeal. There is no need to inspect.

Instead, his gaze moves to the cluster of framed images affixed to the wall behind the flatscreen television standing on an entertainment center. Photographs that largely escaped the gunfire earlier, only a single one punctured by a stray bullet, the remaining glass crumbled into a starburst pattern.

Taking a step forward, he studies each in turn, taking in the attorney who started all this. Her husband, the accountant, with the gelled hair and gleaming smile. A three-legged dog with black and gray and white fur.

And a man looking strikingly similar – if not larger - in military fatigues, with hair shorn down tight and a sleeve of dark tattoos.

"These the guys?" Garcia asks, jutting his chin toward the wall.

"Yeah," Enzo mutters.

Grunting softly, Garcia takes another step, moving close enough he can see his own reflection in the glass. One at time, he studies each of the men, trying to get a feel for them.

Underlying assessments for who he is up against.

Who dares think they can come at him, regardless what he might have done to the woman.

"Get Ramon and Hector out of here," Garcia says, dismissing the accountant and moving to the other man. A twin from the looks of things, the semblance between them too strong to be anything less. "And then burn it."

"Burn what?" Enzo asks.

One last time, Garcia looks at each of the men depicted on the walls before turning to stare at Enzo.

This all began as a means of removing a threat. Taking out the attorney and what would have been unwanted attention.

From this moment on, it is about setting an example.

"Burn the whole damn thing."

CHAPTER SIXTY-THREE

"What the hell happened?!" Tyrell practically yells into the phone. Snatching it up in the middle of the first ring, Remington gets the impression he has been sitting on it since he cut their original conversation short a couple hours ago, waiting for word. Some explanation as to what caused the abrupt departure, and if everybody was okay.

That very thing being his next question in order, barely giving Remington a chance to reply to the initial inquiry before lobbing out the second.

Backside resting on the tailgate of his truck, Remington sits with his cellphone on the cool metal beside him. A centerpiece between himself and his brother, both staring out at the reflection of the moon resting atop the small farm pond before them. A deep pool of water adjacent to a hay barn tucked away in a pasture.

A feeding station for a cattle operation Cortland has done some work for, pointing them that direction after they tore away from his house earlier, both spending a good thirty minutes circling the area, ensuring they weren't followed, before ending up here. A place as good as any for them to sit and regroup after departing, Remington allowing them only a few minutes to grab up essentials before demanding they leave.

A hasty exit in the name of being gone before the man was able to call in reinforcements.

His inevitable return with friends being the only part of this whole damn scenario Remington knows for certain.

"We're okay," Remington replies, the answer drawing a small snort from Cortland beside him. A faint sound letting it be known that they are actually a hell of a long way from okay, but given the sliding scale of their new reality, they are as well as can be expected.

A little bruised and battered, but still breathing, which is more than the majority of their attackers can claim.

"Had a little late-night visit from a few goons," Remington adds.

"How many?" Val asks. Her first words of the conversation, Remington was not aware she was listening in, or even awake.

A new voice that causes Shine to tilt her head, trying to place it.

"Hey, Val," Cortland says. A quick greeting that manages to relay more his exhaustion and the comedown after the fight than any true salutation.

"Hey, hon," Valentina replies. "You doing okay?"

"We're good," Cortland replies. "All three of us, which is two-thirds better than our uninvited guests."

"Three of them, huh?" Tyrell asks, jumping back in. "How'd they came at you?"

"Hot," Remington replies. "On foot. Two from the front, one from the side. Shine was with me when they got here, alerted on them. Cort and I were waiting when they got within range."

"Damn," Val mutters. A single syllable extended for several seconds, still audible as Tyrell asks, "You give them hell?"

"As much as we could with one handgun," Remington answers. "Shot one out front. The other two breached, went to fisticuffs before we got the other one. Third made it out while we were dealing with his friend."

The telling is an extremely scrubbed version of events, though right now Remington isn't in the mood for going through the full blow-by-blow. There will be plenty of time for that later, when everybody is gathered, watching and waiting, or formulating an attack.

Until then, broad strokes are sufficient. A baseline overview, ignoring mistakes that were made and opposition that remains.

Things that will only further piss Remington off. An infusion of angst that is the last thing he needs after the cheap shot from the Hispanic bastard, targeting his prosthetic leg.

A dirty move making it almost certain he was the one to go after Maylinn.

A universal lack of integrity, regardless of opponent.

"You need us to come down?" Tyrell offers for no less than the fourth time. Three previous extensions that Remington parried, this time having no intention of doing so.

"That's why we called," Remington replies. "Think you can close up the shop for the weekend?"

"We already did," Val answers. "Put a sign on the door before we took off this evening. Don't call us, we'll call you."

Whether their relatively new business, just starting to grab a solid toehold in the Memphis market, can afford such a thing, Remington isn't really concerned with right now. Their primary investor currently sits just a few inches away, and the task they've been asked to help with stems directly from him.

"Drive or fly?" Tyrell asks.

"As fast as you can get here," Remington answers. "They won't know you, won't be looking for you."

"There's usually a 6:10 out of Memphis that flies direct," Cortland adds. "I've made that trip myself a couple times."

"We'll be on it," Tyrell replies, not bothering to ask what they should bring or how long to pack for. Questions that can be sorted out later, none of the people on the call in the mindset for travel logistics.

Least of all Remington.

"We'll see you soon," he says, extending a finger and ending the call there. An extinguishing of light and sound that feels especially pronounced, neither brother saying anything for a few moments. Time for them both to continue processing what took place earlier.

An encounter Remington has already been through three times in his head, enough to have pushed by the initial anger and to have begun examining things from a tactical standpoint. The small force that was used and the method of approach and what their intended goal was.

Quick kills, the main difference between this and what happened to Maylinn being there would be no hiding it.

Concerns pushed aside either in the name of making it go away, or simply no longer caring. Confirmation that they have the sheriff on their payroll and an announcement that they are willing to go to war for this.

A feeling that becomes more apparent within Remington with each passing moment.

"I've got to ask," Remington says, "and I don't want you taking it personal, okay?"

Glancing over his way, Cortland asks, "What?"

"How far you willing to take this? Because from this moment on..."

Remington is aware that the timing probably comes off a bit indelicate. Pressure he doesn't intend to exert, more a direct result of the situation than anything else. A scenario they had no hand in crafting, forced to do the best they can with it.

What started as a service to Maylinn, now taken so much further.

"I made Maylinn a promise a couple days ago," Remington adds. "You didn't."

Slowly rotating his gaze back to the moonlight flickering across the water, Cortland bends his left arm upward from the elbow. His fingers splayed and his thumb pointed toward the sky, he lets Remington see the pale inside of his wrist before saying, "Three days ago, my wife was killed. A couple hours ago, we both almost died. My house is probably gone. Same for all my possessions. Every memory Maylinn and I shared.

"I'd say we're past asking how far we're willing to go. I think it's time to start asking what we need to do next."

Grunting softly, Remington whispers, "MCB?"

"MCB."

CHAPTER SIXTY-FOUR

If Tony, with the hair and teeth and necklaces, is what Remington expected a guy who specializes in moving or destroying stolen or criminal vehicles to look like, Victor is what he would draw up as the quintessential used car salesman. A complete reversal of stereotypes and appearances, as if each is trying entirely too hard to lean away from what is expected. A means of hiding out in the open, subverting expectations while maintaining their preferred vocations.

Carrying at least thirty extra pounds of fat, all of it is concentrated around Victor's waistline. Robust girth that gives the impression of impending pregnancy, proudly displayed shirtless and without hair of any kind. A polished pale orb serving as the focal point of his body, everything else growing increasingly thin as it extends outward. Arms and legs without a bit of muscular development, wrapped in skin that has never seen the sun.

The top of his head lost a battle with male pattern baldness years ago, the addition of a mustache doing little to offset.

Perched on a recliner in the center of his trailer, a pair of much younger and much too attractive ladies rest on either arm of it. Both also dressed only in underwear, they lean inward, forcing smiles onto their faces as they run their hands down the length of his chest.

"Working girls," Remington mutters, lowering himself beneath the sill of the front window he has been staring through. Glass so spotted with dried water and covered in dust that he can barely get a clear view into the fishbowl that is the interior of the trailer.

The only upside being that there is not a chance in hell anybody is peeking back out at him.

A visit that was the best answer Remington could give to his brother's question as to what they do next. A choice for movement, being proactive, as opposed to sitting alongside the farm pond and waiting for Tyrell and Val to arrive.

A long night that neither of them would be sleeping through anyway, also providing the best time to pay a visit to the man who first sold them out. The one directly responsible for the silver F-350 tailing them the night before.

The counterpart responsible for tonight's visit likely to be their second stop.

"Huh?" Cortland asks, his face twisted up as he glances over while crouching at the base of the trailer, staring up the gravel lane they just walked down. Eighty yards of dirt and rocks and potholes, framed by pine trees and rusting vehicles on either side.

A location and appearance – both in person and in residence – far from what Remington was expecting.

"He's in there with hookers," Remington replies. Jutting his chin toward the dented Ford Mustang sitting by the corner of the trailer, he adds, "Not a snowball's chance those two came here of their own accord."

"Nice," Cortland spits in derision. "We literally caught him with his pants down."

Snorting softly, Remington replies, "Not quite, but close enough."

Rising back to full height, Remington allows himself one more look inside the trailer. A quick check to make sure the man he assumes to be Victor is still distracted before turning his attention to the rest of the interior. A place that gives the distinct impression of a college frat house, the signs of arrested development on plain display. Beer cans and pizza boxes and carpet stains that no adult who is even semi-functional would allow.

A rat's den that solidifies the initial assumption that the two women inside are here only because they are being paid to be.

Quite handsomely at that, Remington would venture.

"Here's how we'll play this," Remington says. "There's no point in trying to use misdirection, having you knock on the window or go around the back. Those two sets of boobs in there are already doing plenty of that for us."

Cortland's eyebrows rise a bit in surprise, a hint of confusion setting in, though he says nothing.

"We'll go with straight force instead," Remington replies. "The door is probably unlocked, so I'll pull it open, you go in first since you can move faster than me. Yell a few times, get the girls screaming, I'll come in and do the rest."

This time, Cortland nods before asking, "Which is?"

"Depends on what Victor does," Remington answers.

Lifting his feet to get past the tall weeds and rusted beer cans lining the base of the trailer, Remington circles out into the dusty roundabout serving as a driveway. With each step, he can feel the distal end of his left leg aching, the low throb the most lingering part of his fight earlier.

A stiffness that is something akin to an ankle sprain, the shot coming in from the back and twisting the prosthetic away, wrenching his knee. A reminder with each step of what happened. The man he was faced off against and the complete lack of honor – or even basic humanity – he possesses.

A deficit Remington will be sure to remember during their next encounter.

Careful to lift his feet with each step to avoid making any unnecessary noise, Remington comes in straight at the set of rusted metal stairs leading to the front door. A freestanding piece with more garbage and cigarette butts spilling over the side, falling into the weeds pushing up on either end.

"You ready?" he asks.

"Ready."

"You want the gun?" Remington asks, already knowing the answer.

Matching him step for step toward the door, Cortland says, "Doesn't sound like I'll need it."

"No," Remington agrees, increasing his pace. A bit of momentum to allow him to hop straight onto the top stair. "And you won't be there but a second without me anyway."

Saying nothing more, Remington slides his body to the side. His pulse rising, he reaches across and grabs the metal handle to the door. Twisting it open, he jerks it straight back to release a plume of chilled air and smoke, the dank tang of cannabis bursting forth before rising towards the heavens.

A cloud that dissipates in an instant, allowing Cortland to rush in. The bass in his voice amplified by a factor of three, he yells, "Nobody move!"

A single command that does exactly as Remington expected, eliciting squeals from both of the girls. High-pitched cries that reverberate through the tiny space, still echoing from the metal walls as he steps inside behind his brother, pulling the door shut behind them.

"You, you," Cortland yells, pointing to each of the girls in turn. "To the back, now!"

Caught in the middle of whatever twisted game they were playing just seconds before, none of the three moves. All frozen in place, they stare straight ahead, the girls both rigid with hands raised before them, Victor sitting with the slightest hint of a grin on his face.

A smile that is the last thing Remington is up for, reaching straight to the small of his back and drawing his gun. Snapping it out before him, he watches as the girl's eyes widen, focusing on the weapon, before yelling, "*Now!*"

A second round of squeals erupt from the girls. Twin shrill cries as they leap from either arm of the chair and run for the hallway, their feet moving no more than inches at a time in short shuffling steps.

A parade of lace and bare flesh that Cortland follows, going to seal them into the back. An exit Victor tries to take advantage of, his hand sliding over the side of the chair and into the pocket sewn into the side.

A reach for his phone or a weapon, Remington not caring which as he steps forward and swings the gun across his body.

A backhanded pistol whip that makes solid contact, snapping Victor's head to the side, sending bloody spittle into the fetid carpet below.

CHAPTER SIXTY-FIVE

Compared to the threadbare recliner in the living room, the wooden kitchen chair is a seat barely sufficient to hold Victor's bulbous frame. Four spindly wood legs that appear to be visibly trembling, topped by a basic wooden seat and a pair of arms snaking up on either side.

A piece of furniture first made as part of a matching set decades before, somehow having found its way here, alongside three others of varying colors and materials. A hodgepodge collection matching everything else in the trailer, looking like it would be best served as kindling for a bonfire.

A blaze that – if the smell in the air is any indicator – would prob-ably make a decent chunk of the surrounding area high on THC for days.

His prodigious midsection wedged in between the arms on either side, Victor sits with his shoulders tilted to the side, his chin lolling between them. Tongue extended from under his mustache, a string of bloody spittle connects his mouth and stomach.

Each inhalation is forced in through his nose, audible throughout the trailer.

"Victor Korneky," Cortland says, checking the name on the

driver's license in the man's wallet. Holding it up before him, he places the image on it side by side with the man in the chair, trying to draw some parallel between the two.

A task that is damn near impossible, the passage of eighteen years having been especially cruel.

"At least, I think. This thing shows a guy with hair it claims weighs a buck-seventy-nine."

Snorting loudly, Remington stands off to the side, his hands both wrapped in gloves. Thick leather taken from the back of Tyrell's pickup truck where Shine still waits, brought here to act as protective cushioning for the ongoing interrogation.

Coverings not to lessen the blows to Victor, but to protect his own underlying fingers and bones from impact.

"I have a hard time believing Ol' Vicky here ever weighed south of two bills," Remington answers, "but that's just me."

Allowing one corner of his mouth to crease back, Cortland delves deeper into the wallet. An item of cracked and fraying leather that should have been disposed of around the time his driver's license photo was taken, filled with a collection of things from a different time period.

"Let's see here," Cortland continues. "We've got three credit cards, expired-" pulling out the first one, he checks the date at the bottom, before continuing, "last year."

Tossing it onto the floor, he goes to the next in order. "In twenty-sixteen."

Chucking it down with the previous one, he slides out the third, a Visa used so many times the paint is just barely visible. "Oh, and our winner here, from two-thousand-and-eight. Nice."

Balanced in his chair, Victor attempts to respond. A garbled mess that gets no further before Remington steps in, swinging his hand across his body. A backhand shot unleashing a bit of the acrimony that Cortland knows his brother has been carrying since they left the house earlier. Brewing hatred best let loose, before it begins to consume him.

There being no better target than the man before them, clearly affiliated with whoever stormed his house this evening. A man who might not be on the inside, but has a close connection sufficient to have put a tail on them the night before.

No matter how many times he might claim otherwise.

The impact of the blow sends Victor's head to the side, his padded chin acting as a point of contact as it swings all the way out to his shoulder. A pendulum releasing more bloody saliva onto the ground before going back in the opposite direction. Kinetic energy takes it back and forth in increasingly smaller amounts before finally it returns to position, his nose pointed straight down.

Pretending to have seen nothing, Cortland goes back to the man's wallet. A quick search that reveals a Blockbuster card and a student ID at Austin Community College. Potential sources of amusement that he and Remington could banter about all evening, but there is no point.

Victor is on the verge of breaking.

Anything they are going to get from him needs to happen now.

Dropping the wallet into the mess of paper napkins and fast-food wrappers littering the sticky linoleum of the kitchen floor, Cortland heads back toward the recliner in the center of the room. The throne for this derelict palace. The spot from which all business is conducted.

"I think we're going about this wrong," Cortland says. Crossing onto the dirty loop carpet of the living room, he adds, "Something tells me there's a reason our friend here keeps a revolver in the side pocket of his recliner."

Going to the small metal end table just beyond arm's reach of the central chair, Cortland leaves the gun where it lays. A weapon Remington had already confiscated and removed the bullets from before Cortland even made it back from locking the girls inside the bedroom.

A dank and nasty space that he almost felt bad about leaving them in, easing his conscious by promising that they wouldn't be there long.

That alone acting as far more assurance than telling them they weren't going to be hurt.

Reaching instead for the cellphone resting on the table beside it, Cortland picks it up and taps the screen, bringing it to life. Unencumbered by facial recognition or a password of any kind, he goes to the home screen and scrolls through a list of downloaded apps, ranging from Dominos Pizza to something called Pornhub. Offerings that make his stomach turn as he swipes through as quick as he can, starting first with the text messaging center.

The top entry in the list is from the service that sent the two girls. A quick back and forth specifying number and type that has clearly happened many times before, causing Cortland's lip to curl back in a sneer as he goes to the next in order.

Another that is just as fruitless, this one with his pot dealer, asking for two more ounces of something called Purple Haze. A product and amount Cortland can't pretend to be familiar with, though judging by the smell permeating every molecule of the cabin, he is guessing Victor is already most of the way through.

A standard Friday night at the Korneky trailer.

"Anything?" Remington asks from across the room.

"Not in his text messages," Cortland replies. "Though without any names, it's kind of hard to know what to look for."

"Try the phone log from yesterday," Remington says. "Look for a 901-area code, and then see who he called next."

Recognizing the numeric prefix from Remington's own cellphone number, the trio of digits assigned to the entire Memphis area, Cortland grunts in agreement. Retreating back to the home page, he does as instructed, finding the recent log and scrolling down through.

"Alright, we've got one incoming here yesterday at 5:33," Cortland says. "And right after that, we've got an outgoing call to someone named Enzo." Looking up to his brother, he adds, "Gold star beside it, meaning important contact."

Dipping his chin in agreement, Remington rolls his attention over to the side. Putting his focus square on Victor, he asks, "Enzo, huh? That wouldn't happen to be a guy with dark hair and a wicked scar down his face, would it?"

Again, Victor manages nothing more than a string of mumbles. Gurgling that ends with what Cortland guesses to be, "Go to hell."

A directive his brother ignores completely, continuing with, "Thinks he's some kind of Mexican cowboy?"

"Piss off," Victor wheezes.

"Snap button shirts and Levi's and all the rest?" Remington adds.

Gloved hands still curled up into fists, he manages to restrain himself from unleashing another shot. Self-control that isn't from lack of wanting, but understanding that this is their last chance to get anything of use from the man.

The next shot he takes likely to be his last for the night.

Eyelids fluttering, Victor manages to roll his head to the side. Lifting his chin toward Remington, he gives his best approximation of defiance before saying, "You'll have to kill me first."

Matching his gaze, Remington says nothing for several moments. Nearly a full minute before the despisal he harbors for the man cracks, a thin smile tracing his features.

"We'll do you one better," he says. Glancing to Cortland, he dips his head forward, motioning toward the hallway. "Go open the bedroom door. Tell the girls we got everything we need and we're leaving.

"They're free to go and take anything they want."

Turning back, he leans forward a few inches as the smile fades from his features.

"There. Now we don't have to kill you. They will."

CHAPTER SIXTY-SIX

If Enzo had it his way, he'd pile Hector and Ramon onto the living room floor of the Alder house. Side by side, he'd make sure to splash them with more of the gasoline currently saturating the sofa, kitchen table, and staircase banister, providing plenty of accelerant to a hasty cremation.

One less pain in the ass for him to deal with now, having wrapped them both tight and lugged them into the back of his truck, preparing them for transport.

And a far better ending for his friends than ending up as hyena shit, which he knows to be what Leo Garcia intends for them. Fresh meat that won't constitute the same thrilling viewing as a hunt, but will at least keep the taste in their mouths and the smell in their nostrils.

A useful means of disposing of two trusted and loyal employees Garcia had claimed, though Enzo knows the truth. The orders to feed them to the animals is a shot at him. A brutal point made without him having to say a word.

A message that doesn't need to be sent, Enzo already plenty pissed about everything that has happened since running that damned Tesla off the side of the road a few nights earlier. The call from Victor and the sighting of the truck with Tennessee plates the night before and the battle that played out just hours ago.

An easy removal of a problem that has happened a dozen times before, though somehow on this one has spiraled upward, threatening to get out of control. Enemies that were either severely underestimated or research that was hasty and incomplete, which one really not mattering, all that does now being to finish things quickly and definitively.

Otherwise, he too will end up as animal excrement, either at the hands of his sudden nemeses, or from that of his employer.

"What are we waiting on?" Cesar asks. A metal lighter with a spring-loaded top in hand, he flips it open and closed in a practiced sequence, snapping his wrist and letting momentum pop it wide before slapping it into his opposite palm. A nervous tic that is now numbering well into the twenties, adding itself to the list of annoyances for the night.

A habit far outweighing any benefit provided by the kid knowing to largely keep his mouth closed.

"Shut the hell up," Enzo snaps, watching as a flash of headlights moves across what's left of the front windows of the house. Square orbs that slow to almost a complete stop before turning into the driveway. Sweeping across the front of the place, they grow steadily larger, framing Enzo and Cesar inside.

Impromptu spotlighting that the younger man visibly shrinks from, raising a hand to block out the glare.

Movements that Enzo takes no part in, instead leaving the fumes of the house for the front porch, wanting the sheriff to see the annoyance on his features. The injuries he sustained earlier.

The look of outright defiance, daring the man to say a single damn word about what took place, or what is intended.

Pulling even with the truck sitting halfway down the driveway, the driver's side door of the cruiser swings open. From it emerges Jeff Daubenmire in jeans and an unzipped sweatshirt, the tails of it hanging down on either side of his waist. Taking but a single step forward, he pauses alongside Enzo's truck and balances a hand on the edge of the bed, rising onto his toes to peer down inside. A quick glimpse at Hector and Ramon in their makeshift burial shrouds before shaking his head and turning toward the house.

Framed by the front lamps of his cruiser behind him, Daubenmire's silhouette grows increasingly distorted as he approaches. Walking slower than necessary, he buries his hands into the front pockets of his sweatshirt. His head swings to either side as muted grumbling can be heard.

Commentary and admonishments that Enzo is not in the mood for, working his tongue around the inside of his mouth before spitting out the last bits of dried blood that had been stuck between his teeth. Black flecks that he can taste on his tongue, spiking the hostility he feels.

After what took place, there was no way to avoid calling Garcia. The mission was supposed to rid them of a headache, instead creating multiple new ones. An original problem that is now even further from being complete, coupled with the loss of multiple men and the inclusion of the local police, there no way to hide the gunfight that went down earlier once daylight breaks.

To even try would have been taken as a direct challenge. Enzo going into business for himself, acting against the best wishes of Garcia and his mother and the entire organization. A decision that – thirty years together or not – would have got his ass tossed into the compound behind the mansion. The latest spook story to be shared with new employees, listening to his screams as the flesh was ripped from his body.

"Do I even want to know what happened here?" Daubenmire asks by way of greeting. Stopping at the decorative display on the corner of the driveway and the front walk, he makes no effort to come closer, even as his gaze dances across the front of the home. His nostrils rise in a deep sniff, seeming to pick up the combination of gunpowder and gasoline in the air.

"It's not your concern what happened," Enzo says. Walking straight across the porch, he stops just short of the top step, staring down at the sheriff. A perch on high to let the man see the full extent of his injuries. The snarl on his features.

An open dare for him to say something else. Push back in any way that will give Enzo a reason to come flying down at him.

"You're here about what happens next."

His focus continuing to roam, Daubenmire glances to the smears of Hector's blood on the porch. Fixating there for a moment, he then shifts to take in Cesar exiting the front door, still flicking his damned lighter open and shut.

"Please tell me you're not about to-"

"Send a message," Enzo says, cutting him off. "That's what we're about to do. And if you don't want to become one yourself, I suggest you get onboard."

Snapping a hand out to the side, Enzo snatches the lighter away from the younger man. Flicking the top open, he sparks the tip of it, sending an inch-tall flame of blue and yellow upward.

An ignition source that he tosses back over his shoulder, waiting only to hear the telltale woosh of the flames catching before stepping down off the porch and heading across the lawn toward his truck.

CHAPTER SIXTY-SEVEN

One of the first rules Remington was given about having a prosthesis was the need to have it off for at least three or four hours each night. A bare minimum that would preferably be more like six or eight, matching his sleep schedule. Time to let his distal limb rest from carrying the extra weight and to remove the tight sleeves encasing it. Needed hours for the skin to breathe without becoming raw and for proper blood flow to be maintained.

A break that Remington is usually scrupulous about observing, forcing himself to strip everything bare each night, no matter how tired or how many beers he might have had before turning in. His own nightly ritual, the way most people brush their teeth or remove their contacts.

One that tonight, for the first time in ages, there is zero chance he will be observing. Not after what happened earlier, and the very real probability that the man who escaped – and many others – are out looking for them.

Back on the rear tailgate of the truck beside the farm pond, Remington has his left heel propped under him, his knee pointed to the sky. His head cocked to the side, he inspects the shaft of the artificial limb, running his finger the length of it.

"Everything okay?" Cortland asks, standing in the grass between the truck and the edge of the pond. Feet planted perpendicular between the two, he has a bag of treats in hand, tossing them to Shine.

"Yeah," Remington replies. Feeling a small dent, he runs his finger over it, ensuring that the material isn't chipped, before lowering his leg back over the edge of the tailgate. "Damn thing is made of titanium. Going to take more than a piece of cheap pine to break it."

"Cedar, actually," Cortland says, flinging another dog biscuit out before turning to give Remington a half smile. A small crease of his features that is likely the closest to mirth he can manage right now. "And it sure as hell wasn't cheap."

Knowing full well his brother is just trying to lighten the mood, ease the simmering tension that has existed since Remington first woke him hours before, Remington can only manage a similar smile. A small grin paired with a smirk, his gaze rising to the faint smudge of light in the distance. Residual glow from the city that in just a few short hours will be replaced with the rising sun.

The start of a Saturday that for most will include errands and farmer's markets and college football games. Tens of thousands of people congregating at bars and around televisions to watch the Longhorns thrash some overmatched non-conference opponent.

A proper Saturday, even if Remington's own fan allegiance trends somewhere other than burnt orange. An option he would gladly take, though, if only to be back in Austin under any other circumstances.

Instead of sitting on the tailgate of a borrowed truck, he would be back in his adopted room on the second floor. Shine would be curled up near the end of the bed, nuzzled into the opening left by his missing foot. His brother would be asleep in his own bed, in his own home.

With his wife by his side.

The start of a list of things that Remington wishes, even knowing full well he can do nothing to bring them about. A game he played after his own accident with unnerving frequency, lying awake at night and trying to envision different sequences that put him anywhere but in that Humvee at that particular moment.

A ritual that started to border on fetish before he cast it aside, in no small part from the help of Maylinn. Their daily chats out on the back porch and the assistance she provided in helping him secure a professional to talk to.

Things he can specifically remember thanking her for, even if it still feels drastically short of the gratitude deserved.

"Where you at over there?" Cortland asks. A handful of treats cradled in the palm of his hand, he glances over while waiting for Shine to finish the last offering. A job that Remington can hear her going at with vigor, even if he can't make out anything beyond the darkened silhouette of her body along the water's edge.

"Just...Victor," Remington replies. "And next steps."

Forced to wager on it, Remington would say that the man he fought with earlier was the Enzo from Victor's phone. The name and ethnicity fit. So did his age and the way he carried himself. A guy of some standing, who would likely be the one to field such a call.

At the very least, he is a right-hand sort. The person that the real Enzo turns to with such assignments, making him a direct conduit. A solid place for them to begin looking once Tyrell and Val arrive.

"Which are?" Cortland asks.

"Which are - you should sleep," Remington says. A reply that gets much the response he was anticipating, his brother lifting a hand to wave it away.

A dismissive gesture paired with a sound of the same sort, followed by him saying, "So should you, but here we are."

"Right," Remington answers. "Here we are."

After leaving the house in the immediate aftermath of the fight, they had considered going to a hotel somewhere. Finding a cheap place to bunk up, rest, put together some sort of a plan. A pipe dream that they both dismissed quickly, reasoning that if the sheriff was on Maylinn's killer's payroll, he would have an alert out for them by morning.

Even trying to pay cash likely wouldn't insulate them, their descriptions out to every place in the area by dawn.

"Okay," Remington concedes, "well, the way I see it, we now have two things working for us. One, obviously, this Enzo guy from Victor's phone."

"Who may or may not know we're onto him, depending on if Victor decided to tell him about our visit or not."

Forced to wager, Remington would say there is no chance that a word of their recent stop will make it back up the ladder. Whatever loyalty a man like Victor might possess is always going to be outweighed by self-preservation.

He won't want to overthink it and risk putting a target on himself.

"And Reseda," Remington says.

Turning over his hand, Cortland dumps out the remaining treats he was holding. Rubbing his palm against the leg of his jeans, he turns toward Remington and walks a few steps closer, his features coming into view under the pale moonlight.

"Reseda?"

"Reseda," Remington repeats. "Before all this went down tonight, we were talking about how he seemed a little too comfortable with deriding the lawsuit. The sort of thing that hinted he'd talked about it at length."

Pausing there, he gives his brother a moment to pick up on the thread that Remington was considering before the arrival of the men earlier. One of several he was trying to unravel prior to calling Tyrell, still trying to put together how the tail had found them the night before.

A question that had led them to Victor, but still left open the issue of timing.

"If Victor had been the only source," Remington says, "they

would have come for us last night. They wouldn't have waited until tonight to make a move."

Grunting in understanding, Cortland asks, "So you think last night they just sent someone to check on us? Probably saw you, the truck, and let it go?"

"Yes, but when they got a second call today about us snooping around, they decided to act on it."

————

The walk from the rundown Buckhorn Motel where Remington and Cortland were spending the summer to the tattoo parlor was exactly three blocks. One-hundred-and-fifty yards past a string of small businesses including the laundromat where they washed their clothes and the diner where they ate dinner at least four nights a week. The bank branch and lawyer's office they'd been to a dozen times each in the six weeks since their grandfather's death, settling up his affairs.

A task that largely fell to Cortland to handle, though his brother dutifully went with him to every meeting between training runs and trips out to the high school to use the weight room with the kids getting ready for football season.

Preparation of his own for what waited ahead.

Taking it extra slow to account for Shine still getting used to working with only three limbs, the trip to the shop took just over five minutes. Time enough that they were able to discuss things one last time, each asking the other if they were sure they wanted to go through with this.

Confirmation that they both already knew, the original notion for such a thing first broached years ago, when they began working for their grandfather. Cortland, as the de facto CFO for the family business, handling the books even long before he was handed the ledger and sent out to serve as the figurehead. Remington, the driver and muscle for the operation, lugging gallons of homemade moonshine and ensuring none of the customers ever got any ideas.

A track record that was perfect right up to that very last delivery.

Chores of the business that G had handled himself for years before age and lack of interest made him hand them off, making Cortland and Remington both official Moonshine Creek Boys.

Refraining from going through with things then, the topic had again come up after their grandfather's death. An idea that Remington pushed forth originally as a standalone act, the two batting it around before folding it into their larger plans. The first step in a sequence that would be their last act before heading their separate ways in the fall.

A farewell both to their home and the man who took them in, not knowing when or even if they might return.

Something solid to ground them, that they could look at not just in the days ahead, but in the years that followed.

A way to remind themselves who they are. Where they come from.

What they are capable of.

Reaching the door first, Remington grabbed the handle and pulled it open, the string of sleigh bells on the backside announcing their arrival to the three men inside. Guys who looked to have more or less already called it a day, one seated in a tattoo chair with an ankle raised to his opposite thigh, the other two in visitor chairs. Beers in hand, both looked to have been under the needle a number of times before, their exposed arms lined with various images.

In the middle of a lively conversation, all three fell silent as they turned toward the door. The grins they were wearing slowly faded, their gazes tracing between Cortland, Remington, and Shine between them.

A slow bit of dawning that caused the man in the tattoo chair to lower his feet to the floor and slowly push himself upright. Rising to full height, the top of his graying curls stood an inch taller than Cortland, his bare arms a bit thicker than Remington's. Dressed in boots and jeans, he wore a leather vest with the name Chewy stitched onto it over a plain black tank top.

"Help you boys?" *he asked.*

"Yes, please," Cortland answered. "If you're still open. If not, we can come back."

Ignoring the question entirely, Chewy's gaze narrowed slightly. "Your G's grandsons, aren't you? From up Moonshine Creek?"

"Yes, sir," Cortland answered, followed a moment later by Remington adding, "That's why we're here."

Flicking his gaze between them, he said nothing, silently contemplating something before beginning to bob his chin. A slight nod going no more than a centimeter in either direction.

"Go ahead and get in the chair. Whatever you want, it's on the house."

CHAPTER SIXTY-EIGHT

The quartet of young men lining the far side of the ring have barely been awake for a cumulative total of twenty minutes. Just five minutes each separating all four of them from slumber, the looks on their faces confirming as much. A collection of eyes that are still half matted shut, with pillow marks striping their cheeks. Hair that is standing up at odd angles.

Two of the guys are wearing boxer shorts and plain white under-shirts. Another dons gym shorts and a ribbed tank top.

Aguilar didn't even make it as far as pulling on a shirt, standing in jeans two sizes too large, a belt cinched tight the only thing keeping them on his narrow hips. Skinniness made more pronounced by the pair of boxing gloves enveloping either hand. Coverings that look cartoonishly large at the end of his thin arms, hanging just past his waist.

Standing with his back to the ropes on the opposite side of the ring, it is all Leo Garcia can do not to go rushing straight across at them. Running in without warning of any kind, he would love nothing more than to charge their way, mashing into them, sending their unsuspecting bodies flying.

Instant gratification that wouldn't be nearly sufficient, Garcia needing this to serve as actual relief. A way of getting out some of the carnal rage hurtling through him, lowering his acrimony to a level that will at least allow him to think. A clear head so he can plan things moving forward, even if there is no chance at finding rest.

Stripped bare to the waist himself, Garcia can feel the cool touch of night on his skin. The lowest point in the daily temperature cycle, dawn still a couple of hours away. Daylight that will soon enough begin to pass through the sliding doors standing open to either side, though for now darkness is all that exists.

Light spills out in either direction, striping the ground. To Garcia's left, he can see the base of a tree with a rock bed around it, a few junipers snaking up through the center. Framing for a wooden bench that, to his knowledge, not one single ass has ever touched. Decoration that has to be painted twice a year, but nothing more.

On the right, bare lawn stretches into the distance. Grass clipped low and kept free of weeds, the tops sparkling with the droplets recently unleashed from the buried sprinkler heads.

Another expense Garcia is considering when his gaze is pulled to the flash of movement in the distance. An approaching figure that causes palpitations to rise through Garcia's core, his eyes narrowing as he stares out. A pointed look that draws over the attention of the others as well, each head turning as Enzo comes into view.

Emerging from the darkness, he looks to be fresh from the accountant's house. Having not yet even cleaned himself up, the left side of his face is still painted with dried blood. What remains of his shirt hangs at an angle, the shoulder of it and the leg of his jeans both crusted over, tugging at the skin they cling to.

His head still angled down in a mix of anger and shame, he cleaves a path through the droplets resting atop the ground. A trail through the cropped grass that ends with wet footprints on the gym floor as he steps inside, lifting his eyes just far enough to nod at Garcia.

"It's done."

For most men in Garcia's position, the words would be a bit of relief. A task completed in a thorough and timely manner. One less item on a list to be done that has grown almost unwieldy as of late.

The usual business of new arrivals and business acquisitions and ongoing money laundering, now coupled with increased demands and spiking overdoses and fledgling task forces.

The matter with the attorney was supposed to be an easy fix. Something that was snipped clean and swept away before it had the chance to become a real problem.

Which is exactly where it now stands. A litany of errors that have compounded, now including one of his own. The very thing Enzo is here to report, Garcia allowing his anger to push him into a hasty decision. A choice fueled by the sight of the photos of the accountant and his twin on the wall and Ramon and Hector lying dead on the floor.

When this all began, his chief goal was to remove a threat. Take care of a budding lawsuit that wasn't an issue in and of itself, but carried the real potential of exposing them. Opening their enterprise up to scrutiny that would reveal far more than Garcia can allow.

Standing in the Alder's living room, he had let the combination of things around him to make him act in haste. A decision steeped in wanting to send a message, making a point to whoever might dare come for them again.

A move that only now can he see was foolish. Reactive thinking that his mother always warned him against and he has prided himself on avoiding.

The type of shit others succumb to, but never him.

A far better use for the house would have been as bait, having Enzo and Cesar and whoever else sit on it for as long as necessary. A lure that they wouldn't be able to resist forever, eventually walking right into his trap.

The easiest possible means of finding them, instead turned into a damn bonfire. A display sure to both draw attention and prevent the brothers from ever returning.

A mistake that has been sitting in Garcia's core for much of the night, rising like bile along the back of his throat. A bitter taste that was the reason he drew the men across from him out of bed, needing somewhere to aim his frustration.

Venom that has now grown into wrath, the sight of Enzo still in his bloody rags and the news he just came to impart the last bits that Garcia can tolerate.

Without offering so much as a word of warning, he pushes himself out of the corner of the ring. Not bothering even with a mouthpiece, he raises his fists before him, charging straight across the open stretch of canvas.

Long, lumbering strides that leaves the quartet across from him flatfooted, openly staring as he approaches. Dumbfounded expressions on their faces, they remain rooted in place, even as Garcia starts his onslaught.

Beginning with the closest target, Garcia unfurls a vicious right hook. A shot with no opposition, the man not even lifting his gloves to defend himself. Contact that tosses him sideways into the ropes encircling the ring, his limp upper body slapping against them before melting into a puddle on the canvas.

An initial victim Garcia doesn't even bother to watch all the way to the deck, his focus moving to the second in order. A man with shaggy hair and beard who gets as far as his eyes widening before Garcia is on him, unleashing an uppercut that lifts the man up onto his toes before finishing him with an overhand right that drives him into the mat.

A hammer pounding on a spike, the man going flat to his stomach, both arms spread wide to either side.

A speed bump that Garcia steps over, his attention going to the last two in order. Men who opt to go with decidedly different tactics, the one in the ribbed tank top abandoning any pretense and ducking straight out of the ring. A full body dive between the top and second ropes, ending with his bare arms slapping against the concrete outside.

A cowardly exit that Garcia is about to scream out against, ordering him back inside, cut short by Aguilar coming straight at him. A flurry of left jabs and right crosses that pepper Garcia's face, the sting of contact traveling down his neck and into his shoulders. Impacts that push his head an inch to either side, his vision barely clearing one before the next arrives.

The sound of Aguilar's grunting finds Garcia's ears. The tang of his own blood crosses his tongue. The sensory outputs of combat that he absorbs, one after another, bracing against the attack until Aguilar begins to wane.

Fuel that he stows away, waiting until the young man begins to tire and slow, before firing back with every bit of animosity he possesses.

CHAPTER SIXTY-NINE

It was a throwaway line Lance Reseda used barely twelve hours earlier that told Remington everything he needs to know. Mention of the fresh beef that arrives at dawn each morning, Reseda and his brother the kind of hands-on owners who are there to greet it six days a week, helping to kickstart the processing cycle.

A bit of self-congratulations that has become his undoing, informing Remington and Cortland of the schedule the man keeps. The hour that he rises and exactly where to find him between that moment and when the rest of the world wakes.

A starting point that was added to easily enough, a simple online search giving them a home address for the only Lance Reseda in the greater Austin area, one of just seven in the entire country. A unique moniker that pointed them in the right direction, allowing them to make a pair of passes by the oversized house on the western edge of the city.

Reconnaissance runs forming the basis for the loose plan they are about to undertake. A scheme with plenty of room for improvisation, taking advantage both of the layout of the Reseda property and the early hour. A spread large enough to not have any immediate neighbors or a clear line of visibility to the road.

More than ten acres in total, accessible through a winding driveway going on back to a stately brick home.

An ideal setup for them to post up at the end. A vehicular blockade with Cortland at the wheel. A place for Reseda to put his focus, never noticing Remington tucked along the trunk of the enormous trees framing the driveway until the moment he chooses to reveal himself.

As a through-and-through scumbag, it was no surprise that someone like Victor, used to dealing with the criminal underworld, didn't buy what they were presenting. The two of them have each been through their share of shit, both together and individually. Stuff that keeps either from having what could be construed as spotless records. Bits of dirt made more glaring in the last several days by the assorted things happening. A targeted attack on their family that was neither warranted nor provoked.

Actions that have them both roiling with hostility, willing to do far more than they would have only a week before.

Even at that, there are still some lines neither is willing to cross. Killing armed intruders in a shootout at the house is one thing. Busting in and murdering a man tied to a chair in his own kitchen is quite another.

Well aware of such restrictions, it was known when they showed up at Victor's that it would be a long shot. A chance they had to take, hoping that he might try to cut a deal to save himself some abuse, but weren't too distraught when they didn't get anything more than a name and his cellphone.

First, because as Remington pointed out to the man, they know he will get his eventually.

And, more importantly, because they knew they had someone else to lean on. A guy who made a massive blunder in their earlier conversation by alluding to Maylinn. A barb that both pissed them off – Remington having to force himself to remain in the truck – and proved not only that he had discussed the matter, but that he had nothing to fear from it.

Candor that overrode basic civility, spilling out without him realizing it, even in the face of a total stranger.

A strong enough case on its own, solidified by the team of thugs who showed up at Cortland's house barely six hours ago.

Standing with his right shoulder pressed against the rough bark of the tree, Remington bends his left knee upward, emitting a small pop. Stiffness in the joint from the indirect shot taken earlier and the extended wear of his prosthetic. Long hours without a break, unlikely to end anytime soon.

Dressed in the same shorts and ribbed tank top he was wearing at the house earlier, he has added a long-sleeve t-shirt. Light protection against the cool night air, the calendar now resting in early November meaning that while daylight hours may still nudge well into the seventies, the temperature plummets at night. A drop that currently rests in the valley of its daily cycle, drawing goose bumps to his exposed skin.

Chills he will gladly take just to be out of the SUV parked nearby. His post for far too much of the last several days, forced to sit and listen to his brother conducting interviews just like the one with Reseda.

Interactions covering the full spectrum, from infuriating to devastating, the time for action now finally starting to come closer.

Movement that begins with Cortland rolling down the passenger window of his vehicle and saying, "Look alive, we've got lights on at the house."

Snapping his left foot down, Remington inches forward. Bending at the waist, he peers around the trunk of the tree, staring along the length of driveway beside him. Black asphalt that cuts through the lawn, bending away in a long arc before disappearing from view.

In the distance, he can hear the faint moan of gears gnashing. A garage door slowly being raised, followed a moment later by an engine turning over.

Drawing his gun over in front of him, Remington wraps his left hand around the base as well. A combat grip with arms both extended, the barrel pointed into the plush grass between his feet.

Small hits of adrenaline seep into his bloodstream, lifting his body temperature, as the same mechanical sound begins anew. The garage door being lowered back into position, hinting that Reseda is on the move.

Pulling back so that just his right eye can see past the bark of the oak tree, Remington counts off seconds, waiting as the faint glow of headlights appears. A pale light that grows steadily closer, accompanied by the low hum of an engine.

Feeling his pulse tick ever higher, Remington watches as the front of the vehicle comes into view. A midsized SUV with square front lamps that swing into position, moving at a steady clip.

An early morning weekend drive that ends much sooner than anticipated as Reseda spots Cortland parked across the end of the drive.

Forced to mash down on the brakes, the faint squeal of tires fighting for purchase calls out. The scent of scorched rubber crosses Remington's nose. The lights jerk to either side as the backend fishtails, needing ten full yards to come to a complete stop.

A final halt leaving the vehicle in the perfect position for Remington to raise his weapon and step out. Walking directly to the passenger side door, he jerks it open to see Lance Reseda sitting behind the wheel with eyes wide, his gaping mouth hooked downward in shock.

"Don't say a word," Remington says. Sliding down into the seat, he pushes the gun into his left hand, keeping it trained on Reseda as he uses his right to slam the door shut. "Just follow that SUV."

CHAPTER SEVENTY

Gone is any trace of the self-assured man from the previous afternoon, with his thick glasses and haughty smile and smart ass barbs about Cortland's wife. Words that he has played on loop throughout the entire drive to where they now find themselves, the shelter house not unlike the one where they met Louisa Gonzalez, though the location is infinitely different. A structure nestled along what is essentially an open meadow miles from the western outer belt encircling the greater Austin area. The first structure in what signage promises to be a bustling community hub in the near future, with ball diamonds and soccer fields and a central concession stand and restroom.

The kind of thing every suburb needs, this one started in anticipation of the rest of the city rushing out to meet it in coming years. Anticipatory development in the face of rapid expansion that Cortland remembered only because it was one of the last cases Maylinn took before leaving her job at the firm. A pro bono matter that she brought Cortland to scout, disguising it as a Sunday drive before pulling into the same small parking lot where Cortland and Reseda's

SUVs are now parked. A chunk of concrete not big enough to bother lining out into spaces, all of that slated for a later date.

Forced down onto one of the two picnic tables in the center of the shelter house, Reseda sits with his hands folded between his thighs. A pose that causes his shoulders to roll inward, making him appear half his usual size.

His hair, perfectly coiffed the day before, has been mussed, the gel in it making it stand up in a twisted mess.

All color has drained from his face as he stares up at Cortland, the initial bit of hope that appeared based on recognition dissipating as fast as it arose, giving way to open fear. Terror far surpassing anything Victor even began to exhibit, no matter how many threats were lobbed his way or shots from Remington were absorbed.

"Who are you, really?" Reseda asks. A bold move of asking the first question that he recognizes instantly as a mistake. Falling silent, he jerks his gaze down, staring intently at the bare wooden tabletop in front of him.

Four hours ago, the response to such a question would have been a hard backhand. Remington, donning the thick leather gloves, would have turned his arm into a whip, rotating at the waist to maximize impact. A blow like so many to Victor, snapping Reseda's head to the side, if not knocking him clean off the bench.

Physical violence that isn't the tact of choice this time, instead swapped out for psychological.

Fear in the form of the gun he used to gain entry into Reseda's vehicle, slamming it down flat onto the table. Loud contact that causes their captive to jump back in his seat, a single moan sliding from his lips.

Complete understanding that Remington drives home by saying, "You did enough talking yesterday. From now on, you speak only when and if my brother speaks to you. Got it?"

His entire upper body visibly trembling, Reseda manages a nod. A short, terse movement that allows another sound to escape, giving the impression that he may well soil himself soon.

As good an opportunity as they are going to get.

Certainly, far better than the entrenched defiance of Victor earlier.

"Who did you call when I left your office yesterday?" Cortland opens. A start right at the top, the last three days of chasing pictures of trucks or names on a case list having grown well past tiresome.

One of the many layers of bullshit that Cortland is over, the time having arrived for a name. Someone to point their attention to, instead of trying to spot vehicles tailing them or fight off men showing up at their house in the middle of the night.

His jaw sagging open an inch, Reseda lifts his gaze to stare at Cortland. Making a point of avoiding Remington – and the gun between them – his eyes widen as any remaining bit of blood drains from his face.

"What?" he mutters.

The question slides out reflexively, gone before he even realizes it, but that doesn't save him from Remington picking up the gun and mashing it down a second time. Even louder, the sound rolls out through the silent darkness, again causing Reseda to flinch.

"What did I *just* tell you?" Remington hisses through clenched teeth.

"I...you..." Reseda manages to mumble, his eyes pin-balling from Cortland to Remington and back.

"I, you, what?" Remington snaps. "And don't make me go over there and check your phone. We're going to find out, so you might as well just tell us."

Moisture rises to Reseda's eyes as his cheeks flush. Heat that is completely involuntary rising to the surface as once more he flicks his gaze between them. "Please," he whispers. "I can't. You don't unders-"

Cortland knows how the sentence will end, even before it is cut short by his brother snatching up the gun and firing a round into the dirt just beyond the back edge of the shelter house. An unexpected explosion of sound and scent that causes Reseda to visibly recoil, his feet rising from the ground as his entire body curls up on the bench seat.

The tears that glassed his eyes just moments before streak south over his cheeks. His breaths become short, bordering on hyperventilating.

"That was a warning," Remington says. "Next one goes in your ankle. And then your knee. And then your shoulder."

Mashing the gun down on the table, forcing Reseda to flinch again, he adds, "One joint at a time. Shots that won't kill you, but will hurt like hell and keep your body from ever operating right again."

More sputtering erupts from Reseda as he twists away a few more inches. Veins and tendons bulge the length of his neck as he turns over his shoulder, looking like he might either vomit or try to sprint away at any moment.

"And even that would be better than you deserve for what you assholes did to my wife," Cortland says. A segue to both answer Reseda's initial question, and keep him from slipping out of reach. Fear or desperation that could either cause him to clam up, or start spewing whatever he can think of to try and save his life.

Neither of which does them any good.

"You want to know who we are?" Cortland asks. "We are the family of that lawyer you sat in your office and made fun of yesterday."

"Which almost got your ass kicked then," Remington inserts.

"And probably should have," Cortland adds, "but we were trying to play nice then."

Pressing in tight beside him, his hip brushing against Cortland's shoulder, Remington leans across the table. Grabbing the front of Reseda's shirt, he jerks him back around, making him face forward.

"That shit ends here!" he barks. "So either start telling us why you all wanted my sister-in-law dead, or I start unloading this gun into your ass one bullet at a time!"

Hands raised to frame either side of his face, Reseda's features are bathed in a mixture of sweat and tears. Chin tilted away from

Remington's hand, his eyes widen, moving just a fraction of an inch to either side to take them both in.

"Dead?" he whispers. "When? What happened?"

"That's what you're about to tell us," Cortland answers. Leaning forward, he rests his weight on his outstretched forearms, bringing his nose to within inches of Reseda's. "Starting with, who the hell did you call after I left yesterday?"

CHAPTER SEVENTY-ONE

Once the initial dam breaks, the shock of the situation and the fear of the subject matter shoved to the side, Lance Reseda talks at a pace that, at times, is barely understandable. A verbal deluge of details and information that Cortland gets the distinct impression the man has been holding in for years. Release that appears to be almost cathartic.

An impromptu therapy session inside the shelter house, the story coming too thick and fast to be fabricated. One thing after another depicting a full visual of what they are up against.

A burgeoning empire with hooks into damn near everything in the area. An enemy that is both much greater than what Cortland imagined, and at the same time exactly what he would expect.

Someone with interests varied enough to be tangentially connected to something as seemingly benign as an environmental lawsuit, and sufficiently ruthless to go to such a degree to see it snuffed out.

Motivations that Cortland would have never – even if given years to sit and brainstorm every possibility – come up with if not for hearing the story Reseda just shared.

His wife's life ended because some arrogant kingpin was worried

375

it might infringe on one of his money laundering sites. Litigation that would have opened up all aspects of the business to scrutiny, including the massive capital infusion that kept it afloat some years back, and the continued reliance on cash as a means of conducting business since.

One of many funnels controlled by a man named Leo Garcia, worth far more to him than the life of some attorney who was refusing to go away quietly.

Abandoning his spot across the table from Reseda, Cortland now stands leaning against the support pole directly across from the man. Assuming one of his brother's favorite poses, his arms are crossed. Every so often, he flexes his left leg back.

Unable to even look at the man sitting a few feet away, his head is turned to the side, his stare fixed on the growing smudge of dawn just starting to form in the distance. A pale glow that will soon give way to the start of the day, their window with Reseda fast drawing to a close.

After that, people will start to question his absence, the thin story Remington had him call and give about a sick child only able to pass basic inspection for so long.

"How many people we talking here?" Remington asks, having inserted himself as the primary interrogator. An unspoken role switch after the full breadth of why Maylinn was targeted came out.

Another sledgehammer blow to the stomach, this one arguably surpassing all but that very first voicemail received from his wife, the only thing more shocking than her passing being the reason for it. Information he is still fighting to sort out, even while trying to listen to what Reseda is saying.

"Total?" Reseda asks. "I have no idea."

Shifting his gaze to the gun still resting in plain sight at the end of the table, he raises his hands in a sign of preemptive surrender and says, "Like I said before, we're not the only iron in the fire. Far from it. Garcia has an empire built on human trafficking and drug running. They only brought us in as a front to launder funds."

Lowering his hands back to his thighs, he continues, "We only regularly see three guys. Enzo, Hector, and Ramon show up once a week to swap out bags of cash, kind of kick the tires to make sure everything is still running okay. Once in a great while, Garcia himself will show up with a few of his personal security goons.

"But how many in total, I don't have a clue. Hell, I can't even tell you exactly how many other businesses they control around town."

When he falls silent, Remington slowly turns his gaze to meet Cortland's. A silent message relating to mention of the name they found in Victor's cellphone earlier.

"Enzo," Remington says, looking to confirm what they both already suspect. Running a finger down his cheek, he asks, "Dark hair. Facial scar?"

A question responded to in the affirmative, Reseda nodding forcefully enough to cause his hair to sweep across his forehead.

Confirmation that the man is a ranking officer in Garcia's regime, given tasks as disparate as picking up money to visiting Cortland's house in the middle of the night.

A player they will for sure be focusing on in the days ahead.

"Law enforcement?" Remington asks.

"Yes," Reseda replies. "APD, county sheriff, even some of the local prosecutors, if what I've been threatened with is all true."

Again, Remington turns to look at Cortland. A second knowing glance, this one with reference to mention of a county sheriff.

Further confirmation of details that were suspected, without prior sufficient means of proving them.

"And you believe them?" Remington asks. Rotating back to face Reseda, he clarifies, "The threats?"

Opening his mouth to reply, Reseda stops short before any sound escapes. Turning his head to the side, he exhales loudly through his nose, staring at the early bits of dawn on the horizon for several moments.

When he does begin to speak, his voice has shifted into a detached monotone, as if putting distance between himself and the subject matter.

"I explained to you already how it went down with us," he begins. "Rising costs of business, new zoning ordinances, all that stuff that left us in a lurch, thinking we'd fallen under a lucky star when Garcia first reached out wanting to invest."

Turning back to look their way, Cortland can see that again most of the color has bled from his face. His chin is tilted downward, his focus fixed on the tabletop before him, only occasionally rising to meet theirs.

"What I didn't share was how they sealed the deal. Invited my brother and me out to their estate outside the city for a nice dinner. Supposed to be this big kickoff celebration to a new working partnership.

"What it really was was their way of setting the hook. Letting us know that from that moment on, they owned us. And if we ever got out of line, questioned what was happening, tried to go to the cops with this, we'd end up down in that damn backyard compound with the hyenas."

Cortland can feel his brows come together as he stares at the man seated on the picnic table. Not sure if the last line is some sort of analogy or a literal retelling, he waits in silence for the man to continue.

Additional information it becomes clear he has no interest in sharing, his skin taking on a ghostly pallor, even as the first streaks of day pass across his features.

"Hyenas?" Remington asks. "You mean like-"

"Actual hyenas," Reseda says, bobbing his head for emphasis. "His nickname around town is Laughing Leo, because he has a whole damn pack of them in his backyard and he feeds anybody who dares cross him to them.

"Sits on his back porch and watches it happen. Listens to those damn things squeal as they do it. Even makes his new associates come and watch."

Lifting his face, Reseda swallows hard, tracking his gaze from Cortland to Remington and back, "I swear, none of us know until it's too late. We all want out, but how can we? He knows who we are. He knows who our families are."

Just as before, his mouth opens. More details to be shared or explanation to be given that doesn't make it out, his jaw left gaping in silence.

Solitude that settles inside the shelter house as all three men fall quiet. A few moments spent with each deep in thought, working through the shock of what was just shared or the resulting trauma of having witnessed it in the past.

A mountain of new information Cortland has no doubt will occupy his thoughts for days and weeks to come. Details about how his wife was tangentially connected and what was done to her as a result.

Data that for now he is forced to push a few inches to the side, instead focusing on a small reference Reseda made in his final few lines.

"How many others do you know of?"

CHAPTER SEVENTY-TWO

Enzo knows that the beating Aguilar took this morning was really intended for him. Blows that Leo Garcia would never aim his direction for a variety of reasons, none more so than the protected status afforded by Sofia. Protection stemming from some sort of long-standing debt, the woman the only reason Enzo still has a job and a roof over his head.

Hell, is probably even still breathing, something the young man by his side is currently having trouble with.

Kindness extended that Enzo knows is not without limit. This week has been his first error of any real magnitude in ages, granting him a tiny bit of leeway, but he can't bank on that forever.

This entire situation needs to go away fast, or even the umbrella of Sofia will be removed from over him, subjecting him to a fate much worse than his two friends nearby. Ramon and Hector both still stowed in the back of his pickup a few yards away, their bodies wrapped in sheets and blankets stolen from the Alder house.

The only items from inside the place to have survived the night, the rest probably reduced to ash by now.

Once Garcia was done with his little show in the gym this morning, his nitro burst of anger released, he'd stood in the ring over Aguilar's prone body. His bare torso gleaming with sweat and striped with blood spatter beginning to streak south, he'd stared down at Enzo for several moments before issuing two orders.

The first, to wake Aguilar's ass up and get him off the canvas.

Second, take him and Cesar and the others to the same site where they'd deposited the remains from the hyena attack just a couple days before and bury Hector and Ramon. A final resting place affording them the dignity of avoiding becoming wild animal chow themselves and little else.

A decision not steeped in civility, but in making another point. The none-too-subtle argument that the animals would be getting a live hunt soon enough and wouldn't need it.

The only question remaining being who would be the one to enter the compound.

"There's some water in the truck," Enzo says, depositing the load of sandy soil heaped on his shovel over his shoulder. Driving the point of it down into the ground, he balances his forearms atop the handle. Leaning forward, he slides his forehead across the sleeve of his right arm, using the fabric to wipe away the sweat covering his features and stinging his eyes.

After tossing the lighter into the house and stepping down off the porch earlier, Enzo had walked straight back to his truck. A quick march to the end of the driveway before sliding back behind the wheel, a couple of minutes all that was needed for the gasoline to do its job, engulfing the place in flames. Thick fingers of orange and yellow giving off the acrid scent of black smoke.

A beacon shining out into the darkness, without question visible for miles, up to and including any planes passing overhead.

A final lingering sight that Enzo did not agree with, but could admit was at least a little bit satisfying. The wholesale decimation of the place where his friends were killed and he came out on the losing end.

And a giant middle finger to the men responsible. A means of goading them, ensuring that they don't go underground.

"What?" Cesar asks, ceasing his work on the opposite end of the makeshift grave. The head of his shovel partially submerged in the soil, he looks up with his features scrunched, dirt staining his cheeks.

"Not you," Enzo says, flicking a finger toward Aguilar between them. Three men assigned to dig a resting place for Hector, the other trio doing the same a short distance away for Ramon.

Burial plots much deeper than the others, ensuring they aren't disturbed by any scavenging animals in the area.

"Aguilar," Enzo says. "Take a break. Go get some water."

A partial load of loose dirt balanced on the end of his shovel, Aguilar doesn't even attempt to turn and toss it on the growing mound heaped behind him. Simply tilting it to the side, he lets it slide free, keeping both hands on the handle as he rises to full height.

Stripped bare to the waist, his torso is painted in sweat, lined with errant streaks of mud and blood, the latter resulting from the open wounds to his right cheek and the left corner of his mouth. Cuts to go along with the goose egg enveloping his entire left eye, already swollen shut and starting to darken.

The beginning of what will be a purple baseball by morning, courtesy of the battering dished out by Garcia's right hook.

"I'm okay," Aguilar mutters, the words just barely audible.

"You sound like hell," Enzo says, evoking a snort from Cesar. "Go get some water."

His one remaining working eye just barely visible, Aguilar draws in another pained breath. The start of another retort, cut short by Enzo's phone springing to life in his back pocket. A shrill ringtone that causes Cesar to flinch, the three men surrounding the other grave all pausing their work to turn and look as well.

Attention Enzo is no mood for. Even less, the promise of who he suspects is on the other end, Garcia calling to dish out more demands. Thinly veiled threats disguised as tasks to be completed next.

"Water. Now," Enzo says, shooting a finger toward the truck

before taking a few steps back. Letting the shovel fall where it may, he turns away from the gravesite, waiting a couple more seconds before sliding the device out and checking the screen to see a name splayed across it he wasn't expecting.

A saved contact that is markedly better than Garcia, though still doesn't necessarily mean good news.

"Yeah?" Enzo asks, pressing the phone to his ear. Marching on a few more steps, he slides in between a pair of pecan trees, using them to wall him off from the men still working behind him.

"Yeah," Sheriff Jeff Daubenmire says, parroting Enzo's own opening. "Heads up, I'm about to call Alder and let him know what happened. I've kept it quiet all night, but the fire department has now come and gone. Can't sit on it forever."

Grunting softly in reply, Enzo asks, "No sign of them yet, I take it?"

"Nope."

Turning back the other way, Enzo watches as Aguilar does as instructed. Standing next to the truck, he upends a plastic bottle, sucking down a few long pulls before moving it to the side and pressing the cool plastic to his eye.

A makeshift compress that won't get him far, but Enzo can't begrudge him for trying.

"Alright. Keep me posted."

CHAPTER SEVENTY-THREE

Like most things in the greater Austin area, the airport was never meant to handle a city quite so large. Expansion that has outpaced infrastructure, forcing the city to try and adapt on the fly. A constant cycle of construction that never truly ends, simply moving from one area to another, eventually forced to return for the next wave of growth at some point in the future.

An ongoing process that leaves buildings and facilities mismatched, certain chunks easily identifiable by style and color. Parking is a nightmare, open plots of asphalt often the first to go when more space is needed.

To say nothing of traffic, the narrow roadways and perpetual rerouting leaving things a snarled mess. A problem that exists even at such an early hour on a Saturday, with many travelers trying to get the first flight out for the day. Crazed football fans bedecked in orange and white, looking to score a same-day flight to wherever the Longhorns are playing.

Congestion that Remington is not in the mood for, still riding on the concentrated emotions from the encounter at the house last night. Adrenaline that has long since subsided, replaced by thoughts and analysis. Assessments that were decidedly negative to begin with, taken even further by everything just shared by Lance Reseda.

News not just of the opposition they are facing – an enemy spoken of in terms bordering on myth – but also the reasons they had for targeting Maylinn. An even mix of greed and megalomania that has Remington clenching and unclenching his hands, already envisioning the moment when they meet.

Future plans he can only guess are matched by his brother behind the steering wheel, Cortland having not said a word since they left the shelter house a half hour earlier. A sight they will return to soon enough, the final agreement reached by all three before climbing into the pair of SUVs and driving away to reconvene at midday. A second meeting with Reseda and some of the others he claimed are also under Leo Garcia's control, aching for freedom.

Whether or not it was the right move, Remington hasn't yet decided. A story that could be total bullshit, the man talking fast to try and save his ass, or could be true, the manner of delivery and level of detail shared too much to merely be a cover.

Real data that in turn poses another question, that being the veracity of Reseda's motivations. A desire to actually free himself from Garcia's oppression, or merely a means of helping him set a trap.

Luring Remington and Cortland in so the man can wipe them away, just as he did with Maylinn.

Such thoughts swirling at the front of his mind, Remington watches as the first golden rays appear across the hood of the SUV. A bright glare promising another warm day, causing him to squint as they work their way through a series of narrow streets. Redirects and one-ways winnowing them toward the arrivals curb in a stop-and-go pattern, never letting them get more than a few feet before they are forced to pull up again.

Driving patterns that seem to be lifted straight from a game of bumper cars, with vehicles trying to angle their way in and out.

Jerked movements that evoke a pained sound from Shine in the backseat as she rests flat, any attempt at balancing herself on a single front leg long since abandoned.

"Delta, right?" Remington asks, breaking the silence as his gaze sweeps across the signs announcing the various airlines. All of the usual offerings, paired up alphabetically and running the length of the curb. More than eighty yards of shaded sidewalk, already lined with travelers and bags of every shape and color.

A vortex of movement Remington is studying as the faint buzz of an incoming call sounds out from the middle console. Long consecutive pulses that draws Remington's attention over.

"I bet that's them," Cortland says.

"Naw," Remington replies, reaching into the nearest cupholder and extracting the offending device. "That's you, not me."

Rotating it around so he can see the screen, he adds, "512 area code."

A cleft appears between Cortland's brows as he alternates his focus between the traffic and the phone. "512? That's Williamson County."

The divot disappears as his brows rise. "You don't think...?"

Given the events of the last twelve hours, Remington could see it being any of a handful of different people. Victor or Enzo or - as he suspects Cortland was just hinting - Garcia himself.

Maybe even Reseda calling already to say he changed his mind.

"Could be," Remington confesses.

Keeping the device clutched tight in his hand, he stares down at it, actively debating whether to answer. A problem that solves itself as a moment later it falls silent, the front reverting from the plain black of an incoming call to the image serving as Cortland's home screen.

A shot of Maylinn and Shine both curled up on the couch, deep asleep and framed by an incoming shaft of afternoon sun. A lazy Sunday with her wrapped in an oversized Texas Tech sweatshirt and Shine filling the space between her legs, head resting on her stomach.

A picture Remington has never seen before, still studying it as the phone buzzes again. A solitary vibration, accompanied by an icon appearing across the top of the screen.

"Text message?" Cortland asks, glancing over to Remington's outstretched hand before again turning his attention to the loading zone nearby.

"Voicemail," Remington replies. "Want to play it?"

"In a minute," Cortland answers. Extending one finger straight out from the top of the steering wheel, he points straight ahead, drawing Remington's attention toward the far end of the walkway where Tyrell and Val both stand, each carrying a duffel bag in one hand, the other raised overhead to flag them down.

"Might as well wait until they get in here, let everybody hear it at once."

CHAPTER SEVENTY-FOUR

Cortland knew that his house was probably no more the night before when his brother gave him fifteen minutes to load as much as he could into a couple of bags. Clothes and toiletries and Shine's food and medications that soon filled the pair of oversized duffels he grabbed out of the bottom of his closet. Essentials that would get them through the coming days, but would never begin to match the comforts of home.

The first house he and Maylinn bought together after a few years of apartment living, every last detail inside was to their liking. Everything from the color of tile on the backsplashes to the style of Keurig resting on the countertop. Two people who poured themselves into their work every day and wanted to come home to an oasis. A respite away from the hustle and noise of the world, where everything was just as they liked.

A place where they could simply be, free to relax and enjoy each other's company. A thousand memories that Cortland had still harbored hope he might return to as he and Shine reversed out of the garage and tore off into the night, leading Remington to the barn and accompanying pond of the feeding station a half dozen miles away.

Wishes that were dashed in an instant by the voicemail left by Sheriff Daubenmire fifteen minutes earlier, the source of the call from the unknown number with the local area code. Just as gruff and to the point as a few nights before, it was fairly light on details, though Cortland didn't need to hear specifics to know exactly what happened.

A fairly easy tale to decipher, as being told now by Remington behind him. Posted up on one side of the truck, his elbows braced against the top of the bed, he is matched by Tyrell on the opposite side. Between them sits Val on the tailgate, her feet hanging down as she stares across the water of the farm pond. A reflective surface barely thirty yards in diameter, the late morning sun shining bright across it.

"I knew once that bastard jumped through the window and got away, he'd be back," Remington mutters, repeating what he'd said to Cortland before telling him to pack his stuff. "If not for the fact that my damn leg was about half off, I would have tried to chase him down then."

Assuming the same exact position as after paying Victor a visit just nine hours earlier, Cortland stands along the side of the pond. Rooted perpendicular to the bank, he has the bag of treats for Shine in hand. Sustenance she is currently not as interested in, instead attacking the stainless-steel bowl of cold water before her after the excitement of greeting Tyrell and Val at the airport.

Exuberance that lasted the entirety of the trip to where they now are with all three crammed into the backseat. Excitement that has her lapping up the needed hydration, the sound providing a soft background din, interspersed with the rhythmic noises of the autumn landscape around them.

Small bursts of breeze. Dried leaves rattling in the trees above. Tall grasses being pushed back and forth.

"You did the right thing," Val says. Turning over a shoulder, she peers at Remington and adds, "You remember our training. What's the first rule about giving chase?"

Glancing that way, Cortland watches as his brother snorts, his head rocking back an inch.

"Huh?" Val presses.

"Never go after them-" Remington begins, making it only a few words before Tyrell jumps in, adding, "unless you know where and you know how many."

"That's right," Val says, turning back to face forward. "And you didn't know either. Hell, there could have been a damn getaway driver or this Leo Garcia himself sitting nearby, just waiting to see what happened."

So close on the heels of everything Lance Reseda had to share, Cortland has only just started to sift through the message left by Daubenmire. A few quick lines informing him that there has been an accident and his home caught fire. By the time the fire department arrived, there was not much left to salvage.

Please call him back as soon as possible.

Coded speak for what they know really happened, especially given that there was no need to use fire as a forensic countermeasure, a man Cortland has to assume is on the payroll there to control the scene, just as he was the crash days before.

It was a message. One more in the unending blows coming his way the last few days, as if he has cosmically wronged the universe and it is intent on bludgeoning him into submission in retaliation.

Another shot that he has only just started to wrap his head around, still processing the battle last night and the ensuing information from Reseda. Bits and pieces arriving scattershot, preventing him from really thinking about the logistics of things.

Who may or may not have been nearby, or even why the hell this is all happening over a lawsuit his wife was working on.

"I know," Remington begins, ready to defend his position or posit some sort of counter to Val's reason. Words that Cortland barely hears as he reaches to his back pocket and slides his phone free. Stepping past Shine still working on her water, he heads toward the gap between Val and the corner of the truck and brings the device to life.

Flicking his gaze around the group, he checks to make sure everyone has quieted, the conversation dying down, before pulling up the sheriff's number. The most direct route to answer the questions they are debating. Inquiries there is no possible way to know for sure about, leaving them only to speculation.

More data it is best to get all at once, rather than trying to super-impose it onto an incomplete structure later.

Hitting send, he flips the phone to speaker and holds it out across the tailgate. Beside him, Val slides down to the ground and turns to stand by his hip. Remington and Tyrell both move closer on either side.

"Daubenmire."

"Uh, yeah, sheriff, this is Cortland Alder. I got your-"

"My message," the sheriff inserts, finishing the sentence for him. "Which means you've already heard what happened. I am very sorry. I don't know who you pissed off, but they sure have it in for you this week."

In his periphery, Cortland can see his brother shake his head. Opposite him, Tyrell lowers his, peering down between his forearms to the truck bed below.

Silent body language matching Cortland's own response to Daubenmire's comment. A caustic barb or a mindless quip, there is no way of knowing which.

"Sure seems that way," Cortland manages to mutter. "Are you there now?"

"I am," Daubenmire answers. "Where are you? How fast can you get here?"

CHAPTER SEVENTY-FIVE

Football games for the University of Texas are some of the busiest days of the year for Leo Garcia's business interests. With kickoff often slated at one for all but the biggest of games, pregame festivities begin as early as eight a.m. Bleary-eyed frat guys and sorority girls in their best hair and makeup wanting to get a fresh jump on the day, even as many are still feeling the effects of the night before.

Morning tailgating for those with tickets to Darrell Royal Memorial Stadium, the rest flooding into every bar and restaurant throughout the area. A crowd in the tens of thousands on its own, swollen tremendously by fans and alumni pouring in from all over the state.

Stadium capacity right at a hundred grand, easily surpassed by the throng of people gathered into campus and downtown.

Eager hordes that are only nominally smaller on weekends such as this, when the Longhorns are on the road.

A target audience that would have Garcia practically salivating most weekends, anticipating the surge in cash that will soon fill the coffers. A veritable windfall, gifted a dozen times a year through nothing more than proximity. A rare bit of good luck for an empire that was scratched out of the dirt and built one piece at a time.

Karmic forces offering them some well-deserved good fortune that, for a variety of reasons, Garcia cannot bring himself to give a damn about today.

Seated in the rolling chair behind his desk, Garcia is turned to face out the side window in his office. Elbow propped on the desktop, he stares out at the bright sunlight without seeing a thing, his eyes glassed in thought.

A hundred different things all running in parallel, starting with the elimination of the lawyer a few days ago and culminating with the incident in the gym earlier. A scene that he never should have let happen, the young punk just doing what his every instinct told him to and trying to defend himself. A few clean shots that Garcia would have otherwise praised him for.

Not cheap shots like Miguel sent his way a few days earlier. Not just standing there and letting Garcia take him out with one punch like the first two guys.

Sure as hell not diving through the ropes and running away like the third one, sprinting like a scared child into the darkness.

In the moment though, there was nothing Garcia could do to stop it. Brimming with rage from the list of losses sustained recently, he had pushed aside all conscious thought, letting pure instinct takeover. Needed release from the growing angst of the situation with the lawyer. And the press conference from Kennedy Banks. And the loss of Hector and Ramon.

A sum total meaning once he started taking those punches from Aguilar, his reptilian brain took over. Pain and anger were converted into action, causing him to pummel the young man into submission.

And then keep beating on him, even after he had lost the ability to defend himself.

"Shit," Garcia mutters, dropping his hand away from his chin. A freefall with his forearm slapping against the bare desktop before him, his focus remaining on the grounds outside. Manicured grass and shrubbery that normally by this hour is being tended to by part of his groundskeeping crew, today totally void of life.

Staff making a point of avoiding his line of sight, word of what happened in the gym having already made the rounds.

Another damned headache for him to deal with, once more important matters are concluded.

Pulling his focus away from the world outside, Garcia rotates his chair to face forward. Reaching for his phone, he is stopped short by a trio of knocks at his door. Three quick taps that can only have originated with two people, the odds slim that his mother would have made her way down from the third floor.

If she wanted to berate him in person, she would merely sit in her bedroom and yell down until he eventually trudged up.

"Come in, Enzo," Garcia calls, the words still hanging in the air as the knob turns and the doors swings inward. Sliding sideways through it, Enzo pushes it closed behind him, venturing barely a step forward before stopping.

Positioning that could be to either keep from getting any closer or because of the thick film of sweat and dirt clinging to him.

"Is it done?" Garcia asks.

"It is," Enzo replies, "but that's not why I'm here. I got a call from the sheriff a little bit ago. He spoke to the accountant."

"And?"

"And the guy claims he is in Dallas, visiting with his wife's family," Enzo replies. "Told Daubenmire he will drive down this afternoon, meet him at the house this evening."

Offering nothing more than a nod, Garcia lets his gaze drift back to the window beside him. A place to put his focus as he envisions the scene he arrived to find the night before. A home that some would describe as idyllic, shot to hell and littered with dead bodies.

Hardly the type of thing the owner would simply run away from, especially to go and visit his wife's family four hours to the north. A distance that would have taken them half the night to cover, only to have to turn around and drive back later today.

"They're regrouping," Garcia mutters. Audible thinking that goes unanswered, Enzo remaining silent on the opposite side of the room.

The first damn thing he has done right all week.

"Where is the sheriff now?" Garcia asks.

"He was headed home," Enzo replies. "Said the fire department was done and what was left of the place was roped off. He's going back later to meet with Alder, but until then the place is empty."

"Good," Garcia replies, again dipping his chin in a nod. Rotating back to gaze at Enzo, he adds, "Go now. Take the same crew with you. Scout it out and sit on the place until Alder shows.

"Don't do anything stupid, and bring them both to me when you're done."

―――――

Cortland couldn't help but recall the scene the last time he and his brother crossed the threshold of The Smokehouse. A night the better part of three months in the past, neither having returned since for obvious reasons. Strong desires not to relive what took place that night when their entire world was put into a blender and pulsed a few dozen times.

The start of a whirlwind that both had ridden every day since. A pieced-together existence with their impending exit finally upon them, arriving in just a few hours with the start of a new day.

One last night in their hometown before Remington boarded a bus bound for Fort Sill in Oklahoma and Cortland climbed into the Charger with Shine and headed west to Lubbock to begin his college career. Their first time apart for more than a couple of days since the moment of inception.

Yet another massive life transition neither was especially ready for, largely because of the one enormous hurdle remaining before them.

Something they'd both been discussing since just after leaving The Smokehouse the last time.

The night had started simply enough. A farewell gathering for the two of them that soon started to go awry, as things at The Smokehouse so often tended to. Still holding on to a handful of jars from the last delivery Cortland and Remington made, shortly after a buffet spread for the gathered crowd was cleared away, Bill Ketchum had brought the moonshine out.

Libations that were met like conquering heroes, sending up a cheer from the masses. A kickoff to craziness that was now well under way, every chair and table in the place pushed to the outside. Cleared space to make room for an impromptu dance floor, the assorted beats of everything from modern hip-hop to nineties country blasting through the speakers affixed to each corner of the room.

A sound system usually reserved for Sunday football games, commandeered for the purpose of a righteous end-of-summer blowout. A proper sendoff to Cortland and Remington, and a final goodbye of sorts to G as well.

An event that had pulled most of the town out for the first time since it all went down. A chance for them to all breathe a sigh of relief and laugh in public without immediately feeling guilty or casting a sideways glance to see who might be around to hear it.

Considered the guests of honor for the night, Cortland and Remington were given seats at the center table. Prime placement, joined by Ketchum himself - the owner having even changed out of his usual attire for a pair of jeans and Smokehouse polo – to allow each person present to stop by on their way to or from the buffet line.

The funeral that everyone but a select few never got to have, stopping by one at a time to offer their condolences or wish the brothers well. A receiving line that neither would have been able to handle two months before including everyone from Sheriff Myles and Judge Mason getting a second crack at it to Chewy and the owner of the Buckhorn offering firm handshakes.

Solemn pleasantries to match the mood, lingering until the last plate was finished and cleared away. The start of a brief bit of awkwardness before Ketchum disappeared into the back and came out a few minutes later with the familiar Mason jars of clear moonshine in hand.

The proverbial ice breaker that had immediately lightened the tenor in the air, followed just moments later by the music kicking on.

The start of a party that was now more than two hours in, most people present deep in the stages of defilement.

The perfect cover, allowing the brothers to drift to the side before disappearing out the back, unnoticed by all.

CHAPTER SEVENTY-SIX

The mismatched trio sitting three-across on the same picnic table in the shelter house west of Austin isn't exactly the overwhelming show of support Lance Reseda promised. Making it sound before like they were no less than a dozen business owners throughout the area who were trapped and afraid, aching for a way to rid themselves of Leo Garcia and break free of his oppression, Remington knew that his brother had returned expecting at least half that many. A full table, all ready to share similar stories and give plenty of details on the way to best go after the man.

A pipe dream that Remington was never foolish enough to believe, he himself just surprised that the man showed up at all.

When the two of them had climbed back into Cortland's SUV earlier with Shine and headed off for the airport, he'd been convinced that that was the last time they'd ever see Reseda. He'd do just what he did the previous afternoon, calling Garcia and sharing everything he knew, and then he would disappear. Grab his family and a few bags and take them away for a surprise weekend trip.

A getaway, during which Garcia and his crew would wipe out

Remington and Cortland. After that, he would return to a pat on the head and a compliment about what a good boy he'd been.

That was the nature of the control it seemed Garcia had over him.

A fact meaning that even though he is back now, Remington isn't completely convinced it is on the up and up. Standing in the same spot as earlier, his shoulder pressed against a corner post, he is turned to stare out the opposite direction. A constant vigil toward the road running parallel nearby, with Tyrell taking up a similar post on the far end of the structure.

Lookouts bisected by Val pacing between them, Remington still carrying his own gun, his friends now armed with the weapons left behind by the attackers the night before. A limited arsenal with sparse ammunition they can only hope will suffice for the time being.

A meeting that is as peaceful as Reseda continues to claim it will be, seated in the middle of the bench on the far side of the table. Flanking him on his right is a woman named Daisy Reed. The oldest of everybody present, she looks to be fighting a losing battle with aging as she progresses into her fifties, prolonged exposure to the Texas sun and a poor choice in hair dye making her look even older.

Diminutive in stature, she is dressed in a pair of bib overalls and a t-shirt with small flowers dotting it. Her thinning hair is teased out around her head in a halo, framing a narrow face with pointed nose and chin and red lipstick.

An overall look that reminds Remington of someone who should be selling honey at a roadside stand thirty years ago, rather than the owner/operator of multiple dry cleaners throughout the area. Businesses inherited from her parents that she kept running even after things started to dry up, making them prime targets for the vulture that is Garcia to move in.

A story not greatly unlike that of Reseda, or of the man on the far end of the group. Named Guy Thomas, he is at least a decade younger than his counterparts, with smooth black skin and a head shaved clean. A goatee void of grays encircles his mouth.

Dressed in jeans and a dark purple polo shirt tucked in tight, his fingers are laced before him, revealing a University of Texas championship ring of indeterminate sport or year. A bit of local celebrity once upon a time that he parlayed into owning a string of car washes after his playing days were over.

Businesses that did well in their early years, while his name still meant something, but as time progressed, the clientele began to look elsewhere. He was almost forced to shut down operations.

Which was exactly when an angel investor arrived, offering to forge a new partnership. A lifeline Thomas jumped at, never once questioning why his new donor was explicit about keeping everything in cash until it was much too late.

"There would have been more of us here," Reseda explains once Thomas is finished, "but today is a football Saturday."

Not sure what the comment is supposed to mean, Remington turns his attention to the side, glancing to Val and Tyrell. A look of uncertainty matched by both that Reseda seems to pick up on, adding, "Most of the other businesses are bars or restaurants. Things that deal in cash and have a ton of foot traffic for pushing drugs.

"If those people didn't show up today, during one of the busiest days of the year..."

"Any other day," Thomas adds, "there would be more."

"How many more?" Cortland asks.

"Hard to say," Thomas replies. Unlacing his fingers, he flips his palms toward the roof of the shelter house, explaining, "It's not like there's a company phone tree or we have annual barbecues."

"Most of us that do know each other kind of met by accident," Reed adds.

"Right," Reseda agrees, his mouth open to continue when he is cut short by the sound of engines approaching. Loud, resonant motors powering large vehicles that causes him to fall silent.

A palpatory tensing that Remington feels as well, pushing himself away from the pole he is leaning against. Taking a step back, he tucks his shoulder tight against it and slides his gun from his rear waistband.

In his periphery, he can see Tyrell take up a similar post, Val falling in behind him. Three people with weapons out, stowed right along their thighs as they stare to the north, listening to the sound growing stronger.

Mechanical rumbling that soon separates, hinting at multiple approaching vehicles. Sounds that conjure images of the massive truck that ran Maylinn off the road in Remington's mind, this time flanked by more just like it.

An entire fleet sent by Garcia after speaking with Reseda or one of the others. An execution squad that he braces himself for, sweat lining his brow as he peers straight ahead, counting off seconds, listening to the trucks growing ever closer.

An incoming convoy that shows itself seconds later, revealing not a death squadron sent to their door, but a trio of farm vehicles with their backs loaded with corn. Fresh crop just removed from the fields, on its way to be sold or stored.

A sight that takes a few moments to register, allowing the tension to bleed out as Remington exhales, slowly raising himself back to full height.

CHAPTER SEVENTY-SEVEN

Whatever trepidation Daisy Reed and Guy Thomas showed up with had started to melt away during the course of the conversation. Basic introductions that were beginning to get a bit deeper, explaining their respective businesses and why they were targeted by Leo Garcia. The innocuous approach that was made and the nefarious scheme that was underlying it.

Interaction that didn't just bring them out of their shell, but started to unleash a bit of the true emotion they each had about it. Frustration and dread and loathing, matching hints of what Lance Reseda revealed earlier. The feeling of helplessness, surpassed only by the desire to be free.

A willingness to trade whatever expansion or growth their businesses might have had for the right to run it as they please again. The ability to conduct affairs in their own manner, or even to shutter the places up just to have their lives back.

A true peek behind the curtain that vanished instantly at the sight of the trucks approaching. A three-vehicle convoy that proved to be nothing more than a local farmer in the process of bringing in their crop, but was enough to instill that original fear back into them.

Terror brought on by the realization of just how exposed they were. What would occur if Garcia and his team were to discover them.

Concerns Cortland would have empathized with even twelve hours ago, but given what he knows now – both about his home and the very reason why his wife was targeted – he cannot let them stop him from getting what they came for.

Seeing that shift play out before him, Cortland knows that their time for extracting anything useful from the pair is fleeting. A final few minutes before the dams close completely and they are left with more background information, but nothing useful. No operative data that they can build a plan around, hoping to either lure Garcia out or make a move on him directly.

Another like so many of their interviews from the last few days, providing a bit of false hope before ultimately amounting to nothing.

A path they have been down too damn many times to let happen again.

"Tell me how it works with Garcia," Cortland says. A jump from the basics of their respective situations to the nuts and bolts of the operation.

Useful, actionable intel that he knows his brother – and almost certainly Tyrell and Val also – will be especially interested in.

"What do you mean?" Reed asks.

"Like, the cash drops, or...?" Thomas asks, his trailing voice leaving the question open ended.

"All of it," Cortland replies, "but start with Enzo. Who is he?"

Again, the feeling of teetering on a ledge returns to Cortland. Palpable uncertainty that emanates across the table as the three of them exchange glances, each silently imploring the others to be the one to kickstart things. A staring contest, none wanting to be the first to blink.

A line there will be no uncrossing, allowing the others to follow suit.

For nearly a minute, there is no response. Long enough that Cortland half expects his brother to come forward and slam his gun on the table, using fear just as he did with Reseda earlier.

The threat of violence that doesn't quite come to pass, Reed of all people the one to speak first.

"From what I've seen," she whispers before casting a sideways glance to the others, "and it could be different for them, there seems to be two different groups. There's Garcia, who does the initial sales pitch, gets you to sign up, even stops by from time to time just to prove he can, but Enzo and his crew are the ones who do more of the day-to-day stuff.

"They make the pickups and deliveries, handle any problems that arise."

His forearms balanced across his thighs, Cortland's hands hang down between his legs. Splayed fingers that curl up into fists, clenching tight at the woman's last line.

Words that it is clear were not meant as a slight to him, said without a single bit of ill will, though it is impossible for him not to think that it includes his wife. A problem that came up in the form of a lawsuit, and when she kept pressing, refusing to go away, she was handled.

And now that he and his brother are poking around, Enzo is attempting to do the same to them, even taking it the extra step of destroying his house in the process.

"He's the one you interact with the most?" Cortland asks, hearing a bit of strain in his own voice.

A question that is responded to with a series of nods. Three heads bobbing in unison, attention fixed on him.

"And Garcia," Cortland presses, "aside from those first few meetings...?"

"Doesn't come around much," Reseda replies.

"Which is a good thing," Thomas adds. "The less you see of him, the better."

"Any idea where he spends his time?" Cortland asks. "Does he have an office in the area? Work from his vehicle, driving from place to place all the time?"

Once more, the three fall into a game of exchanging glances. Uncertain looks that goes through every possible iteration before Reseda replies, "Far as I know, he runs things from his estate. I'm sure he's out and about some, for new arrivals over the border and such, but..."

As has become a pattern, his voice trails away. An incomplete sentence not meant to obfuscate, but to relay a lack of knowledge. Details he hasn't been made privy to, and never had the means or desire to seek out.

Information Cortland knows his brother wants and needs, but there is no point in trying to demand, it only likely to produce conjecture.

"This estate," Cortland says instead, "you've all been there right?"

On the left, Daisy's eyes clamp shut. Opposite her, Thomas exhales, twisting his focus to the side.

Confirmation of the story shared earlier about the welcoming party and the little display they were forced to watch afterward with the hyenas. Memories it is apparent both are still traumatized by, leaving only Reseda to reply, "We have."

"Tell us about it."

CHAPTER SEVENTY-EIGHT

Since the moment Lance Reseda and the others arrived, Remington has been content to let his brother take the lead. Clearly still fuming after the double shots of finding out why Maylinn was killed and that his house was burned to the ground, he was operating with a poise and directness that Remington had rarely seen from his brother. Purpose, fueled by hatred, handling the meeting exactly as it should be. Latitude to let the newcomers tell their story and get comfortable, followed by just a bit of force when it appeared he might lose them.

A deft transition from a grieving husband trying to help them all into an able interrogator. A man using a bit of gained trust to extract exactly what is needed.

Skills much more impressive than many Remington had seen used during his time in uniform, whenever they were arriving in far flung villages or trying to get valuable data from possible allies.

From start to finish there was no need for Remington to interrupt, waiting until the meeting is about to close, the new arrivals standing to leave, before pushing himself away from the corner post. Turning to stand behind his brother, he keeps his arms folded across his chest, peering down the length of his nose at each of the three in order.

One last point to be made, handled in the best way he knows how.

"We know how much you guys risked coming here," he says, "and we appreciate it, but we also need to ask one more thing from all of you, and it might be the most difficult part of all."

Flicking his gaze up to Tyrell looking over from the corner, he continues, "The enemy you've all described, the force he has at his back, the compound where he is holed up, it's going to take us a few days to make a move. Time to think and plan.

"Time that we're going to need all of you to sit on what we talked about here. Who we are, the questions we asked, even what happened to my sister-in-law, it goes no further." Looking from Reed to Reseda to Thomas in order, he continues, "Not one word. Not to your business partners or your spouses or even your dog.

"Seventy-two hours, total radio silence. You got me?"

Like a flight attendant needing audible confirmation from those sitting in the exit row, he goes through them one at a time, extracting the needed response. Affirmation they all willingly gave, Thomas even adding a firm nod, before they turn as a group and head toward the parking lot.

A departure that is much more hasty than their arrival, all piling into Reseda's SUV and speeding away.

No waves goodbye. No promises for future communication or requests to be updated.

A role fulfilled before removing themselves, content to watch and hope from afar.

"We're not really sitting on this for three days, are we?" Cortland asks, his gaze watching the SUV move away, following the same path as the farm trucks that nearly derailed things earlier.

"Hell no," Remington answers. "I just wanted to give them a false timeframe in case one of them does go running back to Garcia."

For most of the last three days, Remington has been solely focused on finding out who targeted his sister-in-law. A request extended to him by both her and his brother, asking for assistance. A promise he made to her to see this through.

A quest of undulating emotions that started with fear and uncertainty after getting the call from his brother before moving into sorrow at the sight of Maylinn in the morgue.

Only to then give way to wanton hostility. Unbridled anger that has ebbed and flowed, fueled by the image on the Tesla screen, and later the picture of Enzo's truck. The sight of a matching one following them. The late-night visit from the man and his hit squad.

Anger that finally started to subside when speaking to Reseda earlier. Hostility compartmentalized and put aside for the moment, allowing him to focus on what was being shared. Information that was being put forward, coupled with events since.

The beginnings of a plan that again just took a massive step forward. Better understanding both of Garcia's operation, and how he likes to do things.

Inside knowledge that Remington is inclined to believe, one person capable of weaving a tale, but not three. And damned sure not with that much visceral conviction.

"Got to be tonight, right?" Tyrell asks. Lifting one foot onto the closest bench of the picnic table, he leans forward, balancing his forearms across his knees.

"Tonight?" Cortland adds, his brows rising as he turns to look at his brother. "Why?"

"Because of what Daisy just shared," Remington answers. "We know Garcia stays at home, Enzo and his team do the heavy lifting.

"Burning your house was clearly meant to be a trap. A way to draw us out, get us into position so Enzo can nab us, take us back to Garcia and his little hyena pen."

"Hyenas?" Val inserts, having not been present for Reseda's explanation this morning.

Details Remington will share in a bit, wanting to get everything out first. The start of a schematic they can all pick holes at moving forward.

"What they don't know is that we're onto them," Remington says. "They don't know Ty and Val are here, and they don't know about the feeding station."

Lifting his chin slightly in understanding, Cortland says, "You want to set our own trap."

"Divide their forces," Val adds.

"Take out the roaming party," Tyrell finishes, "and then go after the estate."

"That's the idea," Remington confirms.

For a moment, nobody says anything. Each of them retreats into their thoughts, beginning to dissect what was just shared, matching it up with what they learned from Reseda and the others.

Silence that stretches two full minutes before being interrupted by Val reaching to the small of her back. Extracting the Beretta swiped from one of the dead men at the house the night before, she holds it up for each of them to see.

"I don't suppose you've also got an idea on how we get our hands on something a little bigger than these, do you?" she asks.

"Maybe one or two."

CHAPTER SEVENTY-NINE

If Enzo had things his way, he would have brought no less than a dozen trucks to sit on the ashes of the Alder house. Most of the available manpower, with one parked where they were sitting down the road just the night before and the others on standby, roving the surrounding area. Rotating positions every hour or so, more than twenty guys in total would have been ready to come tearing in at the first sign of movement.

A small army, not meant to be some sort of misplaced show of force, but to ensure that it is done quickly and efficiently. None of the same shit he went through the night before, trying to sneak in and hoping to pick the accountant and his brother off in the dead of night, but a full blitz attack.

A concentrated effort, wiping them out and driving away before anybody even knows they were there.

A plan he almost made the mistake of voicing to Leo Garcia before recognizing the state the man was in. A continuation of what happened in the gym earlier in the day, when frazzled nerves and unbridled rage nearly killed Aguilar. A man unaccustomed to pushback in any form, and having no idea how to handle it.

Intent on making a display out of the Alder brothers, Garcia was insistent that they be brought to him if at all possible. Not just their bodies, wrapped in blankets and tossed into the back of the truck like Hector and Ramon. Not even their shattered forms, shot full of holes and down to their last breaths.

Something approaching whole, allowing Garcia to take his time with them. A slow and methodical ending likely to involve some form of what happened in the gym before tossing the remainder into the compound.

Perhaps even one of each, while making the other watch.

Sadistic intentions Enzo knew better than to oppose, merely uttering the words, "Yes, sir," before turning and leaving.

"When did the sheriff say these guys should be back?" Aguilar asks. Having been rotated into the front seat as a beneficiary of attrition, he sits with his right elbow propped in the sill, his fingers pressed against the handle above the window.

Facing forward, his left eye is now completely purple, a large bulge extending outward from his temple. Injuries that make him look like some kind of movie monster from where Enzo sits, his breathing only now beginning to level out.

A broken young man serving as one-fifth of the team Enzo was told to bring along with him, the other four grouped into pairs and stationed in two sedans not far from where they now sit. Nondescript vehicles far less conspicuous than the pickup, allowing them to rotate driving past the charred remnants of the house every quarter hour. A constant vigil in the event the Alders return early or show up without letting Daubenmire know first.

A total force that is much larger in numbers than the last time Enzo showed up, though severely lacking in age or experience. Five guys who combined don't add up to the usefulness of Hector or Ramon, let alone the two of them together.

The fact that neither are still with them a testament to the mistakes made in the last few days. Errors in calculation and judgement that left them exposed and vulnerable against a weaker force.

Missteps that could be attributed to many, none more so than Enzo himself, wishing nothing more than to have the last eighteen hours back.

Or even just a few more minutes of the ongoing banter of his friends.

"Alder said he was in Dallas with the girl's family, was going to drive down this afternoon, be here by this evening."

Turning to glance his direction, Aguilar asks, "So why are we here already?"

Not once has Enzo actually believed the story as anything more than a bit of misdirection. Time to – as Garcia said – regroup and form a response, or simply to get Daubenmire to go away. Law enforcement oversight that the Alders didn't want to deal with in the wake of what happened the night before.

A viewpoint he got the impression the sheriff shares, even if he never said as much.

For three days now, the brothers have been knocking on doors and asking questions. A search making it clear they have no intention of leaving what happened to the accountant's wife alone. A hunt that just last night included engaging in hand-to-hand combat and killing two men.

No chance in hell they now just walk away and drive four hours north to visit with her family.

They are close. So close, Enzo can feel anticipation slipping into his bloodstream. Desire to get back at them for killing his friends and finish the battle that began in that living room.

Urges so strong he has even considered stepping out of the truck and going to stand in front of the ashes of the home. Active bait, hoping to draw them out that much faster.

"Why don't you take a nap or something?" Enzo replies, bypassing the question entirely. "I'll wake you when its time."

CHAPTER EIGHTY

"I hope you know when I asked if you missed it the other day, this isn't what I meant," Remington opens. Climbing from the passenger side of Tyrell's truck, he crunches across the gravel bank acting as a parking area along the side of the road. An expanse of crushed stone wide enough for four or five vehicles, though at the moment it houses only a single other automobile.

A pickup somewhat resembling the one Remington just exited, this one with black paint instead of silver, appearing much smaller than the last time he saw it without the trailer loaded with lawn equipment attached to the back.

"And I hope you didn't really think when you called and asked where you could get some hardware that I was just going to give you an address," Linc Brady replies. Leaning against the side of his rig, his arms are folded, putting both his collection of ink and the underlying musculature on full display.

"No," Remington admits, "I guess I didn't."

Coming to a stop a few feet short of the truck, Remington pauses and rotates at the waist, extending a hand to the side. "Linc Brady, this is Tyrell Walters." Lifting his prosthetic a few inches, he adds,

"He was with me in the sandbox pretty much every day but the one that mattered."

"Yeah, and it wouldn't have happened if I was," Tyrell says, stepping past Remington to shake Brady's hand. "Damn CO overthinking things again."

"Been there," Brady replies, returning the shake.

"Jarhead?" Tyrell asks.

"Somebody has to do the heavy lifting for you boys," Brady answers, a wry smile pulling his mouth to one side. A grin matched by Tyrell, white teeth just starting to peek through as the low groan of a motor sounds out. Gears gnashing that ceases any further conversation as the three of them turn in unison to the gate standing closed across the front of the gravel bar. Dark wood panels with wrought iron fixtures, attached directly to painted concrete block walls stretching wide in both directions.

A version of what Remington imagines the compound Reseda spoke of earlier looks like, the biggest difference being that while one is meant to keep hyenas in, this one is designed to keep them out.

"Do I even wanna...?" Tyrell begins before trailing off, his voice disappearing under the last moans of the metal tracks the doors are mounted on. The start of a question that evokes nothing more than a smile as Brady begins to walk forward. Measured paces through the thick gravel, the stones crunching beneath his feet just barely audible over the sound of the gate continuing to open.

A non-answer that causes Remington to flick a glance over to Tyrell before starting onward as well. A slow march forward that lasts no more than twenty paces before stopping just short of where the gate stood moments before.

A clear demarcation point, separating the rock and grass of outside from the smooth pavement extended out before them. A driveway more than fifteen yards across, stretched out the better part of a football field before ending in a matching gate on the far end.

A corridor littered with vehicles of various types, providing access to more than a half dozen different buildings. Structures ranging from squat concrete bunkers with tan paint and darkened windows to a towering warehouse of some sort.

Space and facilities enough to call to mind images of previous outposts Remington was once stationed at. Places carved out of dense forest or hostile jungle and built from the ground up, providing an oasis for those who drew the short straw and were sent there.

"We *are* still in Texas, right?" Tyrell mumbles, taking things in for the first time as well. "Or America, at least?"

The faint smile Brady was wearing a moment before grows wider. Mirth that Remington can't help but match, a faint smirk rocking his head back.

Levity that lasts for but a moment, falling away at the sight of a golf cart emerging from between two of the buildings on the left. Starting about halfway down, it whips out into the center of the paved lane, moving fast. Keeping with the military motif of the place, it is painted camouflage in assorted shades of green, a lone man seated inside.

A solitary figure who keeps both hands on the steering wheel, maintaining his speed and heading before hitting the brakes just ten yards out from them in a sudden and abrupt halt.

Setting the parking brake, he climbs out and stands with his hands on his hips, openly assessing the new arrivals. A drill sergeant inspecting fresh recruits, his mouth twisted up in a scowl, his gaze hidden behind mirrored sunglasses.

The definition of the words *compact* and *wiry*, Remington guesses him to stand five-eight and weigh somewhere in the vicinity of a buck sixty. Muscle and sinew put into a compressor until as tight as can be and then packaged in dark tan skin, leaving every vein and striation visible.

Physicality on display in the cargo shorts and gray t-shirt he wears, decidedly at odds with the silver tint of his hair.

Remaining completely silent for the better part of a minute, his features completely impassive, he scans the group from left to right and back again. A mental determining process that stretches long enough for Remington to begin feeling pinpricks rising along the back of his neck, questions of where Brady brought them or if he should start looking for cameras or sniper's nests nearby coming to mind.

Inquiries tossed aside just as fast as the man's shoulders begin to quiver. Slight chuckles that precede his features splitting into a grin as his hands slide away from his hips.

Taking a step forward, he extends his right hand and says, "Staff Sergeant Brady. Good to see you."

"You too, Gunny," Brady replies. Stepping forward, he meets the shake before releasing and turning back to Remington and Tyrell. "Guys, this is Master Gunnery Sergeant Ward Turakis."

Rotating back to face forward, he adds, "Gunny, these are the Army boys I was telling you about, needing us to bail them out again."

"Yeah, well, what's new?" Turakis replies. A wry retort enough to pull a laugh from Remington as he steps forward, waiting as Tyrell introduces himself before doing the same.

A bit of levity that lingers for a few more moments before Turakis steps back. His features return to neutral as his hands return to his hips. "Sergeant Brady here tells me you boys are looking to do a bit of shopping."

A statement more than a question, Remington nods in the affirmative anyway. "Yes, sir."

Grunting softly, Turakis glanced over to Tyrell. "And that your list might be a little – shall we say – extensive."

Tyrell's turn to reply, he matches Remington's answer, pairing a nod with, simply, "Yes, sir."

"Hm," Turakis replies, bobbing his head in acceptance of the information. Data he considers for a few moments, his gaze drifting to the side, before asking one final question.

"And can I ask who this sudden enemy is that requires all this firepower?"

"Leo Garcia," Remington replies, adding nothing more. No

further explanation of what Reseda and the others explained earlier, or even mention of what had been done to Maylinn and his brother.

Not even the slightest bit of voice inflection.

Only a name, that alone seeming sufficient as Turakis reaches up and slides the sunglasses down the length of his nose. A slow and deliberate movement revealing a pair of crystalline white eyes framed by scars both above and below.

Chemical burns that Remington would recognize anywhere.

"*Laughing* Leo Garcia?"

CHAPTER EIGHTY-ONE

The back ends of Cortland's SUV and Tyrell's truck are lined up side by side in the shadows of the barn. Facing out toward the water of the farm pond that has become their temporary base of operations, the back ends of both stand open, spreads of drastically different kinds stretched across them.

To the left, the rear of the SUV is loaded with a makeshift picnic. Foodstuffs Cortland and Val grabbed from the local H-E-B while the others were away. Deli sandwiches and chips and potato salad. Two bags of cookies. Bottles of Gatorade and water.

Enough sustenance to feed a dozen people or more, picked up in anticipation of a long night ahead. Fuel to prepare them all for what awaits, regardless of what Remington told Reseda and the others earlier.

One of just a few solid meals Cortland has had all week, the hot dogs from the game the night before long since gone. Depletion that he has gotten used to, barely noticing that another eighteen hours had passed without eating until it was suggested he and Val make a run while the others went to meet with Linc Brady and his contact.

A chore that he had jumped at, if for no other reason than to be doing something. A means of distraction. A task for him and Val to focus on, even if it does sit largely untouched for the time being, the group gathered around the offerings spread across the bed and tailgate of Tyrell's truck instead.

Amassed firepower of various sorts sufficient to conduct a covert operation or engage in siege warfare. Arms of assorted kinds that Cortland can admit he isn't entirely familiar with sandwiched between a pair of black tarps. His gaze dancing across each of the pieces, he listens as his brother and Tyrell outline what they were able to pick up.

After Val's suggestion earlier that they needed to upgrade their firepower, the first thing Remington did was reach out to Brady to ask if he might know of a place where they could pick up some gear. Weaponry that wouldn't require a multiple day waiting period or background checks or even a paper trail.

A request Cortland had lifted his eyebrows at initially, thinking his brother was buying too much into the stories of private militias holed up all over the state. Anti-government types or doomsday preppers or whatever else with private bunkers hidden well beyond the prying eyes of society.

A stance he was wise not to vocalize, Brady replying almost instantly with the request for ten minutes to make a couple of calls. A period of time that ended up being far longer than needed, the group having only just started discussing their next steps when Remington's phone burst to life, an incoming text message giving them a time and address.

"You would not have believed this place," Tyrell says. Standing in the same place as earlier this morning, he leans over the side of the bed, his fingers laced before him. "It looked like its own miniature base, hidden behind a wall with gates on both ends."

Her bare arms folded before her, ropy muscle plainly visible under tanned skin, Val lifts her gaze from the bed to Tyrell just long enough to say, "Sounds like a damned commune."

"Close," Remington admits, drawing her attention to the opposite end of the tailgate. "Except that there's only one family who lives there. An old Master Gunnery Sergeant, along with wife, kids, and grandkids.

"A completely self-sufficient homestead, right down to enough firepower to protect themselves from a damned armed invasion."

Motioning to the bed before him with one hand, he adds, "Minus a few pieces now, of course."

"A few?" Cortland asks, his eyes bulging slightly at the spread before him. "Who the hell are these people trying to protect themselves from?"

"The government," Tyrell answers, "which, oddly enough, are the same people who financed most of it."

"Mustard gas settlement," Remington adds, using the same hand to motion towards his eyes. "Long story. Not important right now."

"Nope," Tyrell confirms. "All that does matter is that he has heard of Garcia, and he is not a fan."

"Clearly not," Val mutters. Her thighs pressed tight to the front of the tailgate, she reaches out and runs her hand over the stock of a rifle with a detachable magazine affixed to the bottom. Matte black in color, it is one of four matching weapons, all lined up with spare ammunition.

"M4. Oh, how I have missed you."

"That's what I said," Tyrell says, his features splitting into a smile. Reaching down, he taps at the tarp directly in front of him, adding, "Thought you might enjoy these beauties, too."

Following his outstretched finger, Cortland's gaze lands on a collection of smaller handguns. Pieces much closer to what Remington was carrying last night, and what they took from the men who tried to break in.

Another haul of arms and extra ammunition that a little quick math brings somewhere in the vicinity of five hundred rounds. More than enough to keep them all pulling the trigger as fast as possible for quite a while, with still more than a few left over.

The smile Val wears grows larger, any thought of the M4 dissipating as she reaches out and takes up the closest handgun. Pulling it close, she works the slide a number of times in order before extending it straight out before her, aiming it at the back window of the truck. Held tilted to the side, she sights in on an imaginary target before pulling the trigger, an audible click sounding out.

"I'm not sure that *beauty* even begins to describe the M17," she replies, putting it back down into position along the edge of the tarp. Deliberate placement, allowing plenty of space for the remainder of their haul. Small packages that looked like bricks spread evenly across the opposite side, the space between filled with Kevlar vests shingled one atop the other.

A shopping trip far surpassing anything Cortland might have envisioned, his mind working to process the full spread before him.

"Five vests?" he asks, jutting his chin toward the body armor splayed across much of the width of the truck.

"Five," Tyrell confirms. "And the big one there is for Brady. Ain't no way that dude's squeezing into a large."

Cutting his gaze to his brother, Cortland sees Remington dip his chin in a nod. "He'll be here in a little while. Needed to go home and see to a few things, pick up a couple items first."

Whether they had asked him to join or it was simply a condition for obtaining the weapons, Cortland doesn't bother asking. Details he doesn't need to know, pushed aside as his focus shifts a few feet to the side.

"And those?" he asks, motioning to the small parcels along the far end. Rectangles that look to be made of putty and wrapped tight in green cellophane.

Plastic explosives, if he was forced to guess, though never has he actually seen any up close.

"Ah, these," Remington replies. Dropping a hand down, he lifts the closest brick a few inches, hefting its weight a time or two before returning it. "These are a little something extra from our benevolent supplier."

"Yeah," Tyrell says, snorting loudly, "or as he put it, a nice big middle finger from him to Garcia."

––––––

What Cortland had mistakenly believed was a site obtained for the sole purpose of hosting backyard brawls and makeshift MMA fights was actually the home address of Wes Callum and his sons. Boys who were now well into their twenties – each a decade older than Cortland and Remington, with no clear intention of ever leaving home. Or getting jobs. Or contributing to society in any meaningful way, their purpose in the world seeming to be to follow in their father's footsteps.

Sponging off the taxpayer dime in one way or another, whether it be through social benefit programs or free room and board during their occasional stints in jail.

Three times in the last month, Cortland and his brother had made the drive. Trips by at odd hours and on different days of the week, each for the purpose of doing reconnaissance.

More steps in what they put together in the wake of what happened at their own home.

Not for one minute did Cortland doubt that they were the perpetrators behind what happened to G. Self-righteous assholes who probably felt they had been slighted in some way. Stiffed by the local moonshine maker, and then embarrassed at the hands of his grandsons.

Egregious errors that could not be abided, causing them to go back that night in retaliation. Physical assault on an old man and a puppy, followed by a statement in the form of actually going through with what Remington threatened that afternoon.

The destructive force of fire, taken further by using G's own alcohol as a starter. An accelerant that had gone up much faster and hotter than anticipated, wiping out their grandfather as he tried to crawl his way to safety.

A horrific visual that Cortland had played through his mind no less than a hundred times. Moments when his subconscious would try to fill the silence, or when his sleeping mind would be left to its own devices.

A scene he had no doubts that Judge Mason and Sheriff Myles had also put together, regardless if they couldn't get the evidence together to prove as much.

Seated in the passenger seat of the Charger, Cortland stared straight out at the cone of illumination before them. A narrow stripe cutting through the darkened world, each mile traveled putting the revelry of the scene at The Smokehouse further behind them.

A place they would return to soon enough, once their reason for slipping away was behind them.

Their cover for the night, making sure they were seen both before and after this little jaunt into the woods.

His vision blurred as he retreated deeper into his thoughts. Recollections both from their last visit to the site, and the final conversation they had with their grandfather about the interaction.

Words of assurance that there was nothing to be concerned with, urging them to go to the party and enjoy themselves.

An erroneous hypothesis, without which they might have stayed behind, and G might still be with them.

Letting the same ideas he'd been debating in silence all summer long spool across his mind, Cortland drew his left hand up into his lap. Rotating his wrist inward, he balanced the pads of his opposite index and middle fingers across it, feeling the ridges of the recently embedded ink.

A simple message he kept tracing over as Remington cut out the headlights and let up on the gas pedal, the Charger drifted forward over the last half mile. A short stretch to the small turnout carved into the forest along the side of the road they had identified the week before.

A launching point for what was about to be done.

Angling the wheel to the side, he nudged the vehicle off the side of the road, needing only a single tap on the brakes to bring them to a complete stop. Twisting off the ignition, he pulled the keys, neither of them attempting to move for several moments.

Lingering silence that ended with Remington putting to words the same message Cortland had been going over, forever etched into both their skin.

"MCB?"

"MCB."

CHAPTER EIGHTY-TWO

Remington is aware that the plan is not without holes. The intel they have has been cobbled together on the fly, a combination of Google Earth images and the recollections of three traumatized business associates of Leo Garcia. People who Remington wants to believe can be trusted - the performances they each put on at the shelter house too much to simply be acting - but there is no way to be completely certain.

Not given what Garcia has on each of them. Families and livelihoods and so much more that could be ripped away if things don't go their way.

Even knowing that, it can be assured that the number of combatants Garcia has on his side heavily outweighs what they have, even with the addition of Linc Brady. Armed security, paired with house staff and groundskeepers and whoever else. People all capable of wielding a weapon if instructed to do so.

To say nothing of Enzo and his special projects unit, down two men, but no doubt having replenished by now.

And the fact that, eventually, they will be moving on a fortified position with walls and gates and even a damned hyena pen in the center. An undertaking matching – or even outpacing – some of the stuff they were tasked with in the sandbox years before.

All of that, Remington can accept. Calculated risks that are far from ideal, but can be planned for. Anticipated to the best of their abilities and schemed around.

What can't be is this initial meeting. The part that will put everything in motion, leaving his brother completely exposed for several long minutes. Time during which Enzo and his team can come screaming in from every direction or the damn sheriff can pull a gun and start shooting. Maybe even reach for a set of handcuffs.

Worst-case outcomes that there is no way Remington is going to let his brother face alone, the final words of Maylinn telling them to find her killer and to take care of each other playing on repeat in his mind for the last few hours. Moments when he was supposed to be trying to rest, instead laying flat on his back in the grass with Shine by his side, staring up at the sky, running two distinct loops through his head.

All that has happened thus far, from that first call received from Cortland to the meeting at the shelter house earlier.

And all that will occur in the hours ahead, superimposing the stories and images shared with how he best envisions it all playing out. Visuals of the plan, trying his damnedest to find any soft spots in it so he can determine how to work around them. Constant reenactments, most of which he feels reasonably good about, this opening portion the only part that still gives him pause.

The desire to protect, rearing up again after so many years.

The reason he is now wedged across the backseat, his feet pinned flat to the floor behind his brother's driver's seat. The rest of him splashed across the bench that is usually Shine's perch, the top of his head is flush against the passenger door.

In his lap rests one of the M17 pistols, a magazine wedged into the pocket on the back of the passenger seat, ready to be snatched up and jammed into position the instant his brother exits the vehicle. On the floor within easy reach is an M4 in case things really get hairy, a magazine resting just a few inches from the port it will be fitted into.

Firepower he keeps reaching out and touching with his fingertips every few minutes, making sure nothing slides out of reach as they drive.

"We haven't had much of a chance to talk since..." Remington says. Stopping there, he scrolls back through the last day, all of it feeling like a headlong sprint since he was on the phone with Tyrell the night before. A mad dash starting with Enzo and his team showing up, encompassing the visit to Victor, and the meetings with Reseda, and even picking up his friends from the airport.

A constant flurry of movement, the last time they were alone together – beyond just a few minutes in the car immediately after the fight or hearing why Maylinn was targeted, when neither felt like talking – being the game the night before. A fleeting moment of normality Remington now almost longs for, third only to wanting it to all be over, and wishing none of it had ever happened to begin with.

"You doing okay?" Remington asks, letting the previous sentence go. "You ready for all this?"

Able to see his brother through the crack in the two front seats, Remington watches as Cortland exhales slowly. Releasing one hand from the wheel, he passes his palm over his face, long shadows starting to form from the sun already getting close to the horizon.

Timing that is not by mistake, explicitly picked for this very reason.

"Did Maylinn ever tell you about her name?" Cortland asks. A reply that is not what Remington was expecting, his brows rising on his forehead.

"Her name?" he repeats.

"Yeah," Cortland answers. "It means precious jade, which in her parents' culture is seen as a symbol of goodness, beauty. They picked it because, well..."

Lifting the same hand, he gestures out in front of him. A self-explanatory movement, hinting at how his wife's name was chosen.

As fitting a moniker as Remington has ever known.

"You ask if I'm doing okay," Cortland continues, "and I think we both know the answer to that. But right now, oddly enough, all I can think about is her name. Not why Garcia killed her or those assholes burning down our house or any of the other stuff.

"I'm thinking about precious jade. And how she was exactly those things. Goodness. Beauty. And how since the moment she left us, all I have experienced is evil and ugliness."

Needing to stay hidden from view, Remington has no idea where they are. A short journey he senses coming to a close, as evidenced by the slowing of the car and his brother hitting the turn signal.

"You also asked if I'm ready for this," Cortland continues, making the turn and slowly rolling forward. His chin dips as he says, "Yeah. Right now, I'm feeling pretty damn evil and ugly myself."

Never before has Remington heard such a summation – especially from his brother – though he knows the feeling intimately. A state he lived in after losing his leg, wanting nothing more than to encounter the men responsible for the bomb and unloading on them with everything he had.

A dark cloud that hovered over him for months before dissipating, not to return until just a couple days ago.

"How ugly?" he asks as Cortland comes to a stop and jams the gearshift into park.

Twisting off the ignition, Cortland pulls his left hand back, rotating it so Remington can see the three dark letters inked into the pale flesh on the underside. Block letters normally covered by the titanium band of the watch Remington had barely noticed he's been without all week.

The same message he called with just a few nights before, dating back to an incident the two of them shared years ago.

"This ugly."

CHAPTER EIGHTY-THREE

Since the moment he first heard the voicemail from Sheriff Daubenmire informing him that there was a fire at his home, Cortland has been preparing himself for what he would arrive to see. Mental images ranging from the frame of the structure still standing with the windows blown out and soot staining the sides to a more macabre version with the roof sagged in and small tendrils of fire still licking at the corner posts.

Pictures that all were woefully short of what is now before him, but still isn't the most jarring part.

That honor belongs to the other aspects of the blaze left to assault his senses. The residual heat still rising from it, keeping him from ever getting within more than fifty feet. The taste of ash that lands on his tongue with every breath he pulls in. The sting of it in his eyes and the smell of it in his nostrils.

Complete annihilation making the pile of rubble before him seem that much more drastic. An entire home reduced to ash and soot, with only a few thick beams and posts left to hint at what was once nothing short of a showplace. A source of pride that he and his wife sunk so much time and expense into.

Monies lost that pale next to the value of the memories destroyed. An entire lifetime together, turned to dust and cast away with the breeze.

"I am very sorry," Sheriff Jeff Daubenmire says, his first words since Cortland's arrival ten minutes prior. An unexpected bit of decorum, allowing Cortland to walk across the length of his front yard and back to where he now stands, examining the damage.

Complete and total destruction there will be no salvaging, exactly as it was intended.

More of the same evil and ugliness he was just telling his brother about.

"Being so far out in the country, by the time anybody saw it was on fire and called it in, there wasn't much the fire department could do." Clearing his throat loudly, Daubenmire turns to the side and spits before continuing, "First on the scene estimated it had been burning for an hour before they arrived."

How much of the story is true and how much is the spoon fed rendition handed over by Leo Garcia, Cortland doesn't bother trying to speculate. More things that will only spike the anger within him, causing him to lash out.

Right now, there is nothing he would rather do than turn and grab the man by the open sides of the same zip-up hooded sweatshirt he is wearing. Throwing him to the ground, he'd love to take a few shots at him before snatching away his phone and calling Enzo to tell him to come on in.

A contact there is absolutely no question will be found there, the odds of the sheriff himself being the one to meet him at both the site of the accident and his burned home too much to be coincidence.

Lashing out that may feel good in the moment, but will destroy their plans. More than that, it will leave him out in the open and force Remington to reveal himself. A repeat of last night, with one of them armed, going against an opponent that outnumbers them.

A divergence that he cannot abide for many reasons, none less than the fact that he has to honor the dying request from his wife.

"What happened?" Cortland asks, just managing to keep his voice even.

"That's what I was hoping you could tell me," Daubenmire replies, arching an eyebrow as he glances over.

Knowing full well that he is being lied to, Cortland offers the same in return. Leaning into the same cover story, he opens his mouth as if trying to find the words. He lifts a hand, motioning to the blackened remnants before him.

"I wish I knew, but like I said, I was up in Dallas. With everything that happened, I had to get out of here for a couple days, so I loaded up the dog and a bag of clothes and took off yesterday morning.

"Never dreamed when I took off it would be the last time I saw this place."

CHAPTER EIGHTY-FOUR

For the second night in a row, Leo Garcia finds himself exiting through the rear door on the first floor of his mansion. A direct path from the center corridor bisecting the ground level, opening up onto a patio of Spanish tile. Flooring coated with multiple layers of sealant, making the pieces and the grout between them gleam beneath the lights overhead, as smooth as glass under the soles of his dress shoes.

To either side, wrought iron tables and loungers with striped cushions are arranged. Seating safely tucked under the shade provided by the second-story veranda above.

Window dressing that has to be cleaned and maintained, though to his knowledge has never been used before, the more preferred location being up top with the better view. The place where he stood with the Kleeses earlier in the week, and then again with Enzo and Aguilar a few days later.

The very same one still where he intends to be soon enough, watching as the ongoing headache that is the Alder family is finally snuffed out for good.

Aware of the pair of security guards posted on either corner of the spread, Garcia continues straight ahead without acknowledgement. His chin angled downward, he passes quickly across the patio, decidedly not in the mood for conversation.

One hand thrust deep into the pocket of his slacks, the other grips the smoldering remains of a Honduran cigar. A means of calming his nerves that he has not been without since Enzo left earlier, waiting to hear back from the man.

A preferred form of release that tonight is proving no match for the job, anticipation thrumming through him. Eagerness that was only barely under control earlier, before climbing the stairs to the third floor with dinner for his mother.

A visit he still wishes he could have pawned onto someone else, the caustic bite of her acid tongue spiking whatever angst he was already feeling. Repeated admonishments about where things now stand and how they should have been handled. Miscues that she attributes directly to him, always believing that he alone is responsible for every single action falling under the umbrella of the family empire.

A fate that somehow Enzo always manages to escape, even in moments like this when much of the trouble is his doing.

A protected status Garcia has long since grown tired of, that one day in the dirt and a little scar on his cheek somehow earning him a lifetime of protection. Maternal hovering far surpassing anything he himself has ever enjoyed.

Stepping out from beneath the overhead coverage provided by the veranda, the ambient temperature drops by a handful of degrees. A gibbous moon appears overhead, flanked by handfuls of stars liberally splashed against a darkened canvas. Early nightfall consistent with the month of November, regardless how warm the days still manage to be.

Underfoot, the path transitions from tile to concrete. The start of the walkway encircling the entire compound, extending thirty yards in front of him before hitting a T. Left, toward the holding pen that he and Enzo visited just the day before. Right, sweeping around to the gymnasium and barracks for the staff and grounds crew who live onsite.

Options that both seem less than appealing tonight, Garcia's pace slowing as he considers the much smaller holding cell directly in front of him. One of only two entrances into the compound, this one reserved for those individuals who have earned the fate of being part of the evening show. People who have made errors egregious enough to become sustenance for the animals roving inside.

Access to the place he intends to end up in, this one without the benefits of the UTV or stun batons. A battle he almost welcomes, trusting that the hyenas will put up a better fight than the pathetic showing from the quartet in the ring this morning.

Slowing himself to a halt on the edge of the concrete, Garcia's gaze glasses as he stares at the entryway before him, letting such a thing unfold in his mind. A fight he is deep in the midst of, envisioning just how it would work, the weapons he could cull together, the order in which they would attack, when the scene is shattered by the sound of his phone coming to life.

The very thing he has been waiting on all night, coming at the most inopportune moment. The rare instance when he was able to put everything else at arm's length, immersing himself in something else.

An intrusion that does nothing for his mood, Garcia flinging the remains of his cigar at the door, the stub disintegrating on impact, before sliding the phone out and pressing it to his face.

"We're on Alder," Enzo says, both men bypassing any sort of greeting. "He's alone, so Cesar is sitting on him now, the other crew is nearby as backup. As soon as they stop and we have the brother too, we'll all move in."

"Good," Garcia mutters, turning to his left and resuming his walk. A stroll toward the other entry to the compound, something similar – if less carnal – to what he just imagined in mind. "Just remember what I said earlier. We have plans for those two."

CHAPTER EIGHTY-FIVE

Every instinct Remington possesses is telling him to sit up in the backseat of his brother's SUV. Swap out the handgun he was carrying in his lap while parked at the house, a weapon far more accurate at close range, and go with the assault rifle resting on the floorboard. A change in weapons specifically designed for their new foe, exchanging the sheriff in jeans and boots for the two silhouettes in the sedan that has been following them since they left.

Pursuit that hasn't revealed itself as such yet, but Remington has no doubt that's what it is. Round headlights sitting low to the ground that appeared less than a quarter mile after they left, tracking their every move since. A series of nonsensical turns that nobody even remotely familiar with the area would follow, this car never wavering.

Not once has Remington even seen the sedan with his own eyes, not wanting to reveal himself to the two men following them, but already he can envision it in his mind. Another pair off the Leo Garcia henchmen assembly line, matching the two that he killed the night before. Guys who think they can hide in a smaller vehicle, disregarding the narrow country roads they are on and the total lack of anybody else nearby.

Targets he is aching to grab up the rifle and unload on, hanging out the side window like a dog, feeling the cool night air pass over his scalp.

"Still there?" Remington asks, already knowing the answer based on the faint glow hitting the backs of the front seats beside him.

Two feet away, Cortland lifts his chin, checking the rearview mirror. "Still there. Eighty yards back. No less, no more."

"No less, no more," Remington repeats, reaching past the rifle resting on the floorboards for his cellphone abutted against the barrel. Snatching it up, he cups one hand over the screen to kill any glare. With the other, he navigates through a couple of screens, finds what he wants, and hits send.

Flipping the call to speaker, he drops it facedown on his stomach, waiting as it connects and a single ring sounds out.

"Yo," Tyrell answers.

"They took the bait," Remington replies.

"Yeah?" Val asks, her voice clear over the line. "It's Enzo?"

"No," Remington says, "at least, we don't think so. These guys are in a sedan. Probably meant to follow us, try to blend in, wait for Cort to come to me."

"And then call in the calvary," Tyrell finishes.

His gaze fixed on the seats in front of him, Remington stares at the dull glow of headlights. Targets in the darkness he would love to punch out before unloading on the engine block sitting between them.

Take out their capability to move, and then really go to work on the two men inside.

"How far out?" Linc Brady asks.

The only question Remington can't answer from where he is hidden, he shifts his focus to his brother in the front seat. His chin still lifted upward, he alternates glances between the rearview and the road ahead, going through the progression a couple of times. Repeated glances that tells Remington something is wrong, prompting him to ask, "Cort?"

"Uhh," Cortland answers, clearly distracted as he gives the mirror one more look. "Two miles and closing, but I think we've got a second vehicle. Same size and shape, just fell in behind the first one."

Again, Remington thinks of the assault rifle stowed on the floorboard nearby, the urge to go for it climbing ever higher within.

"Looks like Enzo brought some more friends this time," he mutters before raising his voice and asking, "Ty, you guys get that?"

"We'll be waiting."

CHAPTER EIGHTY-SIX

"The barn is up here on the left," Cortland says, continuing to narrate their progress from the driver's seat. "Fifty yards until the turn."

Still stretched flat across the backseat, Remington grips the assault rifle in both hands. A two-handed clench that causes veins to bulge the length of his exposed arms and beads of sweat to form on his brow and upper lip. Adrenaline and anticipation that he hasn't experienced in three years, taken to another level by the addition of one more key component.

Something he's never known before, making everything seem even more pronounced.

The promise of vengeance. The first step toward retribution for what was done to Maylinn, and his brother's house, and even the shot to his prosthetic leg the night before.

Retaliation that was specifically requested on the voicemail left by his sister-in-law, days in coming and finally within grasp.

"Use the turn signal," Remington says. "Don't give them any reason to think you're onto them."

Grunting softly, Cortland does as instructed, a faint clicking finding Remington's ears. A sound that seems so much louder than he knows it to be, received in his heightened state.

"We get up there, pull in on the far side of Tyrell's truck and go straight into the barn," Remington says, rehashing the plan they have both been over a number of times. One more retelling to focus them both, pushing aside the urgency of adrenaline in their systems. "Unlatch the back door and then get upstairs with Val and Shine. Don't run, but don't dally either."

"Got it," Cortland says, slowing the SUV and turning the wheel hand over hand. A transition that Remington can feel passing through the seat beneath him as they switch from asphalt to gravel, the ride becoming bumpy and uneven beneath him.

"I don't see anybody," Cortland whispers, slowing the vehicle further.

"You won't," Remington replies. "Not until they want you to."

Hidden in the darkness, he knows that right now Linc Brady is posted up on the far bank of the pond. A vantage with a clear line of sight to the gravel lane, coming with the added bonus of the water reflecting his muzzle flashes, making it much more difficult to pin down an exact location.

A hint of confusion making it easier for Tyrell stowed high in the oak tree nearby and Val peering out through the small window in the hayloft on the second floor of the barn to fire unimpeded.

A shooting gallery that, hopefully, Enzo and his men will not anticipate, their bloodlust for Remington and his brother drawing them in.

"Alright, here we go," Cortland whispers, looping the SUV out a bit to the left before swinging it back to the right. A slow roll into position with rocks crunching under their tires, the brakes groaning low in protest.

Jamming the gearshift into park, he twists off the engine. "Good luck."

"Be safe," Remington replies, his grip on the M4 tightening as his brother steps out.

Pulling back on the handle for the rear door, Cortland opens it just far enough to unlatch it, the overhead light already disengaged. A quick exit requiring only that Remington shove it open with his foot before sliding out once the shooting starts. A fourth point in their onslaught, completely encircling their opponents.

His head cocked to the side, Remington waits, listening as the sound of Cortland's footsteps fade away. Progress that is easy to track through the thick gravel, gone for barely an instant before a flash of light passes through the interior of the SUV.

Headlights swinging in from the road nearby, making the turn into the lane. A bright glare that swings from right to left across his field of vision, matched just a few seconds later by a second sweep.

The two vehicles that Cortland mentioned spotting behind them. At least two hostiles, though more likely four, or even eight. Targets he tries to picture, his pulse climbing as he hears the cars pull forward, easing to a stop not far from where he rests. One engine and then another cuts out, followed by the loud din of car doors opening.

Feet setting down into gravel, accompanied by the low tones of voices. At least a handful or so, speaking with urgency, too low for anything exact to be made out. A debate of some sort that grows louder as they start to move forward, coming ever closer.

Sweat stinging his eyes, Remington slides his right foot forward, resting the ball of it on the bottom of the door, preparing to push it forward.

A fast exit in the face of a progressing enemy, both things cut short by the angry wail of an oversized engine tearing through the night.

CHAPTER 87

The very last thing Enzo said when he called the others and told them Alder was on the move was to follow, but do not engage. Knowing how much Leo Garcia wanted at least one – if not both – of them upright and functional, he made sure he was clear that they could get in position, pin them down, surround them if possible, but under no circumstances were they to expose themselves or make a move on them.

That had already happened once, with less than spectacular results.

In order, both of the men he spoke to had said they understood. Guys that Enzo hasn't worked with in the field before, but at the very least he figured he could trust with such a simple order. Follow a vehicle, keep him posted on where it is going.

Nothing more.

Making the fact that they are already out of their cars and moving on the small barn off the side of the road all the more jarring. Guns in hand, they are fanned out across the front of the structure, their bodies silhouetted in their own headlights.

Open targets for the two men tucked away inside, able to fire from either the main door standing open on the bottom level, or the smaller window hatch in the hayloft above.

"What the-" Aguilar mutters from the front seat. Leaning forward, he points across the dash as if Enzo can't see what is going on.

"Shit!" Enzo finishes for him, mashing his right foot down on the accelerator. Needing to head off whatever is about to happen, he bypasses going all the way up to the turnoff ahead, instead jerking the wheel to the side and tearing across the thick grass along the side of the road. A direct route with wheels spinning, the front end bucking as they dip down into a shallow ditch, spewing dirt and weeds in their wake.

Effort that causes the engine to wail, the red needles on the various gauges across the dash jerking to the right. Vehicular adrenaline to match Enzo's own, shoving the truck up and over the opposite side before catching purchase and hurtling them forward.

Fishtailing wildly through the thick scrub grass, Enzo works the wheel back and forth. Futile effort to put them on something approaching a direct course, the vehicle bouncing beneath them, lifting both him and Aguilar from their seats.

A bumpy ride stretching more than fifty yards before they meet up with the gravel lane, allowing him to jerk the wheel to the left, sending a shower of loose stones out in their wake. Headlights bouncing to and fro, their bright glow flashes across a pair of towering post oak trees before skittering over the top of a small pond sitting out to the right of the barn.

Next up are Alder's SUV and the damned truck with Tennessee plates Enzo first heard about days before. Things that are illuminated for but an instant, just long enough for Enzo to see and register, before his truck finally settles onto the lane, the pair of sedans and the four men incapable of following a simple order coming into view.

Each spread a few yards apart, they stand with guns stretched before them in both hands, arms extended to point the barrels toward the ground in front of them. Turned with their features squinted up against the harsh glare, they stand rooted in place, frozen as Enzo bears down on them. One last goose on the accelerator before hitting the brakes, the massive rig ripping trenches through the gravel as it careens to a stop.

A halt that is just barely complete before Enzo jumps out, Aguilar doing the same across from him. Leaving the ignition on and the lights shining bright, he pulls the Beretta from his hip the instant his boots hit stone, flinging the door shut as he goes.

"What the hell are you guys doing?!" he spits, chewing up the gap between them in long strides. "Cesar? The last thing I told you was-"

The remainder of the sentence dies in his throat, ripped away by the first crack of rifle fire. Words there is no point in continuing with anyway, the man he was just addressing tossed sideways by a pair of rounds that rip through his chest. Heavy caliber bullets that tear divots into his flesh, lifting him into the air and flinging him to the side.

Unintended flight that pulls the gun from his hands, ending in a shower of bloody pebbles.

The first shots fired, serving as a signal to the others laying in wait nearby. A crew significantly larger than just the Alders, muzzle flashes erupting from no less than a handful of sites around them. Bright orange flickers that ignite the night, shredding the three remaining men. Stick figures that convulse to either side, their legs giving out beneath them as their bodies contort back and forth, held upright by the power of shots coming in from opposite directions.

A death dance of sorts that Enzo watches for but an instant before wheeling back in the opposite direction. A hasty retreat that Aguilar would be better served in trying to match, instead standing and firing off a trio of shots. Three rounds that Enzo can hear sound out beside him as he tries to sprint back to the safety of the truck, his boots sliding through the loose gravel.

Traction that refuses to come as he flings stones in his wake, his body folding forward, forcing him to put his hands down to try for balance. Precious moments fighting for traction, allowing their attackers to shift their attention from the quartet up front to the two of them.

Sprays of bullets that roil the ground around them, sending pebbles up into the air. Shards of rock that strafe across Enzo's forearms and face as he pumps his legs twice, fighting against the uneven ground.

Ragged, desperate attempts to reach safety. Get inside the vehicle and get away, or at least get on the phone and alert Garcia what has happened.

One final chance to atone for the mistakes of the week. Show gratitude for the life that he has had.

Goals that fall woefully short, subverted by the first round smashing into his left calf. A shot fired from on high, pinning him to the ground, forcing him to try and crawl forward.

Onward progress that makes it but a few inches before the second bullet hits, pounding into his lower back.

Epicenters of pain that are soon joined by a third.

And then a fourth.

———

For as much time as Wes Callum and his two sons spent with wannabe professional fighters, they had proven to be just as weak and ineffectual as Remington figured they would be. Guys who positioned themselves adjacent to those with actual skill and toughness, acting as if that somehow was imparted to them through osmosis.

Classic posturing that had lasted barely a few seconds after he and his brother arrived, the three combined putting up what could generously be referred to as a weak fight, but nothing more. A little bit of profanity, interspersed with a couple of objects picked up and tossed across the room.

Books and lamps and whatever else they could get their hands on inside the shitty little office and the adjoining room that had appar-

ently become their home. A trash heap piled high with fast-food wrappers and cigarette butts, a broken-down couch serving as a bed for the old man while the boys used sleeping bags on the floor.

An existence far worse than what Remington and Cortland had endured the last few months, even at their age and under such extreme circumstances.

Confirmation of every thought Remington had about the family over the last couple of months. A daily purgatory that he made himself trudge through, knowing that this night was coming. A chance to finally clear the family ledger and do right by G before moving into the next phase of his life in the morning.

Aside from their few stray attempts at using projectiles, the closest either of the boys had come to mounting an offensive was a bit of misdirection. One of them standing and screaming, threatening to shoot them all, as the other attempted to jump over the couch.

An aborted Superman punch that never came close, the scrawny bastard's foot clipping the backend of it, sending him sprawling to the ground. Hard contact that was nearly enough itself to take him out, aided by a single shot from Remington with the length of pipe he carried.

A weapon to match what they held the last time he and his brother were in the office, and what the medical examiner guessed was probably used on G, breaking his legs and preventing him from getting away from the fire. Probably Shine too, after she tried to jump in to help.

A knockout blow that sent bloody spittle across the floor, rolling the guy's eyes up in his head and causing his dad and brother to both rush forward.

A haphazard advance that let both Remington and Cortland go to work, unleashing the angst they'd carried for so long. Blows accentuated by grunts and yells, cracking knees and wrists and ribs. Solid contacts that left them both writhing on the floor.

Poses of surrender, allowing Remington to deliver another knockout shot, sending the second son to sleep with his brother. Two prone bodies resting on the floor as Wes was hauled up and deposited into the same chair where he sat months before and claimed that he had been shorted. Forearms and calves bound to it with duct tape, he stared up at them with his features twisted in pain, blood and spittle both hanging from his chin.

A look tinged with malevolence that he aimed at the boys, accepting his fate even as Remington produced one final item. A jar of homemade product made on Moonshine Creek, taken from G's private store under the kitchen sink.

A final bit of closure, bringing things full circle.

Liquid ignition that Remington splashed far and wide, coating enough of the surfaces inside the decrepit office to kick things off, letting the dried lumber it was constructed of do the rest.

A tinder box that went up with but a single spark, flinging flames high above the forest canopy by the time Remington and his brother made it back to the Charger and drove away.

CHAPTER EIGHTY-SEVEN

For the second time in as many nights, Leo Garcia finds himself alone in the compound behind his house. Sitting at the wheel of the UTV, he is parked just inside the northern wall, the front end of the vehicle aimed south. A reverse angle from what he normally enjoys while standing on the veranda looking down from on high, his gaze tonight fixed on the mansion a couple hundred yards away. A glimmering monolith towering above, light spilling out from nearly every window despite it now being well past evening.

A shimmering crystal, topped by the beacon that is his mother's third-floor suite. One entire corner of the spread still lit up bright, as if the presence of a single shadow might somehow be the end of her.

Another of her many idiosyncrasies ranging from quirky to infuriating, this one managing to find itself just right of center. One more thing Garcia knows to go back years and years, when things like keeping the lights on was a luxury they could ill afford.

A proclivity that remains today simply because it can.

Giving his head a shake to cast aside any further thought of his *madre*, Garcia lowers his focus back to the compound around him. Grounds that aren't nearly as dark when looking back from this angle, the house providing enough ambient light to send long shadows across everything. A perpetual sunset that Garcia will take steps to remedy before the next hunt.

That very thing being why he is out here now.

Alone in the semi-darkness, two things rest on the passenger seat beside Garcia. The first is the same stun baton he used the night before. Electronics capable of producing fifteen million volts, housed inside a sleeve of aircraft-grade aluminum and painted black.

A mandatory precaution whenever venturing into the compound, regardless of time of day.

A few inches past the baton sits his cellphone. A standard iPhone with a rectangular screen that he has been waiting to light up for the better part of an hour now, ever since Enzo called and said that Alder had been spotted.

An update informing him that the two men have been nabbed and are on their way. Garcia can exit the compound and begin to make plans for their arrival.

Festivities that he has been thinking about ever since Enzo first entered his office earlier to say that Sheriff Daubenmire had spoken to the accountant and he would be there later. Fantasies that bordered on fetish, imagining getting the two of them in the ring. A test of manhood that is as mismatched as can be, starting with the accountant before squaring off with the one-legged bastard trying to mask his shortcomings with a sleeve of ink and buzzed hair.

A faux tough guy that Garcia has seen many times, getting a measure of the man from the photos at the house, even long before Enzo detailed what had taken place.

Bypassing the use of gloves, Garcia would do things old school. Bareknuckle brawling opening plenty of wounds on both. Fresh blood that will carry their scent out into the night, ensuring that their time inside the compound will be short. Smell so strong that the hyenas will practically pick it out of the air, descending on both of them with a power and tenacity they can't even imagine.

A rare late-night show that will be worth staying up to see.

A spectacle he almost wishes he can film, sending a copy to every one of his associates throughout the area. A digital file that can be forwarded on the next time Kennedy Banks decides to hold a press conference or some enterprising young attorney thinks of filing a lawsuit.

This is what happens when someone comes after a Garcia. The approach may vary and the punchline might change a bit, but the ending is the same.

Always.

Rolling his gaze to the side, Garcia stares at the darkened piece of plastic that is his phone's screen. So badly, he wants to reach out and tap on it, calling it to life. Check to ensure he hasn't received a message that went unnoticed. Maybe even pick it up and phone Enzo just to see what the hell is taking so long.

If the men really did run all the way back to Dallas like frightened children, and Garcia's men are all now in a convoy, headed north across the state.

Making it as far as lifting his hand and stretching it across the middle console, his attention is pulled away by a flash of movement in his periphery. A black shadow that he senses more than sees, given away by the clump of sage grass shifting in its wake.

A soft rattle of dead brush hinting that at least one part of what he has been waiting on has finally arrived. A sight that brings a smile to his lips as he raises his hands to the frame above, using it to stand behind the wheel.

"Soon," he whispers, staring out into the darkness, hoping to catch another glimpse of the alpha and her clan. "Very soon."

CHAPTER EIGHTY-EIGHT

Based on the overhead images that they were able to pull from the internet for the address Lance Reseda and the others gave them, it looks like a fence and gate of some sort surrounds Leo Garcia's compound. An enclosure that Remington couldn't get too clear a look at, able to zoom in just far enough to determine that it is nowhere near as formidable as what he encountered at Master Gunnery Sergeant Turakis's place. A basic fence and gate that probably has cameras and roving guards, but is far from impenetrable, unlike the enclosure serving as the centerpiece of the spread.

The holding pen for the man's beloved hyenas, outlined in painstaking detail by all three of his associates in the shelter house that afternoon. A carveout able to be observed from the veranda extended from the second floor of the mansion, those two features surrounded by a manicured lawn sprawling for acres in every direction.

Rectangles of differing size positioned adjacent to one another, encircled by a third in the form of the fence running the perimeter of the property. A clear demarcation point between land that is mowed and cared for, and the swath of open fields spread wide thereafter.

Land that Garcia no doubt also owns, insulating himself from unwanted neighbors or surveillance.

An estate design that Remington suspects is meant to serve dual purposes, keeping others at bay while still sitting in plain sight. A middle finger to any who might try to come for him, steeped in the belief that he is untouchable.

A viewpoint that Remington has seen proven wrong the world over, his own plan for how to do just that tonight becoming infinitely easier in the form of an unexpected gift.

The truck that he now sits in, previously the property of Enzo, now only slightly dinged up after the battle at the feeding station, if it can even be called that. A trap putting on full display their hubris and the belief that they are infallible.

A one-sided affair that was far better than Enzo or his men deserved, the need for precision outweighing all else. A quick and complete kill before they could retreat or – even worse – get word to Garcia about what had happened.

Aside from a few bullet holes pockmarking the passenger door panel and front bumper, there is nothing to indicate that anything is amiss. No mirrors or taillights shot out. No interference with the handling, the engine starting on his first attempt and running smoothly ever since.

"Turnoff in one mile," Tyrell says from the passenger seat. His features illuminated by the phone held out in front of him, he alternates his gaze between the screen and the road.

A quiet chunk of country two-lane not unlike the one Cortland lives on, with few structures and sweeping meadows pushed tight up to the pavement on either side. Clearcutting that begins just past where they are headed, confirming Remington's previous assumption. Sight lines stretched wide, making anybody who gets too close to Garcia's property easily noticeable.

"Got it," Remington replies, flicking a glance to the pair of headlights nested in his rearview mirror. Square orbs belonging to his brother's SUV, carrying Cortland, Val, and Linc Brady. A sharing of space that made for a more comfortable ride up to this point, things about to get quite cozy over the last mile ahead.

Five people all tucked into the truck, along with the six bodies buried beneath one of the tarps taken from Master Gunnery Sergeant Turakis earlier. A load that fills most of the available space in the bed, humped up level with the tire wells on either side.

Edges tucked down tight, they are completely hidden even from what he can see in the rearview. Secret cargo about to be delivered back to Garcia's place, disposed of as part of the next step in their plan.

The kickoff for the second phase, first made possible by the gift from Turakis, then made infinitely easier by nabbing Enzo's truck. A vehicle that should get them by any cameras and through the gate without opposition, nobody inside thinking twice about seeing it pull up, even at such an hour.

Still carrying the adrenaline of rolling out from the SUV to help mow down Enzo and his men earlier, Remington's thumbs tap at the top of the steering wheel. A dewy veneer of sweat covers his arms and face.

Anticipatory energy that builds as Tyrell extends a finger before him and says, "Right there."

Nodding his head in silent understanding, Remington flips on the blinker to alert his brother behind him. Forewarning prior to tapping on the brakes and beginning to drift to the side of the road. A soft exit that ends with him sliding onto a small dirt patch forming the corner between the road they are on and a smaller one feeding into it.

A makeshift parking lot also nabbed from overhead images where they will leave the SUV. Their getaway vehicle once all this is completed, the remaining life expectancy on the truck they are in down to just a few more minutes.

An ending far more befitting it – and its owner – than what happened to the Ram 1500 that sent Maylinn off the side of the road.

Taking a shallow angle, Remington flips the headlights off to give the impression to anyone who may be watching that he has turned out of sight before shooting to the side. Swinging into the dirt patch, he shoves the gearshift into park and steps out. An exit matched by Tyrell beside him, going straight for the rear tire and using it to hoist himself up into the bed.

A few seconds later, Cortland pulls to a stop behind them, a cloud of dust rising in their wake. Barely coming to a complete halt, all three people pile out and head straight for the truck.

Weapons in hand and Kevlar strapped on, Val and Brady go for the rear tailgate as Cortland rotates up toward the passenger seat.

"Watch the explosives back there," Remington says as they climb in, alluding to the bricks wedged up tight to the inside of the tailgate. Firepower stowed on the backend to match that strapped to the front bumper.

The special gift Turakis was insistent they deliver to Garcia on his behalf.

A greeting just moments from being delivered, Remington waiting only until everyone is inside and stowed before climbing back into the driver's seat and starting on again.

CHAPTER EIGHTY-NINE

Cortland's brother made it abundantly clear that he didn't need to join him and the others as they moved on Leo Garcia's home. Three men and one woman who are all trained in combat. A cumulative forty years of being in the shit, flung across the globe in places they aren't allowed to speak of, and most civilians probably can't find on a map.

Training so ingrained that not one even seems to be feeling the effects of what happened earlier. A wild flurry of a firefight that saw six men mowed down around the barn and pond they have commandeered as their temporary home.

Bodies that weren't even given the chance to start cooling before being scooped up. Wrapped in an old tarp, they were tossed in the back of the pickup Cortland now sits in, riding shotgun with Remington upfront while the others are tucked in around the outside of the bed.

Five live bodies and six dead ones, all crammed into a single vehicle, aimed at a destination that has no idea any of them are coming.

To even pretend he isn't undergoing some effects in the aftermath would be a lie. A bolt of adrenaline that surged through his system beginning the moment he first exited out of his SUV and began to march toward the barn. Electricity that hurtled through him, growing with each step even after he was well out of sight and strapped on the protective vest he still wears.

Full-body tingling that started around the moment he stepped up beside Val in the hayloft and grabbed a semiautomatic handgun, extending it out through the opening and pulling the trigger as fast he could, even after the magazine was emptied and the firing pin was drawing nothing but air.

Sensation that he can still feel pulsating through him, threatening to overpower his nervous system. Overload there will be no way to contain once this is all complete and his body is forced to come down, looking for any possible means of release.

A problem he will deal with later, no chance in hell that he wasn't going to be joining Remington and the others tonight. Not after what Garcia and his minions have done.

Taken his wife. His home. Very nearly his own life and that of his brother.

Robbed him of the child he and Maylinn were planning. The future they were getting set to embark upon.

"You good?" Remington asks from the driver's seat as he pulls out onto the road, leaving Cortland's SUV parked behind them. Their future exit, left far enough away not to be noticed, but close enough they can still get there quickly on foot and make their departure when they need to.

Glancing over, he waits for Cortland to meet his gaze before turning back to stare at the river of gray stretched out in front of them. A straight tract of asphalt pulled taut and true, their final destination now less than a mile off. The place the two of them have spent all week in search of, circling through most of the greater Austin area, hoping to find themselves here now.

The last thing his wife ever said to him – to both of them – was she loved them, and to go find whoever was responsible for pushing her off the side of the road that night. The driver, whose body is now sprawled in the bed behind them, and the man who ordered him to do it.

Remington was right in expressing his concern earlier. Cortland is not a soldier. Pretty far from it, in fact, most of his life spent staring at figures and spreadsheets.

Still, not once did the thought of staying at the farm with Shine ever cross his mind. Even if he doesn't fire another shot or touch another weapon, he has to be here to see this through.

Otherwise, he will never be able to bury his wife and give her peace, let alone find a minute of it for himself ever again.

Rolling his left wrist inward, Cortland glances down to the three letters etched into the soft skin. The only time in his life a needle has ever touched him, as compared to the full array covering his brother's arm.

A reminder of days past that he usually keeps covered up, bringing it out only on rare occasions. Moments when he needs to steel himself for what awaits.

Obstacles that have never been anywhere near this, though the sentiment is the same.

Reaching across his body, he traces the outline of the letters with the tip of his right index finger. Three in order, reminding him who he is. Where he came from.

What he is capable of.

"Good," Cortland replies, lifting his gaze to see the front corner of the fence encircling Garcia's property pass by on his right. A brick base standing two feet tall, with black wrought iron spikes climbing an additional four above that, backstopped by an even hedge.

A line telling others to come no closer, but by no means a complete barricade. The type of cocksure thing a man like Garcia would erect, believing it all that is necessary to insulate himself from harm.

A man so steeped in his own legend, he can't tell where myth ends and reality takes over.

"Here we go," Remington replies, tapping on the brakes to cut their speed in half. A slowing of pace that causes Cortland's pulse to pick back up, the same rush of natural chemicals spilling into his system.

A potent elixir he feels pulsating through him as Remington makes the turn and eases off the side of the road, both of them staring straight ahead at the gate made of the same vertical spikes. His body temperature climbing under the weight of the body armor, Cortland draws in shallow breaths. His hand reaches for the handgun beside him, counting off seconds.

An interminable wait that ends with the truck doing exactly what his brother said it should. A sensor hidden somewhere inside, or a sleepy guard seeing only the familiar vehicle and waving them through.

A free pass inside in the form of the gate parting in the middle, swinging wide to either side. A painfully slow opening that moves a few inches at a time, clearing the way down the lane directly to the three-story mansion rising before them.

A towering beacon with most of the lights within still on, despite the time of night.

The instant the gate is open wide enough for the truck to squeeze through, Remington taps on the gas. A light hit, giving just enough fuel to push it ahead.

"On three," he whispers. "One."

Using the automatic switch to lower his window, Cortland snakes a hand out into the cool air. Balling it into a fist, he knocks twice against the outside of the door, alerting those in the back to get ready to move.

"Two."

Pulling his hand back, Cortland rests it on the handle of the door beside him. In his left, he grips the gun tight, his heart thumping in his chest as the speed of the truck begins to rise. A steady climb past ten and up to fifteen miles an hour, allowing his brother to set the cruise control.

"Three!"

Jerking open the handle, Cortland pushes the door wide. Leaping down, he hits the concrete square with both feet, his momentum pushing him into a jog, carrying him out a few steps into the plush grass of the lawn. An unceremonious exit that is stopped a moment later by Linc Brady grabbing hold of him with his free hand, an M4 pointed toward the sky in his other.

A hard stop in the man's iron grip, followed by Brady asking, "You good?"

"Yeah. Thanks," Cortland says, collecting himself as he turns back to check the opposite side of the drive. A quick look to ensure that his brother's prosthetic survived the exit okay, the answer coming in the form of Remington already standing with his M4 raised before him.

Battle position that Cortland assumes as well, settling in beside Brady as they begin to move, following the glow of red taillights hurtling forward in front of them.

CHAPTER NINETY

Of the many, many misassumptions surrounding hyenas, Leo Garcia has found there to be two that are larger than most. Fallacies that are so pervasive they have become generally accepted by society, muddling assumptions about other animals and inaccuracies from books and movies into false beliefs.

The first of those is that hyenas are pack animals. While it is true that they do live and interact in groups, they are actually called clans. A name passed down from previous generations by the natives where hyenas have lived and thrived for ages.

A recognition of the magnificent beasts not as just marauding vultures, but as animal warriors. Survivors, in the truest sense of the word.

The second inaccuracy often surrounding hyenas is that they follow an alpha male. An error stemming either from mistaking them for wolves or merely superimposing their own societal expectations onto the creatures, when in fact they follow a strict matriarchal hierarchy.

A female at the lead, much like Garcia's own business empire, all others falling in order behind her.

Another point of kinship he couldn't help but feel as he stood behind the steering wheel of the UTV, his feet planted on the floorboards, his forearms resting across the roll bar forming the frame for the open roof. Details that came to mind as he locked gazes with the alpha, her eyes flashing in the ambient light from the house.

Two animals of different species fixated on each other, measuring one another in silence.

A staring contest that had lasted for nearly two full minutes before being brought to an abrupt halt by the explosion from the residence nearby. An audible blast of metal and brick and stucco that pierced the night, sending the alpha and her clan bounding into the darkness.

The start of a chain reaction followed in order by flickering firelight appearing behind the top outline of the mansion, pushing plumes of charcoal smoke into the sky, blotting out the stars and moon from view. Sights that precede the faint rumble of the earth beneath him just milliseconds later. A palpable tremble that passes through the tires of the UTV, causing the windshield before Garcia to vibrate.

In the distance, he can hear the errant calls of security staff and groundskeepers. Shouted orders about where to go or how to react, mixed with fearful inquiries of what just happened.

Voices that carry through the darkness, snapping him into action.

Dropping straight into the seat, Garcia's first move is for the keys still in the ignition. Turning the engine over, he jerks the gear shift into drive and stamps on the accelerator, sending the vehicle hurtling forward before even bothering to turn on the headlights.

Bouncing over stones and divots, he steers with his left hand, his right going for the phone bouncing around on the passenger seat beside him. Snatching it out of the air a few inches above the padded cushion, he draws it over and thumbs it to life.

A moment later, he has the recent call log up onscreen before him, going down but a single entry before hitting send. Keeping it clutched in his hand, he holds it a few inches away from his face as it begins to ring. Shrill tones that sound out over the speakerphone as he stares ahead at the world lit up by the headlights bouncing along the trail before him.

"Come on, come on," he mutters, waiting until the third unanswered ring before shouting, "pick up, dammit!"

CHAPTER NINETY-ONE

With the relatively modest amount of explosives attached to the front bumper and stowed away in the bed, Remington wasn't expecting the destructive impact to the mansion to be overwhelming. Aimed for the front wall just east of the stairwell climbing to the main entrance on the second floor, Enzo's truck had hit square, exploding most of the surrounding windows and carving a deep gouge into the stucco exterior.

A divot formed from pulverized cement and the underlying concrete block that would be roughly large enough to accommodate the vehicle, if it hadn't been ripped to shrapnel on contact. Black soot and twisted pieces of metal and the remains of Enzo and his team that striped the side of the building and rained down across the stairs and front drive.

Odd bits and pieces of glass and steel and bone that Remington can feel crunching underfoot as he steps forward, his assault rifle nested against his deltoid. His cheek lifted a few inches away from the barrel, he jerks his focus in either direction, scanning for the first signs of movement that he knows are set to arrive at any moment.

The real purpose of using the makeshift bomb was twofold. A

pair of distinct objectives that Remington had in mind that had nothing to do with destroying the mansion, the first of those already accomplished by the smears of blood and ragged chunks of carcasses covering the ground around them. A means of getting rid of the six men who attempted to come for them, this a far better means of disposal than trying to dig graves or sinking them into the bottom of the farm pond.

Temporary solutions that would have eventually been found, bringing along investigations and assorted other attention none of them wants.

The second purpose in sending the front of the truck right at the side of the mansion was what Ward Turakis had in mind when he gave them the material, that being to serve as an announcement. A loud call to be heard by anyone inside or nearby. Shake the whole damn place to the foundation, letting them know that they have visitors.

And then wait as they inevitably come rushing out to meet them. A far more effective means of entry, letting them dictate terms, than trying to slip inside and clear a single room at a time in a spread so large.

A siren call that takes only a few moments to prove effective as the first signs of hostiles appear. Voices and commotion that rises in cadence and volume, culminating in men spilling out from the front entrance. Guys dressed in black slacks and matching t-shirts with automatic weapons in hand, far more worried about speed than precision.

Pushing their way through the main door, they pour across the top landing without any sort of cohesion, the confusion of the moment and their lack of proper experience obvious. Men who, like Leo Garcia himself with his lax estate security, aren't expecting to be attacked at home. Hubris that has made them believe themselves untouchable, leaving them vulnerable in the face of an actual threat.

Reduced to little more than target practice, Tyrell is the first to open up. A burst of four or five rounds that are joined in chorus by

Remington, and then Val and Linc Brady as well. Small clusters that chew through the men, twisting their bodies in unnatural movements or flinging them against the front doors behind them, dark bloodstains marring the pale stone and wood in their wake.

"Left! Left!" Remington hears from his brother beside him. A call that immediately jerks his attention to the side, leading with the front tip of his gun. Tunnel vision centered on the sights affixed to the barrel, his entire world view winnowed to the view along his weapon.

Rotating that direction, his knees remain bent. His shoulders and biceps flex, pinning the gun tight to his shoulder.

Pitched forward at the waist, he scans across the front of the building, making it as far as the corner before the men Cortland was calling out come into view. A ragged line of opposition in more matching attire, most making the same mistake as those now bleeding out on the front steps. Guys more worried with getting there fast than being in any kind of position to put up a defense once they do.

Armed lightly with handguns gripped in one hand or even clutched by the barrel, they come sprinting into sight. One after another that Remington lets get a few paces past the corner of the house, making sure they are completely exposed before tugging back on the trigger.

An effort that he is joined in by Val to one side, and Cortland just a few steps off his hip. A three-person assault splitting the team down the middle, the sound of Tyrell and Brady doing the same to the other side finding his ears. Background noise that fills in the brief gaps between bursts from his own weapon and those to either side.

A sudden outburst that lasts but a minute, leaving misshapen lumps strewn across the lawn.

An all-out barrage, wiping away what he has to believe is a fair chunk of the security staff.

In the wake of the initial contact, the silence feels especially pronounced. Quiet that Remington does not trust signals the end, but rather a break between the immediate response and the ensuing wave. Reinforcements grouping up, looking to make their next attempt more of a cohesive effort.

A gap Remington has seen before, knowing this is their best chance to move.

"You guys good?" Remington asks, turning his chin an inch toward his shoulder.

"Good," Brady replies.

"Six down," Tyrell adds. "You?"

"Five," Val answers, "plus the five on the steps."

"Twenty-two total," Courtland says, "counting the ones in the truck."

Just shy of two dozen, Remington guesses there has to be at least half that many still remaining, thirty-five or so necessary to protect a homestead and keep a business like Garcia's running.

Numbers meaning they still have work to do, up to and including finding the leader himself, Remington guessing him to either be holed up with guards inside, or out back hiding in his beloved compound.

"Ty, Brady, you two stay out here, work cleanup on the grounds. Val, Cort, you guys with me on the house."

CHAPTER NINETY-TWO

After the assorted chaos going on out front, the interior of the home seems eerily quiet. Gone is the earsplitting timbre of gunfire pulsating through the air. Same for their accompanying muzzle flashes. The lingering flames still chewing at the charred remnants of Enzo's truck. The thick scents of scorched tires and gunpowder and blood.

Even the ground beneath Cortland's feet feels like it has been swept free as he no longer crunches over the macabre assortment of debris from the crash.

Positioned in between Remington and Val, Cortland finds himself walking through the interior of a great foyer. A space stretching more than twenty yards in either direction, with artwork in gilded frames on the wall and a chandelier overhead. A light fixture blazing forth, highlighting the smoke and dust hanging in the air.

Directly in front of them, a staircase matching the one outside continues its ascent, rising to the third floor. Wide steps with banisters running upward on both sides, each framing the top floor above.

On the opposite side of the door behind them, they can hear the continued report of weapon's fire. A few errant shots fired by hand-guns, followed by the rapid bark of assault rifles.

A continuation of what was happening just moments before, the guards onsite woefully unprepared and outgunned for such an encounter. A firefight in the purest form that has adrenaline thrumming through Cortland's system, taken much higher than even just a short time earlier.

A magnified state he has only approached one other time in his life, that too with his brother by his side.

The full physiological effects taking hold, sweat leaks from every pore, matting his shirt to his back beneath the protective vest he wears. The lights and sounds around them seem more pronounced.

Every scent, even the air he breathes, feels more exaggerated.

An M17 gripped tight with both hands, Cortland keeps it extended out directly in front of him. Flicking the tip to either side, he alternates his focus between the pair of doorways on either side of the stairs. Open maws that go somewhere deeper in the mansion, both shrouded in shadow.

Possible openings through which more opposition could pour at any moment.

To his right, Remington is turned at an angle, checking over the various doors and hallways to that side. An ongoing sweep of the second floor they are on and the third above, checking to make sure nobody is tucked beyond the banister rails, trying to fire down from up high.

Movements that are matched to the letter by Val on Cortland's opposite side, her shoes squeaking softly against the tile.

"We need to get the hell out of this room before we become fish in a barrel," she hisses.

"Agreed," Remington fires back. Twisting his chin to the side, he peers over his shoulder at the two of them. "Your side clear?"

"Far as I can see," Val replies.

Snapping his focus back to face forward, Remington takes

another couple of steps. Progress to improve his vantage, allowing him to peer further into the rooms before him.

"You two go up, make sure the third is empty. I'll work this floor. Meet downstairs in five."

"Roger that," Val says, doing just as Remington had a moment before and giving the rooms on her side one last check. A move forward that Cortland doesn't bother to match, letting her pull out ahead of him a few steps.

Swinging her assault rifle out in front of her in short, spastic movements, she crosses one foot over the other. Quick steps to move past his position, bringing her up along the side of the closest bannister.

Climbing three stairs, she scans the side of it, checking over the empty doorway Cortland was just watching, before tilting her weapon upward. Attention moving to the top floor, she scans the length of it before turning toward Cortland and dipping her chin, followed by tilting her head to the side.

Silent signaling for him to do the same as she just did. A pattern of movement he matches by slipping to the far side of the stairs and moving up a trio of stairs before stopping. Giving one final check over the last doorway in the room, he swings his weapon upward, beginning to ascend in tandem with Val as Remington moves past him down below.

A slow climb going one step at a time, the top floor coming a bit more into view with each rise in elevation. Eight-inch chunks that reveal more of the same décor as downstairs, with landscape artwork on the walls and runner tables lining the hall.

Climbing with his left foot and bringing his right up beside it, Cortland ascends the last couple steps. With each one his chest constricts, his breathing growing more shallow.

Sweat leaks over his features as he pauses just shy of the top to peer out around the banister. His first clear view the length of the hall running through the center of the mansion, with doors spaced evenly along the far side.

Breaks in the wall with doors pulled shut or the lights off inside, pulling his gaze toward the rear corner. A double doorway standing open with a bright yellow glow pouring out, striping the tile and opposite wall

"I got lights down here," he whispers.

"Clear over here," Val replies. "I'm coming your way."

Grunting softly in understanding, Cortland waits until Val appears in his periphery before rising one final step onto the hallway made of the same tile as the foyer and the stairs. Polished flooring that allows him to move silently along the rail, his pulse rising with each step.

Anticipation that goes far beyond what he experienced outside, moving and reacting to threats unspooling around him.

Creeping forward in measured steps, Cortland keeps pace with Val, moving until they go past the edge of the banister, the wall to the room they are approaching filling in beside him. Additional cover from anyone who might be lurking below, Val stopping him from going any further by raising a fist, alerting him to halt.

A silent order bringing him to a stop, keeping his gun extended before him as she stays tight to the opposite wall, her neck craning forward, trying to see into the doorway before them.

Cutting her steps in half, she moves closer, all sound bleeding away as Cortland holds his breath, watching her grow closer.

Total attention leaving him completely exposed for the old woman who steps out of the shadows at their back. A doorway he assumed unoccupied, letting her hide with a shotgun in hand, waiting for them to get into position.

An optimal angle giving Cortland barely enough time to turn and face her before the massive weapon explodes in a flash of smoke and gunpowder.

CHAPTER NINETY-THREE

From the instant the explosion happened on the frontside of the mansion to the moment when realization hit and Leo Garcia dropped himself down into the seat of the UTV and took off was a full minute. Sixty seconds to see the initial burst of flames and the resulting tufts of smoke and feel the tremor of the ground before the synapses in his brain started firing, spurring him into action.

After that, it was another three to bring the UTV to life and go tearing back through the compound. A bouncy ride in a vehicle decidedly not made for speed, no matter how many times he stamped on the accelerator, threatening to push it through the floorboards.

A drive that was unnervingly slow, more than once giving him the notion of simply jumping out and sprinting up through the center of the enclosure. Spurred on by every chemical capable of being produced by the human body, he would pound straight ahead, following the tire ruts of the UTV where he could, cutting new trail when he had to.

A plan that he might have been willing to go for under the light of day, but was forced to opt against given that just moments before he had been staring down the leader of the clan. A collective willing and able to rip him apart, without question tracking his progress.

As it was, the best he could do was to go straight for the holding pen along the side of the compound. The auxiliary building reserved for herding the hyenas before feeding time and where the UTV is normally parked. One of only two exits, this one much further from the mansion, but offering him freedom of movement.

A chance to get out of the damn rattling cage and move of his own will. Urges growing stronger through the pair of calls to Enzo that both went unanswered.

Barely taking the needed moment to close the roll top door to the compound behind him as he went, he left the keys in the ignition and jumped out, pushing through the side door where he and Enzo had spoken less than two days earlier. The stun baton still in hand, he'd burst through, reaching a full sprint within a couple of strides.

A hard charge with arms hooked at ninety degrees, his quads and lungs both burning as he tore ahead. A forty-yard dash that would rank among the best on the nearby Longhorns football team that puts him right back where he was barely ninety minutes earlier. That spot where the path forks wide to either side, the smaller entrance to the compound at his back.

Just seven minutes having passed since that first initial sound tore through the night, already he can see and feel the manifestations of it around him. Wanton chaos that borders on visceral, touching every one of his senses. Everything from the scattered shouts and gunshots of his men to the acrid scent of smoke in the air.

Sweat streaming over his features, Garcia stands with the stun baton gripped tight. Swinging his gaze to either side, he can see the darkened lumps of bodies laying scattered across the lawn. Amoebic shapes humped in odd intervals, hinting at what has already taken place.

Carnage that continues as the sound of weapons firing continues to draw closer, his opponents sweeping in from either side. A pincer formation, driving everything back toward the compound.

Split forces that will meet in the middle before either going straight ahead or circling back into the house.

Of the many enemies he has amassed over the years, he can only think of one that is recent enough – and stupid enough – to move on him. The same one who just the night before engaged with Enzo and Hector and Ramon, responsible for the latter two's deaths, and likely the sudden radio silence of the former.

An opposing force that, as far as he knows, is only two people, though from the sights and sounds around him seems to have recruited some help. Swollen numbers that have imbued them with false confidence, making them think they can come at his home.

Intruders he will personally be the end of, his hand tightening around the stun baton as he begins to move forward. Determined strides along the concrete, heading toward the polished tile comprising the patio under the veranda. The same path he walked in reverse not long ago, his destination then the compound, his goal now to get to his office and the cache of guns hidden there.

Automatic weapons to match those to either side, their angry retorts and flickering bursts of light both easily identifiable.

Vitriol hurtling through him, Garcia takes but a single step forward. A start to resuming his previous sprinting, cut short by a figure appearing in the doorway to the first floor. A flesh and blood blockade coming closer, an assault rifle gripped in his hands.

Coming straight ahead, he walks with a slight limp, as if compensating for a prosthetic leg. His right arm is wrapped in a sleeve of tattoos.

A man Garcia has been hearing about for a couple days, even saw the night before in the photos on the wall at the Alder home.

A target wearing the same snarl that rises across Garcia's features as the two begin to descend on one another.

CHAPTER NINETY-FOUR

The best approximation Cortland can come up with is someone holding a sledgehammer in both hands and swinging it like a pendulum. A shot not the way it is intended, but with using the top of it as a battering ram. A thunderous blow right into his ribcage, making his entire torso feel like it has been constricted two sizes smaller than usual. Pressure that he can feel emanating out from what is certainly a couple of broken ribs, making it difficult to even breathe.

Pain that manifests in small pops of light across his vision, guaranteeing that once the insulation of adrenaline leaves his system, the hurt will be fierce.

"Cort!" Val says, charging down the hallway and dropping in beside where he was tossed flat on his back. A perfect baseball slide going feet first, bringing her to a halt by his hip. Her gun raised, she swings her focus in either direction before settling over him, blocking the light above from view. "Dammit, are you okay?"

Her eyes wide with concern, she traces her gaze over his face, moving instantly down to his body. Releasing her left hand from the underside of her weapon, she passes it across his Kevlar vest. An exploratory search for fresh blood that ends with her forming her index finger and thumb into tweezers, using them to extract the misshapen twist of metal from the protective plates encasing him.

A small hunk of steel mushroomed into a blob that she examines for an instant before flinging it down the hall behind her. An angry dismissal, wanting to cast it as far away from them both as possible.

"I'm okay," Cortland mutters, the words barely audible as he takes in shallow breaths, fighting to catch his air.

"You sure?" she asks, snapping her focus back up to meet his. "Anything hurt?"

"Everything hurts," Cortland mutters, "But I'm okay."

Once more she scours over him, bypassing his torso for his arms and legs. Quick pats before pulling her hand back to examine the fingertips, finding them void of blood.

Final visual confirmation needed before exhaling loudly, her shoulders visibly rising and falling. "Thank God. If something happened to you, your brother would have killed me next."

"Rem," Cortland says, lifting his head and peering past his feet down the hall to a pair of mismatched items. The same shotgun that knocked him flat, resting right next to a diminutive woman in a blouse and skirt both lined with lace, originally white but since dyed crimson in the woman's own blood.

The end result of more than a half dozen rounds offered by Val, flinging the woman against the corner of the doorway and spattering the wall and ground around her with blood.

An odd enough scene taken even further by the clear oxygen tube wrapped around her skull, pulled taut and keeping her head from dropping all the way to the floor.

A visual Cortland would have never put together, even after hearing about the angry matriarch of the empire who really ran things.

One more for the pile of sights and memories from this last week he would love nothing more than to be without, flushing them from his mind forever.

"We need to..."

"Yeah," Val agrees, drawing a knee up under her. Hooking a hand into Cortland's armpit, she helps him to a seated position. A simple movement that causes more pain to ignite across his torso as his breath catches, his jaw clamping shut.

"You-" Val begins, Cortland stopping the question by holding up a hand.

His eyes pinched shut, he manages to push out, "I'm okay," before rolling to the side and shoving himself to his feet. Stopping there, he bends forward at the waist, sucking in shallow breaths as he waits for the dizziness in his head and the agony along his ribs to subside before reaching down and grabbing up his M17 from the ground.

A weapon he didn't even remember dropping, everything from the impact of the bullet to Val appearing before him a blur. A few darkened moments, self-preservation sealing him off from the sharp stab of such overwhelming pain.

"Can you move?" Val asks.

"Yeah, I'm good," Cortland answers, pulling himself up to full height. A final ascent that brings another pass of nausea before leveling out, the woman beside him moving out and back into focus.

"You sure?" she asks.

"Yeah," Cortland replies, shifting his gaze to the side. "Let's go find Rem."

Answering with nothing more than a nod, Val brings her assault rifle up before her. Resuming her previous two-handed stance, she bends her knees, losing a handful of inches in height, making herself a smaller target as she creeps forward. Going first to the banister, she peers over the side, checking the foyer below, before sliding to the stairs.

"Clear," she whispers, lowering herself to the first one. And then the second. A descent that is much faster than their initial climb, forcing Cortland to move quick to keep up, every step, every breath, making the ache in his side more pronounced.

Pain that he forces himself past as they hit the main foyer and circle around the side, ducking through one of the two doorways Cortland was watching earlier. A passage into a narrow hallway that opens out into an entertaining area. A combination living and dining room, connected directly to the veranda Reseda and the others spoke of before.

An open-air spread running the length of the mansion, bulging in the center to provide a perfect vantage into the compound below. The site of so many private viewings, where Leo Garcia would really set the hook, revealing his true intent to his newest associates.

A place that tonight has born witness to a show of a very different variety, a trio of bodies littering the floor, fresh blood leaking out, pooling across the tile. Evidence of Remington's recent passage, though no sign remains of him now.

Picking up his pace slightly, Cortland falls in beside Val. Both still with weapons extended, they inch forward, careful not to expose themselves too much as they come up on the rail encircling the veranda.

A new vantage, allowing them to peer down to the grounds below.

And the impending battle set to take place there.

CHAPTER NINETY-FIVE

Five minutes ago, Remington hated the idea of sending Cortland up to the third floor with Val. Trepidation stemming not from any sort of skepticism of his friend's abilities or his brother's hardened mindset – having seen them both enough in the past to trust them implicitly – but because he didn't want to run the risk of letting his brother out of his sight.

His sister-in-law's final words again returning to him, telling them to watch out for one another.

A directive he wanted to believe was best served by keeping Cortland by his side, capitulating only with the understanding that it was actually the other way around. By that point, there was no way anybody in the house wouldn't have heard what was happening. Commotion that would have woken even the deepest of sleepers and called them down to the main floors.

By sending Cortland upstairs, he would be safer, away from the heaviest of the fighting, as evidenced by the quartet sprawled out in Remington's wake throughout the industrial kitchen comprising a large chunk of the ground floor. Men unlike the ones they encountered out front or the three lying in heaps on the veranda above, all of those in business casual attire, probably meant to serve as security for the main house or Garcia himself.

A second wave that appeared in various states of undress. Shorts and t-shirts for some, bare chests and feet for others. Guys who came tearing into the main house with whatever weapons they could wrangle, be it handheld revolvers or aging hunting rifles. Staff who knew to come running the instant the alarm was raised, even if they had no real clue how to do it.

Charging straight ahead, they had squeezed off as many rounds as they could. Errant shots that dimpled the stainless-steel appliances and tore divots in the tile floor, porcelain chips scraping across Remington's bare forearms. Open gouges that spotted the floor around him with blood droplets as he fired back, picking them off one at a time.

Shots to center mass that flung them backwards or tossed them sideways, their remains now heaped against the wall or across meal prep tables, streaks of blood revealing how they came to rest there.

A scene lifted straight from a B-level horror movie that he was glad to leave behind as he followed the sound of gunfire out onto the patio behind the house, taking barely a few steps before coming face to face with a man he knew instantly to be Leo Garcia.

An opponent he had been seeking for the better part of a week, fitting to the letter with the description of him given by Lance Reseda and Daisy Reed and Guy Thomas. A beefy man with dark facial hair that he would have recognized even before seeing the stun baton in his hand and the sneer across his features.

Unbridled self-assurance that he wore like armor, still present even now as he stands across from an opponent who is better armed, better trained, and brimming with the desire to unload every remaining bullet he has into the man.

Rage that Remington keeps in check only for the reason of wanting Cortland to be here to see it, the death of the asshole who has wronged them so many times in so many ways far more his victory to claim. A husband's right that Remington is not about to deny him, wishing for the first time that he'd kept his brother by his side, even during the worst of the fighting throughout the house.

"You must be the brother," Garcia says, his perfect English carrying just the slightest hint of an accent. "The one from Tennessee."

There is not a single thing the man can say that Remington has any interest in hearing. No reveals about how much he thinks he knows, or barbs to try and get under his skin. Weak attempts at goading him into pulling the trigger or buying a few extra minutes so reinforcements can arrive.

Aid that he has to know isn't coming. By Remington's count, already twenty-nine are dead, with number thirty standing right in front of him. A figure that doesn't even include whoever Val and Cortland encountered upstairs, or Tyrell and Brady outside, each of them slowly edging into the periphery of his view.

Slow, furtive movements with weapons raised, ready to cut Garcia down.

A split approach, wiping out whatever remained of the supposedly vaunted force. The army that had kept business owners and local politicians living in fear for years.

"I've heard about you," Garcia says. "Saw what you did to Enzo last night."

Pulling back one side of his mouth in a faint smile, he takes a step closer. Snapping a hand to the side, he tosses away the stun baton, flinging it into the manicured grass abutting the sidewalk.

A weapon well suited for playing with his pets inside the compound, but doesn't stand a chance against what he is now facing. A calculation he has clearly already made, opting to go this route instead.

A physical challenge that he issues by saying, "So why don't you try and do the same to me?"

So badly, Remington wants to tell the man that what he did to Enzo last night pales compared to what he did barely an hour earlier.

Just as much, he wants to tell him that he can find Enzo and the others out front.

That he will soon be joining them.

Equally much, he wants to not say a word at all. Start tugging back on the trigger seated against the pad of his right index finger, spitting out rounds as fast as the assault rifle will allow. Or use it as a club and beat the man into submission, showing him what physical prowess really looks like.

Options he is still considering, letting them riffle through his mind, as a pair of figures step up on either side of him. Val to his left, her own rifle raised.

Cortland on his right, the M17 in his hand lowered to his side, his gaze fixed on the man before them. A thousand-yard stare that seems to emanate every last thought Remington was just having.

And more than a few new ones. Rage that causes his face to quiver as he stares on, not a word crossing his lips.

Silence that Garcia himself seems incapable of, the sneer on his lips growing wider, peeking out from the ring of hair encircling it.

The beginning of another smart ass remark. Some challenge to the both of them, or a retort about knowing who Cortland is also, or maybe even some comment about how this all could have been avoided if Maylinn would have simply kept her nose out of his affairs and gone away.

Words that never make it out, anything the man could possibly have to say denied by Cortland raising his gun and firing. A shot that is impossible to miss at such a distance, mashing into the man's leg just above the right knee.

A direct hit causing a bright red blossom to spread across the light tan fabric.

With no warning of the incoming blow, Garcia has no way to brace himself. No way to break his fall as the leg gives out beneath him, his body crumpling to the side. A free fall to the concrete ended by his kneecap slamming down, a mighty yell erupting from the man.

Pain and rage that is interrupted a second time by Cortland

blasting a matching hole into his other leg. A limb extended out to the side, propping him up, that is blown backward, spinning him around and dropping him flat on his back.

The last time Remington and his brother were in any sort of similar situation, they were standing in the ragged wooden barn Wes Callum and his sons called home. The place already soaked in moonshine, they'd made it as far as striking the lighter before Cortland showed the slightest hesitation. A hint of trepidation that Remington saved him from, taking the silver Zippo and telling his brother to wait outside.

Intervention that this time never enters his mind. A finale that is Cortland's alone, the others seeming to sense the same and lowering their guns before them.

Slowly they begin to creep inward, Cortland matching them as he lowers his gun and steps forward. A loop slowly tightening with Remington and Val bringing up the rear, coming together around the man resting flat on his back in the center of the sidewalk, both pant legs saturated with blood.

The one responsible for all of them being here, who could have continued his nefarious affairs for as long as he wanted had he not made the mistake of coming after one of theirs.

Grunting softly, Garcia lifts his chin from his chest. The start of an attempt to sit up, using his elbows to try and tilt himself forward. A partially raised position from which he rotates his gaze, taking in the crew descending upon him.

A sight that causes him to let out a bitter laugh, his focus rotating around to see Cortland picking up the stun baton from the lawn.

"What do you think you're going to do with that?" Garcia spits. "Man enough to shoot me in the legs, but not man enough to finish me?"

Clear baiting that Cortland doesn't fall for, depressing the button on the end of the baton to bring it to life before jamming it into the exposed side of Garcia's neck.

CHAPTER NINETY-SIX

The arrangement is kind of like what Cortland imagined when Lance Reseda, Daisy Reed, and Guy Thomas were describing it. Gone is Leo Garcia and whatever new unsuspecting business owner he has lured in. Replacing them are he and his brother standing on the second story veranda overlooking the compound below, flanked by Tyrell and Val to one side, Linc Brady on the other.

Five of the last six people left breathing on the property, all watching the faint smudge of Garcia's t-shirt fifty yards away. Unable to stand with bullets lodged above either kneecap, he looks to be trying to army crawl his way to safety, his torso shifting to either side in the semi-darkness.

Futile effort in the face of what they all know is coming, the hyenas the man built a reputation on already starting to emit their hellish screams. A death rattle of the purest form, letting all within hearing distance know that the end is near.

Pure animal instinct, oblivious to the fact that their newest prey is the man who brought them here, homing and feeding them for years.

"Bet Ol' Laughing Leo isn't finding things too funny now,"

Remington mutters, cocking his chin to the side without taking his focus from the compound.

A quip Cortland can only offer a smirk in reply to, matched by Tyrell a few steps away.

Otherwise, the group remains silent, watching what is about to unfold.

As recently as a week ago, Cortland would have refused to believe something like this even exists. A sadistic setup designed by a madman, featuring beasts only found in the wild on the far side of the Atlantic Ocean. A scenario that might pop up in a late-night horror movie, but never in real life, and sure as hell not in a place like Austin.

Five days ago, he would not have been able to even consider a life without Maylinn in it. A best friend and partner who stepped in when he and Remington first parted more than a decade before, by his side every moment since. The only real girlfriend he ever had, and the future mother of his children.

This time yesterday, he still wouldn't have imagined he would ever be responsible for another person's death. A stain on his soul that was first put there shortly before he and his brother went their separate ways, fading a bit over time, but never truly leaving. A burden he has carried for so long, hoping to find penance for it in some way.

Absolution that is now his, wiped away not through good deeds but more violence. A promise kept to his wife, cancelling out whatever he has done previously.

Standing with his eyes narrowed, his focus on the small patch of white trying in vain for the closest tree, a place to use for cover or to possibly try to climb to safety, Cortland is aware of the low throb of his ribs. He can still feel the kick of the gun he has fired more tonight than in the rest of his life combined.

A faint ringing has settled into his ears, overpowered only by the shrill cries of the hyenas moving into position. Commands spoken from one to another, informing them where and how to move.

Precursors Cortland can sense getting closer, their pitch and length both increasing. Calls steeped in anticipation and delight that last for several minutes, cresting before dying out completely, replaced by the screams of Garcia below.

Pained cries that reverberate up from the compound, passing over the veranda and into the house.

A horrific show that Cortland knows will join the other macabre sights and sounds of the last few days. A fitting final piece that he will never speak of again, how Garcia and his ilk have managed to watch it so many times for so many years something he would rather not speculate on.

Letting his vision glass over, Cortland watches as the small scrap of white disappears from view. Clothing that is blocked by the surrounding animals or succumbs to the resulting blood and dirt of his demise. Visual indication of death that pairs with the fading of the man's screams, the wild creatures doing what they do best.

The start of what is likely to be a lengthy process that Cortland has no interest in remaining for. No desire to spend even another moment in the hellscape that has been responsible for so much death and destruction, stretching from where he stands into Austin, and all the way to the border beyond that.

An evil void that eventually someone will rise up to fill, but for the time being there will be a moratorium on overdoses and animal attacks and all the rest.

Turning away from the rail, Cortland takes but a single step. The beginning of a return to his SUV and an exit from the premises forever, stalled a bit longer by Remington asking, "What now?"

Remaining with his back to the compound below, Cortland lets his gaze pass over the trio of bodies still sprawled across the veranda. A tiny subset of those just like it spread across the grounds, ranging from the old matriarch upstairs to the shattered remains of Enzo and his men out front.

"MCB," Cortland mutters. "Same as they did to me."

Adding nothing more, he watches as the message lands, the corners of his brother's mouth curling upward. "MCB."

"That damn MCB again," Tyrell mutters. "What the hell does that mean?"

"Means burn it," Remington replies. "All of it."

———

Morning had arrived much, much earlier than either Cortland or Remington would have preferred. The start of a new day barely four hours after the previous one ended, with the assorted events of the last night still roiling through their system. Pounds of barbecue and forced libations and time spent on the dance floor long past when they both would have preferred to knock off and head back to the motel.

One last night on lumpy beds with itchy sheets and threadbare towels.

To say nothing of their short field trip in the middle. A jaunt out into the woods that neither had spoken about since, nor would they probably ever. A promise made and kept to their grandfather's memory, to be buried away with him on the banks of Moonshine Creek forevermore.

An outing that both expected to be the reason why they were awoken so early by the pounding on their door. Heavy fisted knocking that caused the thin wooden panel to reverberate in its frame, snapping both from their slumber.

An unexpected arrival and unceremonious greeting that caused them both to assume the worst. Thoughts of what they had done and who could have possibly seen them, filling them both with dread that climbed even higher as they opened it to find Sheriff Myles standing before them.

The start of what both figured would be a long drive out of town to a very different destination, their future plans suspended permanently.

Expectations that, to both their relief, turned out to be unfounded, the man merely stopping by to wish them well and inform them of what had happened to Callum and his family. An accidental blaze, caused by what was suspected to be an errant cigarette and alcohol.

A loss that Myles even went so far as to say was more of a good riddance before immediately pulling back and glancing in either direction, making sure that the admission wasn't overheard from anybody nearby.

An interaction that, in the moment, had seemed like nothing short of a blessing. A rare stroke of luck in a summer – or even a lifetime – that had been noticeably void of them.

Given a couple of extra hours to ruminate on it though, Cortland couldn't be so certain as he leaned against the side of the Charger. Parked on the small asphalt lot alongside the tiny bus station on the edge of town, Remington assumed the same pose nearby, Shine lowered to the ground between their feet.

"He totally knew what happened, didn't he?" Cortland muttered.

"Totally," Remington echoed, his gaze fixed in the distance on the silver shell of a bus rolling into view. Early morning sun flashing across the windshield and along the aluminum body, the faint call of the engine pushing it forward could be heard.

A sight and sound that both allowed to come closer, cutting the distance between them by half. A few final seconds together before Remington levered his hips away from the side of the car and squatted down, clutching Shine behind her ears.

"You be a good girl, okay?" he whispered. Furrowing his fingers into her thick hair, he shook her head to either side before leaning forward and kissing between the ears. "And you take care of him, you got me?"

Lifting her nose upward, Shine pushed back into him. Silent agreement to the conditions laid out for her, and a farewell of her own.

A goodbye Remington accepted before releasing his hold on her, his gaze turning to take in the bus as the air brakes on it sounded. A decrease of speed bringing it closer to the curb, drawing a handful of people out from inside the station. A small crowd looking to head north into Oklahoma, the tiny outpost earning little more than a quick stop.

A chance for people to step on or off, anybody who wasn't in a seat when the driver pulled back on the road out of luck until the next morning.

"You take care of her, too," Remington said.

Rotating his gaze back to face forward, he extended a hand before him. An offered shake that Cortland slapped away, stepping forward to give his brother a hug.

An embrace Remington stiffened against for only a moment before returning it. Both arms wrapped tight before clapping his brother on the back and retreating, his hands resting on Cortland's shoulders.

"You guys call me when you get to Lubbock, alright?"

"Will do," Cortland answered. "And you let us know when your graduation is. We're coming up."

A wan smile traced Remington's face as he let his hands fall away from his brother's shoulders. Taking a step back, he hefted his duffel from the ground beside him and said, "Only if you promise to bring a carload of those college girls with you."

Matching the grin, Cortland said, "I'll see what I can do."

Dipping his chin in appreciation, Remington drifted a step to the side. And then another. A widening gap that grew ever larger as the doors to the bus opened and those gathered outside began to pile on.

"Good luck," Cortland said, raising his left hand overhead, his fingers splayed wide. A pale flare, marked by a trio of dark letters etched into it.

A gesture Remington matched, letting his own markings be seen, before replying, "MCB?"

"MCB."

EPILOGUE

The resplendent glory of autumn in Texas is on full display as Cortland steps out of the car. Brilliant gold and vibrant orange, mixed with just the slightest tinges of crimson. The last vestiges of an Indian summer, hinting that soon the start of winter will be upon them. One final chance for nature to show off before going dormant to enjoy a well-earned winter's nap.

Pulled in from the road so small the county didn't even bother to paint a stripe down the middle, his SUV rests in the pair of ruts they've been following for the last couple of miles. A path that at one point Cortland traversed multiple times a day, left untouched in the years since and allowed to grow up with the thick grass that is underfoot.

Padding that makes for a soft landing as Shine spills down behind him from the driver's seat, not even waiting for him to open the rear door to let her out of her makeshift bed. A small carveout that is hers for the next day or so, every other bit of space in the car filled with the few remaining items he has to his name.

Stuff that he was able to save from the house before it was burned over a week before. Items culled together from people like Beth

Towner and Eleanor Patrick, with mementos they had saved or items tucked away in Maylinn's office they felt should remain with him.

A small collection buttressed by some things from her parents, bestowed upon him at the funeral just two days before. A surreal experience that he still hasn't begun to process, much like most recent events. A radical life redirection he didn't want or ask for, altering his course in ways he won't fully realize for years to come.

"How long's it been since you were back?" Remington asks. Swinging the passenger side door closed, he tromps around to the frontside of the SUV, a few sticks and dried leaves crunching underfoot.

"Same as you," Cortland replies, moving forward to fall in beside his brother, each of them taking one of the paths carved into the ground before them. Signs of passage from long ago, the forest doing what it does in their absence. Wounds that have completely healed in some places, obscuring the route from view, while in others still resembles fresh scars. Chunks of ground with the underlying gravel visible, signaling back to days long past.

One of many apt metaphors Cortland has encountered since the death of his wife, suspecting that his own growth and recovery will be much the same.

"Really?" Remington asks. "Thought maybe you would have brought her by sometime."

Shaking his head, Cortland says, "No reason to. You were gone. So was everything else."

Extending a hand before him, his palm facing the scattered leaves clinging to the treetops above, Remington begins to respond. Another answer challenging why Cortland had let so much time pass that he thinks better of delivering, instead letting his arm fall back to his side.

Silent agreement or merely an inability to push further, Cortland can't be sure. A differentiation that really doesn't matter, his focus turning to the side.

Much like the lane they just took to get here, the house they called home for the better of a decade has been left to the effects of time. Moss has grown thick over the shingles covering the roof and awning extended out over the porch. Streaks of mold stretch down from the corners of the windows, following the natural flow of water runoff.

Tall weeds obscure the front steps and cover most of what was previously the gravel drive. The remains of the screens covering the front door and windows are streaked with tears, left hanging in ragged pieces.

Damage that would probably look worse, if not for the steady encroachment of the forest around it. Tree branches and new growth that has crowded in tight, doing to the home the same as it did to the lane itself.

A move to reclaim its own, using colorful camouflage to obscure the process.

"You ever tell her about it?" Remington asks, the sound of his voice drawing Cortland's gaze back his way. A quick glance, meeting his brother's, before the two of them begin on again.

A destination that today isn't the derelict structure, but a spot a little further on down the bank. One final step before they leave Texas and head east, neither knowing when they might return next.

"Of course," Cortland answers.

A response that Remington again replies to by raising a hand upward, this time holding his hand in a neutral grip, flashing the inside of his arm.

A thick tapestry of designs etched into his skin that Cortland knows aren't the intent of the movement, but rather the small letters stamped at the base of his wrist. The starting point from which all else sprouted.

"I mean, did you tell her about all of it?"

Saying nothing to that just yet, Cortland falls in beside his brother as they move at a diagonal, leaving the lane they drove in on and heading across the east end of what is technically still their lawn. A piece of ground that for years they were put in charge of caring for, going over it with a mower once a week through the spring and summer before spending most of the fall raking it clear.

Endless chores that their grandfather was insistent upon, the reason why now plainly obvious before them. A forest floor that is a thick mat of dead leaves and pine needles, with only the occasional tuft of wild grass poking up in between.

Uneven ground that the three of them tromp through, using the sound of running water ahead to pull them closer. A signal calling to them amidst the thick trees, leading them to the spot they've come seeking.

A place they've both been to only once before, but could get back to without fail, whether it be obscured by the dead of night or a thick winter snowfall.

"I did," Cortland says, sliding his hands into the front pockets of his coat, the fingers of his right hand easing over the small metal tin stowed there. A personal favor gifted from the crematorium that handled his wife's remains, given to him without mention to anybody else.

Not her parents, who asked to hang onto the urn containing the rest of Maylinn's ashes.

The same thinking as himself, wanting to keep a part of her close forever.

None of the myriad people who showed up at her funeral a few days earlier, the crowd swelling to hundreds of people in size. Well wishers from all walks of life, ranging from the law firm where she spent so many years to people like Louisa Gonzalez and Linc Brady who she spent her final days trying to help.

The full spectrum, once again proving the breadth of her reach.

"Kind of hard not to," he says, raising his own left hand. "She spotted it on the first date we ever went on, knew immediately that it wasn't just a nickname. Kept after me until eventually I told her the whole thing."

Keeping his gaze aimed forward, his body tilted slightly to move through the thick underbrush, Remington asks, "And how'd she take it?"

Up ahead, Cortland can begin to see the river peeking through. Pockets of blue that grow steadily larger as the trees thin, eventually giving way to the band of grass and mud comprising the bank.

An open swath of land littered with leaves, marred only by a single slab of granite sticking upward.

A single headstone with letters carved a quarter inch deep and painted black, it alone seeming to be the only thing not touched by the last twelve years.

"Like she took everything," Cortland says, pulling to a stop in front of their grandfather's resting place. The same exact spot where he and his brother stood so long before, so much having changed since then, but also nothing.

A simple response that causes a corner of Remington's mouth to again turn upward before muttering, "You really out kicked your coverage with that one."

Not a single thing he can say to refute, Cortland instead lifts his gaze to the water rushing by less than ten feet away. The end result of a long summer and autumn season that has left the levels low, resulting in pools that in some places are no more than a couple of feet deep, exposing rocks that are buried deep beneath the surface most months. Small juts that create breaks and ripples in the lazy current, giving the air the slightest tinge of damp coolness.

A feeling Cortland hasn't experienced in ages, touching his skin, filling his nostrils.

"Hey, G. Good to see you," he whispers, lowering his gaze before him. "Brought someone I'd like you to meet."

To his right, Shine settles herself onto the leaves by his feet, her shoulder pressed tight to the calf. On his opposite side, Remington stands no more than a few inches away, his hands clasped before him.

"You know," Remington says, "I've been thinking a lot this last week about Maylinn. What happened, how it all went down."

Flicking a glance to the side, he continues, "And I keep coming back to the idea that it was a lot like what happened to me and my leg."

Raising his focus away from their grandfather, Cortland again puts his attention on the river, the colors blurring as he watches it drift past.

"A violent accident that you didn't see coming, wasn't your fault, and while you did survive, a part of you will be missing for the rest of your life."

Cortland's blinking increases as the surface of the river before him begins to come alive. Shimmering as a result of the moisture covering his eyes, his breathing becoming shallow as he stares out.

"Yeah?" Cortland whispers, his voice thick. "And how'd you get through it?"

"The same way you will eventually," Remington replies, unclasping his hands and draping a thick arm around Cortland's shoulder.

"MCB?"

"MCB."

Turn the page for a sneak peek of *Catching Fire*, Hawk Tate Series Book 8

SNEAK PEEK
CATCHING FIRE, A HAWK TATE NOVEL
BOOK 8

The omnipresent scent of the ocean was the first thing to greet Dayton Myers as he stepped out of the concrete edifice that had been his home for the last twenty-six months and into the dark of night. A single step marking a transition from the sharp and sterile smells of bleach and cleaning products that were constantly scrubbing the walls and floors of the structure to the clear sting of brine.

The long-familiar aroma of the sea, made more pronounced by the ice crystals and winter chill in the air.

The Pacific in its purest form, unadulterated by a thousand other odors that the heat of summer could kick up. A scent so pure it could cleanse from within, Myers drawing it in through his nose as he marched dutifully forward, letting it fill his lungs. Expand his chest and lift his shoulders.

The first truly deep breath taken in more than two years.

A fleeting reprieve from the strictures of prison life, ripped away as fast as it arrived by the firm hand mashing into his left shoulder blade. A downgrade from the usual prodding end of a nightstick used when wanting him to move, replaced with a flat palm and fingers splayed away.

Contact enough to twist his body forward at the waist, his shackled feet needing a pair of choppy steps to keep himself upright.

"Keep moving," the same guard who had just lined up Myers and the others muttered. The proverbial caboose on their train of inmates, all being loaded for transport. An overnight excursion taking them from Federal Detention Center - SeaTac to their new home in California.

Forced relocation, this the last chance the guard had to get in a few final barbs. Verbal jabs like the ones issued while applying the chains to their wrists and ankles earlier, and physical shots such as the one just received.

Open goading, daring Myers or one of the others to lash back. Say something in self-defense. Test the bounds of their shackles and try to retaliate.

Outcomes Myers had envisioned in his head no less than a thousand times over the last two-plus years. The full spectrum, ranging from wicked comments that would leave the pasty bastard with the bald head and fleshy features confused for days, all the way to grabbing a makeshift weapon and supplying receipts for every last transgression incurred.

The absolutely only thing stopping being the promise of extra years tacked onto his sentence. A stay that was already starting to wear on him, the daily rites of checking every corner, forever being aware of who might be passing behind him, already growing tiresome.

A young man's game that he knew he wouldn't have the stamina to keep up forever.

To say nothing of the massive amount of unfinished business still waiting for him on the outside. A return to his family and young son. The burgeoning empire he'd been forced away from at the moment when years of pressing were finally starting to pay dividends.

The woman responsible for taking him away from it all.

Up ahead, the transport vehicle loomed ever closer. A modified bus that was shortened to half the length of the one Myers took until dropping out of high school in the ninth grade, the sliding windows replaced with solid panes of plexiglass and covered with metal screens. A matching barricade had been inserted, separating the driver from those in the back.

On the floor he knew there to be steel rings rising from the floor, meant to secure the leg bindings they were required to wear.

Details Myers could recall from his previous trips in such a vehicle, forced into one on his many sojourns back and forth to court. Customizations he hadn't thought about in well over a year, brought back to the fore by the bright lights blazing from within. A harsh glow putting everything on plain display, the damned bus shining like a beacon in the center of the parking lot.

A lone spot of brightness.

A false deity, leading them not into salvation, but further into the depths of hell.

Fifteen yards ahead, Myers watched as the first in line passed through the guards standing on either side of the door. Moving as slow as possible, hoping to milk every last second of time not spent enclosed by concrete walls, he shuffled along a few inches at a time.

A pace matched by the next man in order.

And then the one after that.

An excruciating crawl that forced the guards up front to become more vocal, drawing their nightsticks and using them to flag the next in order through. Commotion that drew the attention from the rest of the queue toward the front, nobody noticing as the same guard who had just shoved Myers stepped beside him.

Brushing up close enough that their shoulders touched, he reached across his body and shoved a single item into Myers' hand.

A small white tablet, no bigger across than a dime.

"Twenty-three," he muttered, saying not another word as he retreated back to his previous position.

***

Continue reading *Catching Fire Fall 2022*:
dustinstevens.com/CFwb

THANK YOU

Hello all!

Whew! I promise, when I sat down and began to draft this story, I had no idea it would easily end up being my longest work ever. A behemoth of a project that just kept unspooling, the combination of the extreme weight pressing on both Cortland and Remington and the need to keep pushing forward in their search for Maylinn's killer needing plenty of space to fully be told.

If you've made it this far, that means you went the distance as well, and for that I thank you, and hope you enjoyed it!

As for how this story came to be (the part I know many of you check these letters at the end hoping to uncover), it all took root on a late-night walk this past spring when I was thinking about loss and the million different ways it can manifest. A singular event that can look so different, depending on the viewpoint. The thousand different connections we all have in this world, the full breadth of which unfortunately doesn't usually become evident until it is too late.

As I tinkered with the idea, I briefly considered the various story-lines I have, but finding none of them to be a good fit, I started from the ground up, building the world you all just spent a few hours in. New characters and locations that I enjoyed getting to know, filling in their backstories, developing their mannerisms, and I hope you did as well.

While this probably is the proverbial "riding off into the sunset" for the Moonshine Creek Boys, I have plenty of other standalone ideas in mind, and hopefully you'll be meeting a few of them in the near future as well. 😊

Per usual, allow me to end here by thanking all of you again. Taking chances like the one here is only possible because of your unending support, and I appreciate the ongoing opportunity.

Until next time, happy reading!

Much love,

Dustin

FREE BOOK

Sign up for my newsletter and receive a FREE copy of my first
bestseller – and still one of my personal favorites – *21 Hours!*
dustinstevens.com/free-book

DUSTIN'S BOOKS

Works Written by Dustin Stevens:

Reed & Billie Novels:
The Boat Man
The Good Son
The Kid
The Partnership
Justice
The Scorekeeper
The Bear
The Driver
The Promisor
The Ghost
The Family
Coming 2023

Hawk Tate Novels:
Cold Fire
Cover Fire

Fire and Ice
Hellfire
Home Fire
Wild Fire
Friendly Fire
Catching Fire
Coming Soon

Zoo Crew Novels:
The Zoo Crew
Dead Peasants
Tracer
The Glue Guy
Moonblink
The Shuffle
Smoked
Coming Soon

Ham Novels:
HAM
EVEN
RULES
HOME

My Mira Saga
Spare Change
Office Visit
Fair Trade
Ships Passing
Warning Shot
Battle Cry
Steel Trap
Iron Men
Until Death

Standalone Thrillers:

Four
Ohana
Liberation Day
Twelve
21 Hours
Catastrophic
Scars and Stars
Motive
Going Viral
The Debt
One Last Day
The Subway
The Exchange
Shoot to Wound
Peeping Thoms
The Ring
Decisions
Moonshine Creek

Standalone Dramas:

Just A Game
Be My Eyes
Quarterback

Children's Books w/ Maddie Stevens:

Danny the Daydreamer...Goes to the Grammy's
Danny the Daydreamer...Visits the Old West
Danny the Daydreamer...Goes to the Moon
(Coming Soon)

Works Written by T.R. Kohler:

Hunter Series:

ABOUT THE AUTHOR

Dustin Stevens is the author of more than 60 novels, the vast majority having become #1 Amazon bestsellers, including the Reed & Billie and Hawk Tate series. *The Boat Man*, the first release in the best-selling Reed & Billie series, was named an Indie Award winner for E-Book fiction. The freestanding work *The Debt* was named an Independent Author Network action/adventure novel of the year and *The Exchange* was recognized for independent E-Book fiction.

He also writes thrillers and assorted other stories under the pseudonym T.R. Kohler.

A member of the Mystery Writers of America and Thriller Writers International, he resides in Honolulu, Hawaii.

Let's Keep in Touch:
Website: dustinstevens.com
Facebook: dustinstevens.com/fcbk
Twitter: dustinstevens.com/tw
Instagram: dustinstevens.com/DSinsta

Made in the USA
Coppell, TX
17 October 2022

84822880R00308